MURDERED BY THE
BLOOMS

ENDORSEMENTS

Jillian and her lovable family and friends are back—trying to identify and stop a dangerous criminal who is striking way too close to home. Jodi Casstevens-Short has crafted a compelling cozy mystery that offers suspense, humor, kindness, and surprises in every chapter. *Murdered by the Blooms* is a page-turner that will hook you (and shock you) to the very end. I was completely absorbed in this exciting and heart-warming story and its engaging characters. The Willow Springs community has its drama, but it's a place you'll want to visit again and again.
—**Lori Peckham**, writing professor and book editor

As a fan of Jodi Casstevens-Short's debut cozy mystery, *Murdered by the Books,* I was delighted to continue my 'friendship' with familiar characters and furry friends, as well. Once again in *Murdered by the Blooms*—a suspenseful mystery intertwining jealousy, stalking, and vandalism with kidnapping and murder—the author encourages the reader to join amateur detective, Jillian Edwards in speculation, clue-seeking, and sleuthing. If you enjoy the challenge of solving crimes, make your way into Willow Springs and start snooping.
—**Carol Amon McGehe**, author of award-winning *In Search of My Heart* and *Becoming a Widow's Advocate*

The lovers of a good whodunit will enjoy the twists that Jodi Casstevens-Short brings to this cozy read!
—**Claire O'Sullivan**, *Award winning author of Romance Under Wraps, Silk & Slippers*, and *Shanghai Road,* (the Whiskey River series)

If you're looking for a fun murder mystery, you've found it! Jodi Casstevens-Short's second cozy mystery novel, *Murdered by the Blooms,* is full of beautiful flowers, adorable puppies, yummy baked goods, and lots of twists and turns thrown in for good measure. Not to mention the dead bodies that keep piling up! Coming complete with a loving, if exasperating, trio of sisters and their extended family and friends. Jodi Casstevens-Short has you covered with this enjoyable read.

—**Cathy Rueter**, author of *Murder May I*

Jodi Casstevens-Short skillfully combines a cast of quirky characters, mysterious newcomers, and plenty of small-town charm to create a page-turning whodunnit and satisfying romance.

—**Nancy Lavo**, author of the Lone Star Loves series

Murdered by the
Blooms

Jodi Casstevens-Short

COPYRIGHT NOTICE

Cover and Interior Design: Kelly Artieri, Deb Haggerty
Editor(s): Peggy Ellis, Cristel Phelps, Deb Haggerty

PUBLISHED BY: Elk Lake Publishing, Inc., 35 Dogwood Drive, Plymouth, MA 02360, 2025

Library Cataloging Data
Names: Casstevens-Short, Jodi (Jodi Casstevens-Short)
Murdered by the Blooms / Jodi Casstevens-Short
387 p. 23cm × 15cm (9in × 6 in.)
ISBN-13: 9798891344228 (paperback) | 9798891344235 (trade paperback) | 9798891344242 (e-book)

MURDERED BY THE BLOOMS

Key Words: Christian romance cozy mystery wedding secrets; Faith suspense love sisters flower shop murder; Cozy godly mystery autumn proposal wedding secrets; Christian mystery and suspense romance sisters love; Clean romance suspense small town autumn secrets; Christian suspense fiction cozy mystery boyfriend; Jesus murder investigation dogs sleuths cozy loves
Library of Congress Control Number: 2025943590 Fiction

DEDICATION

To my incredible husband. Your love and support
make all things possible.

ACKNOWLEDGMENTS

Many assume writing is a solitary endeavor, and in part, they are correct. I do sit alone at my desk or in my favorite writing chair as I outline, write, and edit each novel. Behind the solitude, however, there's an amazing group of people who are with me every step of the way. They are my village and without them, none of my novels would ever see the light of day.

To Deb Haggerty and Cristel Phelps at Elk Lake Publishing, Inc.—thank you for the faith you've placed in me. I appreciate the chance to keep my cozy mystery series available to readers.

To Peggy Ellis, my editor—two books together and going strong. Thank you for your creative suggestions and attention to detail. My novels are always in good hands with you.

To Kelly Artieri, my cover artist—thank you for creating such beautiful faces for my books. I am in awe of your talent.

To my parents—thank you for instilling in me the belief that I can do anything, for always supporting my dreams, and for teaching me that hard work does pay off.

To my family—thank you for being the inspiration for Jillian's family. You've given me great material to work with.

To my dearest friends—you've been there from the beginning of this journey. You've each been an ear to listen, a shoulder to cry on, a sounding board to bounce ideas off, and my biggest cheerleaders. I am truly grateful to have you all in my life.

To my critique partners—I don't think I can ever thank you enough for the support, suggestions, and advice you've provided. Meeting with you each morning motivates me to keep writing. Discussing the writing process inspires me to keep learning. Having the three of you in my corner feeds my soul. Most of all, I am blessed to call you my friends.

To my readers—you've made this past year nothing short of amazing. So many of you have reached out on social media or during in-person events to tell me how much you loved *Murdered by the Books*. You've spread the word, shared my book with others, and written glowing reviews. It is my sincerest hope that you love this second novel in the series just as much as the first.

And last, but certainly not least, to my husband—thank you for always being there when I've needed advice, marketing ideas, or a strong back to lug books from one event to the other. Thank you for being *my* firefighter and the inspiration behind Travis. Most of all, thank you for believing in me and supporting my dreams—I love you the mostest.

CHAPTER ONE

Jillian gazed at her reflection in the full-length mirror. A cynical frown and furrowed brow marred the image staring back at her.

Ugh. Not the look I was going for.

"Good morning, ladies. I need some fashion advice." She performed her finest pirouette, perfected during years of ballet class as a child. "What do you think of this sweater with these black pants—boring, right? I could add a scarf or necklace for a pop of color. Thoughts?"

Her two sleepy schnauzers peeked from under the covers. Their little bearded faces and soulful brown eyes gazed at Jillian with adoration. Her heart melted.

"You two are so stinking cute. I can't stand it." She rubbed under their chins, earning wet kisses on her hand. "Now, how about earning your keep? Give me some help with my style dilemma."

Jillian talked to her dogs like they were humans. They were great listeners, who never interrupted. Their mere presence brought comfort when she felt sad or anxious. Rubbing their soft fur always calmed her nerves.

Because it was Monday, her children's bookstore, Whimsy & Wonder, was closed. She had a full day ahead, starting with an early breakfast with her sister, Amanda. Jillian had been busy these past few weeks organizing two rooms filled with books for adults. Parents could now browse for something to read while their children looked for their own books. The task had kept her so busy, she'd barely had time to breathe, let alone spend quality time with her sister. They would remedy that this morning.

Jillian's to-do list included running errands in the business district of town, sending her into a tizzy about what to wear. As a new-*ish* business owner, she considered every foray into her community an opportunity to connect with people and promote her bookstore. Her Grandma McGuire used to say the right outfit was a must for every occasion. The reflection staring back at her missed the mark.

Jillian grabbed three scarves and a basket of accessories from a shelf in her walk-in closet, then breezed back into her bedroom. She held them in front of Abbey and Hayley for their inspection.

"Okay, girls. I need earrings, a necklace, maybe a bracelet ..."

Jillian tried on several pieces of jewelry while her thoughts wandered to the day ahead.

Most of her planned errands had been long neglected. Whimsy & Wonder had opened one year ago today. Sales had been steady, so business was good. One downside to opening the store—there'd been little time for her to do much else.

Except solve a murder and fall in love with a wonderful man.

The latter gave Jillian a warm feeling from head to toe, making her smile. Thinking of Travis sent her heart racing.

"Last chance, girls. No advice on my outfit?" She twirled in front of them one final time. Their response—two tired yawns. "Fine. I'll make this work." She chose a pair of sleek hoop earrings, the silver pendant from her friend Maggie, and the diamond tennis bracelet Travis gave her for her birthday. Finishing off her look, she draped a beautiful black, cream, and red ruana around her shoulders in the stylish way she'd learned watching a YouTube video.

Jillian faced her sleepy pups snuggled in bed. "C'mon, lazybones. Let's go outside."

The magic word *outside* sent both schnauzers scampering from bed. They dashed to the door with their tiny tails wagging. Jillian clipped on leashes before taking them out into the warmer-than-usual September morning.

While Abbey and Hayley sniffed every blade of grass, Jillian thought about her bookstore's open house on this day last year—the night that brought a murder mystery to her front door and Travis into her life.

Jillian's friends, family, and neighbors had gathered to celebrate Whimsy & Wonder's grand opening. At the end of the evening, as guests departed, the squeal of tires, a loud thud, and a woman's scream signaled an unfolding tragedy. A hit-and-run driver killed her friend Maggie right in front of the store.

When several important clues fell into Jillian's lap, her inquisitive mind took over. She insinuated herself into the investigation, becoming the killer's target on more than one occasion. Her constant interference had irritated the lead detective, Ethan Harden, who happened to be her best friend Becca's husband.

Shaking her head to dislodge the awful memory, Jillian kneeled to remove leaves from the dogs' beards. "Mama's lucky to have survived the killer's attacks, isn't she?" Hayley rewarded her query with a loud woof, while Abbey licked the proffered hand. She could always count on moral support from her fur babies.

"Let's go get your breakfast." That's all it took to send her girls racing for the porch.

Once inside, two ravenous canines crunched and snuffled through their meal. Jillian enjoyed the sounds of enthusiasm as she packed her tote bag for work.

"You're in charge while I'm gone. Protect our house from trouble, but please don't cause any of your own." Jillian asked Alexa to play *70s on 7*, hoping the music and voices would keep her girls company. She blew kisses as she shut the door behind her.

Amanda had requested they meet at La Casita because she craved their *desayuno especial*—a burrito stuffed with fluffy scrambled eggs, green peppers, crisp bacon, and melted cheese. This delight came with a side of *papas con chorizo*—potatoes with sausage. Loving Mexican food any time of day, Jillian readily agreed.

Parking was easy this early, with plenty of open spaces in the lot next to the restaurant. Jillian pulled in beside a dark green, two-door sports car.

"Never seen this fancy ride here in town," she mumbled under her breath. "Better be careful not to bump it with my door—wouldn't want to pay to fix a ding."

Jillian entered the restaurant, greeting all the staff with a friendly hello or a hug. She ate there so often these people were like family. Amanda waved at her from a booth near the back. She slid in opposite her sister, folded the ruana, and placed it on the seat beside her.

"Why'd you take that off?" Amanda smiled. "Those colors are beautiful on you, and you'd styled it perfectly."

"Too much fabric—makes it hard to move my arms when I eat." Jillian rolled her eyes. "Plus, you know me. Salsa often becomes an accessory. I'll keep the ruana nice and use it to cover up whatever I spill on my sweater."

A waitress appeared with a basket of warm cinnamon *churros* and took their drink orders. Amanda's stomach chose that moment to state its need for food with a loud rumble.

Jillian asked for an *horchata* for herself. "I believe my sister would like a hot chocolate with extra spice," she added.

Amanda confirmed with a nod.

Ready with their food orders too, Jillian chose *gorditas de harina*—a pocket pastry stuffed with scrambled eggs, vegetables, cheese and chorizo. Amanda predictably ordered the breakfast special with an extra side of bacon.

"Skip dinner last night?" Jillian arched a brow.

"As a matter of fact, I did."

"I was kidding," Jillian said. "What in the world were you doing that made you forget to eat?"

A pink flush crept up Amanda's neck. Two rosy apples popped out on her cheeks.

"Oh, I get it. Sam called." Jillian grinned at her sister's discomfort. "How's his trip going?"

Sam was Amanda's boyfriend of the past two-and-a-half years. His career as a professional photographer often took him away for weeks at a time to exotic places. His photos had been featured in high-profile magazines and documentaries. He'd been on assignment in Italy for six weeks and wasn't due home for another two. Amanda's melancholy look said it all—she missed him like crazy.

"He said everything was right on schedule, and he should return by the end of the month." Amanda sighed. "I can't wait for him to come home."

"Did you tell him that?"

"I ... um ... probably." Amanda's hesitation spoke volumes.

"That means no." Jillian let out an exaggerated sigh. "Amanda, how do you ever expect the man to propose if you don't give him some encouragement?"

Amanda coughed and sputtered, wiping hot chocolate from her chin. "Propose? Who said anything about marriage? Sam and I are fine the way things are. We don't need a piece of paper to prove we love each other."

"You sure about that?" Jillian's eyebrow arched.

"When we were younger, I never dreamed of my wedding day or imagined myself in a sparkly white dress like you did. Maybe I'm not the marrying kind." A wistful look flitted across her face, then disappeared. "You and Travis, on the other hand, will make a great married couple. Speaking of that, the one-year anniversary of your first date is coming up. I expect you'll be getting a ring any day now."

Jillian met Travis, a Willow Springs firefighter, the day after the hit-and-run incident that killed her friend. He walked into her bookstore to return the blanket she'd used to cover Maggie. A fleeting touch as he handed it to Jillian sent a spark of electricity up each of their arms, igniting something unexpected between them. The attraction was undeniable. Despite a turbulent first date, they'd been together ever since.

"Travis and I aren't getting married. Not any time soon anyway." Jillian pushed a stray lock of hair from her face.

"Oh, c'mon. You can't tell me you haven't dreamed of a certain tall, dark, and handsome firefighter down on one knee with a sparkly ring in a box. He loves you. You love him. What's the problem?"

Jillian's mouth froze as her brain searched for the right response. Her mind refused to form one coherent thought that would pacify her sister. The waitress appeared with their breakfast platters, giving Jillian an extra moment to compose herself.

"Wow, I've rendered you speechless." Amanda pointed her fork at Jillian. "That's never happened before."

Jillian shook her head. "I'll admit the thought of marriage has crossed my mind a time or two." She put up her hand to stop Amanda's interruption. "Travis and I haven't talked about it. We're taking it slow. Things are good the way they are. Besides, I have too much going on right now. The new book rooms at Whimsy & Wonder have just opened. The upstairs remodel at the shop is close to being finished, so I'll be moving out of Cate's basement and into my own apartment above the store soon."

"Stop." Amanda's curt response halted the flow of Jillian's long list of excuses. "First of all, you know Cate will go ballistic if you move out. She told Mom, Aunt Grace, and me just yesterday how happy she is you've lived with them, saving your money for something important." Amanda lowered her voice to a mumble. "Like a wedding or a house." Raising her tone to its normal volume, she continued. "Second, what do you mean, you two haven't talked about marriage?"

"The subject has never come up." Jillian scrunched her face. "Why were you all talking about me, weddings, and houses? I don't like you discussing my love life behind my back."

"Well ... you know how Mom and Aunt Grace can be."

"Intrusive? Nosy? Pick an adjective." Jillian scowled at her sister. "Next thing you'll tell me is Mom has looked at reception venues, and Aunt Grace has had visions of me in my wedding dress." Her voice rang with frustration. "Isn't her upcoming wedding to Dr. Madison enough for this family? Their nuptials should satisfy everyone's needs for frilly dresses, extravagant flowers, and romance."

Their aunt fancied herself a bit of a clairvoyant, insisting she'd been blessed with the gift of prophecy. She read people's palms, interpreted their auras, saw omens in tea leaves, and had visions foretelling doom and gloom for others. Last year at this time, she had visions of a wedding for someone in the family. No one was more shocked than Grace herself when Dr. Robert Madison put a gorgeous diamond ring on her finger.

"Several of us were having lunch, chatting about ... things, and someone speculated as to when Travis might propose. The whole family made it a little game with everyone picking a different date. I chose the anniversary of your first date." Amanda huffed out a long breath. "Since you two lovebirds haven't discussed marriage, he probably won't propose today."

"I cannot believe you." Jillian's voice took on an icy timbre. "What if Travis hears about this? Instead of proposing, he'll run and never look back."

"Calm down, we're only having a bit of fun. Everyone is thrilled you two are happy and in love. Besides, we all agree you'll make a beautiful bride, regardless of whether or not you wear Mom's wedding dress." A mischievous grin lit up Amanda's face.

"Mom's dress? You talked about me wearing her gown?" Jillian's stomach fluttered. Stunned at the thought of being a bride, she sat without moving or speaking as she attempted to think of a witty comeback. Nothing came to mind.

After an uncomfortably long pause, Amanda reached across the table and tugged on her hand. "Earth to Jillian. Please blink or speak. Are you in a trance or having a vision like Aunt Grace?"

The accusation snapped her out of the mental game of ping-pong bouncing through her head. "Don't be ridiculous. I have no inclinations toward the prophetic sensibilities, as Aunt Grace calls them."

"Your body language screamed your mind had roamed a million miles away." Amanda's wrinkled brow exposed an array of worry lines. "Are you upset with us?"

"Upset? I should be, but no. I'm not even surprised there's been conjecture about a wedding proposal—our family being how they are. But picking dates? That's over the top." She wadded up a napkin and threw it at her sister.

"If you think that's outrageous, wait until you hear the rest of the story." Amanda took another bite of her burrito.

"There's more?" Jillian groaned.

Amanda explained how an innocent conversation three weeks ago at their cousin Bryan's pub, McGuire's, had led to "The Proposal Pool." Ten dollars a pick. The person who guesses the correct date wins all the money in the kitty.

"You're all betting on this? I should report you to Ethan."

Amanda laughed. "Go ahead, but he placed a bet too."

Of course he did.

Jillian rubbed at her temples, a dull headache building. She pushed away her plate, the meal half-eaten.

"Please don't be mad." Amanda begged for forgiveness. "This isn't Bryan's fault alone. We all egged him on."

Jillian took a steadying breath, swallowing the anger boiling just below the surface. This was not the place to have an all-out sister fight. She let calm prevail. "I hope Travis doesn't hear about this. He'll be furious that everyone is sticking their noses into our business. Go ahead with your ridiculous pool, but I'll have no sympathy for any of you if he finds out."

Jillian hunched in her chair, sipping her *horchata*. The sweet, creamy beverage cooled the fire inside her. After a few moments, she sighed. "Becca has always said this family is crazy enough to be entertaining. This proves it."

Amanda's tone was apologetic. "Everyone is happy you and Travis found each other. They're excited for your future together. No one meant any harm. You might be interested to know the pot is over four hundred dollars."

"How is there so much money?" Jillian's words came out in a low whisper. "Forty bets would have to be placed for the total to be so high. There aren't that many people in our family."

"Some non-relatives have joined the pool too." Amanda held her hands palms up in appeal for her sister's mercy.

"Really—like who?" Jillian wondered how far this engagement pool had spread. "Spell it out for me."

"Let's see, there's Becca and Ethan, Trixie, Mike and Max from the pub." Amanda ticked everyone off on her fingers. "A couple of Travis's buddies who frequent McGuire's and a few of Bryan's regulars wanted in on the action. Aunt Grace told some of her friends at the Senior Center—"

"Stop. I get the picture." Jillian blew out a breath.

"Don't be mad, Jilly."

"I'm not mad." She waved off Amanda's concern. "Go ahead. Have your fun. You'll all be waiting a long time to see who wins the money. There's no way Travis has marriage on his mind." Jillian dropped her voice as the waitress arrived to clear empty plates. "Can we please change the subject to a less ridiculous topic?"

"Happy to." Amanda polished off the last bite of her *papas con chorizo*. "What would you like to talk about?"

"Will your new part-time helper—what's her name— help us decorate your window this morning?"

"Her name is Brianna, and no, she won't be coming in until we open at ten o'clock." Amanda signaled for the check. "I hope to get most of the window finished before then."

"This girl has only been with you a few weeks, but you really like her, don't you?"

Amanda swallowed the last bite of the churro she'd popped in her mouth.

"Brianna is my Trixie—personable, responsible, and conscientious. I trust her completely."

Trixie was one of Jillian's best friends and her assistant manager at Whimsy & Wonder. She embodied all those qualities Amanda admired in her new employee.

"High praises coming from you. She must be amazing." Jillian snatched the bill as soon as the waitress placed it on the table. "Brianna's never been in the shop when I've stopped by. Looks like I'll miss her today too, since I have to leave by nine-thirty."

"No worries. If we don't finish before you go, I can keep working. If Brianna needs help with customers, I'll be inside the window."

Jillian handed her debit card to their waitress as she breezed back by.

"Thanks for breakfast, Jilly. I'll pick up the tab next time." Amanda smiled at her younger sister. "Thanks for coming with me to Hobby Mart too. Having another pair of hands to pick up the things I need to decorate my store's window is a huge help."

Each year, all the businesses in downtown Willow Springs designed incredible window displays for the Halloween decorating contest. The Chamber of Commerce selected a winner and awarded the most ostentatious trophy, sure to draw customers' attention to the winner's store.

Jillian stood after signing the receipt, placing her card back in her wallet. She grabbed the ruana from the bench seat, arranging the wrap around her shoulders with a flourish. "C'mon, we need to get busy if you want your display looking spectacular by October first. Let's go create some magic."

"Don't you mean my Halloween display should be *spooktacular?*" Amanda used a creepy voice. "Sorry, I couldn't help myself."

Jillian cringed at her sister's weak attempt at humor, but a silly comeback popped into her head.

"Yes, you'll need to *bewitch* the judges to win that trophy."

Amanda waved her hands in surrender. "Stop. These Halloween puns are awful. They make us sound like—"

"Dad!" they said in unison.

They walked out into the bright sunshine, each turning in the direction of her car.

"Let's take separate cars to Hobby Mart, then I can pick up Abbey and Hayley on my way to Blossoms & Blooms. They can nap while we work on your window."

"Sounds good. Your sweet girls are welcome in my shop anytime." Amanda searched her purse for the key fob. "Please don't tell anyone you know about the engagement pool. They'd be disappointed to know you found out."

"Mum's the word." Jillian mimicked zipping her lips. "See you in a few."

The notion of marriage danced through Jillian's head as she climbed into her car.

Hmm. Engaged to Travis.

Visions of herself in a frothy white dress walking toward the altar where Travis waited, looking handsome in a dark suit, pushed all other thoughts from her mind. She could see and smell the beautiful flowers Amanda would arrange to decorate the church. Strains of traditional wedding music played in her head, making her sigh out loud.

A car backfired, snapping her back to the present.

This *wool-gathering,* as her grandmother used to call it, was getting her nowhere. She'd better hustle to meet Amanda.

Jillian caught herself humming "The Wedding March" as she started the engine. A quick shake of the head dislodged the tune, but the idea of marriage remained and brought a smile to her face.

Engaged to Travis? Maybe someday.

Jillian backed out of the parking lot, distracted by thoughts of wedding cakes and bridesmaid dresses. A flicker of movement over her shoulder made her slam on the brakes. An old man stood behind the car, peering through the back window—his eyes sad, vacant. He didn't move. She put the car in park and hopped from the front seat.

"Sir, I'm so sorry. I didn't see you there." Jillian took in his tattered, dirty pants, the scuffed, worn-out shoes, the military-style olive green knapsack thrown over his shoulder, and the US Army veterans' hat perched on his head.

The man stared at her, silent and unmoving.

"I don't believe we've met. Are you new to Willow Springs or just visiting?"

He nodded yes.

But yes to which one?

Jillian tried again. "Are you lost? Do you need help getting somewhere?"

This time, he rewarded her by shaking his head *no.*

Before she could ask him anything else, he dropped his gaze to the ground and shuffled down the sidewalk, shoulders hunched forward.

No wonder his shoes are worn out.

She'd come so close to running him over. Probably scared him to death—frightened herself a little too. Thinking back to the terrible tragedy last fall when her friend had died, Jillian shuddered. Her carelessness today could've caused history to repeat itself. She waited a moment before getting into the vehicle, taking time to steady her nerves.

Her mind buzzed with questions about this wordless stranger. What brought him to Willow Springs—family, friends, a job? Why hadn't he talked to her?

Something about him pulled at her heartstrings. He reminded her of someone, but she couldn't figure out who.

Jillian headed home to pick up her girls after the trip to the hobby store with Amanda. Halfway home, she gave herself a mental forehead slap. She'd left yesterday's bank deposit at the bookstore. Her pups would have to wait just a little bit longer.

She shot Amanda a quick text, letting her know a pit stop at Whimsy & Wonder would make her a few minutes late. She'd pop into the store, grab the deposit, and be out in seconds. Someone had a different plan for her.

"Hey there, Book Lady. I need to talk to you." Mr. Erickson, her ninety-something neighbor, hollered at her as he stomped across the street. He wore a wrinkled, stained, light blue T-shirt, a pair of plaid boxer shorts, house slippers, and a scowl. Jillian reached for her sunglasses to fend off the glare from his stark white bird legs.

"Good morning, Mr. Erickson. How are you today?" She pasted on the brightest smile she could muster.

Mr. Erickson had entered her world this time last year when he announced his displeasure at her store's presence in his neighborhood. He'd ranted about plummeting property values, increased traffic, and chaos caused by loud, bratty kids. She was certain he'd come to deliver yet another litany of complaints.

"Not good, not good at all thanks to you and this gosh-darned store." He'd worked himself into quite a snit. Spittle flew from his mouth, landing on the sleeve of her sweater.

Add a trip to the dry cleaners to today's list.

"I'm confused. What's happened to upset you?"

"I'm tired and cranky 'cuz of all that racket on your porch last night—kept me wide awake for hours."

"The store closed at six. No one should've been anywhere near the porch."

"You callin' me a liar?" He puckered his mouth, pushing out his bottom lip like a petulant child. "I know what I heard."

A mental eye roll helped take the edge off Jillian's irritation with this old man's audacity.

"What did you hear, Mr. Erickson?"

"Loud voices, laughing, and breaking glass. Quite a ruckus, if you ask me." He gave a sharp nod, then scratched the stubble on his chin. "Sounded like you was havin' a wild party. You promised when this here shop opened that it wouldn't disturb the neighborhood. Well, I was disturbed last night."

"I'm very sorry, Mr. Erickson. I have no idea what went on here last night, but I assure you I'll check into it."

"How you gonna do that? Can you look into the past like your wacky aunt who sees the future?"

Jillian bristled at his slight to Aunt Grace, but chose to let it go. "No, sir. I have security cameras. I'll check the video to see what happened."

"You do that." He jabbed a finger in the air. "I'll expect a full report by thirteen hundred this afternoon." He saluted, pivoted military-style, then marched down the steps and across the street.

Jillian unclenched her jaw. That man could get under her skin like no one else, but as he struggled to get over the curb, her heart softened. She needed to remember his kinder, gentler side, which he'd shown on a few occasions— when her friend was killed, when he began courting her neighbor, Mrs. Taylor, and when he complimented her sister's baked goods. His sweet tooth was renowned at all the eateries in Willow Springs. Jillian smiled.

Lord, let me be that sassy when I'm ninety.

CHAPTER TWO

Amanda arrived at Blossoms & Blooms in a great mood, ready to work. After unloading her purchases, she carried them into the front room and placed them in the window within easy reach. She'd wait for Jillian to arrive before starting on her display.

Two pairs of hands are better than one.

Standing on the sidewalk outside her flower shop, Amanda enjoyed the sights and smells of the season. Fall was her favorite time of year—the changing weather, the riotous autumn colors, and the decorations popping up in the windows here on Main Street. No one could doubt Halloween was only a few weeks away.

Staring at her large undecorated window, Amanda visualized how it would look to the shoppers walking by once the design was finished. A variety of fresh fall flowers in bright colors would attract their attention, but she'd been unsure about how to keep the blooms in her display fresh for the four weeks leading up to the big day.

Sam had devised the perfect solution. Before leaving for Italy, he'd built a sturdy wooden structure out of a piece of plywood, cutting large holes in strategic locations. He arranged the holes in such a way that, when Amanda placed a bucket of flowers in each hole, the blooms would spell out the word BOO. His design cleverly hid the stems and containers while allowing Amanda to switch out the blossoms when they began to wilt.

"This window will be amazing." Amanda clapped her hands.

Sam is amazing.

Thinking of him sent shivers up her arms. She couldn't wait for him to come home. Eight weeks was a long time to be apart.

Too long.

Shaking herself from her own wool-gathering, she entered the shop. The beautiful blossoms assaulted her senses, making her florist's heart sing. An array of pinks, purples, reds, yellows, blues, and oranges captured her eye while the smell of roses, freesia, and lilies tickled her nose. She loved puttering in her store all alone in the hours before it opened.

"I could stand here all morning admiring you beauties." Amanda spoke to her flowers as she circled the room, selecting buckets of bright blooms and setting them on the floor by the window. "Jilly should be here any minute, so I'll go ahead and get started. I want to have most of the set up done before Brianna gets here."

Amanda crawled into the window and draped Sam's wooden frame with yards of sheer, shimmery black fabric, soft folds falling over the high back, down the sides, and across the strategically placed holes. Satisfied with the look, she pushed the buckets of fall blossoms into their slots. The dark backdrop allowed the bright colors of the flowers to pop. She'd used chrysanthemums, pansies, daisies, asters, and sweet alyssum in vibrant shades of orange, yellow, red, and deep purple.

A bang on the window startled Amanda.

"Oh, Jilly. You scared the daylights out of me." Amanda dropped the last bucket into its hole, then backed out of the window to unlock the door for her sister.

"Sorry. I didn't mean to scare you." Jillian bumped Amanda with her hip as she breezed into the shop with her dogs. "The window looks good, but after you left Hobby Mart, I went back in—thought it might need a little something extra." She pulled a plastic bag from behind her back, dangling it in front of Amanda. "I'll get the girls settled in the backroom, then let's see if these add a bit of sparkle and shine to your display."

With her pups snuggled on a blanket under the worktable, Jillian climbed into the window alongside Amanda, where they looped strand after strand of orange and purple twinkle lights around the window and across the ceiling. They scattered more lights all over the plywood frame, where they twinkled happily among the beautiful blooms. Amanda used layers of floral moss across the window's floor for ground cover. She positioned several pots of tall grasses to fill in the corners. An assortment of pumpkins and gourds of different shapes, colors, and sizes surrounded them.

Jillian pulled a few more boxes of lights from the bag. "I thought we could string some lights around the window, maybe even across the floor. The moss you used will camouflage the wires. I mean—can you ever have too much sparkle?"

"Great idea." Amanda reached for a box, then ripped it open. "How many of these did you buy?"

"Every box on the shelf." Jillian's face burst into a playful smile.

"Jillian, that doesn't seem fair—"

"All's fair in Halloween window decorating. Besides, if the other businesses want lights, they can order them from Amazon." Jillian rubbed her hands together. "You're going to win this year. I can feel it. Take that, First National of Willow Springs."

The bank across from the flower shop had won the trophy four years in a row.

"Your mind works in mysterious ways," Amanda said. "I'm glad you're on my side."

A hand-painted banner revealed Amanda's artistic talents. Stretched across the top of the window, oversized, brightly-colored calligraphy beckoned to shoppers— *Come in and see all our BOO-tiful flowers.* Amanda hoped shoppers would appreciate her cheeky Halloween humor.

"Let's check it out from the street." While winning the trophy and cash prize this year would be great, Amanda's main goal was to draw customers to all the downtown businesses.

"What do you think?" She crossed her arms, admiring their efforts. "Looks pretty good, even without those animatronics I ordered. They should be delivered tomorrow. Will this be enough to win the contest?"

"Your design is incredible," Jillian said. "Perfect for this large window. I can picture the witch stirring her cauldron, the little ghost popping out of a pumpkin, and the hairy spider dangling from a web. That big, gold trophy shining from the corner by those pumpkins will be the icing on top. There's no way you can lose."

"I couldn't agree more." From behind them came a soft voice with a gentle southern drawl.

Both sisters whirled around to greet the window's admirer—a petite, young woman who looked like she'd stepped from the pages of a fashion magazine. She wore a deep teal wrap dress that complimented her soft blue eyes and light blonde hair.

"I didn't mean to eavesdrop," their visitor said, "but as I passed by, your lovely window caught my eye. Which one of you owns this charming shop?" Her voice dripped sweetness like honey as she toyed with the large diamond hoops adorning her ears.

"That would be me. I'm the owner of Blossoms & Blooms." Amanda smiled, extending her hand to this potential customer. "I don't open until ten today, but I could make an exception if there's something you need."

"Oh no, that won't be necessary." The woman offered a perfectly manicured hand to Amanda. "I'm allergic to flowers. I can only admire them from a distance."

"Excuse me," Jillian interrupted. "Have we met? You look familiar. Perhaps you've come in my bookstore, Whimsy & Wonder. I'm Jillian Edwards. This is my sister, Amanda."

"I'm sure we've never met." The woman shifted her fancy leather purse from one arm to the other. "I've just moved here from New Orleans for my job—haven't met many locals yet."

"Then let us be the first to welcome you to our town," Amanda said, trying to ignore the way this woman made *locals* sound like a four-letter word as it rolled off her tongue. "Willow Springs is a friendly place, full of good people. You'll like it here."

"That remains to be seen." The woman sniffed. "A little town like this will take some getting used to after living in a big city."

Before either sister could respond, the woman took a few steps toward Amanda, pointing at the store's newly-decorated window. "You did a marvelous job here. I hope nothing stands in the way of you winning that contest. Good luck to you."

Her kind words were in opposition to her tone, which was patronizing, a bit disdainful.

Amanda and Jillian watched the woman sashay down the sidewalk, her slim hips swinging seductively. They weren't the only ones who'd noticed the town's newcomer. She'd attracted the attention of a crew of city workers fixing a pothole in front of the bank. They stopped their work, shouting a few inappropriate suggestions for how she could spend the rest of her day.

"Oh, very classy." Jillian rolled her eyes. "We told her how wonderful the people are here, then those guys have to behave like idiots."

"Hold on, Jilly," said Amanda. "The cavalry is coming to the rescue."

Mayor Sanford had walked out of the bank in time to hear the chorus of whistles and catcalls. He gathered the crew, gesturing emphatically as he spoke to them. Whatever he said sent the men straight back to work without further comments. The mayor then approached the woman, tipping his brown fedora in her direction. She spared him a brief smile as she walked up to a dark green Jaguar.

The woman climbed in without a word to the mayor, stepped on the gas and sped away.

"Is it just me, or was there something odd about her?" Jillian squinted in the direction the Jaguar had taken. "She wouldn't shake our hands or tell us her name. What was that bit about hoping nothing kept you from winning? Weird."

"She seemed nice enough." Amanda dismissed Jillian's concerns. "After all, she had the good taste to agree my window display is amazing. Don't be so suspicious, Nancy

Drew. Enjoy this lovely morning and the view of my winning Halloween display."

"Miss Southern Belle is right about your window—it's gorgeous." Jillian patted Amanda's back. "She's also the second mysterious newcomer to Willow Springs I've met this morning." She shared the story of the elderly gentleman in the parking lot of La Casita.

"I've never seen him around here, but I could swear I've seen that woman before. Something about her has my Spidey senses tingling." Jillian ran her hands up and down her arms.

"Speaking of odd, look who's headed our way." Amanda poked Jillian in the side and tipped her head at something across the street.

Aunt Grace stepped from the curb in front of the bank. As usual, she was a vision to behold thanks to her bold wardrobe choices. This morning, she'd dressed in spicy shades of orange. Her ankle pants, kitten heels, flowing flowery silk blouse, and the scarf tied around her curly hair—all orange. Her signature gold bangle bracelets jingled as she hustled across the street. The scent of her floral perfume reached them before she did.

Aunt Grace was never one to shy away from wearing new styles and bright colors, even ones that didn't quite work. Today's color choice paired with her auburn hair made their aunt look like she'd been lit on fire.

"Oh, my goodness." Jillian sucked in her breath. "That's quite a sight."

"Aunt Grace, what a nice surprise." Amanda greeted her aunt with a hug and a kiss. "What has you out this early on a Monday morning?"

"Hello, Pumpkin." Aunt Grace returned Amanda's hug. "Hello to you too, Kitten." She blew a kiss Jillian's way.

She'd been using these endearments for as long as anyone could remember, rarely using their given names.

"I had some business at the bank this morning. On my way out, I saw you admiring your handiwork on this window. The design is breathtaking. I love all those bright, beautiful colors." Their aunt sighed, the sight of the amazing bouquets of fall blossoms momentarily distracting her. A door slammed across the street, jolting her attention back to the reason for her visit.

"I came to warn you. That woman—the one you were talking to—she's bad news. You both should stay far away from her."

"Do you know her, Aunt Grace?" Jillian asked. "Who is she? We couldn't get her to tell us her name."

"No, I've never met her." Aunt Grace closed her eyes and rubbed at her temples—a sure sign she was having a vision.

"How do you know she's bad news?" Jillian cocked her head, a skeptical look on her face.

"I could see her aura from across the street—a deep green dotted with dark red spots. That's a dangerous combination of jealousy, resentment, and intense anger. You steer clear of that one. She's trouble." Aunt Grace gave each of them a hard stare. "I'm serious, girls."

"Don't worry, Aunt Grace," Amanda said. "She complimented my window—that's all. I'm sure we won't see her again. She's terribly allergic to flowers."

"Worry is what brought me here, Pumpkin. I'm afraid that woman isn't the only danger in your future. My teacup held an ominous message this morning." Their aunt pursed her lips, gnawing on them as she did when upset. "I needed to check that you were okay." Aunt Grace scrutinized Amanda from head to toe.

"As you can see, I'm fine." Amanda put out her arms and turned in a circle.

Aunt Grace shook her head with vigor, unconvinced.

"No, no. When I finished my first cup of Earl Gray and looked in the bottom, the leaves warned me of impending danger for you."

Aunt Grace was known as the eccentric, kooky one in the family. She felt an obligation to use the gift she'd been blessed with to help people—keep them safe. There had been several instances when Aunt Grace's so-called visions had amounted to something. Not everyone in the family, however, would admit she had any real psychic ability. They humored her to keep the peace.

"Tell us what the tea leaves said about her." Jillian winked at Amanda. "What kind of danger should she be prepared for?"

"The leaves were very clear." Aunt Grace dropped her voice to a whisper. "They formed a circle of flames around the letter A. This is a clear warning of fire for you, Pumpkin."

Amanda heard Jillian stifle a giggle and knew exactly what her sister was thinking. The irony of their aunt predicting a fire when she looked like one herself wasn't lost on either of them. Amanda didn't think Aunt Grace would see the humor in this situation or appreciate their opinions of her current fashion choices, so she kept those thoughts to herself.

"Fire. Hmm, that's interesting," Amanda said. "The store was chilly when I walked in early this morning. I cursed that relic of a furnace Sam keeps telling me needs replacing. A quick trip to the basement revealed the pilot light had gone out during the night. Maybe that's what you saw, me relighting the flame."

"Perhaps." Aunt Grace sounded doubtful, continuing to suck her lip. "The fire in the tea leaves seemed bigger than a pilot light. Promise me you'll be careful here at the flower shop and at home."

"Of course. I'll be so careful it will prove your tea leaves wrong." Amanda crossed her heart, shooting her aunt a warm smile. Quirky as she was, Grace had the best intentions.

"The tea leaves are never wrong." Grace leveled a dubious stare at her middle niece. "I will expect you to keep your promise."

"Yes, ma'am."

"I should go." Grace dug around in her orange leather bag. "I have an appointment at the salon in ten minutes. I don't want to be late. My stylist gets cranky at clients who throw off her schedule, then I swear she takes it out on their hair. Have a good day, Pumpkin. You too, Kitten."

Grace hurried across the street to where she'd parked her new Toyota hybrid. Amanda and Jillian stood on the sidewalk in front of Blossoms & Blooms, watching her go.

"Aunt Grace has seen a fire in my future." Amanda let out a loud snort. "What next? A flood? Famine? Plague?" She laughed at the absurdity of the situation, then stopped when Jillian didn't laugh with her. "What's wrong? You don't believe Aunt Grace's latest prediction, do you?"

"Several of her visions during Maggie's murder investigation turned out to be true. How do you explain that?"

"Dumb luck?" Amanda said. "C'mon, you don't honestly think Aunt Grace has some special power. Think about all her visions and predictions over the years that were wrong. There was the 2008 presidential election when she was certain the McCain/Palin ticket would win in a landslide vote. Dad never lets her forget that one. What about the time she was convinced there was a dead body buried in old Ms. Roger's backyard? She gave no one a moment's peace until Ms. Rogers gave the police permission to search the yard. All they found were the remains of two dead possums beneath some bushes. You remember? She's on a lucky streak right now, that's all. Don't read too much into this."

Jillian shrugged. "Maybe. Just in case, be careful with anything electrical. We wouldn't want to add fuel to Aunt Grace's fire."

"Pun intended?" Amanda laughed.

"Of course." Jillian kissed her sister's cheek. "Your window's done, so I should go." She opened the shop's door and whistled for Abbey and Hayley. "I still have a few errands to run and need to drop the pups off at home before *my* appointment at the salon. I don't want to be late and have Kate take it out on my nails. Are we still on for lunch with Mom at noon?"

"After the breakfast we had, I hope I'll be hungry by then. Why did she insist on this little get-together?"

"You know Mom. She claims she hasn't seen or talked to us in ages." Jillian hooked the leashes on her girls.

"I talked to her on the phone last night." Amanda shook her head, smiling to herself. "I'll close the shop and meet you at The Corner Deli. Grab a table if you get there first."

"Will do." Jillian unlocked her car, then shouted over her shoulder. "Hey, Amanda, your display has given me a great idea. I think I'll run a Halloween special at the bookstore. Could you paint me a sign like yours that says, *Halloween books and merchandise 15% off for all ghouls and boys?*"

Jillian's giggle faded as she climbed into her vehicle. Amanda chuckled at her sister's pitiful attempt at holiday humor. On her way inside, she took one last glance at her store's window.

Almost perfect.

Amanda stood in the center of the front room, breathing in the sweet scent of flowers. She appreciated the warm glow of the soft lights and the quiet classical music playing in the background. The sights, sounds, and smells of her shop made her smile.

"My window will be a success if it entices customers to buy some of you gorgeous things." She leaned into the display case to sniff a petite bouquet of gardenias and yellow roses as she pulled a variety of stems for her first arrangement of the day.

Amanda had finished trimming the ends of the blooms when Brianna breezed into the backroom, punctual as always.

"Good morning, Amanda. I hope you had a great weekend." She placed her purse in the cabinet by the supply closet. "What can I do to help you this morning?"

"There are several messages on our voicemail that need attention, but first, would you mind running to the post office? I've run out of stamps." Amanda handed some money to Brianna. "This should cover it."

"I'll head there right now." Brianna retrieved her purse. "Can I bring you back anything?"

"No, but thanks for asking."

"I'll be right back with those stamps." Brianna scurried out the front door.

Standing inside the cooler selecting flowers for the first bouquet of the day, Amanda jumped when the bell above the door jingled, signaling her first customer. She spun around to gaze at a good-looking gentleman in a well-tailored gray suit. By the cut of his clothes, she was confident he had money to spend on flowers for his wife.

But how could she know he'd come to buy a bouquet for his wife and not a girlfriend, partner, or mother? Had she developed *The Sight* like Aunt Grace?

Definitely not.

She *did* know that whenever Cate's husband walked into the shop, he always left with a bundle of colorful tulips—her sister's favorite.

"Good morning, Wes." Amanda greeted her brother-in-law with a sisterly hug. "I'm surprised to see you." She reached into the cooler for some tulips, then carried them to the check-out counter. "However, you're not the first family member to stop by today."

"You've been open two minutes." Wes checked his watch. "Who could have beat me here?"

"Jillian. She came to help decorate the window." Amanda motioned with her thumb. "Then Aunt Grace dropped in to share news from her tea leaves."

"Let me guess." Wes raised an eyebrow. "You're in grave danger."

"Is there any other kind?" Amanda shrugged one shoulder. "Aunt Grace saw flames in the bottom of her teacup and rushed over to warn me. Speaking of fire, you should've seen the outfit she had on."

"Bright red everything?"

"Close. Flaming orange." Amanda let out a belly laugh. "She looked like someone set *her* on fire. Poor Aunt Grace."

"You have to admit your aunt is one of a kind."

"Yes, she is." Amanda snipped the bottoms off the stems off the ivory, pink, and orange blossoms she'd chosen. "How many tulips can I sell you today? I'd suggest eighteen. That would make a nice bouquet for the love of your life."

"I'm not here to buy flowers for Cate."

Amanda stopped fussing with the tulips. She laid them alongside her florist shears on the long metal counter. Fisting her hands on her hips, she stared at Wes through narrowed eyes.

"Not for Cate. You're here to buy flowers for someone else?' Amanda tapped her fingers on the counter, her voice light with amusement. "Coming to my shop to buy flowers for the *other* woman is not your brightest move to date."

The shocked expression drained from his face once he realized Amanda was teasing him.

"No flowers for anyone today. I'm here to check on the plans for Cate's surprise party. Do you or Jillian need anything from me before Friday night?"

Amanda had liked Wes the instant she met him years ago, the day Cate brought him home to meet the family. He was smart, funny, and handsome, newly graduated from law school with a job at a prestigious firm in the city—and head over heels in love with Cate. They dated for over a year before Wes proposed, and the wedding plans commenced.

Ten years later, and happily married, Wes had planned a surprise party for Cate's thirty-fifth birthday. He'd come to Amanda and Jillian two months ago asking for their help. He wanted everything about the event to be perfect.

"The decorations are ready, the flowers I need for the centerpieces will be delivered later this week, and Jillian is hard at work on the slideshow." Amanda ticked the tasks off on her fingers. "Oh, Becca agreed to make a fabulous cake."

"Sounds like everything's under control." His warm smile reached his eyes. "I reserved the back room of McGuire's. The RSVPs have rolled in, and Max assures me the buffet will be delicious."

"Is there anything else we need to do before Friday?" Amanda continued to work on the bouquet of tulips. If not Wes, someone would buy them.

"You've done so much ... I hate to ask ... but yes, there's one more thing."

His sheepish grin tugged at Amanda's heart. She motioned him to continue.

"Cate's present will be ready at Lake's Jewelry tomorrow, but I'll be stuck in a trial all week. Do you think you or Jillian could pick up her gift for me?"

"Of course." Amanda shot him a sly smile. "I can't promise I won't sneak a peek, though."

"Go ahead, but make sure you rewrap it for me. I'm terrible at that." Wes ran a hand through his neatly combed hair, causing his cowlick to stand up. "Did I tell you I had it designed for her?"

Amanda looked up from the blush-colored ribbon she was tying in a bow. "Ooh, custom-made. Can I have a clue what it is, or are you keeping it a complete surprise?"

"No, I trust you to keep my secret. I ordered her a family ring. Cate has always loved the one my mom wears. Mr. Lake set the diamond from my grandmother's engagement ring in the center. On one side, it has Cate's and my birthstones. On the other will be Laney's and Aubrey's."

Laney and Aubrey held a special place in Amanda's heart. From their curly auburn hair, bright blue eyes, and quick wit right down to their love of tulips, they were the spitting image of Cate. Thinking about her nieces brought a smile to Amanda's face.

"Do you think she'll like it?" Wes's voice snapped Amanda back to the moment.

"No, she's going to *love* it!" Amanda looked down at her unmanicured fingers. She tried to imagine what a ring such as the one he'd described would look like on her hand. Or any ring, for that matter.

Another thought popped into her head. "How will we get her to McGuire's Friday night without raising her suspicions?"

"Bryan has it covered," Wes said. "He's telling Cate the pub is having its first Trivia Night, and he needs us all to be there to ensure there's a decent crowd."

"That's perfect. Cate can't resist trivia games." Amanda rubbed her hands together. "This party is going to be so much fun. I can't wait." Finishing the bouquet of tulips, she returned them to the cooler. "Too bad this isn't for Cate—it's gorgeous, if I do say so myself."

"Yes, it's beautiful. I'm sure you'll sell it in no time." Wes checked his watch again. "I should go. Opening statements start this afternoon. There's still a bit of prep to finish. Thanks so much for all your—"

Wes sniffed the air. "What's that smell?"

Amanda wrinkled her nose. "Oh my gosh, something's burning in the back room."

CHAPTER THREE

Wes and Amanda raced toward the offensive odor. They arrived in time to see a hulking figure in the doorway to the alley wielding an extinguisher directed at a quickly growing fire in the trashcan. A few well-aimed shots of the dry chemical powder controlled the flames. Placing the canister on the floor, Amanda's savior stepped farther into the store.

"Rick? What are ... how did ... you put out the fire. Thank you."

Amanda knew the disaster Aunt Grace predicted had been averted thanks to some quick thinking. A shuddering breath escaped her lips.

"Glad I was here to take care of it." Rick set down the extinguisher.

Distracted by thoughts of what could've happened if Rick hadn't walked in, it took Amanda a moment to find her manners and introduce her two visitors.

"Wes, this is Rick. His family has a wholesale flower business in Rochester. They've been my supplier since I opened. Rick, this is Cate's husband, Wes."

The men shook hands.

"Amanda, you should be more careful about what you throw into the trash." Rick reached back to close the door.

"And did you know you left this door standing wide open? You don't want all the cool air escaping into the alley. Not on a warm day like this."

"I didn't leave it open." Amanda shook her head. "I unlocked it, disarmed the alarm, and then picked up some boxes I'd carried from the car. My hands were full, so I kicked the door shut—hard."

"Maybe it didn't latch and popped back open." Rick shrugged. "When I walked into the backroom to deliver your flower order, I saw the flames shooting out of the trash. Did you put something hot in there?"

"No, I wasn't working back here this morning. Jilly and I were too busy out front."

Rick always wore gloves when he made deliveries, which came in handy now as he reached into the still-hot ashes and pulled out a melted plastic object.

Amanda peered at the mangled mess in his hand. "My hot glue gun! I used it last night on some ribbons in an arrangement." Amanda twisted the ties on her apron. "I can't believe I left it turned on all night. I must've knocked it into the trash today when I put down my boxes. Thank goodness you walked in when you did, Rick. I could have lost my shop."

"I was in the right place at the right time." He ducked his head, a slight blush creeping across his cheeks. "I better get your flowers unloaded. We don't want them to wilt in this heat."

Amanda watched Rick stride into the alley where his delivery truck idled.

Right place, right time—that's an understatement.

Wes placed a hand on her back. "Looks like everything's under control, so I'm going to head out. You need anything before I go?"

"Yes, could you do me a favor?"

"Name it."

"Please don't mention the fire to anyone. Not to Cate, not my mom, and especially not to Aunt Grace. I'd never hear the end of it."

While Rick worked up a sweat placing buckets of blooms into the walk-in cooler, Amanda took a phone order for a birthday bouquet.

"Yes, of course. The arrangement will be delivered to her office tomorrow around ten a.m. What would you like the card to say?" Amanda wrote the note as she listened. "Okay, that sounds perfect. Thank you for your order. I know she'll love it. Have a great day."

Amanda finished typing the sender's message as the jingle of the bell signaled a new arrival. She walked from behind the counter to greet the customer, who stood in the middle of her shop.

Amanda noticed the woman's disheveled appearance. Her petite frame, swallowed up in a shapeless gray dress and an oversized cream sweater hanging off one shoulder, shifted rhythmically from side to side. Limp, mousy blonde hair framed what might have been a pretty face but for the sallow complexion and dark circles under her eyes.

A quiet cooing sound drew Amanda's attention to the tiny infant strapped in a sling nestled on its mother's chest.

This poor woman. She looks hot and exhausted.

Amanda put on her warmest smile.

"Good morning. Welcome to Blossoms & Blooms. How can I help you today?"

The woman managed a weak smile, mumbling an inaudible greeting. She wandered over to the front of the huge cooler, placing her delicate fingers on the cool glass. After several awkward moments, she turned and spoke to Amanda.

"I passed by your window and saw the gorgeous flowers. I don't know why, but they drew me in." The woman's last words breathed out in a whisper Amanda could barely hear, but still, she detected the slightest hint of a drawl.

Two southern belles in one morning. What were the odds?

"I'm delighted the window grabbed your attention. My goal for the display was to draw people in to buy flowers for the people they care about."

"Hmm, that would be nice." The woman spoke the words aloud but seemed to talk mostly to herself. "I love fresh flowers. They brighten up a room."

"Could I pull together an arrangement for you? Something cheerful for your kitchen table, maybe?" This woman exuded sadness. Amanda had an inexplicable urge to cheer her up.

"Oh, no thank you." The woman ducked her head, averting her eyes from Amanda. "I'm not sure why I stopped in. Are you the owner of this shop?"

"Yes, I am. My name's Amanda Edwards." She reached to shake the woman's small, cold hand.

"Hmm, Amanda." The woman swayed faster, which jostled the baby, who now fussed and struggled against the cloth sling. She murmured, patting its back.

"Your baby is beautiful. Boy or girl?" Amanda peeked at the sweet face with long, dark eyelashes lying against full pink cheeks.

"Boy."

"How old is he?" Amanda tried her best to draw the woman out.

"Six weeks."

This woman perplexed Amanda. Okay, she was not a scintillating conversationalist, but didn't most new mothers gush about their newborns?

Amanda sensed her visitor might be struggling with the demands of an infant. She decided to brighten this poor woman's day if even in a small way.

"Excuse me for just a moment." Amanda walked to the cooler where she'd placed the colorful tulip bouquet she'd arranged earlier.

This should bring a smile to her face.

"I'd like you to have these flowers—a thank-you for your first visit to my store."

"Oh no, I'm not buying anything today." She patted the baby harder as she rocked faster and faster.

"These are on the house." Amanda wrapped the bouquet in her signature pink floral paper. "Take these home. Enjoy them. When you have an occasion to buy flowers, come see me." She handed the tulips to the young mother.

"Oh, they're beautiful. Thank you." The woman reached for the flowers. "I think they'll look nice on my—"

"I'm done. Flowers are unloaded and in the cooler." Rick stood in the doorway to the backroom, holding a clipboard. "I need your signature on—oops, sorry. Didn't know you had a customer."

The woman startled at Rick's voice and shrank against the cooler, hiding herself from his line of vision.

Amanda stepped away to sign the delivery invoice Rick handed her. "Thanks. I'll have another order ready for you middle of the week."

"I'll be by on Wednesday with the flowers you need for Cate's party on Friday." Rick stuck his pen into his shirt pocket. "See you then."

The bell sounded on the front door. Amanda turned to see her peculiar visitor hightail it across the street.

"Wow, your customer was sure in a hurry to get out of here." Rick let out a low whistle. "Hope I didn't scare her off."

"I doubt it." Amanda watched the woman's back as she scurried away. "She seemed sad, depressed maybe. She wasn't much for talking—never even told me her name."

"Must be new in town if you didn't recognize her. I've only been back home a few months, but I bet everybody still knows everybody in Willow Springs." Rick chuckled. "I mean, some things never change around here, right?"

Jillian arrived early for lunch, snagging a table in the corner where she had a view of the street and the people walking by. She had the perfect vantage point to watch a tall, handsome man with the most attractive brown eyes approach her table.

"This is a nice surprise." Travis pulled up a chair and leaned in for a quick kiss. Overt public displays of affection were not his style.

No sooner had they moved apart, Amanda and their mother strolled into the deli.

"Don't you two look cozy." Amanda hung her purse over the nearest chair. "We can sit at another table if we're interrupting something."

"No, please sit here." Travis jumped up, pulling out a chair for Jillian's mother, then one for Amanda. "I was keeping Jilly company while she waited for you. I'll be out of your hair just as soon as my take-out order is ready."

"Keeping her company—is that what the kids are calling it these days?"

"Amanda Siobahn Edwards. Stop teasing poor Travis." Joy gave him a motherly kiss on his cheek.

"You know how much she enjoys toying with people." Jillian cast a withering glance at Amanda.

"You can relax, Travis. I'm messing with you." Amanda gave him a playful pat on the shoulder. "I'm glad you're here to keep an eye on Jilly. We all know from experience, when left to her own devices, she can get herself into trouble." She shot a triumphant smile at her little sister.

Touché, Amanda.

The waitress brought a large, brown paper sack to the table and handed it to Travis. She batted her eyes, shot him a flirtatious smile, and rubbed his arm before walking away, hips swinging.

"What was that?" Amanda pointed at the waitress. "She flirted with Travis right in front of you, Jilly. She has some nerve."

"Flirting? She didn't even say anything." Travis's furrowed brow revealed his confusion.

"Are you serious? You didn't notice her brazen smile, the come-hither eyes, or the way she touched your arm. No?" Amanda gestured her thumb at Travis. "Jillian, you have this one under a spell if he doesn't even recognize when a *very young*, beautiful girl comes on to him."

"I'm a lucky woman." Jillian took Travis's hand and squeezed.

"What can I say? I only have eyes for your sister." Travis used one arm to pull Jillian closer. "I better go. If I'm gone much longer, Jack will think I've ducked out on the rest of the work at his house."

He stood, nodding to his right. "Always good to see you, Mrs. Edwards, Amanda." Turning to Jillian, he smiled. "I'll see you tonight for dinner at six. Bring the pups. Blaze will love having a play date with her friends." Travis grabbed his food and left.

"He's such a sweet man, Jilly. A keeper for sure." Joy gave her youngest daughter a pointed look. "You don't want to let that one get away."

"I don't intend to, Mom."

"Dinner at his place *and* he cooks. You hit the jackpot with him. Neither Sam nor I can boil water without burning it." Amanda laughed at her own shortcomings in the kitchen.

"Yes, we can all agree Travis is great." Jillian unfolded her napkin, placing it in her lap. "Now, on to a new topic. How was your morning, Mom?"

"Busy. I baked two loaves of banana bread, worked in my garden, then waited over two hours for the technician to arrive to service the furnace for winter." The irritation in Joy's tone made her feelings unmistakable.

Her daughters knew all too well how their mother felt about tardiness.

"How were things at the flower shop after I left?" Jillian asked.

Amanda's mind flashed back to the fire at the store, and how much worse it could've been. She chose not to mention it. At least not yet.

"After you left, Wes stopped by to check on the party plans. I took a few phone orders. Rick delivered some flowers, and a very odd woman with a baby stopped by for no apparent reason other than my window display drew her in. She seemed depressed, so I gave her a bouquet of tulips I'd made—hoped they'd brighten her day."

"Gave them to her? That was a thoughtful thing to do." Joy gave Amanda an approving smile.

"A bit fiscally irresponsible, but very kind." Jillian winked at her sister. "Hopefully, they'll cheer her up each time she looks at them."

"That was my plan. She wasn't the strangest visitor I had though. That honor goes to my last customer." Amanda blew out a long breath. "He tried my patience."

"A bit difficult, was he?" Jillian could sympathize with her sister.

"Difficult would be an understatement." Amanda ran her fingers through her shoulder-length, auburn hair. "I had locked up for lunch when this old man banged on my door. He called me Flower Lady and demanded I sell him some of my *posies* from the window."

Flower Lady?

Sounds like Mr. Erickson paid a visit to the flower shop.

"Before I could even ask what he was looking for, the old coot told me to save my breath. He wasn't interested in my sales pitch. '*I'm just here to buy a few posies for a hot date I have later today. Don't you be thinkin' I'm gonna spend an arm and a leg, either.*'" Amanda did her best impersonation of a grouchy, old man's voice.

"He picked out three each of my orange, yellow, and white Gerbera daisies which only cost three dollars per stem. He still had the nerve to complain about my prices—accused me of highway robbery. I made him a bouquet with greenery and added a ribbon all for ten bucks just to get him out of my store."

"I'm sure his date will appreciate your efforts," Joy said.

"Wait, there's more." Amanda took a big drink of her Diet Coke.

"As I crawled into the window to grab his flowers, I caught him ogling my behind. When I called him on it, do you know what he had the audacity to say?"

"I'm afraid to guess." Jillian cringed.

Amanda used her old man voice again—deep and throaty. "He snickered and said, *'Just enjoying the scenery.'* Can you believe that? I mean, how rude. I pity the poor woman who said yes to a date with him."

"If I'm not mistaken, your crabby customer was Mr. Erickson. You remember him. My not-so-friendly neighbor across from Whimsy & Wonder. You met him at McGuire's the day Maggie's murder was solved. I know it's been a long time, but that man's hard to forget."

Amanda snapped her fingers. "I thought the old guy looked familiar."

"The poor woman, as you called her, receiving those daisies would be my other neighbor, Mrs. Taylor. They've been dating since this time last year. Who knows? Maybe before long you'll be putting together their wedding flowers."

The horrified look on Amanda's face spoke volumes, but any words she might've uttered were cut off by the appearance of the waitress.

"Hello, I'm Shannon. What can I get ya?" The girl managed to ask this while smacking the large wad of gum in her mouth. She couldn't have been more than eighteen.

They gave her their order, then Jillian changed the subject from nonagenarian romance to event planning. "You talked to Wes—what does he think of our plans for Cate's party?"

"He liked everything, especially the color scheme of orange, ivory, and pink we chose to match the tulips he always gives Cate. I rented tablecloths, chair covers, and linen napkins in soft shades of pink and orange from The Party Palace in Westhaven. They also had these great cream dishes with tiny pink tulips around the edges that will be perfect. The party store will deliver the balloons to the bar by four on Friday. Rick will bring the flowers I need for the centerpieces on Wednesday. What do you think?"

"McGuire's backroom will look beautiful. Cate will be so surprised." Joy stirred sweetener into her tea. "I'm glad Wes decided to do this for her. Thirty-five is a big birthday for some women—you know—halfway between thirty and forty, when laugh lines stop being cute and start looking suspiciously permanent."

"Poor Cate. Next thing you know, she'll be moisturizing like it's her full-time job." Amanda's words belied the grin on her face.

"You two are nuts," Jillian said with a mock frown. "Cate doesn't have one line on her face—she still looks like she's 25. Now, can we please get back to her party? I was thinking—what if Bryan or Mike made pink and orange cocktails? One that's fruity, the other a little bolder."

"I love that idea, Jilly. I'm sure they can come up with something delicious. How's it going with the video you're making?" Amanda asked.

"Despite your doubt of my technology skills, I'm happy to report the video is done." Jillian puffed out her chest. "Everyone's going to love it. One of Travis's buddies helped me incorporate several of Cate's favorite songs and some cool graphics, along with all the pictures of her that we chose."

The waitress brought their lunch orders, placing a delicious-looking bowl of chili and half a grilled cheese sandwich in front of Jillian. Amanda had settled on her usual grilled chicken slider with fries while their mom chose a cobb salad. The conversation paused as they dug into their food with gusto. Who knew planning a surprise party worked up such an appetite?

"Wes asked for help with Cate's gift." Amanda described the ring he'd designed, making them promise to keep his secret. "He's going to be busy in the city all week, so he needs one of us to pick it up tomorrow."

"A family ring. What a wonderful idea." A wistful look shrouded Joy's face.

"We'll be sure to mention it to Dad before your birthday," Amanda said.

"What a romantic gift—a ring from the man you love." Jillian let out a long sigh.

"Are you going to get all sappy on me?" Amanda shook her head. "I suppose you're hoping for a ring from your guy."

"Enough with the engagement talk." The words flew from her mouth before Jillian could stop them.

"What do you mean?" Joy narrowed her eyes. "You know about the proposal pool at McGuire's, don't you? Who told you—no, wait. Cate blabbed, didn't she? She cannot keep a secret."

"No, Amanda gave me the heads-up." Jillian toyed with the silver locket around her neck. "I promised to keep quiet and not spoil everyone's fun, but just so *you* know, the money in the pot will be sitting there for a while. There isn't going to be another wedding in this family anytime soon. Aunt Grace can have the spotlight all to herself."

The waitress brought the check, signaling the end of lunch.

"I'd better get back—open the shop. Those flowers won't sell themselves." Amanda dug in her wallet, pulling out a twenty. "I'll pick up Cate's ring and hold on to it until the party."

"Put your money away, sweetheart. Lunch today is my treat." Joy waved away the money.

"Thanks, Mom." Amanda tucked the cash into her jacket pocket. "We'll talk again soon. Love you both."

"Love you more," her mom replied, like always.

"Love you the mostest," Amanda and Jillian chimed in together, falling into their familiar family routine.

After the bill was paid, Jillian walked her mom to the car.

"Thanks for lunch, Mom."

"You're welcome, sweetie. Please behave yourself." Joy patted her youngest's face. "Try to stay out of trouble."

"Why do you always say that?"

"Because I know you, and I'm your mother. Love you more." Joy climbed into her car and waved goodbye.

Jillian had arrived at The Corner Deli before noon when parking spaces were hard to come by. She'd found a spot several blocks away in front of Sugar & Spice, Cate's bakery. She welcomed the walk to burn off the calories from lunch.

Not far from her car, Jillian discovered a bunch of discarded flowers on the sidewalk—droopy tulips with a B & B ribbon. The flowers Amanda had given the woman with the baby.

She'll be disappointed when she realizes she dropped them.

Jillian picked up the bouquet and slid it into one of her totes. Maybe the blossoms could be salvaged if she put them in water soon. She stowed her bags in the back seat, then opened the driver's side door. A slip of paper folded under the windshield wiper caught her eye.

Her first thought was someone had placed flyers from a local business on all of the cars, but none of the other cars had one. Wrong color for a parking ticket. Then the childlike handwriting captured her attention. Jillian snatched the paper.

Roses are red, violets are blue.
Flowers die. Someone you love will too.

Jillian slumped against the car with the ominous note clasped in her hand. Her heart and mind raced. This could not be happening again. Maggie's killers had used notes to communicate their intent, but they were all dead or in jail. Who was this copycat?

The author of the poem stated someone she loved would die. Did the overt reference to flowers point to Amanda? That would make sense.

The poem said *too*. Did the writer plan to kill more than one person?

Jillian's pulse quickened. She'd been through one murder investigation and knew the correct way to collect evidence. She pinched the paper between two fingertips before sliding it into the outside pocket of her purse.

On her way home, she called her favorite Willow Springs detective. Ethan agreed to meet her at Blossoms & Blooms in an hour.

Amanda needs to know if someone is out to get her.

CHAPTER FOUR

Walking back to her shop, Amanda's brisk pace slowed as the vibrant fall colors outside the storefronts caught her eye. Gold, crimson, and burnt orange blooms spilled from flower pots, tugging at her attention and nudging her thoughts off course. So much so, it took her a moment to notice the familiar car parked six spaces down from her shop—a vintage 1965 Shelby GT350 Mustang, cobalt blue with white racing stripes. Her heart gave a little jolt. That little beauty was Sam's pride and joy, and if his car was here, so was Sam—home early from his trip to Italy.

Could this day get any better?

A dark-haired man with a lean athletic build leaned one hip against the driver's side of the car, his back to Amanda. Completely engrossed by something on his phone, he didn't hear her approach. She snuck up from behind, stood on her tiptoes, and covered his eyes with her hands.

"Hey, Sailor. If you don't have plans for tonight, I might be free."

The man turned and grabbed her. He slid one hand to the small of her back, easing her into a slow dip. Then he kissed her—slow and tender, like something straight out of a Hollywood movie.

"Sam, let me up before all the neighbors come out to stare." Amanda laughed, pushing against his chest as he restored her to a standing position. "You were quick with the moves, buddy. What if it hadn't been me, but some strange woman propositioning you on the street?"

"Well, you are sometimes a strange woman."

Amanda narrowed her eyes at him.

He chuckled, softening. "Still, I would know your voice and the smell of your perfume anywhere." Sam kissed her again before taking a good, long look at her. "I've missed your face—six weeks is too long to be apart."

"I couldn't agree more, but you're home now." She laid a hand on his cheek. "Wait a minute. Why *are* you home early? Nothing wrong, I hope."

"The exact opposite. The shoot went smoother than expected. The weather and my subjects cooperated. I took some amazing photos. My client will be very happy."

"That's wonderful—a reason to celebrate. Where would you like to go for dinner?"

"While the food in Italy was incredible, I craved Max's barbeque ribs by week three."

"McGuire's it is. I can meet you around six-thirty after I close." Amanda traced a finger across the dark circles under Sam's eyes. "I need to open the store, and you look like you need a shower and a nice, long nap."

"Is it that obvious?" Sam scrubbed his hands over his stubble. "I'm not sure if it's the seven-hour time difference or the long flight that's kicking my behind—maybe both. A shower followed by a nap sound like a great way to pass the time until I have dinner with you." He pulled her in for another kiss—this one deeper, more urgent, heat curling through her. A warm tingle swept over every inch of her body. When he finally broke the kiss, he rested his forehead on hers.

"I missed you, babe."

"The feeling's mutual." Amanda placed a quick kiss on his lips. "Now get out of here. I have work to do, and you're dead on your feet. I'll see you tonight, Sailor."

Amanda stood on the sidewalk, watching Sam climb into his car and drive away. She let out a soft sigh.

Tonight can't get here fast enough.

Inside Blossoms & Blooms, Amanda tied her florist's apron around her waist. She sang along to the radio while finishing the bouquets for this afternoon's deliveries. The shop was doing well, her window display looked fantastic, and Sam was home early. Her heart was full.

Amanda stood in the backroom's cooler, grabbing a few stems of freesia when there was a knock on the alley door. Before she could respond, the door creaked open and Jillian peeked around the door frame, hesitant.

She wasn't alone. Ethan and her pups had come along too.

The dogs pushed their way in and rushed to see Amanda. They flopped over, baring their hairy bellies for her immediate attention. She dropped to the floor, scratching them in all their favorite places. They rewarded her with soft grunts and quivering bodies. She pulled a container of dog treats from under the counter. Each dog received one more rub, followed by a biscuit.

"What brings you two into the shop together? Wait, don't tell me. Ethan's in the doghouse and needs flowers for Becca. Jilly came to help pick them out. Am I right?" Amanda teased.

"I *wish* we were here for that reason." Ethan shifted from foot to foot.

"You wish your wife was so angry with you that flowers were needed to make amends? You feeling okay, Ethan?" Amanda quirked an eyebrow in his direction.

"Becca's anger would be preferable to this." He took a deep breath and jumped right in. "Amanda, we believe you've made someone angry enough to want to kill you."

"Geez, Ethan," Jillian chastised. "What happened to breaking it to her gently?"

"Hang on. What are you talking about?" Amanda blinked, trying to make sense of what she'd just heard. The arrangement of roses she'd been working on was momentarily forgotten.

Once settled at the worktable, Ethan pulled a plastic bag from his jacket pocket and handed it to Amanda. "Read the note through the plastic. We don't want to contaminate evidence."

"Evidence of what? You two are acting strange." Amanda took the baggie, reading the paper inside. As the meaning of the words sank in, a wave of nausea left her unsteady on her feet. She sank onto the nearest stool.

"Why would anyone write such a horrible thing? Where did you get this?"

"Someone put it under my windshield wiper while we were at lunch. After I read it, I called Ethan." Jillian rubbed her sister's arm. "We need his help."

"This is ridiculous, probably a stupid Halloween prank." Amanda shoved the bag back at Ethan. "I've never done anything to make someone want to kill me."

"If it's a prank, it's a sick one." Jillian's tone sizzled with anger.

Ethan cleared his throat. "Prank or not, I will have to investigate. We need to put our heads together and figure out who wrote the note. Find the poet, then we'll know if the threat is real."

Ethan interrogated Amanda for thirty minutes about her friends, customers, neighbors, and casual acquaintances. He asked about the places she frequented often.

"I still say this is a twisted Halloween hoax." Amanda rubbed her temples. "How will all these questions help you catch the pranksters who wrote this rhyme?"

"I'm creating a picture of your daily routine—the people you come in contact with and the places you go. Whoever wrote this note could be someone you know and see often."

Jillian put up her hand like a policeman halting traffic. "Whoa, wait a minute. You think the person threatening Amanda is someone she knows?"

"Yes, I do. In ninety percent of cases like this, the perpetrator is someone the victim has met or has a relationship with. Most often, it's the person you least expect."

Jillian had a vague recollection of him sharing that information during Maggie's murder investigation. The statistic hadn't set well then—or now.

"If that's the case, how do we keep her safe?" Jillian's voice rose in frustration. "Someone needs to be with her 24–7 to protect her from this lunatic."

"Uh, hello. I'm standing right here." Amanda waved her hands. "You two talk about me as if I have no say in this matter. I don't need protection. I can take care of myself."

"Funny you should say that," Jillian said. "I seem to recall when my life was threatened, you jumped in with a plan for how to keep me safe while ignoring my wishes. Now it's my turn, so you hush."

"You're being ridiculous." Amanda huffed out a long breath. "This is a juvenile Halloween prank by some of our local teenagers."

"What if it isn't?" Ethan's deep voice punctuated the tension. "Amanda, we have to treat this as a serious threat. I'll have a squad car patrol by the store and your house every hour."

"That's it? Your guys will check on her *once* every hour?" Jillian glared at Ethan. "What about the other fifty-nine minutes? Anyone could walk in off the street and—I need a minute." She grabbed the dog leashes and snapped them onto her girls' collars. Jillian stomped into the alley behind the shop, letting the door bang shut behind her.

"Hope she can calm down out there." Amanda laid her hands flat on the worktable, staring at Ethan. "I promise to keep my eyes and ears open. I'll be wary of anyone acting suspicious, and I'll keep my gun close at hand."

"Your gun?" Ethan leveled a concerned stare, one skeptical eyebrow raised to his hairline.

"Yes, Detective, I own a gun. I've taken the sixteen-hour concealed carry class, received my license, and had a background check done." She returned to the vase of white roses, adding purple delphinium. "Sam took me to a reputable shop in the city—all above board and legal—to buy a weapon. He and I logged over fifty hours at the shooting range in Weston. I'm very comfortable with my gun, and I know how to use it."

"What kind of gun did you get?" He narrowed his eyes at her. "Where is it now?"

"I have a SIG Sauer P238—which is locked in my home safe." Amanda pursed her lips at him. "I have all the paperwork if you'd like to see it."

"Not at the moment, thanks." Ethan had his serious cop face in place. "I'd suggest you keep your gun with you all the time until we solve the mystery of this note. Should you have to use it, *then* I'll need to see that paperwork."

"Will do." Amanda sighted down her fingers. "Someone tries to take me out, I'll be ready for them."

Jillian stormed through the door, her face like a dark storm cloud ready to burst. Her pups struggled to keep up on their short legs.

"Didn't expect you back so soon, Jilly. I figured the girls would want a longer walk." Amanda wiped her wet hands on her apron. She grabbed a bowl and filled it with water for Abbey and Hayley.

Jillian ignored Amanda. "Um, Ethan? Could you come into the alley with me?" Her voice quivered. "I need to show you something."

"What has you so upset?" Amanda took a few steps toward the door. "Did someone do something out there—oh no, not my new car?"

"No, it's not your car. The store is fine ..." Jillian let her voice fade away.

"You're making me nervous. Tell us what's wrong." Amanda tapped a staccato rhythm on the tabletop.

Jillian's shoulders drooped. "Come outside—it would be better if I showed you."

"Take it easy. I'm coming." Ethan finished a text, then shoved his phone into his pocket.

"Not without me, you're not." Amanda raced for the door. "Brianna, I'll be out back for a few minutes if you need me."

"No worries." Brianna called out from the front.

"Has she been here this whole time?" Jillian asked.

"Yes, she's been watching the front of the store, so I can work on orders back here," Amanda said. "Now c'mon."

Out in the alley, Jillian hustled them toward the west corner of the building where Amanda's car sat parked and unharmed. Babbs Barker, the owner of Yips & Clips, the upscale doggy spa next door waved as she threw a bag of garbage into the dumpster they shared.

"Hey, Amanda. How's it going?"

"All good, Babbs. How about you?"

"Can't complain. Business is great."

"Yeah, me too. Hope it stays that way." Amanda enjoyed chatting with Babbs, but now wasn't the most opportune time. She waved at her neighbor, then turned to Jillian as Ethan's patience wore thin.

"Okay, what did you see back here that has you so bent out of shape?" Exasperation reverberated from every word Ethan spoke.

"This."

Jillian had led them to a large, white delivery truck backed into the alley and parked two doors down from Blossoms & Blooms. The rear doors hung wide open, showing no merchandise inside.

"Big deal." Ethan shrugged one shoulder. "You found an empty truck."

"Not completely empty." Jillian's voice held a chill.

"Looks abandoned to me. I'll call for a tow since it's parked illegally." Ethan pulled his phone from his pocket.

Amanda didn't say a word. She walked around to the passenger side and spotted the familiar logo. "This is Rick's floral delivery van. Why would he leave it here in the alley?"

"I don't think he had a choice." Jillian pointed to the front seat.

Ethan stepped onto the passenger side running board to get a closer look. Whatever he saw caused him to swear under his breath.

"What is it? Is someone in there?" Amanda climbed up beside him on the truck step. Her hand flew to her mouth, stifling the shriek bubbling to the surface.

Rick, his face partially hidden from sight, slumped over the steering wheel. A neat, round bullet hole darkened his right temple. Yellow carnations were scattered inside the cab of the truck.

"Please. No." Amanda stumbled off the truck's running board and backed away.

"Amanda, do you know the man in the truck?" Ethan's cop voice was sharp.

Her head bowed, she nodded. "Yes, yes I do."

He turned to face Jillian. "Did you touch anything? The door handle, maybe?"

"Nope. I didn't touch a thing. Despite what you think, I do know better." Jillian scowled at him.

Ethan muttered something under his breath, but Jillian ignored him, choosing instead to put her arm around her sister, pulling her close.

"I thought it was weird—the van sitting here with doors wide open," Jillian continued. "I peeked inside, saw that poor man, then rushed to get you. He's dead, isn't he?"

Amanda's stomach churned. Not Rick. He couldn't be dead.

"Appears to be." Ethan sighed, pulling latex gloves from his pocket. He moved to the driver's side of the truck and tried the door. Unlocked. He pulled it open, blocking Jillian's view. Reaching in, he put two fingers on Rick's neck to check for a pulse. "Needed to be sure."

Amanda fought her trembling legs as Ethan placed two calls, first to dispatch to get the forensics team on the scene, the second to the coroner's office.

"What happens now?" Jillian stood on tiptoes, peeking over Ethan's shoulder. "We need a positive identification of the body to notify next of kin, right?"

Ethan pulled at the collar of his shirt. "We, Jillian? Did you become a sworn officer of the law without telling me?

Because if not, *we* won't be doing anything. You found the body and reported it to me. Your job here is done. End of story."

Jillian tsked. "How soon you've forgotten my part in your last murder investigation. If it weren't for me, you wouldn't have had key information that helped solve your case." A pained expression crossed Ethan's face. Jillian softened her tone. "Maybe I could assist with this case too. Another pair of eyes and ears never hurts."

Amanda, who'd hunkered against the dumpster in stunned silence, snapped out of her stupor. "Stop it!" She screamed at them. "Just stop. A good man is dead. He deserves better than you two bickering like this."

Jillian took her sister's hand "You're right, sweetie. We're both really sorry. Right. Ethan?"

"Er... yeah... I'm sorry." He averted his eyes from Amanda. "How about we move this conversation somewhere else?"

They gathered in the corner of the alley, away from the delivery van—away from the dead body.

"What can you tell me about that man? What's his name?" Ethan's tone was much gentler now.

A shuddering breath escaped Amanda's lips.

"His name is Rick Westbrook. He is ... *was* ... my floral supplier. He brought a delivery earlier this morning. I can't believe this." Amanda swiped at warm tears trickling down her cheeks.

A police car pulled up, distracting Ethan from his questions. A young officer climbed from his cruiser and approached. The two men spoke in hushed tones, then the rookie took a roll of yellow crime tape from the trunk. He cordoned off the alley.

"Let's go inside." Ethan fussed with his polo, yanking the collar away from his neck. "I need to get out of this heat before I melt."

While the past week had been cool and pleasant, the weather had experienced a drastic change in the last two days—an unusual late September warm up. A cloudless sky with the sun blazing down had raised temperatures to over ninety degrees. Summer seemed determined to hang on a little longer.

Ethan grumbled to no one in particular. "This heat won't help preserve that body, either. Evidence is deteriorating as we speak."

A quick check showed Jillian's pups slept curled together on the blanket they kept under Amanda's long worktable for their visits. Jillian grabbed three bottles of water from the mini fridge, handing one to Ethan. He rolled it around on his forehead before cracking the seal and taking a long swig. She set a second bottle in front of Amanda.

The room fell into oppressive silence, broken without warning minutes later, when Ethan cursed under his breath, slamming his stool into the table. The pups yelped and ran to their mama.

"You ladies stay cool in here. I forgot something outside." He drained his water, tossing the bottle into the recycle bin. "Don't go anywhere. I have questions for both of you."

Jillian waited for the door to close behind him before she pelted Amanda with questions of her own. "You saw Rick had been shot, right? I didn't see a gun, did you? Who could have done this? How well did you really know him? What's with the yellow flowers?"

"Jilly, stop. My head is pounding." Amanda rubbed at her temples. "Yes, I saw the bullet wound. No, I didn't see a gun. I have no idea who would do this. Rick was a nice guy—friendly, funny, kind. I've known him since kindergarten."

She took a sip of water. "And I have no clue why there were yellow flowers or where they came from.

"He left Willow Springs after high school to attend Louisiana State. He returned home when his dad became ill. He passed away two months ago, so Rick stayed to help his family run their floral business. I could count on my delivery being correct and on time. He sold only top-quality flowers. He loved his wife and their newborn. They were planning a trip to Louisiana soon to show the baby off to her family. That's what I know about Rick."

There. She hoped that would pacify her sister's thirst for answers.

Jillian pursed her lips. "No one's that perfect, Amanda. He must've ticked someone off."

Amanda drew a slow, unsteady breath. "This is unbelievable. First, you find the note threatening more than one murder, then Rick turns up dead in the alley behind the store. The two must be related, right?"

Jillian hesitated. "We have to let Ethan invest—"

"Of course, they're related, and I'm the common denominator." Amanda's voice exploded, vibrating with frustration.

"Stay calm." Jillian massaged Amanda's back. "Ethan's here. He has everything under control, but even he can use a little help now and again. Let's make a list of details we know about each crime, so when he comes back, we'll be ready with something helpful."

"That's a good idea." Amanda managed a weak smile. "You'd make a fair detective if you weren't already a successful business owner."

"Who says I can't do both?" Jillian asked with an easy confidence that left no doubt.

Amanda threw up her hands. "The law says so. You are neither a police officer or a detective. Those people are trained to solve crimes. You, on the other hand, are too nosy for your own good. Don't get involved, Jilly. Remember what happened last time?"

Jillian sat on the nearest stool, scooting closer to the table. "Last time? Yes, I remember. Ethan struggled to solve two murders. He hit one dead end after another until information I provided helped him close the case."

"You seem to remember quite a bit." Ethan's voice, as frosty as icicles in January, brought a chill to the room. He'd returned inside just in time to hear Jillian boast about her contributions to his last murder case. "I'm concerned about what you've forgotten—the fact you were attacked *three* times because you stuck your nose into my case."

"I survived the attacks. When information in that case fell into my lap, I brought it straight to you." Jillian's voice ratcheted up several notches. "I didn't go looking for clues. I can't help it if people trust me and are comfortable talking to me."

"Hey, hey, hey." Ethan's wife, Becca, burst into the back room. "What's all the yelling about? I could hear you before I opened the door. Bring it down a few notches unless you want everyone on Main Street to know your business."

Amanda's gaze flitted between Jillian and Becca, landing on Ethan.

Uh-oh, this could get interesting—bestie vs. wife vs. husband.

Becca and Jillian met on the first day of kindergarten and had been best friends ever since. Amanda envied their close friendship—except at times like this. Jillian possessed a knack for getting involved in Ethan's investigations, which put Becca squarely between the two people she loved most.

"Hi, Becca. Welcome home." Amanda greeted her with a warm smile.

Becca grunted a *hello* as her gaze volleyed between the two who remained silent.

"Really—not going to speak to me? Fine." She pivoted, giving Amanda her full attention. "Maybe you can tell me what's going on between these two stubborn mules. Does it have anything to do with all those cop cars in the alley?"

"Yes." Amanda fussed with her apron strings. "I'm just not sure how much I should tell you."

"Nothing. You should tell her nothing." Ethan spoke through gritted teeth.

"Ah, ah, don't be rude." Becca jabbed a finger at Ethan, then turned to her friends. "C'mon you guys, out with it. I leave town for a week, then come home to some major happenings. Bring me up to speed."

"I need to see if the forensics team is here yet." Ethan stormed out, letting the door slam behind him.

"Hi, sweetheart. Welcome home. I missed you so much." Sarcasm dripped like melting ice cream from Becca's tongue. "Which one of you managed to make my husband so angry he couldn't bother to give me a proper hello?"

Amanda stared at Jillian, who raised her hand. "That would be me."

"Humph, of course, it is." Frown lines creased Becca's forehead. "What's going on? Why is Ethan waiting on the forensics—"

BOOM. CRACK. CRASH.

CHAPTER FIVE

The women startled at the sound of breaking glass and splintering wood. The noise sent the pups scampering into the supply closet.

Amanda wished she could hide there with them.

"What in the world was that?" Becca said.

"Whatever it was didn't sound good." Amanda handed the dogs' leashes to Jillian. "To be safe, maybe we should grab the pups and get out of here."

Coaxing Abbey and Hayley with treats, Jillian snapped on their leads just as the back door was wrenched open.

Ethan rushed in.

"Stay here." He barked the order, bolting for the front of the store where the noise had erupted.

The women exchanged wary glances, then nodded their silent agreement to ignore Ethan's instructions. With the dogs in tow, they slipped from the backroom and followed him through the shop and out the front door—stopping just short of the chaos, keeping a cautious distance from Ethan.

Jillian, Amanda, and Becca joined the crowd gathered on the sidewalk, doing their best to blend in. The sight of the destruction drew a mixed reaction of curses and gasps.

The shop's plate-glass window had been shattered. A few remaining shards clung in the corners. Amanda's beautiful floral display lay in ruins. The wooden frame Sam built was split in half, upending the buckets and scattering fresh stems across the floor of the window. Water puddled everywhere. The twinkle lights no longer hung where they'd been strategically placed, and they definitely no longer twinkled.

No one needed to wonder what caused this awful mess—the answer stared them in the face. A metal flower planter recently installed along the street sat upended in the middle of the Halloween display, having wreaked havoc on the window and its contents.

"This is terrible. All our hard work—ruined." Jillian said.

Amanda bit back a response—too overcome with anger to trust herself to speak.

"Jilly, it's not safe out here for your girls." Becca motioned at the scattering of sharp fragments on the sidewalk. "They could get glass stuck in their paws."

"Good call." Jillian scooped the pups into her arms. "I'll take them to my car around back, get them settled with the AC on, and be right back." Cradling her dogs, Jillian wove through the uneasy hush of the crowd and the crunch of glass underfoot, disappearing around the corner.

Becca put an arm around Amanda's shoulder. "I'm so sorry. I can't imagine who would do something like this. Or why."

Finding her voice, Amanda shared her theory. "My money is on the same person who threatened my life in that pathetic poem." She twisted and untwisted a strand of hair, a sure sign of her distress.

A strangled cry drew everyone's attention to the shop's front door. Brianna stood with her hands covering her mouth, her eyes stretched wide.

Amanda took her by the arm. "Bri, are you okay?"

"Why are you asking about me? Look at your beautiful window." The young woman gestured at the destruction. "I was in the restroom when I heard a loud crash. Amanda, I'm so sorry. If I'd been in my position when this happened, maybe I could've done something to catch the vandal in the act."

"Don't apologize. This mess isn't your fault." Amanda patted her back. "I'm thankful you weren't near the window. You could've been hurt by flying glass."

"I hadn't thought of that." Brianna managed a weak smile. "Appears I was lucky then."

"Go home for the rest of the day," Amanda said. "There's nothing you can do here."

After many assurances that Amanda didn't need her, a police officer retrieved Brianna's purse and she left, but not before making Amanda promise to let her know when to come back.

"I'll be here whenever you need me to help clean up."

The whispers of people huddled around the flower shop reached Amanda's ears. They echoed some of the same questions racing through her mind. Was this vandalism an isolated incident, or should all the shop owners be worried about their businesses? How did someone get away with this in broad daylight?

The others had no idea what had happened behind Blossom & Blooms, not yet anyway. The Willow Springs rumor mill would bring them up to speed soon enough. With her knowledge of Rick's death, Amanda speculated, not if but how, the two incidents were related.

Greg Weaver, the owner of The Chocolate Factory, the candy store on the corner, stepped forward. "We should call 9-1-1. The police need to know about this."

"There are cops out back—"

Ethan cut Becca off by addressing the assembled crowd. "The Willow Springs police department is on the scene. We'll be conducting a thorough investigation and would appreciate everyone's cooperation."

"How come the cops were already here?"

"Yeah, what's with all the police cars in the alley?"

"What aren't you telling us?"

"How could this happen in broad daylight?" Jillian's voice rose from the crowd as she rejoined them out front.

As Ethan fielded questions shouted by onlookers, Amanda studied the faces in the crowd. Matt Carpenter, who owned the pharmacy next to the flower shop, stood next to the Harrisons, who ran The Corner Deli. They whispered with the Garcias who owned La Casita. Babbs Barker and her partner, Jen Green, co-owners of Yips & Clips, huddled with Greg Weaver. The entire staff of the bank looked on from across the street.

These people belonged here on Main Street. They were Amanda's neighbors, fellow business owners, and, in some cases, friends. But could one of them be responsible for this damage or the threat to her life? Ethan said it could be someone she knew. This made them all suspects.

Who can I trust?

"I don't know what to do," Amanda muttered to no one in particular. "What should I do now?"

"We need to secure your store—get the window boarded up until you can arrange to get it fixed." Greg Weaver came to the rescue. "I have a buddy who works at the lumberyard in Red Hill. I'll give him a call and get some plywood for you."

Amanda's gaze found focus on Greg's face. "Thank you. I appreciate your help. Seeing my busted window ... finding poor—"

"Ahem." Jillian cleared her throat, a reminder that Ethan warned them against talking about Rick's death.

"Er ... yeah. Thanks." Amanda shook hands with Greg.

"No worries—wish I could do more. I'm sorry about all of this, Amanda." He pulled out his phone, stepping away to make the call.

Jillian took Amanda by the arm, leading her off to the side. "Well, wasn't he Johnny-on-the-Spot—a little too eager to help if you ask me. How well do you know this Greg guy?"

"Greg and his wife Allie are wonderful neighbors and friends. He has a kind heart—helps others whenever he can." Amanda dismissed the concern.

"All the same. Their store's only been open a few months. They haven't lived here long. What do we really know about them?" Jillian squinted at him.

"You suspect the Weavers of destroying my window? That's ridiculous." Amanda rolled her eyes. "Weren't you the one welcoming our southern visitor earlier—telling her our town is full of wonderful people? She's only been in town a few weeks. Maybe you should put her on the suspect list too?"

"Maybe I will," Jillian said.

"You read too many mystery novels." Becca nudged Jillian with an elbow. "Suspicious of everyone."

Greg returned. "You're all set, Amanda. The plywood is on its way." He gave her a one-armed hug. "Let me know if there's anything else you need. Are you okay if I head back to my shop? Allie needs me to look at one of the ovens."

"Thanks, Greg. I'll be fine. Go fix that stove, so your wife can churn out more delicious chocolate confections." Amanda managed a weak smile.

Ethan finally succeeded in dispersing the crowd, leaving the sisters and Becca alone in front of the flower shop.

"I'll help you clean up when we get the green light from Ethan," Jillian said. "Until then, let me take the girls for a quick walk, and after that, we can pop next door to the pharmacy for a fountain drink at the counter."

"I can stay too." Becca bounced on her toes. "I'm an expert with a dustpan and a broom."

"That's not necessary, you two. All the chaos here at the store has ruined a lot of people's afternoon plans. Both of you, go. Try to salvage part of your day."

Amanda moved closer to inspect the damage.

"Whether you want to admit it or not, you'll need help cleaning up this mess." Becca sidled closer to Jillian. "We're not going anywhere."

"That's right. There's so much to do here."

Amanda had a sneaky feeling Jillian wasn't just talking about the clean-up.

The techs collected evidence from both crime scenes. They processed Rick's body quickly, so the coroner could rescue it from the heat. Only the delivery van and the yellow crime tape remained in the alley. Ethan, Greg Weaver, and the young police officer nailed large sheets of plywood over the gaping hole in the store window. Every pound of the hammers broke a tiny piece of Amanda's heart.

The idea of fountain drinks was abandoned when Amanda announced she had a few arrangements to finish.

"I can't offer beverages like the pharmacy, but there are sodas in the fridge." She took an etched crystal vase from the cabinet.

"I'll get them." Becca retrieved three ice-cold Diet Cokes from the refrigerator, along with a box of leftover cookies from Sugar & Spice. She placed everything, including napkins, on the table. The sleepy schnauzers snuggled on the blanket underneath, exhausted from their walk. Soft snorts and snuffles drifted from below.

Amanda fetched an armful of red, pink, and white roses from the back cooler.

"Whoa, that will be a huge bouquet if you plan on using all those flowers." Jillian inhaled as she picked up a rose. "I love the pink ones."

"One of the tellers at the bank is celebrating her eighteenth anniversary. Her husband wants six red, six pink, and six white ones in the arrangement."

"That won't come cheap," Jillian said.

"Happy wife, happy life. Isn't that the saying?" Amanda snipped the bottom of the stems on an angle.

"Enough about flowers. I've been gone—missed some of the excitement. I need information." Becca's attendance at a culinary conference since the previous Monday had her out of the loop.

"Okay, I heard Ethan whispering with the other cop. Who was the guy in the truck? How was he killed? Why would someone break Amanda's window? What's this about a crazed poet?"

"Take a breath, Becca." Jillian pushed a drink toward her bestie. "We'll tell you everything we know."

Amanda and Jillian launched into their versions of the day's occurrences, talking over and drowning each other out. Becca waved her white napkin in surrender.

"Stop. I didn't understand a word you said. You have to take turns." She pointed to Amanda. "You start, then Jillian can fill in the details. I want to hear it all."

Amanda began with Jillian's discovery of the ominous note. Jillian added information Amanda left out. They fell into an easy storytelling rhythm which highlighted the discovery of Rick in the alley and the vandalism to the Halloween display.

"Wow, that'll teach me to leave town," Becca muttered, shaking her head. "I still have questions, but I'm not sure where to begin."

"Let's start with one of mine." Ethan marched into the room, his face dripping with perspiration. He locked eyes with Jillian, his steely blue gaze challenged her piercing green. "Then, we need to come to an understanding about your part in this investigation."

Amanda winced at his remark, knowing his tone wouldn't sit well with Jillian. Unless she did something, another argument was inevitable.

A diversion was needed. Quick.

Amanda grabbed a stool for Ethan since Becca sat in the seat he'd vacated earlier. She retrieved another beverage and opened the bakery box sitting on the table to reveal the chocolate chip cookies Cate dropped off yesterday. These were Ethan and Jillian's favorites. Amanda hoped the treats would distract them from arguing or at least take the edge off their anger toward one another. She'd read eating chocolate releases endorphins which make us happy.

She slid the cookies to the center of the table within both their reach.

C'mon endorphins, do your thing.

Ethan threw out the first olive branch. "I'm sorry I yelled at you earlier, Jillian. I should've been more professional than that."

"Apology accepted." She offered her hand, which he took. "I'm sorry too. When there's a mystery to solve, my curiosity gets the best of me. I can't seem to help myself, but I'll try."

Amanda and Becca let out derisive snorts. Jillian volleyed with a withering glare in their direction.

Ethan ignored the women and pressed on. "I appreciate that, Jilly. Your inquisitive personality doesn't make it easy for you to let the trained professionals do their jobs. How about we make a deal?"

"What kind of deal?" Jillian narrowed her eyes.

"I'm going to ask you and Amanda some questions. During the process, I'll give you any details I'm allowed to share to satisfy your need for information. Then, you promise to step back and let me do my job."

Amanda sucked in a tiny breath. Step back? That was a bit vague for Jilly. She'd find a loophole in this agreement.

"You have yourself a deal, Detective." Jillian pumped his arm, grinning like she'd won a prize.

Amanda sighed.

Poor Ethan. He has no idea what he just agreed to.

"That was too easy." Ethan's face crumpled. "Why do I feel like, once again, I'm getting the short end of the deal?"

Or maybe he does.

"Be happy she agreed to step back." Becca patted her husband's arm. "You know our Jilly. That's a huge promise from someone like her—an inquiring mind who needs to know all."

"Fine, let's get started." He pulled out his notebook. "I'd like to narrow down the time frame for the flower guy's death. Amanda, when did he deliver your flowers this morning?"

"I wasn't staring at the clock, but it was before nine-thirty. Wes was still here when Rick put—" Amanda almost let it slip about the trashcan fire. She still couldn't believe she'd been so careless with the glue gun.

"Put what?" Ethan waited.

"Put ... er ... the flowers in the cooler for me." Amanda hoped no one noticed her hesitation.

"How long would you say the flower guy was here?"

"Give me a minute." She tapped a finger to her chin. "Wes left a little after nine-thirty. I answered the phone and took orders while Rick unloaded his truck. I'd say he was done before ten—oh, wait. I can check the delivery invoice I signed. Rick dates and time stamps them."

Amanda rushed to her office, returning with a slightly damp receipt. She offered the soggy paper to Ethan. "Sorry, job hazard in a flower shop."

"Nine fifty-seven. Wow, your flower guy liked to be exact." Ethan entered the receipt as evidence. "Did he tell you where he was going next?"

"No. Rick promised to be here Wednesday with my next order, then he left." Amanda swiped at a lone tear. "At least, I thought he left."

"How could this have happened, yet no one heard a shot?" Jillian threw this question into the mix. "And the window. Surely someone saw something that will help catch the vandal."

"The shooter probably used a silencer, but I'll interview everyone on the street to see if they heard or saw anything relating to his death or the smashed window. Maybe we'll get lucky." Ethan took a long drink from his soda.

Jillian put down the cookie she nibbled. "I don't envy you those conversations. Talking about a dead body makes people nervous."

"Could you stop calling him *my flower guy* or the *dead body*? He has a name—Rick." Amanda snapped, then gentled her words. "His name is Rick." A few more tears ran down her cheeks.

"You're right, sweetie. We're being insensitive." Jillian nudged Ethan with her hip. "Right, Ethan?"

"Yeah ... sorry." He averted his gaze from Amanda's face.

The sound of the air conditioner working double time punctuated the silence in the room as they gave Amanda a minute to pull herself together.

"Speaking of Rick, did the forensics team uncover any evidence?" Becca brought them back to the point of their discussion.

"If so, did it point you toward a possible suspect?" Jillian's eagerness was palpable.

"Ah, ah, ah." Ethan waggled his finger at her. "Curiosity rears its pretty little auburn head."

"C'mon, Ethan," Jillian said. "You promised to share information with me if I promised to step back. Your words, not mine."

"Patience, Jilly. I mean to keep my word. All in good time."

Amanda couldn't help an inward smile. Ethan enjoyed stringing Jillian along. Before he could satisfy her need to know, the young officer interrupted them. He hung back in the doorway, fidgeting with the uniform cap in his hands.

"O'Neil." Ethan nodded at the officer. "What can I do for you?"

"I'm sorry for intruding, sir, but you're needed back at the crime lab. The forensics team wants to show you what they've found so far inside the victim's truck."

Ethan left without a backward glance. His complete disregard for Becca rankled.

"That man is unbelievable," Becca ranted. "Gone a week—no greeting, no kiss, no goodbye. Just wait until he gets home."

Amanda understood Becca's resentment, but pitied poor Ethan. Things would be ugly at his house later tonight. Jillian, on the other hand, wasn't finished sharing her thoughts on the two cases.

"This is incredible. A murder behind your shop and the vandalism of your display window." She blew a strand of hair from her face. "Both on the same day."

"I can't believe no one heard a commotion in the alley when Rick was ... killed." Amanda choked out the words.

"Or saw someone throwing a planter through the shop's window," Becca added. "They must've chosen the perfect moment when no one was around."

"Or they were just lucky," Amanda said.

Only partially listening to their conversation, Jillian's analytical mind was working hard to sort things out. "Rick was killed during the day when all the businesses are open, but no one heard a shot."

"You can have a silencer made for just about any gun." Amanda arranged the red roses in the vase.

Jillian gasped at this off-hand comment. "When did you become an expert on guns?"

"Since I took the class for concealed carry and bought one of my own. The instructor was very informative." Amanda added a stalk of baby's breath.

"Wait, you own a gun? Never thought you, of all people, would be packing heat." Jillian shook her head. "However, knowing you have protection makes me feel better about you being here alone—until the killer is caught."

"Oh shoot! I have to go." Becca jumped from her stool. "I have a haircut in five minutes. I expect you two will let me know if you hear anything more about the murder or the broken window."

"You live with the lead detective. You can pump him for details." Jillian waved at Becca's retreating back.

"You should go too, Jilly." Amanda surveyed the partially finished bouquet, choosing where to stick the white blooms.

"No, I'll keep you company while you perform your magic on these flowers. Ignore me and get back to work. I'll do the same." She pulled a laptop from her tote bag.

"What are you doing? Go home." Amanda scowled. "I don't need a babysitter, if that's what you're thinking."

"Nope—not leaving."

Amanda knew arguing with Jillian was a waste of time. She'd focus instead on these roses and the last two funeral arrangements of the day. Tim, a high school junior who delivered for her, would arrive around four to take the bouquets to their destinations.

They worked for the next hour or so, talking little, while the radio provided background noise. Tim came, loaded the flowers into the Blossoms & Blooms van, and headed to his first stop—Whispering Pines Funeral Home.

At five o'clock, Amanda locked the front door before changing the *Open* sign to *Closed*. She swept the floor in her workroom and prepared the daily deposit to drop at the bank in the morning.

"Okay, let's go." At the word *go*, Jillian's pups jumped up and ran to the door.

"Good girls. You and your mama head on home." Amanda patted them on the head. "I'm going to do the same since I have a hot date with Sam tonight."

"Sam is home?" Jillian stopped with only one dog fully leashed. "Why didn't you tell me?"

"I'm sorry. I guess with all the excitement, it slipped my mind. He was here waiting for me when I came back from lunch. His photo shoot wrapped early, so he hightailed it home to see me. Or it might be the ribs at McGuire's he hurried home to enjoy." Amanda didn't care one way or the other. All that mattered was Sam had come home.

Jillian sighed with relief. "I'm glad he's back. He can help keep an eye on you."

Amanda frowned.

"I know. I know. You don't need a babysitter." Jillian wouldn't be deterred. "Think of him as a handsome bodyguard."

"No, it's not that." Amanda laughed at the suggestion. "The whole family will find out what happened today if they haven't already. They'll be upset if they hear about it from someone other than us. Maybe we should invite them to dinner tonight?" Amanda put out her hands, palms up, and shrugged. "What do you think?"

"Won't that ruin your cozy welcome home date with Sam? He'll be disappointed."

"One of the things I love most about Sam is his thoughtfulness—he'll understand. Besides, he loves our family dinners at McGuire's." Amanda caught herself smiling. "I'll be sure to make it up to him later."

Jillian pulled her phone from her back pocket. "I'll text everyone—tell them their attendance is mandatory. That will get them all there." Her fingers flew. "Done. Family dinner at McGuire's around seven-thirty."

She rounded up the girls who'd wandered back to their blankets under the table. She clipped on the second leash and herded them toward the alley door.

"The pups will need a minute before I put them in my car. You're coming right behind me, aren't you?" Jillian looked over her shoulder. "I don't want you here alone. Not after today's events."

"I'm leaving in a few minutes. See you at dinner."

Amanda did a quick pass through the shop, making certain the lights were off and nothing dangerous was still plugged in. She didn't need another incident like the glue gun.

Once everything met with her approval, she stepped out of her shop and into the alley, the door clicking shut behind her. Jillian waited in her car, headlights casting long shadows against the brick walls. Amanda raised her hand and waved. Jillian responded with a soft honk, then pulled away into the dark, leaving Amanda alone in the hush of the evening.

Amanda hit the button on her key fob, unlocking the car. As she opened the door, her purse slipped from her shoulder and fell to the ground. A surprised grunt escaped as she bent down to retrieve it from the gutter.

"Are you kidding me?" Her front left tire was flat. "Could this day get any more frustrating?"

Years ago, when the sisters began driving, their father insisted they learn how to change a flat tire. He said they should be prepared in case of an emergency.

Thanks, Dad.

Amanda walked back to the trunk to get the spare and stopped dead in her tracks. She blinked, then looked again, as if her eyes were playing tricks on her.

The back tire was flat too.

"Come on!" She kicked the offending rubber orb. "I can't change *two* tires when I only have one spare."

She leaned against her car, pulling out her cell phone to call Sam for help. She did her best to ignore the tiny niggle of worry building in her brain. Sam promised he'd be right there. They'd have one of the mechanics from Shorty's Garage take care of the flats in the morning.

The call lasted less than a minute. Amanda was in no mood to talk. She needed to blow off this foul mood before dinner with her family.

Slamming the trunk shut, she stepped around to the right side of the car ready to power walk her frustration away. One look at this side of the car had Amanda wishing she knew more curse words. Anger boiled to the surface as she screamed into the empty alley. The two right tires were flat.

Two might be a strange coincidence, but all four? No way.

A tingle of apprehension crept up her spine as she stewed over her misfortune. The threatening words from the note echoed in her brain. She could no longer blame today's mishaps on some teenager's Halloween prank. Someone had a vendetta against her.

An unexpected breeze lifted a loose curl and tossed it across Amanda's face. Goosebumps skittered up and down her arms.

A dog barked. Amanda flinched. The rumble of a car engine signaled she was no longer alone in the alley.

CHAPTER SIX

Amanda's pulse quickened. The sound of the approaching car grew louder. A scary thought popped into her head.

Who would be driving in the alley after business hours?

That's when it hit her—standing here alone with a killer on the loose was a terrible idea.

Amanda ducked back inside Blossoms & Blooms, leaving the door open a crack. She held her breath as the sound of the rumbling engine faded into the distance. Leaning back against the wall, she reminded herself to breathe.

The car is gone. I'm okay. Sam will be here any minute.

Another car pulled into the alley, sending her heart racing. She peeked around the door frame, then sighed. The cavalry had arrived in a beautifully-restored blue Mustang. Sam stepped out of his car, dressed for their date.

Warmth spread through Amanda's chest as he walked toward her.

He wore a pair of impeccably cut dark jeans, a light blue button-down shirt, and his favorite soft brown, suede Keens.

Hands off, ladies. He's all mine.

Amanda glanced at her wrinkled work clothes. She'd wanted to put on something nice for Sam, but that wouldn't be possible now.

"Babe." Sam's smile made her weak in the knees. He wrapped her in his arms. "How did you get yourself into this mess?"

She breathed in the musky scent of his cologne, which calmed her nerves—a little. Irritated and confused, she couldn't decide whether she wanted to cry or scream. She chose the latter, leaving the shelter of Sam's hug.

"What did I do to deserve this?" Amanda paced in front of her car, gesticulating at the infuriating tires. "I'd like to get my hands on whoever thought this was funny."

"They're just tires, babe. Shorty's guys will have those two fixed in no time tomorrow."

"Great. Do you think they'll have time to fix all four of them?" She crossed her arms over her chest, glaring at Sam.

"All of them?" Sam ran his fingers through his still-damp hair. "How did that happen?"

"I have no idea, but look at my car. All four tires are flat as a pancake." She stomped her foot like a petulant child.

"Okay, calm down. We'll get you *four* new ones in the morning." Sam rubbed his hands up and down Amanda's arms. "Could you have run over something—like in a construction zone?"

"I haven't been anywhere near a construction zone." She threw her hands in the air. "Considering my car is less than a year old, these tires are practically new. Unless," she poked an accusing finger at Sam, "that dealer you sent me to scammed me with a crappy set on my brand-new vehicle."

"I checked your car myself before you bought it, remember? I can assure you those tires were as new as the car." Sam pointed at the deflated pieces of rubber. "Besides, Brett Highland and his dealership have an excellent reputation. He wouldn't do something shady or underhanded to his customers."

"Someone's been shady and underhanded." Amanda mumbled several expletives. "They did this on purpose, but I don't know why. Jillian and Ethan are going to have a field day with this."

"What do they have to do with anything?"

"Um ... I was going to tell you later, but I guess now is good." She told Sam about the menacing note, Ethan and Jillian's visit, as well as his plan to keep an eye on her.

"Ethan wants to have police surveillance at the shop and my house. I argued it was a harmless Halloween hoax, but I see that he's right. Bring on the cop drive-bys."

Sam leaned forward, his arms extended for a hug.

"Wait, there's more." Amanda stopped him with a hand on his chest.

He let out a big sigh. "Why do I get the feeling you're going to tell me about something worse than a pesky poet and four flat tires?"

"Because I am." Amanda described the vandalism to her display window, then segued into finding Rick's dead body in the alley. Tears ran down her cheeks by the end of the story. "I don't understand why all these things happened. My window can be fixed, but poor Rick didn't deserve to die. He was truly a nice guy."

She held her breath, waiting for Sam to explode. He'd demand to know why she hadn't called him when these horrible things happened. That was his usual reaction—always wanting to rush in and rescue her. They'd had several arguments about his need to be a knight in shining armor and her need to be independent.

This time was different.

Sam wrapped Amanda in a fierce hug, resting his chin on top of her head. They stood like this for the longest time— no words, only the silent support of two hearts beating in rhythm together. She knew him well enough to understand he was giving himself time, gathering his thoughts, and calming his anger. His body relaxed little by little until he pulled back and steered her toward his car.

"Call Ethan. Tell him about your tires. This is another case of vandalism for him to investigate." Sam opened the passenger side door for her. "We're going to dinner. I want a delicious meal with the woman I love, whom I missed while I was gone."

"Oh, Sam." Amanda breathed a sigh of relief. "You have no idea how much I missed you. Tonight will be a great evening—a date with my favorite photographer, a relaxing drive in your sweet ride with four functional tires, and dinner with my entire family."

The final words were whispered in a rush as Amanda delivered a quick kiss on Sam's cheek before ducking into the car.

"Everyone's coming? Our intimate dinner has become an Edwards family function?" He leaned into her open window. "Let me guess. You and Jillian invited them to McGuire's, so they don't hear about the note, the window, and the murder from the Willow Springs rumor mill." Sam motioned toward Amanda's car. "Now this too."

"You know me so well." She flashed him her most endearing smile. "We didn't want the family to hear about the threat from someone other than us. I hope you don't mind a few more people joining our romantic date."

"I don't mind at all. I love your family. After what happened to Jillian last year, I understand your need to tell them about this threat." Sam put a hand under Amanda's chin, tipped it up and winked. "But after dinner, you're all mine."

"That's a deal, Sailor." Amanda leaned back into the cool leather seat. She closed her eyes, letting out a shuddering sigh.

Sam made her feel safe and loved.

After a five-minute drive, he pulled into a newly vacated spot across the street from the pub. They ran into Ethan and Becca at the door.

"Ethan, good to see you, man. You taking your lovely wife to dinner too?" The two men exchanged a bro-hug.

"Yes, I am." Ethan pulled Becca in for a side-armed hug. "The little woman's been away for a few days, so I'm treating her to a night out on the town."

Becca bristled. "I'm the little woman, am I?" She gave him a hard look. Her mouth disappeared into a thin line. She hooked her arm through Sam's.

"Well, this *little woman*," Becca huffed, "chooses to eat dinner with Amanda and Sam tonight. You, dear husband, can dine alone."

Amanda stifled the laughter that threatened to erupt.

Sam escorted his two lovely dinner dates into McGuire's while Ethan followed, grumbling the whole way.

Amanda watched Jillian scurry around, arranging two more chairs for Becca and Ethan. Sam had invited Jillian's bestie and her husband to join this impromptu dinner. With a group now numbering more than ten, hugs and greetings took a few minutes. Seeing the people she cared for most under one roof, ready to share a meal, warmed her heart.

Bryan's wait staff took drink orders, while Max, the chef, delivered serving trays of appetizers to the table. Skewers jammed with antipasto, jerk chicken, marinated steak bites, and grilled fall vegetables filled the room with an intoxicating aroma of herbs and spices. The drinks arrived as the trays were passed. Everyone settled in.

Conversation and laughter flowed until Cate brought them around to the reason for their gathering.

"Jillian, you called us all together. To what do we owe the pleasure of this spur-of-the-moment family dinner? Are we celebrating Sam's homecoming or some other good news, maybe?" Cate raised an eyebrow, then discretely tapped her left-hand ring finger.

"His early arrival is reason to celebrate." Jillian raised her glass in Sam's direction, ignoring her sister's innuendo. "However, that's not why you're all here. Something's happened."

Amanda clenched her jaw, waiting for Jillian to break the happy mood with their somber news. Before she could, Aunt Grace squealed, hopping from her chair.

"You're getting married." Glasses and cutlery skittered across the table. "I've had visions of you in your mother's wedding dress. Oh, this is wonderful news." Aunt Grace pulled Travis into a big hug. "I knew I was right."

"Congratulations," everyone shouted.

"Bryan, check the board to see who wins the proposal pool." Ethan rubbed his hands together. "Somebody's winning a chunk of money today."

"No, no, no. I'm not getting married." Jillian waved her arms. Travis's face blanched. "We're not getting married."

"You're not engaged?" Aunt Grace's enthusiasm deflated like a balloon pricked with a pin. She sank back into her chair. "You didn't pop the question?" She looked at Travis, who shook his head.

"Then, what's going on?" Cate wrinkled her nose. "Start talking, Jilly."

"She texted you because of me." Amanda cleared her throat. "I received a note today—a death threat. At first, I thought it was a Halloween prank, but my opinion has since changed."

The table exploded. Everyone talked at once, firing questions at Amanda. She waited them out without saying one word, overwhelmed by their concern. Sam came to her rescue, raising his voice.

"Hey, hey, everybody. Settle down." Sam moved his chair even closer to Amanda, placing his hand on her back. "Jillian and Amanda can bring you up to speed when you're all quiet."

Seats were reclaimed. Voices silenced. Concerned faces waited.

Amanda nodded at Jillian, who began by explaining the details of the note—how and where they found it, along with the haunting message.

"After I read it, I called Ethan. We went to Blossoms & Blooms to warn Amanda. Anything I left out?" Jillian looked to him for support.

"No, you summed it up well." Ethan made eye contact with each person at the table. "I want you all to know Amanda will have police surveillance at the shop and at home until this mystery is solved."

"Please don't say mystery in front of Jilly." Becca shuddered. "We know how that will turn out."

"Jillian will *not* be involved in this investigation." Ethan's cop tone came through loud and clear. "Her assistance is not needed. Until this threat is eliminated, my job is to keep Amanda safe—can't afford any distractions."

"Oh, I'm a distraction, huh?" Jillian sniffed. "I take offense to that, Ethan."

Amanda intervened before things became heated between the pair.

"I'll do my part to stay safe. My gun will be with me all the time." She put up a hand to stop them. "Before you hammer me with questions again, I've taken the concealed carry class. I'm very comfortable shooting my weapon."

"Let's hope shooting isn't necessary." Sam squeezed Amanda's hand. He turned to Ethan. "Find this lunatic fast before Annie Oakley here does anything we'll regret." His comment earned him a jab to the ribs.

"You're a riot, Sam." Amanda followed her jab with a soft kiss. "You're also the best."

"This is dreadful news, Amanda." Aunt Grace tsked. "I saw fire in the teacup this morning, not death threats and guns. I don't know how I could've been so far off."

Amanda considered mentioning the trashcan incident, but their aunt had already switched her attention back to engagements and weddings.

She turned to Jillian. "You're really not getting married?"

"Sorry, but no." Jillian patted Grace's hand.

"That's so strange. I clearly saw you walk down an aisle wearing your mother's beautiful wedding dress." She peered in Travis's direction, but he avoided eye contact. "Maybe someday soon."

"Mom," Bryan's tone held a hint of warning. "Enough with the wedding talk. Can't you see you're making Travis uncomfortable?"

"Am I?" Grace cast a mischievous look at Travis. "I simply call it like I see it."

Furtive glances were shared around the table. No one liked to encourage Aunt Grace's so-called visions. Even though they would love to see Jillian and Travis engaged, no one pressed the issue. Amanda wasn't surprised when their attention swung back in her direction.

"Ethan, how will you find the person who wrote this note?" Bryan asked.

"Good, old-fashioned police work." Ethan said with a confident nod. "I'll follow wherever the clues take me. I promise I'll do everything in my power to find this lunatic before they can act on their threats."

"You're sure it isn't a hoax?" Cate twisted her wedding band, a sure sign she was worried.

"I can't be sure of anything until I find the person responsible for writing it. That's why Amanda must be on guard all the time." Ethan threw her a cop-like stare.

Amanda, Jillian, and Ethan were still fielding questions about the note when the main course of barbecue ribs arrived at the table. Max had prepared his hand-cut crinkle fries, fresh coleslaw, and spicy baked beans to serve alongside the main course. The sound of utensils clinking against serving platters interrupted further conversation while everyone filled their plates.

"While you enjoy this delicious meal, there's more news to share." Amanda took a big swallow of water, her mouth as dry as a farm field in a drought. Dread at telling them the rest of the day's incidents coiled in her stomach.

"You're getting married." Aunt Grace clapped her hands as Sam choked on his drink. "It was you, not Jillian, in my vision. You girls all look so much alike."

"No one is getting married," Amanda snapped at her aunt. "Except you."

With Grace seated contritely in her chair, Amanda relayed the story of her four flat tires.

"How is that possible?" Jillian shook her head. "I've never heard of anyone having all their tires go flat at the same time."

"I'd say they had a little help from Amanda's note-writing psycho." Ethan growled and rocked forward in his seat. "What I can't say is why I'm just now finding out about this." He glared across the table at Amanda.

She fired back. "Before you grumble at me anymore, Detective, you might want to check your voicemail. I called you on our way here."

"All right, you two, truce." Amanda's father, Drew, spoke from the end of the table. "Ethan, you think someone did this to her car—they deliberately slit the tires?"

"I'll be investigating it along with the note, but yes. That's probably what happened." Ethan pulled his phone from his pocket. "Amanda, where's your car now?"

"Parked in the alley behind the flower shop," she said. "We're going to call Shorty's in the morning to have it towed."

"Let me take care of it. I'd like your car off the street and locked up at Shorty's to protect any evidence." Ethan left the table to make the call.

"I agree with Ethan." Bryan took a long swig of his beer. "This has to be the work of the crazy poet. You need to be careful, Amanda."

"I will." She smiled at her cousin. "I know in the grand scheme of things this is silly, but it's going to be expensive to replace four tires if my insurance won't cover it."

Her dad came around the table to place a kiss on his middle daughter's forehead. "Don't worry, sweetie. Mom and I can help you out." He slipped a few crisp fifty-dollar bills into her hands amid protests.

"Daddy, no. I can take care of this on my own." Amanda handed the money back, but her father shoved both hands in his pockets.

"Shorty'll get the job done and give you the best deal he can." Travis entered the conversation, attempting to ease the stalemate between father and daughter. "If he doesn't, you let me know. I'll rough him up for you." Travis punched one hand into the other.

Everyone laughed at the image of sweet, easy-going Travis beating up a seventy-year-old man.

"My big, strong hero." Jillian dropped a kiss on his cheek. "You'd never hurt a fly."

"Could if I needed to."

"Yeah, yeah, Lieutenant. We know you're a tough guy." Ethan returned to the table, shoving his phone in his pocket. "Shorty's guys are on their way to pick up your car now. He said to tell you not to worry. He'll take care of everything." Ethan signaled the waitress for a refill. "Give me your key fob. I told Shorty I'd leave it at the hostess stand."

Before Amanda could thank Ethan for his help, Max arrived at the table to serve his latest dessert—a double chocolate caramel cake with homemade chocolate whipped cream. The gooey caramel oozed from every inch of the cake as he sliced into the moist layers. In no time at all, every crumb on every plate had been devoured.

"That has to be the most decadent of all Max's desserts, and I ate too much." Becca pulled on the waist of her pants. "Do you think he'd share the recipe, so I could make a cupcake version for the bakery?"

"He's secretive about his recipes, but it won't hurt—" Bryan didn't bother to finish. Becca had jumped from the table, making a beeline for the kitchen.

"Tell him he has another hit on his hands," Jillian called after Becca's fleeting back.

Chairs were shifted. Napkins were placed on the table as people prepared to leave.

"Before you go ..." Amanda cleared her throat to regain everyone's attention.

"Was there something else, dear?" Her mom's face radiated concern.

"Er ... yes ... there are two more things I've put off because there's no easy way to say them." Amanda took a deep breath before diving right in. "Someone threw an iron planter through my display window, and my flower delivery man was found shot to death in his truck behind my store." Her words came out in one long, frenzied stream.

No one moved. No one spoke. Amanda wasn't sure they breathed.

"We know this is a lot to take in." Jillian moved to stand beside her sister. "Just remember, the important thing is Amanda is safe, and Ethan's on the job."

The women surged toward Amanda offering comfort and support. The men pounced on Ethan, demanding to know more details.

One of the perks of hosting these family dinners at McGuire's was Bryan owned the place. They could stay as late as necessary for Ethan to address each question and concern while calming every nerve.

"Death threats, vandalism, and murder. What's going on in our quiet, little town?" Cate snuggled in closer to her husband. Wes draped a protective arm across her back.

"When Maggie died, Ethan told me murder can happen anywhere, and the killer is most often someone the victim knows."

"Kitten, that information doesn't assuage our nerves." Aunt Grace toyed with the multitude of gold chains adorning her neck.

"Just speaking the truth, Aunt Grace."

Time crept toward ten. As the family made their way to the exits, Amanda reassured her parents and aunt she'd be fine. Ethan reiterated her safety was his top priority. The elder Edwards trio departed for home, only somewhat pacified by their assurances.

The ladies grabbed all their coats while the men squabbled over who would pick up the check. The waitress arrived without one. She informed them it had been taken care of along with a generous tip. When Jillian asked who'd paid for their dinner, the waitress shrugged.

"I'm not supposed to say." She gave them a nervous smile before walking away.

"Bryan," Amanda said.

Everyone agreed it could've been him. Bryan was known to pick up the tab for some of his favorite diners.

"C'mon, let's go thank him." Travis motioned for the ladies to go first.

Amanda led the group of sated diners back to Bryan's office, barging in without bothering to knock. The room was empty. They checked with Mike, the bartender and Bryan's business partner.

"Sorry. You just missed him." Mike wiped up a spill on the wooden bar. "He left not five minutes ago—said something about a late-night date."

"Do you know if he picked up our bill before leaving?" Becca said.

"No clue about that, it looks like this is your lucky night." Mike winked and went back to filling bar orders as fast as the waitresses could place them.

"The bigger question would be who is Bryan's mystery date?" Cate said. "He didn't mention anything during dinner. Why's he being secretive about it?"

"Ooh, two mysteries in one evening." Jillian tapped her bottom lip with a Positively Pink fingernail.

"Uh-uh, no detective work for you." Travis put his arms around Jillian. "We know what happens when you get involved. I'm not going through that again."

"Don't be silly." Jillian wiggled out of his grasp, turning to face him. "I'm talking about an unknown benefactor and a clandestine date. The police won't be investigating those cases. My life won't be in danger if I poke around. I'm curious, that's all."

"You've heard the expression, *curiosity killed the cat,* right?" Sam tugged on Jillian's sleek French braid. "Don't tempt fate. You seem to rub people the wrong way when you start asking questions."

"Aw, Sam." Jillian batted her eyes at her sister's boyfriend. "Does this concern mean you care about me? That's so sweet."

"Leave it to you to change the subject rather than agree to mind your own business." Amanda made a face at Jillian.

"I hate to break up this party," Travis looked at his watch, "but I'm relieving a buddy an hour early tomorrow morning. I need to get some sleep before my shift starts at six."

The day's heat and humidity had broken. They walked out into a cool, crisp fall evening. Goodbyes were exchanged, then each couple headed in the direction of their car.

Halfway across the street, Amanda stopped. "Hey, Jilly," she shouted. "Can you give me a ride to the flower shop tomorrow since my car is out of commission?"

"Can do. I'll pick you up around eight." Jillian waved. "Have a good night, you two lovebirds. That goes for you old married couples too."

"You can count on us having a great night." Sam grinned like a kid on Christmas morning. He swung Amanda around and planted a long, loud kiss on her lips. "I've been on the road for over a month. I've missed my girl."

"Yeah, he missed me so much, he informed me he's sleeping over—on the couch," Amanda said.

"With some lunatic on the prowl, I'll take up my sentry post on her sofa with a bird's-eye view of the front door. Somebody tries to get in, I'll be waiting for them."

"My knight in shining armor." Amanda rested her head on his shoulder. "You might want to bring coffee and cinnamon rolls, Jilly. If we're having a slumber party, we'll need sustenance in the morning."

"I'll have breakfast goodies boxed and ready," Cate called out.

"Since I'm picking up treats for your boyfriend, I'll be there a little *after* eight," Jillian yelled back across the street.

Despite the brave face she chose to show others, relief at having Sam home flooded Amanda's body along with a warm, tingly feeling. As they climbed into his Mustang, a long-suppressed thought exploded like a bomb in her head.

Sam really does love me, and no matter how much I might protest otherwise—that feeling is entirely mutual. I'm in love with Sam. Maybe marriage isn't out of the question.

Amanda gave herself a mental slap.

Where did that come from? I'm starting to sound like Aunt Grace.

Jillian settled in the cozy front seat of Travis's truck. He'd barely closed his door when she blurted out.

"Do you think Sam's ever going to ask Amanda to marry him?"

Travis clutched the steering wheel. The skin stretched tight across his knuckles.

"Why're you asking me? I don't know anything about anybody getting married." Travis snapped out his words.

Whoa, what was his deal?

An awkward silence filled the truck's cab. Jillian stewed over his reaction until a lightbulb blinked on.

"Travis ... um, look. About my aunt tonight. You know ... that whole engagement thing. I don't know where she gets this stuff." Jillian shook her head.

"No worries, we all know how your Aunt Grace can be." Travis refused to make eye contact.

"R-i-ght." Jillian dragged the one syllable into three. "She's way out in left field with this one. I mean, *us* getting married—it's crazy."

"I don't know if I'd use that word." Travis gazed at Jillian. "I could think of crazier things."

Her heart skipped a beat as a goofy grin spread across her face. She hoped to explore this topic further, but Travis pulled into the circle drive in front of Cate's house and her apartment. They walked hand in hand to Jillian's front door.

As she put the key in the lock, he spun her around, initiating a kiss that left her weak in the knees and out of breath. Pulling back enough to place his hands on both sides of her face, Travis stroked her cheeks with his thumbs. His stare was intense—those brown eyes flecked with gold bored into her soul. He said the one thing that always made Jillian shiver.

"I love you. Probably more than you know." His smile reached those sexy eyes, crinkling them around the edges. "Maybe we could talk about this whole marriage thing sometime soon." A brief kiss this time, then he reached behind her, opened the door, and nudged her inside to the joy of her pups. "Sleep well. Talk to you tomorrow."

He pulled the door shut.

Jillian counted to ten, waiting to make sure he'd walked away before she let out a squeal and sank to the floor. The girls jumped in her lap, showering her with puppy kisses. Her heart raced, both hands shook, and a lump formed in her throat. Tears threatened to spill over, but she willed them away.

"He wants to talk about marriage. What do you think about that, ladies?" Abbey and Hayley snuggled deeper into their mama's lap, happy for whatever was making her so generous with the cuddles.

With thoughts of frothy wedding gowns, sweet-scented flowers, and honeymoon destinations taking up space in her head, it took Jillian a minute to register the loud commotion coming from her front yard. Raised voices, then someone cursing was followed by the squeal of tires. Shooing her dogs back, she opened the door and peeked out.

Travis stood on her porch, one hand on his forehead. Blood trickled between his fingers, dripping onto the cement steps. She backed up as he stumbled into the house.

CHAPTER SEVEN

"You look awful." Amanda opened the door to Jillian and her pups, ushering her morning visitors into the kitchen. "Hey, furballs. Did your mama have a rough night?"

Jillian followed, carrying a blue Sugar & Spice box. She shoved it at Amanda. "Here." She threw her jacket over the back of a chair and slouched into the seat, resting her head on the table.

The dark circles under her little sister's eyes didn't escape Amanda's notice. She slid a steaming mug in front of Jillian. "I know you don't drink coffee most days, but it looks like you could use this." She tossed a few dog biscuits to Abbey and Hayley while Jillian sipped the proffered java. Amanda poured herself a cup and settled in with a warm pastry, groaning with the first bite. The heavenly cinnamon scent made her nose twitch.

"Talk to me. What has you looking like something the cat dragged in?" Amanda nudged her sister with her knee.

Jillian raised her head long enough to mumble Travis's name.

"Romeo kept you up late, huh?" Amanda arched a brow with a grin. "I thought when you left McGuire's, he planned to head home and go to bed. You must've done a great job convincing him sleep is overrated."

"I didn't convince him. The brick someone threw at his head did."

"Are you serious?' Amanda put down her muffin, unable to eat as a knot formed in her stomach. "What happened?"

"We said goodnight. I closed the door. Then, I heard shouting and tires squealing. I opened the door to find Travis standing there, bleeding from a gash on his forehead."

"What ... why ... who threw it?" Amanda struggled to find the words. Anger muddled her thoughts.

"I don't know. They drove away before Travis could get a good look at them. But they said—" Jillian stopped, staring into her coffee cup.

"Said what?"

"Travis heard them shout some nasty slurs about his girlfriend, *Amanda*." Jillian's brow furrowed, a pained look on her face.

"Wait. They thought Travis and me—they attacked him because of me?" Amanda lurched to her feet, knocking into the table.

"Amanda, it's not your fault." Jillian held up her hands.

"You and I both know this is the work of whoever wrote that note. Whatever I did to incur their wrath has now hurt poor Travis." Amanda paced, stomping out a rhythm on the kitchen floor. "How is he? Will he be okay?"

"A trip to the ER, seven stitches, and a prescription of painkillers—he'll be good as new." Jillian attempted a smile, but the catch in her voice gave her away. "He has to take it easy for a day or two. Stitches come out in two weeks."

"Jilly, I'm so sorry this happened." Amanda wrapped her in a hug.

Sam walked in, hair tousled, rubbing his eyes. "Hey, I smelled ... oops. Am I interrupting a tender sister moment?"

He grabbed a cinnamon roll from the box and leaned against the sink. "Uh-oh, this looks serious."

The sisters filled in the details while Sam sipped his coffee, his eyes darting between them. "Ethan knows about this, I presume?"

"Despite Travis's protests," Jillian said. "I called him as soon as we reached the emergency room. He took a statement, then headed to my house to search for clues."

"I don't understand why someone could think Travis was Amanda's boyfriend when they attacked him outside your house." Sam scrunched up his face. "Makes no sense."

"Ethan has a theory." Jillian reached for a blueberry scone. "He thinks the attacker didn't know where Amanda lived and followed the wrong Edwards sister home in the dark."

Amanda sank back in her chair, her spirit deflated like the tires on her car. "What happens when this wacko realizes they made a mistake? They'll come after Sam next." A quiet, suffocating fear curled in her chest, whispering worst-case scenarios she couldn't silence. Amanda reached for him, entwining her fingers with his and holding on tight.

"Ethan will catch this nutcase before that can happen." Jillian refilled her sister's coffee cup. "He mentioned you should be careful, Sam. 'Watch your back' were his exact words."

"I will certainly do that." Sam nibbled his cinnamon roll. "I feel bad about Travis, though. Is there anything I can do for him—or you?"

Jillian smiled. "That's sweet, Sam. If you don't mind, there is something you could do."

"Name it."

"The kitchen sink at the bookstore has sprung a leak. I'd ask Travis, but he's out of commission for a couple of days. Could you look at it?" Her hands steepled in appeal.

"Consider it done. I'll hop in the shower and be ready for duty by nine." He saluted as he left. Abbey and Hayley followed him up the stairs.

"He's a good man, Amanda. You should marry that one."

"First Aunt Grace. Now you." Amanda wadded up her napkin, then threw it at Jillian. "I'm sure a proposal is the furthest thing from Sam's mind."

"Travis wants to talk about marriage," Jillian mumbled into her now cold cup of coffee.

Amanda widened her eyes. "I'm sorry. Did you say Travis wants to get married?"

"No. I said he wants to *talk* about it." A sappy grin spread across her face.

"Did he mention this before or after he took a brick to the head?" Amanda winked.

"Before," Jillian said, a slight frown tugging at her lips. "He knew what he was saying."

"Well, what do you know? One of us might win the engagement pool after all." She rubbed her hands together. "I hope it's Sam. Then, maybe he'll let me borrow a little for a new set of tires."

Jillian helped Amanda tidy her kitchen, then climbed the stairs to round up the dogs. Her two small charges in tow, Jillian barked out an order to her sister.

"C'mon, Amanda. Those flowers and books aren't going to sell themselves."

They marched the pups out into the clear fall morning. Mother Nature had cooled things off after the past few days' heat wave. Abbey and Hayley made quick work of their business, then hopped into the backseat ready to roll. Their humans stowed their bags before climbing into the front.

Amanda felt Jillian's stare as she buckled her seatbelt.

"What?" Amanda wiped a hand across her mouth and reached to check both ears. "Do I have toothpaste on my face? Did I forget to put on an earring?"

"No. You look fine. I'm making sure this latest turn of events hasn't rattled your nerves too badly."

"My nerves? My boyfriend wasn't the one attacked by a projectile brick." Amanda's attempt at humor fell flat.

Jillian let the matter drop, changing to a safer subject.

"Do you need to stop anywhere on the way?" She pulled into traffic, turning left on Sycamore.

"Nope. I need to open the shop. There are several arrangements to be finished for another visitation tonight at Whispering Pines."

"Your funeral bouquets are beautiful. I love how the scents don't overpower you when you walk in the room. Most bouquets for visitations are too cloying." Jillian signaled another left turn. "Who died, by the way?"

"Mr. O'Leary." Amanda pulled down the sun visor to reapply her lipstick in the mirror.

"Our high school science teacher? Oh, that's sad. I liked him. His classes were fun."

Amanda snorted, a brief chuckle escaped. "Who're you kidding? The only thing you liked about those classes was David, your lab partner."

"That's not true." Jillian flicked Amanda on the arm, accidentally knocking the lipstick case from her hand. "And don't be disrespectful. Poor Mr. O'Leary. I didn't even know he'd been ill."

Amanda retrieved her errant makeup from the floormat. "Lottie at the pharmacy said he suffered a stroke a few weeks ago—never recovered. Considering the number of bouquets I'm making, he lived a long life, loved and well-respected by many."

They reminisced about Mr. O'Leary and the science

projects they'd done in his class—swapping stories of experiments gone wrong—until Jillian pulled into a parking space not far from Blossoms & Blooms.

"Look at that." She pointed to a crowd gathered in front of Amanda's boarded-up window. "Why are all those people staring at the plywood?"

Amanda's stomach tightened into a hard knot.

This can't be good.

"Let's check it out," Jillian said. "I'll leave the windows cracked for my girls." She looked at her sleeping pups in the backseat and smiled. "I'll only stay a few minutes—long enough to see what's going on."

They shouldered their way through the assembled group to get to the front door of the store. Amanda froze, her feet unwilling to budge. "You have to be kidding me." Her voice cracked with disbelief, then rose in anger. "Not again." She let out a sharp guttural sound—half shout, half growl—before muttering a string of colorful words that would've made her mother gasp.

"Oh my gosh, Amanda. I'm so sorry." Jillian placed a hand under her sister's elbow. "We need to call Ethan—again."

"Several of your neighbors called it in." Both jumped at the sound of Ethan's voice at their backs. "Our dispatcher gave me the message, so I rushed over. Looks like you had more excitement around here. A threatening note, a murder, a smashed window, and four flat tires weren't enough for you?" He raised a sardonic eyebrow. "Here we thought Jillian was the overachiever in the Edwards family."

Under cover of darkness, Amanda's vandal had returned with bright orange spray paint. They'd created a mural of inventive expletives across the front of Blossoms & Blooms, accusing her of every sin under the sun.

Amanda's chin dropped to her chest.

Why is someone targeting me?

Ethan pulled Amanda into a one-armed hug. Leaning into his shoulder, she took a moment to pull herself together. She brushed away a lone tear, straightened her shoulders, and whispered to Ethan.

"I don't care what you have to do. I want this person caught. We all have businesses to run." She raised her voice, gesturing toward her neighbors. "None of us have the time, patience, or money for these outrageous acts of vandalism." A spattering of applause broke out.

"What's that hanging on the plywood?" Jillian took a step forward to get a closer look. Ethan blocked her with a firm hand on her arm. Without a word, he pulled on a pair of gloves, then gripped the pair of garden shears jammed into the plywood and yanked them free. A yellow carnation and a light pink paper fluttered to the ground. He bent to retrieve them.

"Your polemic poet strikes again."

"What does it say?" Jillian hovered behind Ethan, attempting to get a peek at this latest sonnet from Amanda's foe.

"Let's take this inside." Ethan nodded toward the others nearby. "We don't need everyone on the street hearing this."

Jillian stepped through the assembled crowd to get her pups from the car. A store owner shouted at Ethan.

"What's going on? You're the police. What's being done to catch this crackpot and keep our town safe?"

"Yeah, yeah." Muttered agreement from the crowd swelled in volume.

"People aren't gonna want to shop at our stores with these threats and vulgar language emblazoned on the wall."

"Everyone, please." Ethan waved his arms for attention. "The Willow Springs police department is investigating these incidents. At the moment, they've all been directed at Ms. Edwards and her flower shop. There is no reason to believe any of you or your property are in danger. I suggest you go on about your daily routine. Let us worry about the crimes here at Blossoms & Blooms."

The crowd was slow to disperse, muttering and complaining as they wandered back to their businesses. Anger bubbled inside Amanda. What did the note say?

Ethan left an officer outside to contend with any stragglers. He tasked the rookie with keeping an eye out for the tech team, who'd once again been called to collect evidence. The young cop guarded his scene like a dog with a bone.

"He's going to be a good cop someday—still has a lot to learn." Ethan strolled into the flower shop, heading for the back workroom with a gaggle of females on his heels, both human and canine. Jillian settled the girls on a blanket with Kong toys filled with peanut butter to keep them entertained.

Ethan put the evidence face up on top of Amanda's worktable. Both sisters leaned in close to get a look.

"Amanda, are these scissors yours?" Ethan pointed to the black-handled tool used to hold the flower and note in place on the plywood.

"Nope, mine have green handles."

Much like the pruning shears, the wilted carnation held no clues, but the new note warned of more trouble to come.

Roses will wilt, violets will die.
As the Bible says, an eye for an eye.

Amanda stared at Ethan and Jillian, her heart pounding out such a frantic rhythm she thought it might burst form her chest. She worked to slow her breathing.

I can't afford to fall apart. Not now.

"Amanda, you should know—" his ringtone halted Ethan's next words. He stepped into the storage room to take the call.

Jillian filled the silence his departure created. "We will figure this—"

"Stop. Give me a minute." Amanda walked toward the front of her store.

There, she let out an ear-splitting scream lasting for a good five or six seconds. Jillian hoped none of the neighbors heard it, or they'd come running with pitchforks to fight off the evil within. The noise drew Ethan back to the workroom. An angry scowl had taken up residence across his face.

Amanda returned, looking calm, but determined. "Okay, I have flowers to arrange. You ..." She pointed at Ethan. "... can talk while I work."

"Are you sure you're up to being here today?" Jillian wrinkled her nose. "No one would blame you if you took the day off."

"All the people who ordered arrangements for Mr. O'Leary might not be happy with me." Amanda chose a large, clear vase from the shelf. "I'm the only florist in town, and his service is this evening."

Ethan cleared his throat. "Your enemy struck in the middle of the night, so I doubt there will be witnesses. I plan to check the surrounding stores' video surveillance cameras to see if they caught anything."

"Sounds like a great place to start." Amanda walked to the cooler, grabbing a variety of white flowers and greenery. "Jillian, stop looking at me as if I'm going to shatter into a million pieces."

"I'm sorry. You're being so nonchalant about all this. Why aren't you crying, pacing, or railing at the idiot who's threatening you?"

"I screamed. Isn't that enough?" Amanda used scissors to cut small strips of floral tape to create a crisscross pattern over the top of the vase to hold each stem in place. "Ethan's on the case. I'm safe here in the shop. My gun is right over there." She motioned to her purse.

"I guess that's something." Jillian widened her eyes at Ethan, nodding toward her sister.

"Amanda, I promise we'll catch the person responsible, but I do need to impress upon you how serious this is."

"Thank you, Ethan. I understand the threat is real. I'll be careful." Amanda snipped the ends off several calla lilies, placing them none too gently into the vase. One of the stems snapped in two. "But I refuse to let this lunatic run my life. I'll carry on as usual."

She plucked the offensive blossom from the arrangement and tossed it onto the floor, where the discarded bits of stems and leaves landed. Sweeping came after all the bouquets were done.

"Be on the lookout for anything peculiar—don't hesitate to call me."

Amanda's head snapped up at Ethan's stern tone. She met his cop stare with a determined one of her own.

"I promise to have my head on a swivel, watching for any signs of danger." She crossed her heart.

A soft knock at the back door ended their conversation for the moment.

"Come in," Amanda called to her unexpected visitor, earning her a reprimand from Ethan.

"Really, Amanda? You promised to be careful, yet you invite an unknown person into your store."

Officer O'Neil pushed the door ajar, poking his head in. "Ladies, sorry for the interruption. Sir, I need to see you about an urgent matter."

Ethan joined the young officer in the alley, closing the door behind him so curious female ears couldn't eavesdrop on what appeared to be police business.

"O'Neil looked so serious." Jillian pursed her lips. "I wonder what that's all about?"

Amanda slammed a pair of shears down on the table. A crack in her calm façade surfaced.

"Let's hope he's found a clue that will blow this case wide open."

Before my stalker does any more damage.

The heavy steel door banged open announcing Ethan's return. The angry scowl on his face sent Amanda's heart plummeting to her stomach.

"Problem out there?" Jillian risked his wrath by asking.

"Yes—a big one. When a crime tech bungles the handling of evidence, it's a huge issue." He yanked a plastic bag from behind his back. "This was delivered to the police station. O'Neil intercepted it, knowing I'd want to see it immediately. Some idiot missed this inside the cab of the flower truck yesterday. Thank goodness for the work ethic of the people at the state crime lab."

"What do they have to do with anything?" Amanda plopped onto the nearest stool—her current funeral arrangement abandoned for the moment.

"We had the vehicle towed there because they have a larger, more secure facility to house a truck that big. One of their technicians did a sweep of the cab and found a piece of paper stuck between the seat and the console. How one of our people missed it is beyond me." Ethan's cheeks had bloomed bright red. "They'll be lucky if they don't lose their job over this."

Amanda rubbed her temples. "Could you please tell us what you're talking about?"

"This." Ethan gave the plastic bag a vigorous shake.

"What is that?" Jillian bounced on the balls of her feet. "Did they find a letter from a scorned lover or a receipt for the murder weapon?"

"Why in the world would you think they found a receipt for a gun?" Amanda squinted at her sister.

Jillian shrugged. "I read a book once where the police found the victim shot in his car. A bill of sale for the gun surfaced during the investigation. They were able to arrest the murderer from his credit card number on the receipt."

"That was fiction. I doubt Rick's killer would be careless enough to leave an incriminating piece of evidence for the police to find." Amanda dismissed the theory.

"Jillian, you watch too many real crime shows." Ethan shook his head. "We didn't find a love letter or a receipt for the murder weapon. The paper in the truck appears to have been written by the dead ... er, Rick."

"Like a to-do list or something?" Amanda asked.

Ethan cleared his throat. "No, it's a suicide note."

CHAPTER EIGHT

"A suicide note—that's not possible." Amanda twisted and untwisted the ties on her florist's apron. "There's no way Rick committed suicide. He's not the kind of person who'd kill himself."

Rick didn't do this, did he?

Amanda shook her head to dispel the notion.

"I'm sorry, Amanda, but there's no *type* of person who commits suicide." Ethan let out a long sigh. "If I've learned anything on this job, it's that anyone can be at a low enough place in their life to attempt it." He lowered his voice. "His name is signed on the note."

"How can you be sure it's Rick's signature?" Jillian inserted herself into their exchange.

"I can't, so I'll let a forensic handwriting expert examine it to be certain."

"Why'd he do it?" Jillian pressed Ethan. "Don't most suicide victims tell why they killed themselves in the note?"

"Some do, some don't." Ethan shrugged. "Rick didn't. The note simply said he couldn't do '*this*' anymore and to tell his wife he was sorry about everything."

"That's all it said?" Jillian's shoulders slumped.

Amanda rubbed at her temples, one of her migraines building. "I cannot believe Rick committed suicide."

"I'm sorry about your associate, Amanda, but I have to ask. How well did you know him?" Ethan pulled out his notebook.

"Like I told Jillian, we started kindergarten together and went all the way through high school. He left Willow Springs after high school to go to college at LSU." Amanda rolled a flower stem between her fingers. "I ran into him a few times over the years at reunions or when he came home for holidays. He moved back here in February to help his mom take care of his dad, who suffered a stroke. His dad passed away two months later. Rick took over the family wholesale flower business."

"Apart from his mother, does he have other family?"

"He has a younger brother Jillian's age. Rick has a wife—married a girl he met in college." Amanda gasped. Her hands flew to her face. "Oh, his poor wife. This will devastate her. They had their first baby a few weeks ago."

"Am I the only one who thinks this is all too coincidental?" Jillian cleared her throat. "A man turns up dead in the alley the same morning Amanda's shop is vandalized—followed by her car tires being slashed, a brick thrown at Travis, and the graffiti out front. There has to be a connection."

She leaned on the counter, staring at Ethan. "Do you disagree?"

His face morphed into serious cop mode before he delivered a typical law enforcement response. His words were clipped, harsh.

"I've told you everything I can about these cases—no more questions. And no investigating on your own." He leveled his gaze at Jillian. "If you'll excuse me, I have to get back to work." Ethan jammed his notebook and pen into his pocket. He stomped from the backroom without another word.

"He knows more than he's told us." Jillian stared at Amanda as she tapped her foot. "I hate it when he does that."

"You aren't thinking of doing anything silly, are you?" Amanda's pointed stare rested on Jillian.

"Me? Do something silly? Of course not." Jillian feigned her innocence. "I told Ethan I'd step back." She took three steps backward to drive home her point. "If information happens to fall into my lap like last time, that's a different story."

"How would information pertaining to these cases fall into *your* lap?" Amanda tilted her head, scrutinizing Jillian's face. "These crimes weren't committed against you. They didn't occur outside your shop this time. A friend of yours hasn't turned up dead."

"Willow Springs is a small town. People talk. They could decide to talk to me." Jillian's cavalier attitude worried Amanda.

"Yeah, right," she muttered. "Sounds to me like you're thinking about talking to people close to this case. Please stay out of it. We don't want a repeat of the last time you poked around in Ethan's case."

The bell above the flower shop door jingled, ending the sisters' conversation—for now. Abbey and Hayley raced to welcome Amanda's customer.

"Yoo-hoo, anybody here?" Becca poked her head in the backroom. "Here you are—two of my favorite people."

"Good morning, Becca. Nice to see you." Amanda greeted Jillian's best friend without looking up from her work. "What brings you here so early?"

"I'm here on a three-part mission." She plopped a light blue Sugar & Spice box onto the worktable. The scent of chocolate and caramel wafted into the air.

"Mm, smells like heaven." Jillian sighed.

"Wanted you to try my newest muffin recipe inspired by Max's dessert last night. You're the first two to get a taste. I need honest opinions."

"You're timing is impeccable, Becca. Especially since we left an entire box of breakfast pastries at Amanda's house." Jillian peeked into the bakery box. "I'll bet Sam's eaten half the cinnamon rolls by now."

"Brought us breakfast, check. What's part two of the mission?" Amanda carried napkins to the table.

"Cate sent me to grab the flowers she ordered for the brunch she's hosting at the bakery today."

"The bouquets she requested are done and in the front cooler. Tim, my delivery helper, is out of school today. He can run them over as soon as he clocks in—wouldn't want them spilling water all over your pretty, new car."

"Oh, that's right," Jillian said. "Cate's hosting their foster parent group at Sugar & Spice this morning. She's been so nervous about it, stressed about making everything perfect."

"Foster parent group? What's that about?" Becca asked.

"Cate and Wes completed the classes to renew their foster parents certification. They hope to have an infant or toddler placed with them soon." Jillian put a still- warm muffin onto her napkin.

"They fostered kids before Laney and Aubrey were born," Amanda added.

"Oh, yeah. I remember a few little ones they took in," Becca added. "Cate and Wes have big hearts."

Amanda took her first bite of moist muffin and groaned softly.

Worth every calorie.

Jillian peeled back the paper and bit into her muffin. The taste of semi-sweet chocolate burst in her mouth. A little pocket of caramel oozed onto her tongue. "Oh, Becca. This muffin is unbelievable—your best yet."

"Completely agree," Amanda mumbled around the bite in her mouth.

Becca beamed. "Thank you very much."

"Baked goods and flowers, done. What's the third leg of your objective?" Amanda wiped the crumbs off her shirt.

"I hoped to connect with my husband. We were on the phone earlier—said he was headed here. Has he left already?"

"You missed him by mere minutes." Amanda returned to the flowers she'd been arranging. "He verbally sparred with Jillian, then blew out of here like a Midwestern tornado."

She plunged a floral stick into the arrangement with the sympathy card attached. "Is he always this intense when working a case?"

"Yes," Becca said. "He becomes oblivious to things going on around him. What's set him off today besides Jillian?"

Amanda brought Becca up to speed on the latest twists in Ethan's case—a suicide note and her poet's newest threat.

"An eye for an eye? That's creepy enough to make my skin crawl." Becca shivered, rubbing her arms. "Any idea what they're talking about?"

"No, but I wish I did. Then, maybe we'd have a clue who this person is. Ethan could arrest them for slashing my tires, breaking my window, and defacing the front of my store. Who knows—they might have killed Rick too."

"You don't believe he killed himself?" Becca asked.

"No, I don't." Amanda shoved two tall gladioli she'd cut too short into a spare vase. She'd use them in another arrangement later. Wiping her forehead with the back of her hand, she slumped onto her stool. "I've ruined so many flowers this morning. My focus is a bit off today—no surprise there."

"Why don't you take a break for a second? I'll get you something to drink." Becca headed for the mini-fridge in the corner.

"Yeah, sit. Relax." Jillian pulled her seat closer to Amanda. "Let's talk about who this poet might be—see if we can figure out why they're coming after you."

"Uh, Jilly." Becca's tone carried a hint of chastisement. "Do you think that will be relaxing for her?"

Amanda stifled an unladylike snort. "Don't worry about it, Becca. My little sister's inquiring mind needs to know."

"Yes, I do. We all do. Once we uncover who's behind these attacks, they can be stopped. Who knows? Amanda might be right. Her bizarre bard and Rick's killer might be the same person."

"*If* he was murdered." Becca waggled her index finger. "We can't forget about the suicide note."

"Ethan's having a handwriting expert analyze it for authenticity, so we'll know soon," Jillian said.

"That's my man—always on top of things." Becca exhaled a lovestruck sigh.

"Yes, yes, he's wonderful." Impatience rolled off Jillian's tongue. "Can we get back to Amanda's problems, please?"

"Okay, Miss Marple. What's your take on these threats?" Becca fisted her hands on her hips.

"Sounds like someone feels Amanda's done something to them. They want payback." Jillian pounded one fist into the palm of her other hand, punctuating her points. "We should—"

"Hold it right there." Becca's firm order stopped Jillian's rant. "Enough with the *we* business. I need to remind you once again you're not supposed to get involved in Ethan's case. He'll get annoyed with you, then he becomes a bear for me to live with."

"Relax, Becca. I meant if we—the three of us—put our heads together, maybe we can come up with a list of people who want to hurt Amanda. We give the names to Ethan."

"Are you serious, Jilly?" Amanda's face flushed at the insult. "You think I've offended so many people we could make a list?"

"I'm sure it's not a long one, but let's think about it." Jillian said. "Is there anyone who could be jealous of you or the flower shop? Both attacks did happen here."

"Hey, that's a good point," Becca chimed in. "Maybe Blossoms & Blooms is the source of their anger. A rival, perhaps?"

"I'm the only florist in town. You know that, Becca."

"Maybe someone dreamed of opening one, but the success of yours thwarted their plans. They've held on to their jealousy until they can't stand it." Jillian's enthusiasm for Becca's idea shone through her face.

"That could be almost anyone." Amanda took a deep breath, trying to rein in her frustration. "We don't know what goes on inside someone's mind, what their dreams might be. Four flat tires, a broken window, some graffiti, two cryptic notes, yellow carnations, and a brick to poor Travis's head aren't enough evidence to point the finger at anyone specific."

Jillian and Becca remained silent following this tirade. Amanda appreciated not having to hear anyone's thoughts for the moment. She stepped into the cooler to gather flowers for Mr. O'Leary's final funeral arrangement. The frosty air inside cooled the sweat from her brow, taking the edge off the anger bubbling inside her.

"Change of subject." She held up two different types of blue flowers. "Forget-me-nots or cornflowers. Someone wants blue sprinkled into their order since that was Mr. O'Leary's favorite color."

"I don't know much about flowers." Becca pointed to her choice. "Just the name forget-me-not seems appropriate for a visitation."

"I agree," Jillian said. "Doesn't everyone want to be remembered even after they're gone?"

A shiver inched up Amanda's back. Rick was gone—either by his own hand or someone else's. How many people would remember him years from now?

Amanda was certain she would never forget him.

Jillian took her pups outside for a mid-morning break. She and Becca stood in front of the flower shop, discussing the best way to help Amanda. Becca's stomach announced it was ready for lunch a bit early today. Two rosy pink spots bloomed on her cheeks.

"Oops, sorry. I was running behind schedule this morning and skipped breakfast."

"You baked those delicious muffins, but didn't try one?" Jillian chuckled at Becca's sheepish grin. "Trixie's opening the bookstore today, but I still need to stop by. Sam's playing Pete the Plumber fixing my kitchen sink—better check if he needs anything. I'll have to run Abbey and Hayley home first, but we could meet at, say, eleven-thirty at Manny's if that sounds good to you. We can continue brainstorming ways to help Amanda over a slice of pizza."

"Great idea," Becca said. "Should we ask Amanda to come with us? I don't like talking behind her back."

This was one of Becca's most admirable qualities—always thinking of others' feelings—and Jillian loved her for it.

"The glass installation company has a technician coming to assess the damage and give her an estimate for the repairs. They gave her the window of eleven to three for his arrival."

Becca laughed. "Window, ha! Pun intended?"

"What ... oh, window." Jillian palm-slapped her forehead. "No, I'm not that mentally sharp today."

Manny's Pizzeria was a few storefronts down from Amanda's shop on Main Street and was Jillian's favorite place for a quick lunch. Even though Manny's was the only pizza place in town, it had rightfully earned quite a reputation for its thin-crust pizzas, calzones, and cheesy garlic knots. People came from towns around Willow Springs to experience Manny's gastronomic delights.

Jillian arrived ahead of Becca and chose a booth near one of the windows. She sipped her iced tea and people-watched until the young waitress who'd once had a huge crush on Travis showed Becca to the booth, then took their drink orders.

Becca pointed at her retreating back. "Isn't she the one who flirted with—"

"Yes, that's her. She's been nothing but polite since she found out I was dating Travis."

"Speaking of your hunky fireman ..." Becca motioned toward the counter.

Three good-looking men in dark blue uniforms placed their takeout orders with Lola Russo, who owned the pizzeria with her husband, Manny. The tallest of them sported a stark white bandage over his right eye. Becca caught their attention.

"Excuse me, gentlemen. We could use the assistance of Willow Springs bravest over here." Waving her arm straight up in the air, she was hard to ignore.

Travis's eyes found Jillian. His smile lit up his face and sent Jillian's pulse racing. He finished paying for his meal, then sauntered over.

"Hello, ladies." He kissed the top of Jillian's head. "What a nice surprise to see you here. Is this a casual lunch, or is this one plotting something?" He gave Jillian's shoulders an affectionate squeeze.

"I take offense to that," Jillian said. "Why would you assume I'm up to something?"

"Because he knows you, and your track record speaks for itself." Becca high-fived with Travis. "Good one, by the way."

"Hmm, my boyfriend and best friend in cahoots against me. What have I done to deserve this?" Jillian touched Travis's forehead. "How're you feeling? I thought you were told to take today off to rest."

"Hmm, funny how you only hear what you want to hear. Doc also said I passed the concussion protocol and could work as long as I felt up to it, which I do." This last was uttered before Jillian could object.

The pager strapped around Travis's chest emitted several loud squeaks, followed by a dispatcher's voice calling out instructions and an address.

"See you later." Travis kissed Jillian again, on the lips this time. He and his crew snatched their orders from the counter before bolting out the door.

Mrs. Russo shouted at their retreating backs. "*Stai al sicuro là fuori.*" 'Stay safe out there' in her native Italian.

The waitress arrived to take their food orders—two slices of meat lovers and a side salad for Becca, a sausage calzone for Jillian.

"Okie-dokie! This'll be up in like five minutes," the girl chirped, flipping her hair with a little too much flair.

With their server gone, Becca couldn't wait any longer. "Jilly, what happened to Travis's head? I have a sneaky feeling it has something to do with Amanda's troubles these last two days."

"You're very perceptive."

Jillian regaled her friend with the details of Travis's attack and their trip to the emergency room.

"Amanda's enemy thinks *she's* dating Travis?" Becca scrunched up her face. "That's ridiculous. Everyone in town knows he's head over heels in love with you."

Jillian told her of Ethan's theory of mistaken identity.

"He thought maybe the attacker followed the wrong couple home from McGuire's last night." Jillian unrolled her silverware, placing the napkin on her lap. "In the dark, I suppose that's possible."

"Wouldn't Amanda's stalker know where she lives?" Leave it to Becca to add a wrinkle to her husband's hypothesis.

"Unless they're new in town." This thought popped into Jillian's head and out of her mouth. Two newcomers to their little community came to mind—the old man in her driveway and the mysterious southern belle who complimented Amanda's now ruined window. Why would these strangers have it in for her sister? They didn't even know her.

"How could someone who's just come to Willow Springs have a vendetta against Amanda? That makes no sense."

Becca put words to Jillian's thoughts. "I feel so sorry for your sister. I wish we could do something to help."

"Maybe we can." Jillian sat straighter in her seat. "We could identify the crazy poet helping Ethan put one of his current cases to bed. We could also stop at The Corner Deli and take lunch back to Amanda. She told me this morning she was craving their mushroom bacon burger."

"Your enthusiasm is admirable, but Ethan won't appreciate your interference. Drop it, Jilly." Becca laid her napkin on the table and stood up. "Taking lunch to Amanda, however, is a great idea. Food always cheers me up. Maybe it will work on her. I need a quick stop in the ladies' room. Be right back."

Jillian slumped in her seat, mulling over her next move. She understood Becca's reluctance to cross Ethan. She didn't want to cause conflict between husband and wife, but she was determined to help stop these threats against Amanda.

"What Ethan doesn't know won't hurt him," she mumbled to herself.

"What's that you said?" Jillian jumped at the sound of Becca's voice.

"Oh, nothing."

"Mm-hmm. Sounded like you said something about Ethan." Becca cocked her head. "Jillian Saoirse Edwards, tell me you aren't planning to interfere."

Ooh, she pulled out my middle name.

"Of course not. I want nothing to do with the murder/suicide case he's working on."

Jillian smiled. This was the truth. She had no intention of engaging in anything to do with Amanda's flower supplier's death. She'd make no promises about the lunatic threatening her sister's life.

Her phone vibrated deep inside her purse. Amanda wanted to Facetime.

"Hey, what's up?" Jillian answered on the third ring. Amanda's smiling face came into view.

"You don't have to be at the bookstore until after lunch, right?"

"Yep. This is Trixie's full day at the shop. I have to be there by four for my middle school book group. Do you need something?"

"A favor." Amanda fussed with some stems of hydrangeas. "Could you go to Hobby Mart again—pick up a few things for me? I'll pay you back when you get here."

"Sure. What do you need?"

"Everything to redo my Halloween display—lights, black gauze, acrylic paint, fabric—I'll text you a list. The glass company is here, thanks to Sam calling in a favor. The technician said it's an easy fix. I should have a new window installed by close of business today." Amanda's cheerful voice relayed her upbeat attitude.

"That's great." Jillian returned her sister's broad smile.

"Good for you." Becca poked her head into the screenshot. "Don't let that wacky wordsmith get you down. We can help you put things back together."

"Thanks. The more people working, the faster the decorations go back up." A determined scowl replaced her grin. "I refuse to let this nut job ruin my plans for a fun Halloween and a first-place trophy."

Amanda's spunk warmed Jillian's heart. She was thrilled her sister had pulled herself up by the bootstraps, making plans to move forward.

"Becca and I will grab your supplies and head straight back to Blossoms & Blooms as soon as we've finished lunch."

The call ended as the waitress placed their food on the table. They made quick work of their meal and paid the bill on their way out, walking the short distance to Jillian's car.

"We'll pick up yours when we get back to town." Jillian had offered to drive.

"Sounds good." Becca buckled her seatbelt. "I'm glad we can help Amanda with this. Recreating her window will show everyone—including her poetic enemy—she's one tough cookie who won't back down from a threat."

"Mm-hmm." Jillian managed a mumble as her brain raced. "Maybe I should have left the girls with her. A couple of pups with loud barks could've deterred any pranks while she's there alone."

"Doesn't Amanda have her gun with her at the shop?"

"Yes, but let's hope that isn't necessary." Jillian shuddered. "One person shot and killed is enough, don't you think?"

CHAPTER NINE

Jillian and Becca headed to Hobby Mart in Stonefield in search of the replacement items on Amanda's list. The twenty-minute drive gave them time to chat about Becca's recent trip.

"Tell me everything." Jillian turned down the radio. "Was the cooking seminar worth the time spent away from Ethan and the hard-earned money you paid to go?"

Becca had worried herself into a tizzy during the weeks leading up to the trip.

"The whole thing was fantastic." Her voice emanated excitement. "The instructors taught us baking techniques I'd never seen. We explored unexpected flavor combinations. I caught up with three old friends from culinary school. The best part ..." She paused for dramatic effect. "... was winning a private lesson with Chef Rousseau from Le Cordon Bleu on the art of *patisserie*. Our Sugar & Spice customers will be blown away by the French pastries I plan to add to the menu." Becca clapped her hands in delight. "A little taste of France in Willow Springs."

"I'm glad the week went so well." Jillian reached over to pat Becca's leg. "See, you worried for nothing. Ethan and the bakery survived without you."

"Survived, maybe, but it doesn't seem like he missed me much." A scowl adorned Amanda's face. "Who knows how the bakery fared in my absence? I did feel bad leaving Cate with all that work."

"Cate managed—with help from the rest of her staff. She's a talented baker in her own right, you know." Jillian chose her next words with care. "I know Ethan missed you. Perhaps your expectations for a romantic reunion were a bit unrealistic—knowing how your husband feels about showing affection in public."

"Unrealistic. Me?" Becca stuck out her bottom lip. "I have no idea what you mean."

"C'mon, Becca. You expected Ethan to take you in his arms and give you a passionate kiss. You thought he'd tell you how much he'd missed you, proclaiming his undying love." Jillian put a hand over her heart. "You wanted a love scene reminiscent of Richard Gere and Debra Winger in *An Officer and a Gentleman*."

Becca frowned. "You think you know me so well."

"Am I wrong?" Jillian arched an eyebrow.

"No." Becca expelled a long breath. "He could've at least acted like he missed me, though. He barely acknowledged my presence at the flower shop. That peck on the cheek—pathetic."

"You know as well as I do when Ethan is in the middle of a case, his attention to other things suffers. You caught him at a bad time yesterday. I'm sure when he gets home tonight, he'll make it up to you with some nice, romantic gesture."

Jillian made a mental note to call Ethan—give him a heads-up, so he didn't disappoint his wife twice in one week.

"He better, or he might not live to solve this latest case," Becca growled.

Once in Stonefield, they made quick work of filling their carts with the items Amanda requested. They loaded bag after bag of Halloween merchandise into the back of Jillian's SUV, then headed home.

"Since we'll be in the neighborhood, let's stop at the bakery. I'd like to pick up some treats for my middle school book club. Those tweenagers are always starving after school."

"Great. That will give me a chance to check out how big a mess I'm coming back to tomorrow. I couldn't bring myself to look in the bakery's kitchen when I popped in earlier." Becca let out a dramatic sigh.

"Every time I went into Sugar & Spice, things seemed—"

Becca raised a hand, placing it over her brow. "Stop. I won't be able to bear it if you tell me they didn't suffer without me. First, Ethan, and now the bakery."

Jillian groaned. "Quit being such a drama queen."

Becca laughed. "Aw, c'mon. What's life without a little drama?"

Jillian parked in a space in front of Sugar & Spice. A late lunch crowd was visible through the front window. Most of the tables were full. The wait staff scurried around filling orders. Becca pushed open the door and breezed in with Jillian right behind her.

"Hey, it's good to see our head pastry chef has returned." Jenny, one of Cate's part-time employees, called out to Becca as she handed a customer his to-go bag. "We've missed you around here."

"Thanks, Jenny. I'm glad to be back," Becca said. "Is the boss lady in the kitchen prepping for tomorrow's breakfast menu?"

"No, Cate's in her office. The cooking's all done." Jenny wiped the counter with a rag. "While you were gone, she let Melanie take a shot at some of the baking and cooking responsibilities—turns out she's pretty good. They prepared all of today's menu items together and prepped what they could for tomorrow morning."

"Super." Becca's tone sharpened, all friendliness gone, as she turned and marched toward Cate's office.

"Uh-oh," Jillian muttered. "I know that tone."

Ethan hadn't properly welcomed her home. Cate had let someone else cook in the bakery's kitchen. Becca wasn't going to handle this well.

Jillian followed her friend, prepared to intercede in the upcoming battle to prevent any casualties. Ethan had enough crimes on his plate right now. He didn't need another, especially one involving his wife.

Becca knocked on Cate's door, then entered without waiting for a response. Cate was on the phone, placing what sounded like a supply order. She smiled at her visitors, waving them into the room. Ending the call, Cate sprang from her chair. She flew around the desk like a whirlwind, grabbing Becca in a fierce hug.

"You have no idea how happy I am that you're home," Cate said. "Things weren't the same around here without you."

"Looks like you didn't miss me at all," Becca grumbled.

"What are you talking about?" Cate stepped back, looking Becca in the eye. "The kitchen was crazy. I couldn't keep up with morning requests or lunch orders. I had to ask poor Melanie to pitch in, but our attempts fell short most days." Cate pulled her into another hug. "Please don't ever go away again."

Jillian admired the skill her oldest sister used to handle Becca. Cate knew just how much to flatter and praise to soothe Becca's frayed feelings.

"I'm not proud to admit this, but I secretly hoped things would be a wreck with me gone. When Jenny told me Melanie did a good job cooking, my feelings were hurt." Becca averted her eyes from Cate. "Not my finest moment."

"Everything took us twice as long—food prep, baking, kitchen clean-up—you don't even want to know how many batches of cinnamon rolls we burned." Cate threw her hands up in the air. "Oh, then there was the customer who threw part of his lunch at Jenny."

"That was rude. What happened?" Becca plopped into the chair across from Cate's desk.

"We don't know what made him angry. The man didn't speak—at all—just gestured at his bowl of loaded potato soup. Poor Jenny offered to bring him more toppings or a fresh bowl, but nothing seemed to appease him. He became frustrated and threw the buttermilk biscuit he'd slathered in butter at her. Hit her right between the—" Cate pointed to her own chest "—left a greasy stain on her apron."

"That's awful," Becca said. "Did he apologize?"

"No. He never said a word the entire time he was here."

"Older guy, kind of scruffy-looking with a green backpack wearing an Army veteran hat?" Jillian asked.

"Yes, that sounds right. Do you know him, Jilly?" Cate grabbed her apron from the hook on the wall, draped it over her head, and tied it in the front.

"I sort of met him yesterday when I almost hit him with my car."

"Oh, my gosh." Becca grabbed Jillian's arm. "That must've been scary—for both of you."

"We need to hear the whole story." Cate motioned them to the front of the shop, where they found a cozy table in the corner with a window view. She filled sugar dispensers while listening to Jillian's story of the man she'd almost backed over in her driveway.

"Sounds like the same guy," Cate said. "I wonder who he is, and why he can't—or doesn't—talk."

"You've never seen him before this?" Becca steepled her fingers under her chin.

"Nope. He's not from Willow Springs, but I'd love to find out more about him."

"Uh-oh, Jillian's curious mind is at it again." Cate let out an exasperated sigh. "Don't do anything silly, Sis. You tend to get into trouble when you stick that nose of yours into other people's business."

The jingle of the bell above the bakery door signaled new customers. Jillian was thankful not to have to defend herself against Cate's warning. The sight of her mom and Aunt Grace arm in arm made her smile.

The two older women, fraternal twins in their sixties, bore a striking resemblance, but their fashion styles were polar opposites. Joy wore navy slacks with a crisp, white button-down shirt under a light blue cardigan paired with her favorite slip-on shoes. The sole piece of jewelry was the gold wedding set on her left hand.

Aunt Grace was the antithesis of her sister with her ensemble of choice. She'd paired a red and white floral pleated skirt with a bright red bateau-neck blouse with an asymmetrical hemline. She dripped with gold jewelry— from the chunky statement necklace to the huge hoop earrings and her signature set of bangle bracelets.

"Don't you two look chummy." Jillian hugged her mom, then her aunt.

"Hello, Kitten." Grace returned the hug, then directed her attention to Becca. "Nice to see you back from your trip, Cookie."

Becca and Jillian's friendship went back to grade school. The girls spent so much time together in those early years that Becca became an honorary member of the Edwards clan—the fourth daughter. This required Grace to choose an appropriate nickname for her to go along with Kitten, Pumpkin, and Sweet Pea. No one, except perhaps Aunt Grace, could've guessed back then how appropriate her choice of name would be for adult Becca.

"Joy and I spent a delightful morning being pampered at the new day spa in Red Hill." Grace prattled on. "We had a fabulous time. You girls should go—would be a nice treat for someone who has a birthday coming up." She let her suggestion hang in the air like party balloons.

"I hope you don't mind us dropping in unannounced." Joy fluttered her hands. "I told Grace the lunch rush would be in full swing."

Cate wrapped her mom in a hug. "You're welcome here any time of day."

"See, they don't mind us coming by. Hello to you too, Sweet Pea." Grace blew a kiss at Cate. "What's this we hear about Amanda? While we were in the hardware store a few minutes ago, some ladies were whispering about new problems at the flower shop today."

Aunt Grace was not only known for having visions, but for her bat-like hearing. "Is everything all right? I've been worried about Amanda since my vision of that fire yesterday."

"Fire? What's this about Amanda and a fire?" Joy's voice resonated with fear.

Jillian jumped in to reassure her mom. "Turned out to be an unlit pilot light. Everything's fine, Mom."

"Pilot light, my patootie. What I saw was bigger than that," Grace grumbled.

No one wanted to encourage Aunt Grace's visions, so Becca swooped in and changed the subject.

"The gossipmongers must be asleep on the job if you have no clue about today's drama."

"What happened—is Amanda okay?" Joy sprang into concerned mom mode.

"She's fine, but yes, there has been another incident at Blossoms & Blooms." Jillian checked her watch. "Becca and I are headed to the flower shop to drop off supplies for Amanda. Why don't you both meet us there to hear all about it?"

"Perfect. I'd feel better seeing Amanda for myself, anyway." Joy exhaled a loud sigh.

"We'll meet you there in fifteen minutes. I have one other quick errand."

"What about lunch? Those tiny tea sandwiches they served at the spa did nothing to satisfy my hunger." Grace's bright red lips formed a perfect pout. "I had no idea being pampered worked up such an appetite."

"We're picking up lunch for Amanda at The Corner Deli." Becca put her arm around Grace's shoulders. "We can grab something for both of you lovely ladies too."

"Oh, Cookie. You're the sweetest." Grace delivered a peck on Becca's cheek. "Jillian knows what I like."

"Mom, what about you?"

"I could eat a little something, a chef salad perhaps." Joy watched her calories like a hawk, making sure she kept her slender figure.

"Great. We'll stop at the deli, pick up lunch, and meet you at Amanda's in less than twenty." Becca grabbed her purse from the chair and slung it over her shoulder.

"Cate, I almost forgot." Jillian snapped her fingers. "Could I get a box of sweet treats for my middle school book club? They'll need an afternoon snack."

"You sure can. I'll put one together, then I'm coming

with you." Cate took off her apron. "Jenny and Melanie can handle the rest of the lunch crowd."

"Wonderful, it's settled." Aunt Grace stood, straightening the pleats in her colorful skirt.

The elder Edwards women left the bakery as they'd come in, arm in arm and whispering to one another. Aunt Grace's gold bangles jangled as she waved goodbye. Her signature floral scent lingered long after she'd gone.

"A morning at the spa seems to have done them a world of good. Maybe we should try it," Cate said. "I could book a girls' day to celebrate my birthday like Aunt Grace suggested."

Becca gave an enthusiastic, "Count me in."

Jillian worked hard to maintain her poker face as thoughts of Cate's surprise party flitted through her head.

"Sure, we could do that," she said. "All of us getting together to celebrate your special day sounds like a great idea."

"Super. I'll book it." Cate's cell phone buzzed in her pocket.

"You go ahead," she said. "I'll meet you at the flower shop—with a goodie box—after I take this call. I can't wait to hear about Amanda's morning." She moved off to a corner of the bakery.

"Hello, this is Cate."

Jillian and Becca walked the five blocks from the bakery to The Corner Deli. Becca seemed a million miles away. Repeated attempts at conversation failed to get her attention.

Jillian clapped her hands. "Earth to Becca, you've been

in a funk ever since we walked into Sugar & Spice. What's going on?"

"Oh, it's silly," Becca sighed. "Despite what Cate said, the bakery didn't fall apart without me. My ego took a hit, that's all.

"Don't be ridiculous. Cate couldn't have been happier to see you. The only reason Sugar & Spice ran smoothly in your absence is because you've organized the kitchen and trained the staff. They learned everything they know from you."

"You think?" Becca's question held a hint of uncertainty. "I hate to admit this, but I'd hoped things would be a disaster while I was gone. Is that petty of me?"

"Yes, but I still love you." Jillian pulled Becca in for a hug as they walked through the door of the deli.

The warm, friendly face of Steve Harrison, the owner, greeted them along with some delicious aromas—the yeasty smell of freshly baked bread, spicy grilled meat, and something made of cinnamon and apples.

"Good afternoon, ladies. Can I get you a table or is this a to-go order?" Steve's deep voice bellowed from across the room.

"We're taking lunch to go today, Steve. Could we sit at the counter while we wait for our order?" Jillian pointed at two empty seats.

"Absolutely. Come sit right here." Steve gestured to the stools in front of the cash register.

"Special today is a roast beef sandwich with your choice of two sides." Steve hollered at his wife. "Macy, we have a couple of hungry customers out here." He winked at them before returning to the kitchen.

"He's so friendly to everyone who comes in here," Jillian said to Becca. "Do you suppose he ever loses his temper and gets cranky?"

"Yes, he most certainly does." Macy came through the swinging doors separating the kitchen from the rest of the diner. "When he's trying to watch football on TV and our boys are misbehaving, he yells at them something terrible."

"I didn't mean for you to hear that, Macy." Jillian's cheeks warmed with embarrassment. "Steve's just so nice to everyone. Nothing ever seems to ruffle his feathers."

"Trust me, two rambunctious four-year-olds can get him all riled up." Macy took a notepad from her apron pocket. "Especially if the Bears are playing. Now what can I get for you ladies?"

Jillian ordered lunch for her mom, Grace, and Amanda. Becca placed an order for Ethan. This move surprised Jillian.

"Ordering food to be delivered to your hubby? Does this mean you've forgiven his earlier transgressions?"

"No, but a busy detective needs to eat." Becca shrugged an indifferent shoulder. "If I don't feed him, who knows what he'll grab on the go—a Snickers bar with a Dr. Pepper is a safe bet. The man's diet is atrocious."

Macy repeated their orders back to them, making sure she had everything right. "This sounds like Grace's and Joy's usuals. That's sweet of you to take them a bite to eat."

"They've had a rough day at the new spa in Red Hill. They're famished." Jillian rolled her eyes, then smiled. "There's been some drama at the flower shop the last two days, so we're converging on Amanda to provide moral support."

"One of the good things about families." Macy clipped their order onto the spinning wheel hanging from the window between the counter and the kitchen. She gave it a whirl as she shouted at her husband, "Order in the queue."

"Coming right up." Steve's deep voice boomed like thunder.

Macy served Jillian and Becca some fresh-brewed iced tea while all three ladies chatted.

"Now, what's this nonsense about someone damaging Amanda's car and vandalizing her store?" Macy said. "I overheard a few of our breakfast customers this morning talking about it."

"They left out some important details." Jillian lowered her voice to a whisper.

"Let's hear it then." Macy threw her cleaning rag into the bucket of soapy water and leaned across the counter. "If you have dirt, start dishing."

Before Jillian could give Macy the abbreviated version of events, her cell phone vibrated in her pocket. Amanda's number flashed on the caller ID. Jillian excused herself to answer it.

"Hey, Sis. What's up? Becca and I are at The Corner Deli waiting for an order. Mom, Aunt Grace and Cate are joining us ... Uh-huh. ... Yeah, okay. We should be at your place in ten or fifteen minutes. Yes, we have everything from your list."

Jillian listened, nodding at her sister's words.

"Sure, that's no problem. I'll order it now. See you soon." She ended the call and dropped the phone into her purse.

"Macy, we're going to need to add to our order. I've been informed another hungry party will be joining us at Amanda's place. We need a double cheeseburger, hold the onions, and a side of waffle fries, please."

"No problem." Macy yelled into the kitchen at Steve. "Slap two patties on the grill and turn on the fryer for some waffles. Load up the beef but hold the onions."

Her husband shouted back in the affirmative.

"Who else is stopping by the flower shop?" Becca swirled the tea in her glass.

"Sam. He was at another meeting in the city—second one

this week—when Amanda called him about this morning's events. He wrapped things up and is headed home. She wants him to join us, so he can hear all the details. Much like you, she's feeding her man."

Jillian's gaze turned to find Macy staring back, her mouth agape.

"Becca, why's Macy staring at me like that?"

"I might have told her some upsetting news while you were on the phone."

"What did you say?" Jillian gave her friend an accusing stare.

"I told her about the dead guy behind the flower shop." Becca raised her palms to the ceiling. "What? Ethan never swore us to secrecy. I figured the news is all over town by now, anyway."

"That poor man—your poor sister." Macy pursed her lips. "Is there anything Steve and I can do to help?"

"That's sweet of you, Macy," Jillian said. "According to the police, the best thing all the business owners can do is keep their eyes and ears open. If you hear or see anything suspicious, don't hesitate to let me know."

"Let you know?" Becca grabbed Jillian's arm. "You mean let *Ethan* know, don't you?"

Jillian waved off the reminder. "I know what you're thinking, Becca, but I *will* tell Ethan if I find out anything."

Becca opened her mouth to object further, but Steve's boisterous yell cut her off.

"Order's up." He stuck his head through the window from the kitchen. "I tasted everything to make sure it was perfect for you. Just don't tell my wife."

"I heard that." Macy returned to the counter after seating a few more lunch customers. "I figured there was an explanation for why your pants keep getting tighter and tighter."

Steve retreated to his kitchen. Macy chuckled under her breath at her husband. "Can you believe that man? He's around food all day, but still can't get enough of it. Do your men fixate on food?"

"Yes," they spoke in unison.

"Ethan asks what's for dinner before he's finished breakfast," Becca said.

"I've seen your men," Macy said. "Ethan and Travis might like to eat, but it's obvious they work out and take care of themselves. Have you seen my husband's growing gut? He's never met a food he didn't like."

"I heard that," Steve shouted from the kitchen.

"Good, I wanted you to," Macy yelled back. "You need to do something about your expanding waistline before you lose sight of your feet."

Steve walked from the kitchen carrying a cardboard box stuffed with brown paper sacks. The most incredible smells wafted into the air. The aroma had both Jillian's and Becca's mouths watering even though they'd eaten lunch earlier.

"Ladies, here's your order. I thank you for patronizing our deli. Apologies for airing our dirty marital laundry in front of you today. My wife doesn't seem to understand my waistline is a reflection of my love for food. Customers won't trust a skinny cook. Am I right, Becca? You know how it is. Nobody wants to buy sweet treats from an emaciated pastry chef."

Steve tipped his ballcap and disappeared into the kitchen, leaving Jillian in stunned silence.

She'd winced at his parting comment. Becca had always been sensitive about her figure—like so many women—and his words wouldn't sit well with her.

Becca's response caught her off guard.

"Steve's right. Why do you think I became a pastry chef?

My job gives me the excuse to pack on a few extra pounds without beating myself up about it."

Becca smiled as she handed Macy enough cash to cover her part of the bill. "I love your husband. He tells it like it is. If I weren't already married, I'd make a play for him."

"I might just let you." Macy grinned at Becca. She opened the old-fashioned cash register with a loud *ding* and pulled out the change. "You ladies take this food to our hungry patrons—be sure to come back soon."

As they walked outside, Jillian stole a glance back into the deli. Steve and Macy stood close together, deep in conversation about something. She gazed up at him with a look of pure love in her eyes as he brushed a stray piece of hair back behind her ear. He bent and placed a kiss on her forehead before returning to the kitchen.

Their interaction made Jillian smile. Here was one business on Main Street running smoothly today. If they hurried to Blossoms & Blooms, maybe they could get another business back on track by the end of the day.

Taking out her phone, Becca settled in the passenger seat. "Let me text that man of mine and tell him to get over to Amanda's for lunch. He should be starving by this point in his day."

Jillian walked around to the driver's side. She startled when someone tapped her on the shoulder just as she reached for the door handle. She spun around and came face-to-face with a woman she'd never seen before.

The stranger looked disheveled and weary. Her long blonde hair was pulled into a messy bun, greasy at the roots. Dark circles under her pale blue bloodshot eyes stood out in contrast to her ashen skin. She wore a long-sleeved, black dress, much too big for her petite figure and a gray cardigan with two missing buttons. The woman shifted from one foot to the other, as she rocked the infant strapped to her chest. The fabric of the sling muffled the baby's cry.

"I ... um ... are you Jillian Edwards? The woman who owns the bookstore?" She failed to make eye contact, her voice coming out in a raspy whisper.

"Yes, I am." Jillian put a cheery tone in her voice. "Have you visited my bookstore?

"No, I haven't been in," she said softly. "But I've heard it's ... nice. I'd like to come by sometime. Maybe you could help me find something—for my son?" Her voice lifted at the end, as if she were asking for permission to visit the store.

"Of course," Jillian assured her. "I'd be happy to help you anytime."

"Isn't your sister the woman who owns the flower shop on Main Street?"

This quick change of subject sent warning bells clanging in Jillian's head.

"Y ... e ... s." Jillian drew out the word, giving herself time to regroup. "My sister, Amanda, owns Blossoms & Blooms. Do you know her?"

"No." Her response, loud and curt, bordered on defensive. "I heard she's had some trouble at her shop. Is she terribly upset?"

"Someone has vandalized her property. That would make anyone upset, don't you think?"

The woman stared at Jillian with a glint of steel in her gaze, then brought the conversation to an abrupt end.

"I should go. My son needs a nap." She made a clumsy turn and stumbled, tripping over the hem of her oversized dress. The infant's faint cries carried on the breeze as his mother raced off.

Jillian scrutinized her retreating form, questions swirling

like fall leaves inside her head. Waiting in the car, Becca had some questions of her own.

"Who was that? Did you see her dress? That thing was at least three sizes too big." Becca took a breath.

"I've never met her before, and our conversation was strange." Jillian replayed their brief exchange in her mind. "She asked about my store and Amanda's, but said she's never been to either one. She mentioned coming to Whimsy & Wonder to get books for her son, then, out of nowhere, she asked if Amanda was upset about the problems at her shop. That was a weird thing to say, don't you think?"

Becca muttered something unintelligible under her breath, then added, "Yes, it's weird. Or perhaps she's a nutcase who walks around saying wildly inappropriate things to total strangers."

"Be nice." Jillian chastised Becca with a playful slap on the hand. "She seemed unhappy or depressed, a little confused maybe—needed someone to talk to. The poor woman is dealing with a tiny baby, which has to be difficult."

"Why is it always you these sad sacks gravitate to?" Without waiting for a response, Becca answered her own question. "You're too kind and easy to talk to. People sense that about you. If you're not careful, you'll end up ..."

Jillian stopped listening to Becca's rant when she spotted the piece of pink paper folded under her windshield wiper.

Not again.

CHAPTER TEN

The midday sunshine poured through the broken window of Blossoms & Blooms. The cooler morning temps had risen into the eighties. The AC unit chugged along, doing its best to cool things down. The repairmen had promised to return by two o'clock to begin work on the window. The Methodist church bell tower had tolled one-thirty a few minutes ago.

Amanda stood with a view of the street, wiping sweat from her forehead. Seeing the new pane of glass, protectively wrapped and leaning against the brick storefront just waiting to be installed, brought a smile to her face. Worry over the loss of expensive flowers was replaced by a wave of appreciation. All would be right soon.

Voices rose over the chime of the doorbell announcing Cate, Aunt Grace, and her mom's arrival. They burst in, a cacophony of happy chatter, just as Becca, Jillian, and her pups came in through the back. With their hands full of bags, boxes, and dog leashes, the two friends were in a more somber mood than the rest of the group.

"Give me a minute," Jillian snapped at Becca. "I don't relish the thought of adding one more thing to Ethan's or Amanda's plate right now."

Uh-oh. What's that all about?

Becca wrestled with her purse and a cardboard box that emanated the most mouthwatering smells. "They need to know about this sooner rather than later."

"I know, I know. But timing is everything." Jillian carefully slipped a piece of paper into her purse before kneeling to release the two pups who pranced at her feet.

Amanda frowned, wondering what the pair argued about. Their quarrel sent a tingle of apprehension down her spine.

"We can set up the food on my table in the backroom." Amanda motioned for everyone to join her.

"Help, someone call off the dogs." Becca laughed as she juggled the box, sidestepping to avoid Abbey and Hayley.

Amanda whistled, then uttered the word *treats.* Jillian's pups scooted across the room, ears flapping. Abbey let out a few excited yips as the two schnauzers begged their Aunt Amanda for attention or treats—in whichever order she pleased.

"Could your furballs be any cuter?" Amanda rubbed their soft, pink bellies. "Someday, I'd like a dog as sweet as you. Don't know if I could handle two at a time, though."

Jillian's head jerked up. "You want a dog?"

"Yeah, sometime in the future. I have to finish the renovation at the house first. That includes replacing the dilapidated fence in the backyard."

Amanda gave one last vigorous scratch, then stood to reach into the pocket of her apron. She tossed two dog biscuits into the air. They were devoured in seconds. Every crumb licked from the floor.

On the heels of this canine cuddle-fest, Ethan had entered through the back door. He grabbed the box from Becca, whisking it onto the long worktable, which had been covered with a cheerful yellow tablecloth. Joy and Aunt Grace put out paper plates, napkins, and utensils, while Cate poured ice-cold tea into plastic cups. Amanda had rescued some of her older blooms, setting out three vases filled with colorful and aromatic flowers.

"These bouquets are beautiful." Jillian leaned closer to breathe in their scent. "You were busy while Becca and I were gone."

"I had to do something with those blossoms slightly past their peak." Amanda shrugged off the compliment. "I made some arrangements for my neighbors too."

"That was thoughtful of you, Pumpkin. Your flowers will brighten their workspaces." Aunt Grace motioned to the table. "Let's sit and enjoy what smells like a delicious lunch."

Sam strolled in as the food hit the table. He wrapped his arms around Amanda, greeting her with a kiss, one full of quiet promise. Aunt Grace patted the seat next to her, prompting Sam to sit down. Everyone else grabbed a stool and dug into their lunch. The silence that followed was proof that Steve Harrison had succeeded in putting a little extra comfort into his comfort food.

Since they'd already eaten, Jillian and Becca shared the details of Amanda's latest vandalism, while the others enjoyed their meal.

"Are there any new leads?" Becca quizzed Ethan, who choked on the bite of burger he'd taken.

"Geez, Becca. You were gone less than two hours." He took a drink of tea to clear his throat. "You can't expect these crimes to be solved that fast. Haven't you learned anything from being a detective's wife?"

Everyone stopped eating as they stared at the couple. A thunderous look spread over Becca's face. Ethan's good-natured teasing hit a sore spot.

"Why, Detective Harden," she launched a verbal assault on her husband. "I'm glad you remembered you *have* a wife. Could've fooled me with the pathetic welcome home I received yesterday after being gone for a week."

The table fell silent. Becca carried on.

"Yes, I know all about being a detective's wife. I know how you become self-absorbed when you're involved in a case. I know how insensitive you can be to other people's feelings. I know sometimes you can be a big jerk." Brushing tears from her cheeks, Becca stormed from the workroom and into the alley, slamming the door behind her.

All eyes stared at Ethan.

"Um, I should go after her, right?" Ethan scrubbed his fingers through his military-style haircut. His question was directed at Jillian.

"Yes, you should go." She brought out her best teacher voice. "Becca was gone for a week, Ethan. You barely acknowledged her arrival home yesterday. The first time you two are apart since you were married, and you don't act like you missed her. You know how Becca is. She expected a mushy reunion. Instead, you pecked her on the cheek and went outside to deal with a dead body. Imagine how that made her feel. You acted as if a corpse was more important than her." Jillian took a breath after her long tirade.

Amanda studied Ethan's face. He looked like a three-year-old being scolded for sneaking a cookie before dinner.

He remained seated, staring at the door Becca had slammed upon her dramatic exit.

"Get out there. Apologize to your wife." Jillian flapped her hands, shooing him away. "Make this right."

Ethan wiped his hands on a napkin and headed for the door. He turned at the last moment.

"Becca texted me about the new note you found. Hiding it in your purse, aren't you, Jilly? I'll expect you to hand it over as soon as I come back inside." He straightened his shoulders before entering the alley.

Jillian clicked her heels and saluted. "Yes, sir."

"Let's hope they kiss and make up." Sam grinned around his mouthful of fries. "Happy spouse, happy house—isn't that how the saying goes?"

The bell over the front door sounded, sending Amanda to wait on a customer. She needed to sell more flowers before the heat killed them. Gone only minutes, she returned smiling like she'd won the lottery.

"They're here to fix my window." She rounded the table to deposit a huge kiss on Sam's cheek. "This wonderful guy called in a favor, and the glass company put me on today's schedule. I owe this man of mine big time."

"Like I said, happy spouse, happy house." Sam winked at Amanda, who rewarded him with another quick kiss.

"Nice sentiment, but she's not your wife." Cate raised an eyebrow at Sam. "Perhaps you should do something about that."

Sam's cheeks flushed. He averted his eyes from the group.

"Cate, how about you mind your own business?" Amanda spoke through gritted teeth. "Sam and I will decide if, and when, we get married. We don't need a marriage license or wedding ceremony to know how much we love each other. *If* we ever choose to get married, we'll let you know. End of discussion."

"Girls, let's not embarrass poor Sam with this talk of weddings." Aunt Grace tsked and patted his hand. "Even though Amanda would make a beautiful bride." She shot a brazen look in her niece's direction.

Sam pulled Grace in for a quick hug. "She most certainly would."

One of the glass technicians entered the backroom. "Sorry to intrude on your meal, folks. Ms. Edwards, we need you in front to show you the plan to fix your window. Once you to sign the repair agreement, we can get to work."

"You all keep eating. I'll be back in a few." Amanda left to supervise the installation of the new window. She called over her shoulder. "No more talk about weddings."

Amanda stood a safe distance away on the sidewalk, watching the glaziers clear away the remaining shards of broken glass. The sound of the door opening drew her attention. Relief flooded through her as Sam approached. His concerned expression unhinged the tight control of her emotions she'd clung to all day. He opened his arms to her, and she walked into his embrace.

Finally, a chance for them to be alone.

Away from my nosy family.

Holding her tight, he said, "I'm sorry for everything that's happened."

She rested her head on his chest, allowing her frustrated tears to fall. For once, she didn't care who might see their PDA. Being held by the man she loved soothed the stresses of the day.

After a few moments and with reluctance, Amanda stepped back to look Sam in the eye. She laughed at the wet stains her tears left on his shirt. "Looks like I owe you a dry shirt, Sailor. Or at least to launder the one you're wearing."

"No need for that." He tugged on a loose curl and kissed her cheek. "Why didn't you text or call me *before* my meeting? I would've canceled it and come straight home."

"To do what—hold my hand? Bring me a tissue? You had important business to take care of." Her fingers tightened in his shirt, but her words tried to soften the weight he was carrying. "There was nothing you could do here. I'm fine. The shop can be fixed."

Sam stared into her face. "I want to be here to support you when things get tough. Even someone as strong and independent as you can use a little help once in a while."

"You do help me. You arranged for new tires for my car. You built the structure to hold flowers for my window display, then agreed to build another one. You made a call to your friend and, *voilà*, my window is being repaired in record time. Let's not forget, I couldn't do the renovations on my house without your expertise and skill." Amanda pressed a hand over Sam's heart.

"More important than the tangible things, you help by letting me be that strong, independent woman. You've never tried to change me. I appreciate that more than you know." She took Sam's face in her hands, placing a tender kiss on his lips. "I love you for letting me be me."

"I wouldn't want you to change. I love who you are, the way you are." Sam rested his forehead against hers and lowered his voice to a whisper. "While I hate for this moment to end, we've attracted a small audience. Maybe we should take this conversation somewhere more private."

Amanda glanced at her fellow business owners who stared in their direction. She gave them a brief wave, took Sam's hand, and led him into the fragrant front room of her shop.

"I'm sorry about Cate's comment earlier." She kept hold of his hands, looking into his eyes. "You know, about us not being married. Please ignore her or other family members' future remarks on this subject. I'm fine with things the way they are, as long as you are."

"Yeah, about that. I've been thinking—"

"There you are." Jillian entered the room. "Sam's back. Your window's being fixed. I'm going to head to the bookstore. Time to go set up for my middle school group."

By all means, come in, Jillian.

"Leaving so you can avoid Ethan?" Amanda raised an eyebrow. "Didn't I hear him say something about another note?"

Jillian whistled for Abbey and Hayley, who scrambled to join her. She clipped on their leashes and slung her purse over her shoulder. "Just wanted to say goodbye before I left."

"Wait, I asked you about the note." Amanda blocked her path to the door.

"A note? I don't ... I'm not ..." Jillian fussed with the leashes as they'd become wrapped around her legs in the dogs' excitement. Sam came to her rescue. He grabbed Hayley's lead, helping free Jillian from the tangle.

Ignored my question twice. Must be bad.

Amanda narrowed her eyes. She wasn't done with her little sister.

"Thanks for being here today." Sam gave Jillian a quick hug. "We know Amanda can handle things on her own, but I feel better knowing family is close by."

"Anytime," Jillian said. "Speaking of family—"

"What now?" Amanda sighed. "Did Aunt Grace have another vision about me? What is it this time, flood, or famine?"

"None I'm aware of." Jillian rolled her eyes. "Let's hope she doesn't have visions of *you* in mom's wedding dress."

Amanda winced and sucked in a breath. "That was awkward. Poor Travis looked like he'd been punched in the gut." The memory of his pained expression last night at dinner played through her head.

"Hey, take it easy on Travis. The mention of marriage makes some guys nervous no matter how much they love their girl." Sam came to Travis's defense.

"Are you speaking from personal experience?" Jillian opened her eyes wide. "Does the M-word make you nervous, Sam?"

"Not at all, but I'm not like most men." A smug grin crossed his face. "I'd marry your sister in a heartbeat if only she'd say yes."

Jillian's mouth flopped open. "Oh, really?"

Amanda ignored them both, moving the conversation away from the subject of marriage. "You started to say something about family?"

"Oh, right. Mom asked me to tell you she's buying dinner at La Casita. Late supper since I close the bookstore tonight. We agreed on seven-thirty-ish." Jillian handed Amanda a set of keys. "She also wants you to use her car until Shorty brings yours back. She'll get a ride with Aunt Grace."

"Leave it to Mom to solve my transportation problem, but an Edwards family dinner two nights in a row. Did she say why?" Amanda sensed her mother had an ulterior motive. This impromptu dinner was unusual behavior for a woman who planned everything in her life three weeks in advance.

"She didn't give a reason," Jillian said. "But if I had to guess, she's making sure you're surrounded by people who'll look out for you."

"I don't know. Doesn't this make you both suspicious?" Amanda's eyes darted between Sam and Jillian. "Mom doesn't do anything spur of the moment. My gut tells me this is no ordinary get-together. Something's up, and I'm afraid to find out what it is. I've had enough drama in my life in the last two days." She leaned on Sam for support.

"Your mom wants everyone to come for dinner." Sam made light of her qualms. "We do this all the time. We'll go and enjoy the evening. Besides, you know how Jilly and I love Mexican food."

"Sure, we could do that, but you'll have to excuse my skepticism. After four flat tires, a smashed window, poor Rick's death, and two threatening notes—or is it three now?—I'm a bit cynical." Amanda's eyes bore into Jillian, who let out a long sigh.

"Yes, there's a third note."

"Has Ethan seen it?"

Jillian confirmed with a nod. "He's putting it into evidence as we speak."

"Why didn't you say something earlier?" Amanda ran her hands through her hair, pulling it from its current updo. "C'mon, then. What does it say?"

"Maybe Ethan should tell you." Jillian backed away, shooing Abbey and Hayley toward the door.

"Don't you dare leave." Amanda's icy command froze Jillian mid-step. "Tell me what the note said."

"Okay, but this one is more cryptic than the first two."

"Spill it." The chill remained in Amanda's voice.

"Beware of yellow carnations." Jillian's gaze flit from Amanda to Sam. "That's all it said. No clue what it means, but it's yet another threat."

Amanda gripped Sam's sleeve. "My stalker's counting on me understanding since I'm a florist."

"Babe, what is it?" Sam's forehead creased. "Do yellow carnations mean something to you?"

"Yes, they do. The SAF, that's the Society for American Florists, has a list of flowers and what they represent, both positive and negative." She paused. "Yellow carnations, in their negative context, stand for rejection, disappointment, and heartbreak."

The seconds of silence that followed this statement crawled by like snails on the pavement. Sam rallied first.

"Never send yellow carnations to anyone. Check."

"Everything will be okay." Jillian said, with the practiced steadiness Amanda had come to expect from her in a crisis. "Your window's fixed, and, Sam, you can make a new wooden structure for the flowers, right?"

"Of course. I'll start on it as soon as I get over to Amanda's house. Plenty of leftover wood in her garage." His eager smile lifted Amanda's spirits, if only a little.

"Great," Jillian said. "And Ethan's working hard to find this nutcase. We'll get to the bottom of this soon." She gave Amanda's hand a quick, reassuring squeeze before letting go. "See you both tonight."

Jillian hustled her pups out the door before Amanda could warn her not to meddle in Ethan's case.

"You noticed she said *we*, right? Is she actually getting involved in this mess?" Sam rubbed at the stubble on his chin.

"You've met my little sister." Amanda let out an exasperated sigh. "That girl never shies away from a mystery—ever. She'll be up to her eyeballs in this investigation by tomorrow morning, putting herself in danger."

"Hmm, maybe I should warn Travis. He'll want to know what Jillian's up to."

"He's a smart guy, Sam. He knows Jilly, and after the attack on him last night, I'm sure he knows my vandal's behavior is escalating."

Amanda's heart ached for Travis. Judging by Sam's expression, she wasn't hiding her concern as well as she thought.

"I know that look. Stop beating yourself up about Travis. His injury wasn't your fault." Sam touched Amanda's cheek. "And the doctor is sure he's all right?"

"He's fine—just a few stitches. He even went on shift today." Amanda shook her head, a frown pulling at her lips. "A little too tough for his own good, if you ask Jillian."

"Glad he's going to be okay." Sam rubbed his own forehead, a subconscious gesture of solidarity, perhaps. "If this fruit loop is coming after people close to you, I better be on guard."

Amanda had pushed the thought of Sam being in danger to the darkest recesses of her mind. With that seed now firmly planted by Sam himself, she felt sick to her stomach.

Everyone wandered up front to inspect the progress on the window. Becca and Ethan held hands, suggesting all had been forgiven.

"They're doing a fabulous job fixing your window, Pumpkin." Aunt Grace tilted her head, studying the space. "I can picture your new Halloween display. This one will be even better than the first."

After the goodbyes and hugs, Amanda and Sam were finally alone. They stood shoulder to shoulder, surveying the mess left behind by the vandal, the crime scene techs, and now the glaziers.

Amanda picked up a broom to sweep some broken glass, dumping it into the trash bin. "I have a lot of work to do to put this place back together."

"You mean *we* have work to do." Sam dragged a lined trashcan close to the back side of the window. He picked up handfuls of ruined, dripping stems and shoved them in the garbage. "The two of us can get it done in no time."

"While your help here would be great, I want to recreate the window display as soon as possible." Amanda dumped more broken glass into the trash. "No Halloween prankster or lunatic stalker is going to stop me. I *am* going to win the trophy this year."

"That's my girl." Sam grabbed her around the waist. "You want me to go home and work on the new structure, don't you?" Sam delivered a steamy parting kiss, sending a rush of warmth through Amanda's body. "Consider it done."

"Thank you." She pulled Sam closer. "You're the best, and I love you like crazy."

"I love you more." He gave her a playful nudge. "We'll figure out a way for you to repay me."

"I'm sure we will." She tilted her head, smiling at him. "You know—we make a good team."

"We certainly do." The buzzing of his phone interrupted Sam's next words. Amanda continued to clean while he took the call. His conversation, the part she could hear, only took a minute or two.

"Shorty?" Amanda asked.

"Yes," Sam said. "As we knew, all four tires were flat, but he'd hoped to patch the old ones. That's not possible because of how they were slashed. He can get you a deal on a new set and have them installed by the end of business tomorrow." Sam dumped more wilted flowers into the trash. "Shorty wanted to make this as easy as possible for you, so he called Joe over at the insurance office and had him start your paperwork. You'll be happy to know the deductible is waived in the case of vandalism."

"Shorty is one of the good guys." Amanda made a mental note to take him some cookies from Sugar & Spice.

Another good guy is lying in the morgue.

Amanda's stomach tightened as the thought of Rick hit her like a punch in the gut. She stood there a moment, letting the pain pass.

After they agreed to meet at her house a little after five, Amanda kissed Sam goodbye. "Thanks for spending the afternoon rebuilding that flower frame. I appreciate you, Sailor."

"You're welcome." Sam smiled as he headed out the door. "You know I enjoy hanging out at your house—it's a great space. See you later, babe."

I do love that man of mine.

Amanda had also fallen in love with her house—the first moment she set eyes on it—with its stately porch across the front, the gabled roof, the open floor plan and all that gorgeous wood. She'd already spent hours removing wallpaper, stripping and repainting cabinets, and replacing flooring.

She'd purchased the two-story house on Rosewood Lane six months ago. The property had been owned by an elderly couple and had fallen into disrepair. The home's rundown condition helped her negotiate a great deal, but now she'd spent all the money she'd saved on the asking price to pay for the remodel. The thought of all those expenses made her head hurt. She needed a distraction from her money woes.

Amanda closed her eyes and took a slow, deep breath, envisioning what the house would look like once all the planned renovations were complete. She couldn't wait for that day to come.

Sam and I could be very happy living there after we're married.

Whoa, why had that thought popped into her head?

Amanda's heart skipped a beat, and she suddenly felt weak in the knees. She stopped working and leaned on the cold glass door of the flower cooler.

"Must be all this talk about Jillian and Travis, the proposal pool, and Aunt Grace's upcoming wedding." She once again spoke to the room full of flowers. "Me—married?"

Amanda had never dreamed of the perfect wedding like her sisters had. Marriage, and all it entailed, had never been something she pictured for herself—until now.

Until Sam.

Her mother had always said when the right guy came along, she'd change her tune.

Sam was definitely the right guy—for her. No question about that.

While visions of bridal bouquets danced in her head, Amanda finished cleaning the front room.

I get this done, then I can prepare my midweek floral order.

Amanda gasped. A sharp pain seized her chest as she remembered Rick wouldn't come for that order. He'd never walk through her back door, smiling and booming out his usual greeting. They'd never share bad floral humor or commiserate over difficult customers. Rick's impish grin and sweet personality had been extinguished by a bullet.

Amanda slumped against the counter, allowing sorrow to wash over her. Tears fell, uninhibited. How could this happen to a great guy like Rick? How would his wife and infant son move on?

"What am I going to do for flowers this week?" She spoke to the empty workroom. "I have no choice but to call the supplier in Henderson. They might help me out."

The receptionist at Wholesale Flowers took no more than five minutes to get things lined up for a delivery tomorrow.

"We've all heard about poor Rick." The woman sniffled into the phone. "He and his family might be our biggest competition, but they're such nice people. His death is tragic—and so soon after his dad passed away. My boss directed us to help Finest Florals' customers any way we can. He's increasing our weekly orders to cover the demand."

"Please pass on my thanks to him. I appreciate his generosity." Hanging up the phone, Amanda was overcome with gratitude. There really were good people in this world.

I'm going to need a lot more cookies.

Amanda stopped cleaning and reorganizing the front of the store at three-fifteen. Tim, her delivery help, would be there in half an hour to deliver the funeral arrangements for Mr. O'Leary's visitation. She'd taken phone orders for two other bouquets—a birthday and a get-well—Tim would need to take.

Whenever Amanda worked with flowers, her hands took over, letting her mind wander. She thought about the evidence in Ethan's investigation of Rick's death.

There was the suicide note. She still struggled to believe a man like Rick, upbeat and full of life, would kill himself, but she supposed Ethan was right. Anyone could feel low enough at some point to consider taking their own life. The handwriting analysis would confirm whether Rick had written the note. Ethan had said other tests would be run too. Rick's hands would be checked for gunpowder residue and after the autopsy, the—

Autopsy.

The finality of this word made her heart ache. The picture of her friend slumped over the steering wheel popped into Amanda's head causing a cold shiver. She took a sip of the now warm soda sitting on the table. A steadying breath, then she returned to work.

As she completed the last bouquet and deliberated over Rick's death, she chastised herself.

"Look at me. If I don't watch it, I'll be just like Jillian—sticking my nose into Ethan's case."

She tied a large cream ribbon around the vase, then attached the get-well card to the floral stick before placing the arrangement back in the cooler. As she shut the door, a memory popped into her head.

"Wait a minute," Amanda shouted into the empty room. "There won't be any residue on Rick's hand because this wasn't a suicide. I can prove it."

CHAPTER ELEVEN

Amanda paced the floor of the flower shop, wringing the towel in her hands. "To shoot yourself in the right side of your head, you'd hold the gun in your right hand. I must have seen Rick sign my copy of invoices a thousand times—with his *left* hand. He couldn't have pulled the trigger. Rick didn't commit suicide. He was murdered."

"Who was murdered, Miss Amanda?" Tim strolled through the front door.

"Oh ... um ... nobody. Just talking to myself."

"You talk to yourself about murder?" The boy rolled his eyes. "People think we teenagers are weird."

Amanda ignored his comment. "I finished the last arrangement, so you can put them in the van."

Tim—a tall, strapping seventeen-year-old football player—took no time loading the flowers. "Anything else need to be delivered?"

"No, it's been kind of a slow day for business." Amanda snipped the ends from a dozen colorful Gerbera daisies before taking some cash from the register. "There were repairmen here all afternoon—they just finished."

"Yeah, I heard about your broken window, the graffiti, your tires, and the dead flower guy. Somebody must be super angry with you. That's a bummer."

Amanda knew his sympathies were heartfelt despite the lack of finesse in his delivery. Typical of a teenager, she supposed.

Amanda handed Tim the key, along with sixty dollars. "Before you bring the van back, please fill the tank."

"Can do." The boy grinned. "I'll be quick. Don't intend to spend any more time than necessary at the funeral home. Dead people freak me out."

"You and me both, kiddo."

Tim strolled out the back door as the bell in the front signaled a customer.

Make that two customers.

An elderly couple stood arm in arm at the cooler, their heads bowed together. The silver-haired woman sighed over the array of beautiful flowers.

"Oh, my goodness. They're all gorgeous and smell wonderful. How will I choose?" She offered a smile to the man whom Amanda could only see from the back. Then, he opened his mouth.

"Hey, Flower Lady," he grumbled. "I need to buy more posies for my gal."

That voice. Like fingernails on a chalkboard.

Amanda squared her shoulders, summoning every ounce of patience she possessed.

"Good afternoon, Mr. Erickson. Mrs. Taylor." Amanda hoped her greeting rang genuine. "I'm happy to see you in my shop again. How can I help you?"

"Not so fast, missy. How do you know our names?" Mr. Erickson scowled at her. "I never introduced myself when I was here before."

"We met about a year ago at McGuire's Pub—you had lunch with my family. The day the hit-and-run killer was caught. My sister, Jillian, runs the bookstore across from your house." Amanda searched for any flicker of recognition on his wrinkled face. "I told her about your visit yesterday. She knew right away from my description it was you. Funny, isn't it?"

"I don't see nothin' funny about it." The old man snorted. "Now The Flower Lady and The Book Lady bein' sisters—that's funny." He cackled like a hyena. "And you're both related to The Cookie Lady. The legs on that one." He whistled long and slow. "Quite a looker. Tell her I could sure use some of her delicious treats sometime soon."

"Henry, don't be rude." Mrs. Taylor tapped him lightly on the arm, stopping his laughter and sending his gaze to the floor. "A gentleman shouldn't be so cheeky with a sweet, young woman like Miss Edwards."

"Uh, sorry. Didn't mean to leave you out. You're darn good-lookin' yourself, Flower Lady." He wiggled his bushy eyebrows at Amanda.

Her face warmed.

"Henry, stop. You're embarrassing her." Mrs. Taylor pursed her lips. "We've talked about this. You can't always say what's rattling around inside that head of yours. You'll offend people."

Amanda found this censure of his crass behavior amusing. Jillian might be right about Mrs. Taylor being the one to smooth out this old man's rough edges. The thought of a more refined, genteel Mr. Erickson made her smile.

"Whatcha standin' there grinnin' for?" he asked. "We got things to do, places to go. Let's get crackin' on them posies."

This earned him a soft clearing of the throat from his lady friend and a tsk, tsk under her breath.

"Er ... I mean ... could you please help me with some flowers for my purdy gal?" The attempt at manners garnered him an approving nod from his date.

"What kind of blooms do you have in mind?" Amanda addressed Mrs. Taylor. "Did you like the ones in yesterday's bouquet?"

"Oh yes, dear. They were lovely." Mrs. Taylor fussed with the lace handkerchief she clutched in her hand. "I told Henry I don't need more flowers today, but he's insisting. He's such a thoughtful man." She laid a hand on his face, her compliments turning the apple of his cheeks a warm pink.

Amanda couldn't wait to tell Jillian about this visit. She'd be amazed at the changes Mrs. Taylor had made in Mr. Erickson's personality, like Beauty taming the Beast.

"What are your favorite flowers, Mrs. Taylor? I can create a wonderful bouquet with blossoms you like best."

"Oh goodness, I love them all. You're the expert, dear. I trust you'll pick something nice, but not too expensive." She lowered her voice. "Henry is retired and on a fixed income."

"Give me a few minutes. I'll pull something together for you." A rush of cold air escaped as Amanda walked into her cooler. She gathered small yellow mums, purple asters, and white Japanese anemones with sweet alyssum for filler, then set to work cutting the ends so they'd take plenty of water.

"Would you like these in a vase or a floral box?" Amanda directed the question to Mrs. Taylor, but Mr. Erickson jumped in.

"Neither. She's gonna wear them posies."

"Excuse me?" Amanda tilted her head. "Mrs. Taylor can't wear a bouquet of flowers."

"Didn't ask for no bouquet, Flower Lady. I need one of them thingies—you know—you pin it on the lady's blouse. I'm takin' my girl dancin' at the VFW tonight." He plucked at the striped suspenders under his tweed sportscoat. "She needs some pretty posies for her dress."

"Henry, what a wonderful surprise. I love dancing." Mrs. Taylor beamed at her escort for the evening. "You should've told Miss Edwards you needed a corsage before she pulled all these beautiful flowers."

"Don't worry, Mrs. Taylor. I can use them for a different arrangement." Amanda found a vase for the cut flowers and returned them to the cooler. "May I suggest a wrist corsage since you'll be dancing? The delicate flowers won't get crushed."

"That sounds good, 'cuz I plan to hold this gal real close while we're dancin' the night away." He giggled like a schoolboy, grinning at his date.

"Coming right up." Amanda was thankful she stood in the cooler with her back to the old man, so he couldn't see the disgusted face she'd made.

Mrs. Taylor wore a deep burgundy dress, so Amanda chose a fragrant white gardenia, two petite pink roses, and a bit of delicate greenery. A burgundy ribbon to match her dress would finish it off.

While she worked, Mr. Erickson interrogated her.

"What's this I hear about some troubles you've had around here?" He tapped the counter with a gnarled finger. "Vandals are bad enough, but a dead body? What kinda place you runnin' here?"

Once again, Mrs. Taylor reprimanded his ill-mannered queries. "Henry, please. Miss Edwards has a lovely establishment. She can't control some lunatic who has targeted her store." She smoothed down the front of her dress. "We should be supportive, not discouraging."

Amanda appreciated the elderly woman's kindness.

"Here we go." She handed her creation to Mrs. Taylor. "I hope this meets with your approval."

Mrs. Taylor buried her nose in the gardenia. "This corsage is the most beautiful thing I've ever seen—and smelled. You've matched my dress to a *T*. Thank you so much." Her smile lit up her eyes.

Amanda's heart swelled. The magic of flowers had brought joy to this kind lady. That was why she loved her job.

"You're welcome. I'm so happy you like it."

"If you two hens are done cluckin' about these posies, I need to pay for 'em, so we can skedaddle." Mr. Erickson pulled out his worn, leather wallet. He handed a twenty to Amanda, not bothering to ask if it covered the cost, which it didn't.

She said nothing as she slid the bill into the cash drawer. *Not a hill I'm willing to die on.*

"All the good tables fill up quick. Dinner starts in just a few minutes—the band at seven." He took the corsage, placing it on Mrs. Taylor's delicate wrist. She raised it to her face, inhaling the scent again.

"Thank you, Henry. You are such a dear." She dropped a brief kiss on his cheek.

"You two have a great time tonight." Amanda ushered them to the door. "Thanks for coming in."

"If you ain't got plans later, come out to the VFW. I'd love to see if The Flower Lady can cut a rug with this old guy." He poked a thumb in his chest.

Mr. Erickson held the door open for Mrs. Taylor like a real gentleman. Then, tucking her arm in the crook of his, they navigated their way across the street to his behemoth of a car. Amanda wondered if he could see over the steering wheel, let alone handle a car that big.

Lord, look out for the other drivers on the road tonight.

One glance at the clock had Amanda flip the *OPEN* sign to *CLOSED*.

Mr. Erickson had just opened the car door for his date when a movement to Amanda's right caught her attention. A face appeared, staring at her through the newly repaired window.

Amanda startled and jumped back. The visitor—a woman with long hair—jerked away from the glass when their eyes locked.

Amanda dashed to open the door to confront the stranger peeking into her shop. She looked up and down the street, but her window peeper had vanished like a wisp of smoke.

"That was creepy." Amanda whispered into the dusky air. She'd glimpsed the face only briefly but could swear she'd seen the woman before—here at the store—with her baby. "She was probably checking to see if I was still open."

Amanda locked the door and headed home. She would've preferred a romantic evening alone with Sam, but another family dinner would keep that from happening tonight.

Tomorrow. Definitely tomorrow.

Amanda was curious about why her mother had called them all together. There'd been enough bad news in the past two days. She hoped her mom had something good to share.

Her drive home took only ten minutes. Amanda hopped from the car, feeling restless and jumpy. An hour of hard labor might help shake off her sour mood. She changed into work clothes and grabbed a paintbrush from Sam's bucket.

"Hey, Sailor, can you use another pair of hands?" She deposited a kiss on the top of his head as she walked into the dining room.

"From the sexiest woman wearing paint-spattered overalls? Absolutely." His broad grin made her heart flutter. "I finished the new flower holder for your window. I'll bring it by the shop early tomorrow."

"Thank you, Sam. You're the best." She could always count on him—if he said he would do something, he followed through.

They worked side by side, talking while they made good progress on the baseboards and wall trim. Until her grandmother's clock chimed seven.

"Oh my gosh. We're going to be late for dinner." Amanda dropped her brush into the cleaning bucket. "I need a shower."

She took the stairs two at a time, leaving a trail of messy clothes. With her eyes shut, Amanda stood under the warm water and exhaled her first truly relaxed breath in the last twenty-four hours. Times like this made her happy she'd decided to move in before all the renovations were complete.

The faint creak of the door rose above the cascade of water. A current of air moved the shower curtain, slapping it against Amanda's legs. Her heart slammed against her ribs like a trapped bird in a cage. Every instinct screamed—she was not alone.

"Don't mind me—just need to grab my razor."

Sam.

A few deep breaths steadied her racing heart.

"Ever heard of knocking, Sailor?"

Amanda couldn't see him through the shower curtain, but she heard the cabinet door open and close.

"I know how your mom dislikes it when we're late," Sam said. "I'll be done and out of your hair in a few minutes."

"Beat it, Sam. Go use the guest bathroom, then we have a chance that both of us will be ready on time."

"You're no fun," Sam muttered. The sound of the bathroom door shutting behind him didn't quite cut off his snort of laughter.

Fresh from their showers and dressed in clean clothes, they tromped downstairs only a few minutes late. Sam laughed at a joke Amanda shared as he stepped onto the porch ahead of her.

Suddenly, he thrust out his arm to stop her, his laughter frozen.

"Amanda, don't come out here."

CHAPTER TWELVE

Amanda sat in a wicker chair, staring at the yellow carnations and four dead rats scattered on the unvarnished floorboards of her front porch.

That's a disgusting calling card.

A new thought popped into her head.

Where were these flowers coming from? Certainly not her shop.

Before she could process the thought further, Ethan arrived. His quick response to Sam's call settled her rattled nerves—if only slightly. While he processed the scene and took the deceased vermin into custody, she seized the opportunity to share her revelation about Rick.

"There's no way a left-handed person could shoot himself in the right temple." Amanda mimicked holding a gun with her fingers. "Rick was a leftie, so it's safe to say he did not commit suicide."

"You're sure he was left-handed?" Ethan scrunched his nose as if her theory reeked like the dead rat.

Amanda stood, facing him down. "Yes, I'm sure. Do you know how many times I watched him sign floral invoices?"

"If you're right, the forensics will support you. If you're right, I'll be working on a murder investigation." Ethan scratched his chin. "Until the test results are in, don't mention this to anyone—especially Jillian. I hear you're all meeting at La Casita tonight."

"Yep, another enjoyable evening with the Edwards family." Sam nodded at Ethan. "You and Becca care to join us?"

"Thanks for the offer, but no." Ethan started down the porch steps. "I promised Becca a romantic evening to make up for my—what'd she call it—oh yeah, insensitive behavior. Although she loves you guys, I'll be in deeper trouble if I accept your invitation."

"Too bad," Sam said. "I know how much you love the tamales."

Ethan waved him off with a grin. "I love my wife more."

Amanda and Sam weren't the only ones running late. Jillian and Travis pulled up at the same moment. Jillian scurried across the street, flailing her hands in the air like a wind-up monkey Amanda had received one year for Christmas.

"Jilly must be having a day like mine—seems a bit distraught." Amanda nudged Sam and pointed at her sister.

"Hello, you two. Looks like we won't be alone in getting the punctuality lecture from Mom." Jillian greeted them both with a hug. Sam and Travis shared a fist bump. "Strength in numbers, I guess."

"Hope you two have a good excuse." Sam winked at them.

"It's my fault—had to stay late at the bookstore. Our computer system crashed this morning. After we closed, I had to key in all the sales Trixie had handwritten." Jillian shoved her car key into her purse. "What's your excuse?"

Sam shrugged. "Nothing that needed tech support. We lost track of time while staining woodwork."

Amanda sighed, bowing her head. That excuse wouldn't mollify her mother, but this one might.

"Someone also left a surprise on my doorstep—one requiring Ethan's attention." Amanda shivered thinking of the rats.

"What happened? Are you okay?" Jillian put an arm around her sister.

"Let's go face the music before it gets any later." Sam held the door for the ladies. "We'll tell you about it once we're inside. No sense having to share the story twice."

Hanging their coats in the vestibule, they let their noses lead the way through the restaurant to the large table in the back where the family waited. The sweet smell of cinnamon *churros* as well as something peppery and spicy filled the air. Amanda's stomach growled in response to the delectable smells.

Bryan headed them off with a reproving shake of his finger.

"Ooh, you four better get a move on. Aunt Joy's been working up a good head of steam, muttering about timeliness being next to godliness—or something to that effect. Wouldn't want to be you right now."

Conversations stopped as the latecomers approached the table. Her mother's scowl wasn't lost on Amanda.

"So nice of you to join us—thirty minutes late." The clipped words stopped both daughters in their tracks. "I'm sure you boys had nothing to do with my daughters' tardiness." Joy bestowed her sweetest smile on Sam and Travis, then patted the chairs closest to her. "Please, come sit by me."

Sam took the seat to the right of Joy as instructed, while Travis settled into the chair on the left with a polite nod.

Amanda pulled out the chair next to Sam. He'd been gone for weeks, and after the chaos of the past two days, she wanted—no, needed—the comfort of having him close.

The smell of warm tortilla chips and spicy salsa signaled the waitress' arrival. She set several baskets and bowls on the table as she took their drink orders. Joy waited until she left, then cleared her throat.

"Dare I ask what held you girls up? I thought I raised you to know the importance of being punctual."

"Joy, don't be so hard on them." Davis came to his daughters' defense. "They're here now. Isn't that what counts?"

Amanda took her dad's hand, giving it a squeeze.

"I'd like to hear the excuse." Aunt Grace put down the menu and peered over the top of her reading glasses. "Knowing these two, there's a story to be told. Kitten, would you like to go first?"

Jillian recounted the story of the computer crash at the bookstore. "After closing, I had to key in handwritten sales before preparing the bank deposit—busy taking care of business." With a kiss on her mom's cheek, she took a seat. "I am sorry for being late."

Joy nodded, pacified by her explanation. "What about you, Amanda? I hope there weren't more problems at the flower shop."

"No, thank goodness. Our tardiness," Amanda pointed to herself and Sam, "had nothing to do with my store. We lost track of—"

Aunt Grace let out a sharp cry. Sitting ramrod straight in her chair, her eyes drifted shut. Her arms fell limp at her sides. An eerie strangled whisper replaced her usual cheery voice.

"There was happiness and laughter." Her eyes flew open. "But the air chilled. Darkness came, followed by death and destruction."

Amanda closed her eyes, taking several deep breaths.

"Aunt Grace, what's going on?" Jillian rubbed her aunt's arm. "Talk to us."

Jorge Garcia, the owner of La Casita, arrived with two large trays of appetizers. "Fiesta Platters for our best customers—on the house. You'll be sampling our grilled shrimp with chili lime mayo, shredded chicken and cheese empanadas, and Mexican street corn quesadillas. Enjoy— *buen provecho!*"

His appearance had allowed Grace time to recover. Color returned to her cheeks as she sipped a glass of water.

"I'm sorry. I've done it again." She wiped away tears trailing down her face. "I don't mean to ruin our family get-togethers, but these thoughts just pop into my head. I have no idea what they mean except to warn of danger."

"As always, Mom, you sure know how to throw a damper on a party." Bryan crossed his arms over his chest, then leaned back in his chair. "What's all this about a chill followed by death and destruction?"

"Amanda and I can shed some light on part of your vision, Grace." Sam swallowed a gulp of the ice-cold beer the waitress handed him.

He described the discovery of the dead rats and the carnations. Jillian gasped.

"That crazy stalker-poet knows where you live. He left a warning right on your doorstep." Jillian set her glass down a bit too hard, sloshing her iced tea onto her hand. Cate handed her a napkin. "You have to call Ethan."

"Already did," Sam said. "He came, took the critters into evidence, and left. Nothing more he can do tonight."

"What about the destruction Aunt Grace saw?" Cate's glance bounced from Sam to Amanda. "What has been destroyed?"

"Nothing new that we know of." Sam raised his glass in salute. "Let's drink to that."

Amanda shuddered, a chill creeping up her arms.

Nothing new had been destroyed, but how soon before the other shoe dropped?

Everyone joined Sam's toast before helping themselves to the appetizers. The waitress returned to take their food orders, assuring them their meals would be up in less than twenty minutes.

They chatted while enjoying the appetizers Jorge had provided. Laughter rippled around the table. Bryan grabbed another empanada, then brought the conversation around to the reason they'd all gathered this evening.

"Aunt Joy, didn't you have something you wanted to tell us?" Bryan bit into the crispy, fried treat. Cheese oozed down his hand. "Nothing bad, I hope."

Joy put down her fork and wiped her mouth. "What I have to say seems insignificant now, but this family needs something positive to think about."

"Good news for a change?" Amanda sat straighter in her chair. "Go ahead, Mom. We're all ears."

Toying with the gold pendant she wore—her telltale sign of nerves—Joy took a deep breath.

Mom's nervous—must be something big.

"As you know, I've been at loose ends since retiring from the hospital two years ago. A person can only do so much cooking, cleaning, and reading."

She paused as several waitstaff delivered fresh chips and more salsa. Glasses were refilled to prepare for the arrival of their meals. Once settled, Amanda's dad steered them back on topic.

"Sweetie, I think we're ready for you to continue."

"Thank you, Davis." She beamed at her husband of forty years. "I received a call from the Human Resources director at St. Francis a few days ago. She and Dr. Ramsey, my former boss, are good friends. He recommended me for a job she's looking to fill."

"That's incredible, Mom." Cate patted Joy's arm. "Will you be nursing again?"

"Are you sure you want to lose the freedom of retirement?" Jillian asked.

"Yeah, Mom. You used to complain about the demanding schedule." Amanda echoed Jillian's concern.

"The job they've offered has flexible hours. I'll be able to design my own schedule. Work when I want, take time off when needed. I'll have the best of both worlds."

Their mom's excitement was palpable.

"What will you be doing?" Jillian asked.

Her mother's words came out in a rush. "My position would be to hire, train, and supervise the nursing staff for the Katherine Marie Flannery Cancer Center which opens soon. Can you believe it? Jilly's friend's inheritance isn't only helping cancer patients, but it's giving your old mom a new career."

"You'll be working with Dr. Madison, Aunt Grace's fiancé," Cate said. "That could be interesting."

"Would you please call him Robert?" Grace mumbled. "He'll be family soon, for goodness sake." Her lip protruded in a pout any four-year-old would be proud of.

Amanda ignored her aunt's petulance. "This is amazing, Mom. The Cancer Center is lucky to have someone with your experience in that position."

All three girls jumped from their seats and snatched their mom in a hug.

Bryan returned from outside where he'd taken a 9-1-1 call from his bartender at the pub. He sat next to Sam and grabbed the nearest glass, taking a long swig. "What's going on with the ladies over there?"

"Dude, you're drinking *my* beer." Sam punched him in the arm. "You owe me a new one."

"*Una cerveza, por favor.*" Bryan called out to the waitress who nodded, heading to the bar to fill his request. "Now, tell me. What'd I miss?"

Grace told him the good news. "Isn't that wonderful?"

"Congratulations, Aunt Joy." Bryan winked at her from across the table. "The HR lady is smart to bring you on board. You'll have the place running like clockwork in no time."

The waitress arrived with their food. Small, quiet conversations broke out while tamales, fajitas, and burritos were devoured. As plates were cleared away, Señor Garcia brought over a bottle of champagne and a tray of flutes.

"Someone told me this table has cause for celebration tonight." He popped the cork on the champagne. "*Felicitaciones a ustedes.*"

Bryan helped Jorge fill the glasses before raising his own. "To Aunt Joy. Congratulations on your new career. May it make you as happy as you make all of us. *Slainte.*"

"Thank you for that lovely toast." Joy blushed a rosy pink. "You've all helped make this evening so—"

"She's very angry." Aunt Grace shouted in a strangled voice. She rose to her feet, knocking over her chair. "The woman feels betrayed by him. She's coming for you." Grace pointed at Amanda. "You're the one she blames."

She flopped into her chair, weeping softly. Bryan flew to his mother's side and patted her hand until her eyes fluttered open. Grace shrank at her family's concerned stares.

"I'm sorry. You must all think I'm crazy." She took a sip of water. "Another vision hit me out of nowhere. I saw the same blonde-haired woman." Tears cut a path through Grace's impeccably applied make-up.

"No one thinks you're crazy, Mom." Bryan wrapped a protective arm around his mother's shoulders. "Just relax for a minute."

The assembled group remained silent, allowing Grace time to recover.

Two creepy visions in one night.

Aunt Grace's 'sight' is working overtime.

"Who is this woman, Aunt Grace? What does she think I've done?"

Amanda hoped for answers, but her aunt had none.

"I'm sorry, Pumpkin. I couldn't see her clearly, but I could feel her anger—sense her thoughts." Grace looked around the table. "We need to keep a close eye on Amanda. She needs protection from this woman."

This latest clairvoyant episode was a wet blanket on the evening. With leftovers boxed and the bill paid, they called it a night. Bryan walked his mother to her car. Jillian's parents said their goodbyes too. Those remaining discussed Grace's strange declaration.

"What do you think of her eerie prediction?" Cate's voice quivered.

"Seems to have shaken Aunt Grace," Jillian said. "If I'm being honest, it's spooked me a bit too. These visions of hers are happening more often. Does that worry any of you?"

"Your aunt's always been sensitive to people's feelings." Sam put on his coat, helping Amanda with hers. "She could've picked up on something from one of the patrons in the restaurant. Maybe it has nothing to do with Amanda." Despite his attempts to make light of the vision, he pulled Amanda close.

Bryan returned in time to overhear the end of Sam's comment. "Do you truly believe my mom channeled some sinister plot against Amanda? I mean, you all know her. She has visions, spouts off dire predictions, then nine times out of ten nothing happens."

Jillian cleared her throat. "What about that tenth time, Bryan? She's been right quite a few times in the last year. You can't deny someone out there is angry with Amanda. They've slashed her tires, smashed the display window, graffitied the front of her shop, and written threatening notes."

"Don't forget the dead rats on her porch," Cate added. "And the carnations."

Listening to her sisters list the heinous acts against her, an alarming thought wriggled its way into Amanda's head.

What if the fire in the backroom of the shop hadn't been due to her carelessness? The door had been open. Maybe her stalker had set the trashcan ablaze.

Bryan's frustrated outburst jerked Amanda's mind back to their conversation.

"Yet here we are again. Mom brought another family dinner to an end with one of her wacky visions." Bryan let out a bitter laugh. "Don't you get tired of the drama she creates?" He whirled around, slamming right into Ethan, knocking him back a few steps.

"Not sure who created drama here this evening"—Ethan took off his baseball cap, shaking off the rain he'd been caught in—"but it looks like I'll be adding to it. I'm sorry to be the bearer of more bad news, but there's been an accident."

CHAPTER THIRTEEN

There it was—that other shoe.

No one moved or spoke. They gaped at Ethan, each one afraid to ask the burning question.

The goosebumps on Amanda's arms had goosebumps of their own.

He stepped in from the rain, closing the door behind him. "Could we sit somewhere quiet and talk?"

Jillian snapped to attention first. "I'll ask Jorge for a secluded table." She scurried off in search of the owner, who ushered them to a curved corner booth—perfect for a private conversation.

"I see some of your party has left, but can I bring coffee and dessert—*café y postre, sí*? We have a delicious vanilla custard, *natillas*."

"Thank you, Jorge. That sounds great," Travis said. "Take your time. We're in no hurry."

"Depending on what Ethan says, we might need something stronger than coffee," Sam muttered.

"There's no easy way to say this." Ethan placed his clasped hands on the table. "Amanda, your floral van was involved in an accident, but don't—"

"Oh my gosh! I didn't check to see if Tim made it back from deliveries before I left." She cut him off. "Is he okay? Have his parents been called?"

Ethan put up his hands. "Yes, Tim will be fine. His football season is over, but his injuries aren't life-threatening."

"What happened?" Cate asked. "Did he lose control in this rain?"

"No, this had nothing to do with the weather. According to witnesses, another car ran him off the road. He hit a tree."

Señor Garcia brought the coffee and custard, giving everyone time to process Ethan's news.

"Please enjoy. Isabella will check on you in a bit."

As soon as Jorge left their table, everyone erupted with questions.

"Who would do this?"

"Why would someone want to hurt Tim?"

"Where did it happen?"

"Did the witnesses get a good look at the other car?"

Ethan waited them out. "If I may continue?"

Heads nodded as voices quieted.

"Tim was on Route 4 heading back to town when a white SUV sped up, bumping him from behind. He retained control of the van until the SUV pulled alongside, ramming him several times. That's when he lost control and headed straight for an old tree. Tim doesn't remember anything after that—he hit his head on the steering wheel. Your van looks like a total loss."

"Any witnesses?" Travis asked.

"The crash happened right outside the VFW. Big dance for the old folks tonight. Several people in the parking lot saw the white car run Tim off the road. One old guy had many good details to share."

The pained expression on Ethan's face wrenched a moan from Amanda. "Don't tell me—Mr. Erickson?"

"Yep." Ethan's shoulders slumped. "I don't know why that grouchy old man keeps turning up in my cases."

Travis clapped him on the back. "You're living under a lucky star, my man." This caused a riff of laughter around the table.

"Whatever," Ethan grumbled. "Erickson did get a good look at the driver and a partial license plate. I'll give it to him. He might be old, but he has the eyes of a man half his age. I'm hopeful his information will help us find the woman who did this."

Amanda's head jerked. "Woman? A blonde woman?"

"Yeah. How did you know that?" Ethan scowled at her, then noticed the others around the table. "What's with the funny looks?"

"We might take a while to fill you in," Jillian said.

"We're going to need more coffee. Or tequila." Sam's comment garnered mumbled agreements.

The rain had stopped by the time they left the restaurant. Sam and Amanda drove to the ER to check on Tim. Wes and Cate went home to relieve the babysitter, while Ethan headed home to Becca.

Jillian placed her hand in the crook of Travis's arm as they walked the few blocks to her car. He attempted to engage her in conversation, but she remained silent. She flexed and unflexed the fingers that rested on his sleeve—a sure signal her nerves were on edge. Travis turned her to face him.

"You're a million miles away, babe." He played with a loose tendril of hair. "Need to talk?"

Jillian's heart beat a little faster at the feel of his hand brushing her cheek.

"I'm sorry," she said. "When a mystery like this rears its ugly head, I revert to last year's poor date behavior—distracted, not really listening. Let's just hope I don't fall asleep on you again." She let out a breath and gave a small shrug. "Though in my defense, being attacked and passing out in your truck wasn't exactly an ideal first date."

"You ..." Travis pulled the collar of her jacket up around her ears. "... are not a bad date. A lot has happened in the past two days. You're worried about Amanda, busy processing clues, and creating your suspect list. You might as well tell me who's made the cut."

"I'm not sure." Jillian searched for her keys in the depths of her bag. "Whoever the guilty party is appears to be escalating—five incidents in less than forty-eight hours. Who knows when or where they'll strike next."

"No persons of interest?" Travis squinted one eye at her.

"There are a few mysterious newcomers in town, but none of them have connections to Amanda." She told him about the elderly man and the fashionista, then remembered the sad woman with the baby. "Besides, Ethan says most of the time it's someone the victim knows."

Jillian rubbed at her tired eyes. She let out a shuddering yawn.

"That's it. Get in the car." Travis opened the door. "I'll follow you home."

She climbed in and started the engine. "That's not necessary. I'm not the one being targeted this time."

"Yeah, I didn't think I was either. Look what happened." He patted the bandage on his temple. "Wait for me to get to my truck."

A quiet nod sent him jogging the extra blocks to his vehicle.

Turning on the heat to combat the evening's chill, Jillian's mind played ping-pong with thoughts of the threats on her sister.

"This needs to stop. I *will* figure out who's behind these attacks." Her promise was visible in the cold air.

Jillian flicked on the windshield wipers to clear the leftover raindrops from her window. The blades dragged a piece of pink paper across the glass as they traveled back and forth, back and forth. She turned off the wipers, then bolted from her car to snatch the note.

"Please let this be a parking ticket." Her plea carried to the heavens on a brisk wind. "I will be more than happy to pay it."

The paper was damp, the ink slightly smeared, but the message was clear.

> *Some flowers are purple, some of them red.*
> *Your sister is evil, she should be dead.*
> *She stole what's mine, I won't forget.*
> *She should be warned, I'm not done yet.*

Instead of fear, anger coursed through Jillian's veins. She shouted her frustration into the darkness.

"Enough with the stupid poems."

Amanda's enemy might be good with a rhyme, but unoriginal when it came to the use of the notes. Jillian's friend Maggie had died at the hands of a message-writing murderer. She could only hope this copycat didn't intend to leave a trail of dead bodies like before.

Amanda woke before the alarm clock could signal the new day. Not surprising since she'd tossed and turned all night. She hadn't been able to stop her mind from replaying the previous night's events—her aunt's ominous predictions plus the attack on poor Tim.

Her visit to see him last night had eased part of her worries. He'd been sitting up, smiling, and eating the cheeseburger his dad had smuggled past the nurses. He'd apologized repeatedly for wrecking the van. She assured him the van could be replaced. He couldn't.

The house was quiet. Amanda burrowed under the blankets, warding off the early morning chill. Sam's snores drifted up the stairs. He'd insisted on sleeping on the couch for the second night in a row to keep watch and protect her from a potential intruder.

Stepping into her fuzzy crocs, Amanda pulled on her robe. She crept down the stairs, tiptoeing past Sam. She smiled at his wrinkled clothes, slightly open mouth, and tousled hair. He'd even fallen asleep with his shoes on—in case he had to chase her stalker.

"My hero," she whispered before planting a soft kiss on his forehead.

The nip in the room sent her to adjust the thermostat. Sam had installed a new furnace before leaving on his last work trip. For this, she was thankful. Maybe she could talk him into doing the same at the flower shop. She didn't need Aunt Grace having visions of more fire.

Amanda rubbed her arms as she wandered into the kitchen.

Coffee. Must have coffee.

Sam had surprised her with a Keurig last Christmas, making the morning routine much simpler and her wait for that first invigorating cup much shorter.

Amanda stared out the window, pondering the joys of flavored coffee. She didn't hear Sam shuffle in, jolting when his arms snaked from behind to wrap her in a hug.

Shivers ran down spine at the soft kisses he sprinkled on her neck. He spun her around and backed her against the sink, where they shared an intimate kiss.

She could get used to this every morning—a lovely thought if only Sam wasn't gone so much.

His constant work travels had been a sore spot in their relationship over the years they'd been together. They'd dated off and on for the first two years, but he was gone more than he was home. She would get frustrated with his absences, break it off, then he'd return, convincing her to take him back. This frustrating cycle was finally broken when they admitted their love for each another and committed to making their relationship work. That was six months ago. Things were going well. Sam was being incredibly patient. Maybe soon they would spend every morning just like this.

Amanda was unaware they had an audience until a tap on the window startled them—Jillian's face was pressed to the glass.

"What's she doing here, skulking around my yard at this hour?"

Amanda extricated herself from Sam's embrace and stomped to the front door to give her too-early visitor an earful. She opened the door, ready to blast her baby sister, but was taken aback by what greeted her on the porch.

Travis grinned at her, holding a blue box from Sugar & Spice in one hand and a cardboard tray of coffee in the other.

He came bearing breakfast?

Yes, he can come in.

Jillian had two leashes wrapped around her right hand, reining in her adorable schnauzers. She held a third leash in her left hand. This one came attached to the pink collar of the cutest puppy Amanda had ever seen.

The small creature's incredibly large paws suggested it would grow up to be a big dog. The long fur—a mix of white, tan, and brown—created a brindled look. When the pup cocked its head to one side and stared at Amanda, she noticed its unusual eyes—one the color of a bright blue sky, the other the color of milk chocolate. The little thing raised her paw to Amanda as if to shake hands and introduce herself.

"Good morning, Amanda." Jillian's voice dripped with sweetness. "I brought a few furry visitors. After your crummy day yesterday, some puppy love is just what the doctor ordered." She stepped into the house with all three dogs in tow.

"Oh ... um ... Jilly," Amanda stammered. "I'm happy to see you and the girls—you too, Travis—but there's a new friend tagging along, and you're all in my house before eight o'clock in the morning. What's going on?"

She couldn't help notice how the younger dog took its cues from Abbey and Hayley. If they sat, the pup sat. If they lay down, so did she. The dogs acted like they'd known each other for quite a while.

"How long have you had this dog, Jilly? Or is it yours?" She shifted her gaze to Travis.

"Nope, not mine." He shook his head. "Blaze is my one and only."

"Why don't we take a seat at the table? Then I'll tell you all about this sweet girl," Jillian suggested.

Amanda's radar pinged, sensing something was off, but she didn't press the issue.

"Yeah, you're going to want to be sitting down." Travis laughed, earning him a playful jab in the ribs.

With the pups leading the way to the kitchen, Amanda followed like a fourth well-trained, obedient dog. A sleepy-looking Sam waited for them at the table with his coffee mug in hand. Jillian set her bag down and took a seat. The dogs lay at her feet.

"What do you have there?" Sam eyed the blue box in Travis's hands. "Judging by the incredible smell, it must be some of Cate's famous cinnamon rolls. Please tell me there's at least one in there for me." His eyes begged her to confirm.

"There's at least one, Sam." She handed him the box, smiling as he popped open the lid, grabbed a roll, and took a huge bite. Enjoying the baked goods, it took Sam a minute to notice the hairy visitors in the kitchen.

"Well, who do we have here?" He reached down to scratch behind Abbey and Hayley's ears. "I'm acquainted with you two, but who's your friend? She's awful cute."

"I wondered the exact same thing." Amanda pointed at the dog. "Jilly, would you care to introduce us to ... her, I believe you said?"

"Maybe you should sit. I have some not-so-good-news to share first."

"You brought bad news with you this morning." Amanda dropped onto the nearest chair. "This puppy is here to soften the blow, I assume?"

Travis came to Jillian's rescue. "Keep in mind, Jilly didn't go looking for trouble—for a change." His chivalry was rewarded with a stony glare from both sisters.

"There's no easy way to say this." Jillian sat in the chair next to Amanda. "Your front yard is covered with yellow carnations. That's why we came to the side door."

"Carnations again? Where are they coming from?" Sam looked to Amanda. "You haven't sold a large quantity of them lately, have you?"

"Why, yes, I have and I know exactly who my stalker is." Amanda's sarcasm dripped from every word. She rolled her eyes at Sam, then turned to Travis. "Are there any deceased furry vermin this time?"

"Not that we saw." Travis crossed his arms over his chest.

"We didn't touch anything," Jillian said. "Before you ask, we've called Ethan. He's on his way."

"Here I'd hoped today would be drama-free." Amanda shook her head. "How silly of me."

"Wait, there's more." Travis helped himself to one of the cinnamon rolls, receiving the stink eye from Sam. "Enough with the looks, dude. Cate packed plenty of rolls for all of us."

Jillian grabbed her sister's hand. "Your poet left another note on my windshield outside La Casita last night—not sure why it's always *my* car." She pulled a Ziploc bag containing a sheet of pink paper out of her tote bag.

Amanda's head pounded. "I ... can't ... even—" She closed her eyes, pinching the bridge of her nose. "What's it say this time?"

The threatening message was etched into Jillian's brain. She repeated it word for word.

Amanda sucked in her breath.

Sam closed the distance between them, pulling her gently to his side "You're going to be okay. We won't let anything happen to you, right?" He locked eyes with Jillian and Travis, who nodded their agreement.

"What could I have done to make someone hate me this much?" Amanda put her head in her hands. "What did I steal from her—I've never stolen a thing in my life." Her voice ratcheted up a few notches. All three pups scampered to her feet to offer comfort. She bent to pet them.

"This woman, if Aunt Grace's visions are correct, believes you stole her man." Jillian paced the length of the kitchen. Her thoughts flowed like chocolate from a dessert fountain. "Maybe somewhere in your past, you dated someone she was in love with?"

Amanda's head jerked up. "I've been with Sam for the last two and half years, and no one serious for many years before that. Even if you're right, who carries a grudge for that long?"

Three sets of eyes fell on Sam. "What? Why're you all gawking at me?" He flinched under their intense stares. "Oh wait, you think this crazy person is someone I know?"

"Could be," Travis said. "I mean, what's the saying about a woman scorned?"

"Who was the last woman you dated before Amanda?" Jillian asked.

"Her name was Victoria." Sam tried to take Amanda's hand, but she pulled it back. "She and I dated for about a year. We broke it off two years before I met Amanda."

"Did Victoria have blonde hair?" Jillian's left eyebrow raised, disappearing into her hairline.

"Jilly, where are you going with this?" Amanda's question was laced with suspicion.

Sam's shoulders slumped forward. "Yes, she did."

Jillian snapped her fingers. "Ah-ha. The angry woman in Aunt Grace's vision was a blonde. So was the lady driving the car that ran Tim off the road. Maybe it's this Victoria person. We have to find her and stop this evil plot of hers."

Travis stepped in front of Jillian, blocking her frenetic pacing. "Think about what you're saying. You can't accuse a woman Sam dated almost five years ago based solely on her hair color."

"Yeah," Sam agreed. "Victoria was a nice woman—not insane at all."

"I'm no expert, but women often change their hair color, right? Look at Trixie. Her hair has been four different shades in the last six months." Travis sided with Sam in his defense of the former girlfriend.

"Okay, okay." Amanda made a T-sign with both hands. "Timeout, you guys. Can we agree this old girlfriend *might* bear further investigation, if only to eliminate her as a suspect?"

"Agreed." Jillian nudged Travis aside and walked to the table. She kneeled in front of Amanda. "Ethan swore he wouldn't rest until this fruitcake is caught, so we need to tell him about Victoria. Oh, he also wants you to have someone with you *at all times*. He said having your gun close by isn't enough."

"A babysitter?" She shook her head, then reached for her purse. "My gun's right here. I've felt helpless these last two days, but Hazel gives me strength."

"Hazel?" Jillian frowned. "You named your gun Hazel?"

"Don't judge me. Hazel is a good strong name." Amanda's smile reached her eyes. "Can we please move on to the good news?"

"We can if you promise to keep an open mind." Jillian looked at Sam and Amanda. "Both of you." Their nods encouraged her to continue. She scooped the puppy into her arms.

"Someone dumped this poor little thing at Travis's fire station a week ago." She stroked the dog's soft head. "The guys took her in, fed her, gave her a bath, even made an appointment at the vet. Dr. Curtis has given her a clean bill of health. She's going to make some family a great pet."

"Why don't the firefighters keep her at the station?" Sam suggested. "You know, like a mascot or a firehouse dog?"

"Can't—department policy says no pets. Plus, she gets freaked out by the sirens whenever we leave on a call." Travis scratched the dog under her chin. "The guys are all disappointed."

"Which means this sweet, little girl needs a good home." The puppy wiggled in Jillian's arms. Sam reached out to take her. The puppy licked his face.

"Oh no," Amanda shook her finger. "You want me to take her, don't you?"

"The idea crossed my mind." Jillian steepled her hands. "You're great with dogs. Abbey and Hayley love you, and just yesterday, you said you'd like to have a dog of your own."

"I said *someday*, like in the future." Amanda pushed back her chair, grabbed a clean bowl, filled it with water, and set it on the floor. All three dogs scurried over for a drink.

"I'm too busy for a dog—let alone training a puppy. Plus, the fence in my backyard is practically falling down." She ticked off the points on her fingers, but one look at Sam cradling the pup made her resolve crumble.

He sat cross-legged on the floor with the dog cuddled in his lap, stroking her silky fur and whispering baby talk.

This wasn't helping her win the argument with her sister.

"Aw, look at them. They're so cute together." Jillian's voice softened, almost coaxing. "She seems taken with Sam. Maybe he can help you take care of her."

"Hey, yeah. That's a great idea." Travis was swept up in Jillian's enthusiasm.

"What do you say, babe? This sweet girl needs a home." Sam's sexy blue eyes begged for her permission. "We could have shared custody."

Amanda laughed at his ridiculous attempt at coercion.

"You'll do half the work?" Amanda shot Sam a look, half skeptical, half amused.

"I'll do more than half," Sam said, his smile widening as he nuzzled the pup. "You'll see."

"That sounds like a deal you can't refuse," Jillian said.

Amanda took the puppy from Sam, holding it like a baby.

"Does this mean she's found her forever home?" Travis asked. "The guys at the station will be happy to hear Puppy will be taken good care of."

"Puppy? They called her Puppy?" Amanda shook her head at Travis's shrug. "Bunch of geniuses."

She stuck her face into the soft fur on the dog's neck. "Don't worry. We'll find you a better name than that."

"She wants to name her." Jillian squealed and grabbed Travis's hand. "Puppy has found her home."

Amanda joined Sam on the floor, placing his new furry girlfriend back in his lap. "This is a really bad idea. You know that, right?"

As if on cue, the little dog raised her head to meet Amanda's gaze. Then, to seal the deal, Puppy gave her several kisses before curling up and drifting off to sleep. Amanda's resistance melted along with her heart.

"Oh, aren't you a smart one? Did Jilly teach you that move?" She ran her fingers through the soft fur on top of the dog's head.

"There you go." Jillian clapped her hands. "She's adopted the two of you. Looks like a match."

"Sam told me you'd discussed getting a dog once the renovations were finished." Travis plucked a cherry turnover from the bakery box.

"Yes, when the house was *done*." Amanda poked Sam with one hand while fondling the pup's floppy ears with the other. "What am I going to do with a puppy in all this mess?"

"This'll be great." Sam hopped from the floor. "The backyard fence will be installed next week—she can go out on a leash until then. The entire first floor is almost finished. She can stay here with me when I work on the house or at my place if you're busy. She can go with you to the shop, like Abbey and Hayley do with Jillian."

Amanda let out a resigned sigh. "She's going to need a better name. I refuse to keep calling her *Puppy*."

"We need to choose a name as pretty as she is," Sam said. "We could name her after one of the flowers in your shop. Let's see—Rose? Lily? How about Petunia?"

"The flower idea is good." Amanda scratched the dog's belly. "I like Poppy—sounds like 'puppy,' so it should be easy for her to learn. And it's perfect—her one blue eye is the exact color of a Himalayan blue poppy."

"What do you think, girl?" Sam ruffled the fur at the nape of her neck. "Is it okay if we call you Poppy?"

The sleepy, little dog let out a small *woof* without even opening her eyes.

"Sounds like we have a winner," Jillian said. "You won't regret this, Amanda. Poppy's going to be great fun and good company. Who knows, maybe having a dog will deter your crazy stalker from doing anything else here at the house or the shop."

Sam stood with Poppy in his arms. Her tiny head tucked under his chin.

"She can walk, you know. Or do you plan carrying her everywhere you go?" Amanda teased Sam.

Without warning, Poppy woofed, struggling to jump from Sam's hold. He put her on the floor where she made a beeline for the front door with Abbey and Hayley in hot pursuit, barking their heads off.

"Do they have to go outside to take care of business?" Amanda's inexperience with dogs was showing.

"Abbey and Hayley don't usually bark like that unless they hear or see something that upsets them."

"I didn't hear anything, did you?" Sam started for the living room.

They all followed the canines who jumped and scratched at the door. Jillian darted to the bay window overlooking the yard to see what had the pups all riled up. She let out a strangled gasp.

"Amanda. Sam. You need to see this."

CHAPTER FOURTEEN

Four humans and three canines stood in the driveway staring at the damage. Amanda's stomach churned. Her pulse thundered in her ears. Her car, parked amongst a scattering of yellow carnations, had fallen victim to another attack. The weapon of choice—Day-Glo spray paint in an obnoxious shade of green. One word had been graffitied across the hood, rear, and both sides of the vehicle—a crude, five-letter word aimed squarely at Amanda.

Amanda couldn't believe this was happening. Less than twelve hours ago—while they'd been at dinner—Shorty had dropped off her car, complete with four new tires.

And now this.

After a tense silence, Jillian attempted a little levity. "Aunt Grace did mention destruction." She gestured toward the car with a dramatic sweep, channeling her best Vanna White. "Ta-da!"

Travis smothered a laughed. Sam ducked behind him, suddenly very interested in his shoes.

Amanda shot them a withering look. "Glad to know I'm surrounded by adults."

"She's right, you two. Try acting your age." Jillian's teacher voice left no room for debate.

"This is great." The sarcasm in Amanda's voice dripped like ice cream on a summer day. "First, my delivery van is totaled, and now I get to drive around town in this ... this ... colorful new symbol of personal disgrace." She motioned to the defaced car. "Exactly the look I was going for—public humiliation in fluorescent green."

Her remark earned a round of juvenile snorts and laughter from the men, neither of whom seemed to notice Amanda's scathing glare.

"Sure. Go ahead. Laugh." Amanda pulled her hair into a messy bun with a tie from her robe pocket. "You won't be the one behind the wheel of this monstrosity. I have errands all over town today. Everyone and their grandma will see me in this thing." She fisted her hands on her hips, glaring at the distasteful ride.

Sam swooped in and caught Amanda in his arms. She sank into the embrace. His body offered comfort, a refuge from the nightmare she was trapped in.

"I'm sorry, babe." He glanced at his co-conspirator. "We shouldn't laugh."

"One more thing for Ethan when he gets here." Amanda dropped her hands to her sides.

"I called him before we came outside." Sam dropped a kiss on her cheek. "He should be here any minute, and I'll be right back." He picked his way through the yellow blooms, heading toward the house.

Amanda paced. "Today's Wednesday—the one day my shop opens late. I have so many errands to run before going to work—pick up the rest of the decorations for Cate's party, run by Sugar & Spice to finalize the cake with Becca." She pursed her lips as she thought of her to-do list. "Oh. I have to swing by Lake's Jewelry to pick up the ring Wes had made." She took one last look at her odious car. "I better pull myself together and get moving. My chariot awaits."

"Let us help," Travis said. "I don't know anything about decorations or cakes, but I can stop by Lake's and pick up the ring."

"I can grab the rest of the decorations after Trixie clocks in at the store." Jillian's smile and their offers to pitch in chased away part of Amanda's bad mood.

"That would be great." She hugged them both.

"I'll take care of your car." Sam had returned. He dropped the key fob to his Mustang into her hand. "I'm sure the body shop in Stonefield can give it a makeover."

"You're letting me drive your car?" Amanda's eyes grew wide. "You never let anyone drive the ''Stang.' She's your baby."

"No big deal. Besides, I have a new baby now." He scooped up Poppy, cuddling her close. "Just be careful with my car, please."

Amanda touched her lips to his—quick, but unmistakably grateful. "Thanks, Sailor. You're the best."

With a dog in one arm, Sam didn't miss a beat. Using his free arm, he leaned Amanda back and returned her kiss. Poppy wiggled between them.

"Okay, you two. Enough." Travis shielded his eyes with his jacket. "Stop all this mushy stuff, or when Ethan gets here, he'll have to arrest you for lewd and lascivious public behavior." He whispered to Jillian. "That's a thing, right?"

She nodded.

The sound of an approaching vehicle forced Amanda and Sam apart. Ethan's unmarked police car rolled to a stop behind Amanda's.

"Sorry it took me so long to get here." Ethan climbed from his cruiser, then reached in to grab his department-issued iPad. "A resident went missing from Magnolia Manor. We found the old guy asleep in a barn." He straightened up and shut the door, then froze, his gaze landing on Amanda's car.

Ethan let out a long, slow whistle. "Whew, that's a fancy paint job. Not a color I would've picked, but to each their own. The shade does complement those yellow flowers."

He fist-bumped Sam, squeezed Amanda's shoulder, then greeted Jillian and Travis with a nod. "This shouldn't take long." He grabbed a camera from the trunk of his car. "I'll take some photos, check for fingerprints, and be on my way in no time." He looked at the car from all sides. "I'm sure you can't wait to get behind the wheel of this beauty and cruise Main Street."

Amanda wished she held something heavy she could throw—at him.

Jillian parked behind the bookstore and climbed out, eying her heavy tote bag, a box of books, and two leashed dogs in the backseat. Juggling all three while unlocking the door and disarming the alarm would take some finesse.

She set the box down and reached for the keypad—

A deep voice from behind made her jump.

"Hey, gorgeous, can I help you with any of that?"

She turned to face her favorite firefighter.

"Hi, handsome." With a smile, she passed him both leashes. "We said goodbye less than fifteen minutes ago. I didn't know you were coming to work with me."

"Consider it penance for my previous immature behavior." Travis kissed her cheek. "Sam and I shouldn't have laughed at Amanda's car."

"No, you shouldn't have, but you apologized. She forgave you." Jillian silenced the alarm and nodded toward the dogs. "You can let them off their leashes."

Once Travis obliged, Abbey and Hayley scampered into the main room with their noses to the floor.

"You never answered my question," Jillian said. "Is there a reason you followed me here?"

He pulled a brown sack with a familiar logo from behind his back. "This morning's graffiti artist interrupted what promised to be a delicious breakfast. You didn't eat a thing, so I made a quick stop—picked us up a little something. Figured I'd hang out here until the jewelry store opens."

Jillian sniffed the fragrant air. "Smells amazing. I'll get everything ready to open, then we'll dig in. Sam can have his silly old cinnamon rolls."

Jillian set about her morning routine—raising the window blinds, straightening tables and chairs, and filling empty spaces on the shelves with new books. She flipped the window sign to *OPEN* before unlocking the door.

"We're ready for business, now let's see what's in that bag." She patted the counter. "Put the food here—we'll eat while I keep an eye out for customers."

Hearing one of their favorite words—*food*—the dogs abandoned their exploration of the bookstore, running to the front with their ears flapping and tongues panting. Hayley announced their presence with a few excited woofs.

"These poor dogs," Travis teased. "Don't you ever feed them?" He reached into the bag, grabbed two warm tater tots and tossed them to the girls. "There you go, ladies. I'll take care of you since your mama doesn't." His generosity was rewarded with happy grunts. Both pups devoured their crispy snack in seconds, then begged for another.

"No more," Jillian chastised Travis. "They had their kibble earlier—one tater tot each is plenty. We have to keep an eye on their girlish figures."

"Sorry, girls. Mama said no more." Travis eyed the pitiful furry faces staring up at him. When Jillian looked away, he slipped them each another tot.

"I saw that." She snapped without turning around. Digging into the sack Travis set on the counter, Jillian pulled out the cardboard container of tots followed by three soft, warm bundles wrapped in aluminum foil. "Please tell me these are Jorge's specials."

Travis nodded. "Take your pick."

Jillian reached for the burrito marked *carnitas*. Peeling back the foil, she took a huge bite. The flavor of the perfectly seasoned pork paired with the fluffy eggs, melted cheese, and crisp potatoes exploded in her mouth.

"Never disappoints," she mumbled around her mouthful of food. "You know I love you, right? I love you even more today because you brought me this burrito." She savored the next bite. "This is so good, I don't even care that I ate at La Casita for dinner last night."

The bell above the door jingled.

"Sam. Poppy. I'm surprised to see you both again so soon." Jillian leaped up from the stool. "Everything okay?"

"Sure. No worries." Sam gave her a sheepish grin. "Except for the scene I created driving Amanda's newly decorated car through town. More than a few heads turned."

"You actually drove it? Bold move, my friend." Travis clapped Sam on the shoulder. "The things we do for the love of a good woman, right?"

"You know it." Sam turned to Jillian. "I'm hoping I can ask you for a favor."

"Name it." Jillian sat on the floor, greeting her new hairy niece with a vigorous belly rub. Her girls pounced on the pup, vying for their own slice of attention.

"After Ethan left, I called the body shop. They can get Amanda's car in today if I get it there before noon. I'm afraid to leave Poppy alone on her first day in the house, and I don't think Amanda would welcome her at the flower shop after the last two days she's had."

"Say no more. Poppy is welcome in my bookstore anytime." She stood up and brushed the dog hair from her pants. With three dog biscuits in her hand, she whistled to the pups who followed her like the Pied Piper. They all settled on the big Kong bed in her office for a treat and a mid-morning snooze.

"Do you need me to follow you and give you a ride back to Willow Springs?" Travis asked.

"Thanks for the offer, but it's not necessary," Sam said. "They'll give me a loaner to drive until Amanda's car is finished."

He turned to Jillian. "I should only be gone an hour or so." He stopped halfway to the door. "I plan to stop at the pet store to pick up dog supplies for Amanda's house and the flower shop, so Poppy will feel at home. Amanda will blow a gasket when she realizes how much these things cost. Do you have any advice to soften the blow?"

"I'd tell my other buddies to take their wives some flowers, but since you date a florist, you better upgrade to a nice piece of jewelry." Travis winked at Sam.

"Uh ... er ... sure. Jewelry might work." Sam twisted the leash he still held in his hands. "Yeah ... well ... I better go." He handed Poppy's lead to Travis. "See you later." He turned tail and ran out the door.

Jillian snorted. "What was that all about? He couldn't get out of here fast enough when you mentioned jewelry."

"Oh? I didn't notice." Travis's answer rang a bit too casual.

Jillian narrowed her eyes at him. Something was going on with Sam, and Travis seemed to be aware of whatever it was. He bowed his head, refusing to make eye contact with her. His attention focused on what remained of his burrito.

Fine. Let them have their secret—for now.

The sound of the bell broke the silence. Jillian stepped out from behind the counter to greet her customer.

"Good morning. Welcome to Whimsy & Wonder. How can I—"

Jillian stopped short.

Miss Southern Belle had returned.

The woman's beautiful golden hair fell over her shoulders in soft, loose curls today. Her perfectly manicured hands were wrapped around a Kate Spade handbag the same red color as her stylish coatdress. Her outward appearance exuded money and class.

Looks can be deceiving.

Last year, Jillian had been fooled by appearances during her first meeting with Maggie's identical twin sister. She'd fallen for Moira's alligator tears and her sob story about how she'd looked for her long-lost sister for years. She'd believed every word that came out of Moira's lying mouth. Based on that life lesson, Jillian now doubted her ability to read people based on first impressions. She'd reserve judgment about this newcomer.

"Well, aren't you the kindest. Thank you for that friendly welcome."

Jillian bristled at the woman's accent. The syrupy southern drawl made her skin crawl.

"I happened by and saw your adorable little shop. Thought I'd come on in and check it out." The visitor flashed a pearly white smile at Jillian. She'd probably spent a fortune on extensive dental work.

No teeth are that white on their own.

Jillian shocked herself with this catty mental commentary. She shook her head to dislodge the chatter.

"I'm happy to see you again." Jillian returned her smile. "Is there something in particular I can help you with?"

"Again?" The woman's bright blue eyes opened wide. "Do I know you?"

"We met on Monday morning in front of my sister's—"

"No, I don't believe so," the woman drawled. "I never forget a face."

They'd met two days ago at Blossoms & Blooms. Was she that forgettable or was this woman up to something?

Fine. I'll play along.

"Oh, I'm sorry." Jillian narrowed her eyes at her visitor. "You look exactly like a woman who stopped by my sister's flower shop to compliment her Halloween display. She had the same accent."

The woman chuckled, fussing with the belt on her dress. "Don't you fret, sugar. You Yankees think all us Southerners sound the same, and apparently, we look the same too."

Her smile seemed genuine, but it never reached her eyes. While this woman's words were delivered in a saccharine tone, Jillian felt like a child who'd just been chastised—southern style.

"What can I help you with today?"

"I have a nephew I adore reading to," the woman purred. "I'd like some books to share with him." She wandered between the shelves, trailing her polished nails across the spines of the books. "You go on ahead and help that handsome gentleman over there. He was here first. I'll look around on my own." The woman batted her eyes at Travis.

Now there were two things about this woman getting under Jillian's skin.

"That gentleman isn't a customer. He's my boyfriend." Jillian caught a brief flash of something—annoyance perhaps—in the woman's gaze. "He has no problem waiting while I take care of customers."

"My, my, aren't you a lucky girl?" The woman fidgeted with the chunky gold chain around her neck. "Not all men are as thoughtful as yours. Some are downright disloyal and deceitful." Her friendly demeanor turned ugly. She spit out the words like they tasted bitter on her tongue. "Most men can't be trusted."

Travis laid the remainder of his breakfast on the counter. He squirmed in his seat.

Jillian felt sorry for him—all this trash talk about men. Time to get this conversation back on safer ground.

"How old is your nephew?" Jillian led her guest to the area of the store that should interest her.

"He's just a baby, but I know how important reading to a child is at any age. I've been sharing the Eric Carle books with him. He loves *The Very Hungry Caterpillar* and *The Very Busy Spider*."

"Those are wonderful choices. As your nephew grows, the repetitive text and colorful illustrations of those books will be perfect for him." Jillian gushed about two of her favorite things—literature and kids. "By reading to him early, you're building his vocabulary and fostering a lifelong love of books."

"Well, aren't you a font of knowledge." The woman pulled a book from the shelf, thumbing through the pages. "Sounds like you know a lot about children. How many do you two have?" She pinned Travis with a lustful stare.

Jillian's heart ached for him. She'd never seen him look this uncomfortable.

"Travis, didn't you need to pick something up for Sam?" He jumped from his seat so fast, the stool teetered on two legs before righting itself.

"Yep, sure do." He deposited a peck on Jillian's cheek. "Be back in a sec."

Jillian straightened her shoulders, preparing to face down her customer. "We don't have any children. I taught elementary school for years before I decided to open this bookstore. I've taken a lot of courses in literacy and child development."

"Oh, I see. No children." The woman sniffed, placing the book back on the shelf. "Well, it's nice to meet a young couple whose values are in the right place. As the good Lord says, marriage should come first, then children. You wouldn't want to be damned to hell for all eternity for being one of *those* women who trap a man into marriage by getting pregnant." The woman scowled—all sweetness and light gone.

There it was again—that creepy personality switch. How many people lived inside her head anyway?

"I'm sure you were a fabulous teacher, much loved by all your students."

Southern sweetness returned. Jillian was getting whiplash from this conversation.

"Um ... thank you," Jillian said. "Let's pick out some books."

Jillian pulled three of Sandra Boynton's board books and handed them to the woman. "My nieces enjoyed these when they were younger."

"You have nieces." The woman carried the books to the counter without even looking at them. "Would they be your sister Amanda's girls?"

"No. My sister Cate is their mother." Jillian frowned, looking at the woman with suspicion. "Do you know Amanda?"

"No, but you mentioned her a few minutes ago when you thought you'd met me in front of her flower shop. I assumed—incorrectly it seems—she was your nieces' mama."

Jillian didn't recall having said Amanda's name earlier. This woman's claims not to remember their meeting and now this odd behavior sent her skyrocketing to the top of Jillian's list of stalker suspects.

The woman opened her expensive purse, digging around for her wallet. "Oh, silly me. I don't have any cash with me today."

"We accept most forms of debit and credit cards." Jillian took the point-of-sale unit from under the counter.

"Oh, sugar. I don't use those ridiculous plastic things. Someone can use them to steal your personal information. I pay for everything in cash. Could you put those books behind the counter for me? I'll come back later this afternoon."

"Of course. Let me get a hold slip to fill out your name and phone number." Jillian squatted behind the counter to reach the bottom shelf. She heard the bell above the shop door jingle to signal another customer. Her heart soared at the sound. Looked like it would be a busy morning.

Abbey, Hayley, and Poppy could no longer contain themselves as they rushed to greet the new arrival with enthusiasm. Jillian noticed her peculiar customer shrank away from the exuberant canines.

Jillian smiled at her favorite police detective as he walked through the door.

"Hey, Ethan. I'll be right with you." Jillian put the hold slip on the counter and reached for a pen.

"No hurry," he called back. He held the door for the woman who was rushing from the store. "Here you go, ma'am."

"Why, thank you, Detective Harden. I'm pleased as punch to know there are still gentlemen who hold doors for ladies." She breezed by him onto the porch.

"Wait ... um, ma'am," Jillian called after her. "I need your name to hold these books." The woman had moved down the porch steps out of earshot.

"She was in a hurry," Ethan said.

"Looks like," Jillian grumbled. "I can't put a hold on books without a customer's name. What do I write—peculiar woman with annoying accent?"

Ethan's frown wrinkled his forehead. "You have no idea who she is?"

"None. We spoke for about five minutes, but she never introduced herself. Then, she rushed out of here before I could have her fill out the hold form." Jillian wrenched open the drawer and dumped the pen and paper in. "I can't shake this weird feeling I have about her."

Jillian recounted the odd conversation she'd had with her visitor, hoping to get Ethan's thoughts.

"Don't you find it strange she denied having met me? Why would she do that?"

"Are you absolutely sure she's the same person?" Ethan's face turned from friend to cop in a heartbeat.

"I'm positive. She's the kind of woman who leaves a very strong first impression, don't you think?"

Ethan nodded. "Why'd she come into the store?"

"She wanted books for her nephew. She realized she had no cash and asked me to put the books on hold until she came back with money."

"Why didn't she use a debit card?" Ethan asked.

"I suggested that, but she prefers to pay for things in cash. She said 'those plastic things' make her vulnerable to identity theft."

"She isn't wrong about that. Paying with cash is safer than using credit, but definitely a bigger inconvenience." Ethan stroked his chin with one hand. "You said she gave you a weird feeling. Why?"

"Several things. For one, I think it's odd she didn't have any cash." Jillian returned the books to their proper place on the shelf. "Judging by the way she dressed, she reeks of money. Her behavior was strange too. She was pleasant as could be one minute, then downright ugly the next—like she had multiple people rattling around inside her head."

"You know what else is weird?" Ethan asked. "She called me Detective Harden. How would she know my name—I've never seen her before."

CHAPTER FIFTEEN

Jillian had just rounded up the dogs after a romp outside, shutting them in her office when Travis returned from his errand to Lake Jewelers. They joined Ethan at a table in the Reading Room where Jillian had a perfect view of the front door. She could watch for customers while the trio talked.

Travis offered Ethan the third burrito which he slathered with Tabasco he'd found at the bottom of the bag. Jillian covered her mouth with her hand. Watching him use that much hot sauce made her stomach heave.

"Thanks for sharing—left the house without breakfast." Ethan wolfed a huge bite, chasing it with the black coffee Jillian set in front of him.

"Looks like we have another mystery to solve, don't we?" Jillian looked over the rim of her teacup.

Ethan put his food down with a sigh. "Not again with the *we*, Jilly. What mystery is this?"

"The identity of our mysterious stranger with the irritating drawl." Jillian bounced on the edge of her seat. "A newcomer in town with odd behavior. Aren't you curious about who she is?"

"Not unless she's broken the law." Ethan took another large bite of burrito. "I have enough real crimes to investigate. I'm not looking for more."

"Her behavior was bizarre." She crumpled the foil from Ethan's breakfast and threw it in the trash. "She's up to something. We should check her out."

"I've listened to your story, but being odd isn't illegal. Leave it alone, Jilly." Ethan polished off the last drop of coffee and tossed his paper cup into the garbage.

"Fine, I'll let it go, but I wouldn't be surprised if that woman has done something illegal." Jillian grabbed a handful of Clorox wipes from the closet and cleaned the table. "Change of subject. I've thought about your current cases. I've come up with a theory—"

Ethan cut her off. "You have a theory? I thought you agreed to step away from my investigation. What happened to your promise to stay out of my case and out of trouble?" Ethan stared at her, intimidating cop face firmly in place.

"Lighten up, will you? There's nothing dangerous about *thinking*. I can't be arrested for that, can I?" She returned his steely glare.

"Don't tempt me." Ethan growled between clenched teeth. "I've had my own strange day so far."

Travis put an arm around Jillian's shoulders and faced Ethan. "Let's relax. No need to get riled up before ten a.m. Why don't you tell us about your morning, Ethan?"

He popped the last bite of the burrito into his mouth. "I met Rick's widow for the first time—needed to ask some questions."

"I figured you saw her on Monday to tell her the bad news," Travis said.

"The chief and our department chaplain notified Rick's widow of his death right after the identification was made. I was there today for a follow-up visit."

Jillian's mood softened. "She must be devastated. I can't imagine what it would be like to lose the man you love." She gazed at Travis.

"Devastated isn't the word that comes to mind," Ethan said. "Rick's wife—her name's Stacey—showed no emotion the entire time I was there. No matter what I said or asked, she never cried or even seemed upset. Her face was blank, no expression whatsoever."

"She could be in shock or denial," Travis said. "We see that a lot on calls when people have suffered trauma. They need time to process their emotions."

"Maybe." Ethan hesitated. "My gut tells me there's something off about that guy's wife. While I tried talking to her, a TV blared in another room, the neighbor's dog barked nonstop outside, and her cell phone rang twice. She never flinched, just sat there with a vacant look on her face. Then her baby cried, and she didn't react—nothing. I finally asked if she needed to go check on the child."

"Oh, the poor woman. Sounds like she has post-partum depression," Jillian tsked. "Cate had a mild case after Aubrey was born, but some women suffer so terribly, they have to seek professional help and take medication to get through it."

"That's awful." Travis's tone was sympathetic. "As if giving birth isn't hard enough."

"There are support groups she could attend," Jillian said. "She'll need people to rely on, especially now that she's a widow." Her heart broke for this young mother. "Does she have family nearby who can help?"

"I have no idea. She wasn't forthcoming with much information." Ethan shrugged. "I talked. She listened. That was about it."

"Maybe one of the department's social workers could pay a visit," Travis suggested. "You know. Check on the welfare of the mother and her baby."

"Amanda and I could stop by as well. Take her a meal, perhaps." Jillian warmed to the idea. She knew Amanda would be on board, considering how much she'd respected Rick.

While Jillian considered ways to help Rick's widow, the men moved on with their conversation. She caught the tail end of Ethan's last comment.

"... so there isn't much that's new. The forensic team's report on the evidence they collected inside the flower shop isn't finished yet."

"Then while you wait, finding Amanda's crazy stalker can be our focus," Jillian said. "Until the evidence report comes back, of course."

"Jilly, I'm not going to discuss—"

"Did I say *our*? I meant *your*." Jillian attempted her most apologetic look.

"Yeah, right. You're going to sit back and let me do my job. Why don't I believe her, Travis?

"Her previous track record." Travis bowed his head to hide his grin.

"You're supposed to be on my side." Jillian poked him in the chest, then addressed Ethan. "Is there anything you can tell us about either of the cases?"

"Matt Carpenter told me on Monday night he took some garbage out into the alley behind his pharmacy at nine o'clock. He spotted a person dressed in dark clothes skulking around. When he shouted, they took off." Ethan rubbed his chin. "If I can find that person, they might know something about Rick's death or Amanda's troubles."

"Or the person he saw might be the killer." Travis stated the obvious possibility.

The bell signaled the arrival of a customer, saving Ethan from Jillian's eager inquisition. Sighing in frustration as she left the room, her mood was instantly brightened when she saw her best friend walked through the door.

"Hey, Ethan," she called out. "Your much better half is here."

Becca juggled an armful of bags as she walked through the door. She'd volunteered to pick up and donate the materials Jillian needed for the next elementary group book project here at the shop.

"Thank you for grabbing these art supplies for me. You're the best." Jillian tried to take a bag or two off her hands, but Ethan rushed to relieve his wife of her packages. He stopped long enough to kiss her before depositing the bags on the counter.

"That's more like it, Detective Harden. I'm glad our chat yesterday made a difference in your attitude—no more ignoring your delightful wife." Becca kissed him back, then used her free hand to smack him on his backside.

Jillian giggled as Becca's PDA caused Ethan's face to turn three shades of red. She was delighted to see the couple getting along so well.

The sound of excited dogs barking sent Jillian to open the office door, setting them free. Three frantic, furry creatures burst from the room, scrambling to greet the new arrival.

"Wait a minute." Becca raised her voice above the noise. "There's an extra furball today. Did you get another dog without telling me?" She dropped to the floor and loved on all three pups. Her attentiveness silenced their canine cacophony just in time for Jillian to hear the door jingle again.

She was thrilled with how often the bell was ringing this morning.

It's like Grand Central Station in here.

"No, she didn't." Sam had arrived, overhearing Becca's question. "Poppy is Amanda's dog—well, we have joint custody. She joined the family a few hours ago, thanks to her wonderful Aunt Jillian, who let her hang out at the bookstore while I ran some errands."

He rummaged inside a plastic bag he'd carried in from the car. Ripping open a smaller bag, he tossed a biscuit to each dog. They abandoned Becca's lap for the possibility of a snack.

"I see how you are." Becca sounded hurt. "Someone rustles a bag of biscuits in your direction, and I'm discarded like an old chew toy."

The pups couldn't be bothered with Becca's bruised feelings. They gobbled their treats, then stood on alert in case more goodies were forthcoming.

"Did I miss anything around here while I was gone?" Sam trained his gaze on Ethan. "No more 9-1-1 calls to the flower shop, I hope."

"Nope. Things have been quiet." Ethan faked a swipe to his brow. "I have enough to investigate without further incidents."

"I'm not sure Amanda can take much more from her deranged stalker," Jillian said.

"Poppy and I will swing by the flower shop to check on her." Sam pulled the price tag off a brand-new purple, flowered leash and clipped it on the puppy's collar. "See you all later."

"Hold on, Sam. I'll walk out with you." Travis gave each of Jillian's dogs a parting scratch, then kissed her goodbye. "Blaze needs a walk before I mow the yard. The weather forecast says rain later this afternoon."

"The stack of paperwork on my desk isn't doing itself. I'm leaving too." Ethan pushed in his chair. "Oh, Jilly. I meant to tell you something. Forensics discovered fingerprints on a gun they found on the floorboard in Rick's truck. The prints were not his." He kissed Becca, then shoved Travis and Sam out the door, hustling right behind them.

Jillian whirled around to face Becca.

"Your husband is the most infuriating man on the face of the earth."

"Yes, but he's one of the most handsome too." Becca's smile lit up her face. "I'm a lucky girl."

The joy on her friend's face cooled the anger Ethan had triggered.

"He might be good-looking, but can we agree he's frustrating?" Jillian asked.

"No doubt. That man of mine could teach a course called Exasperation 101."

"I can't believe he waited until he was leaving to tell me Rick's death was murder as I suspected, not suicide. Coward." Jillian's anger returned.

"I didn't hear Ethan say anything about murder." Becca scowled at the offensive word.

"Think about it. The dead man's fingerprints weren't on the gun." Jillian paced the floor. "Amanda said Rick, the victim, was left handed. There's no way he shot himself in the right side of the head. Put these two clues together—it spells murder."

Becca let out a long breath. "What is happening to this town? I used to believe Willow Springs was one of the safest places to live. Now, I'm not as confident."

Jillian sat on the floor, burying her face in Hayley's soft fur as she muffled her next words. "Don't worry. When I solve these mysteries, everything can go back to normal."

"I heard that." Becca crossed her arms. "Those dogs won't tell Ethan, but I might have to."

"I'm goofing around," Jillian said. "I'll mull over the mysteries in my head, while Ethan goes out there and solves them for real."

"Mm-hmm, right," Becca mumbled. "And those two dogs might sprout wings and fly."

"Ooh, that would be fun—"

BAM!

The front door banged open. All eyes turned to Ethan as he stomped inside. His cheeks blazed bright red. His chest heaved with every breath.

"Do you mind if I wait in here? Dispatch says it will be thirty minutes before the tow truck arrives."

CHAPTER SIXTEEN

Jillian watched as Ethan's police cruiser was hauled away. The car's tires rested like deflated balloons against the steel flatbed. Travis and Sam stood shoulder to shoulder in the driveway amid a small scattering of yellow carnations, heads together, whispering. Ethan stood with legs apart, arms crossed over his chest, and a thunderous grimace on his face.

Four slashed tires—again. This time in full daylight in view of the street. Ethan had incurred the wrath of Amanda's stalker.

"Someone must've seen or heard something. My store sits on a busy corner with lots of traffic." Jillian tapped her lips with the pen she held in her hand.

"Don't even think about it." Becca came up behind Jillian. "No interfering in Ethan's case."

"Wasn't even on my mind."

Not at this moment, anyway.

A twinge of guilt over this half-truth flit through Jillian's mind, but she had no intention of sitting idly by now that the stakes had been raised. This lunatic had vandalized a police car, showing no fear of the law. There was no predicting what they'd do next.

The bell above the shop door tinkled. Jillian spun away from the side window, expecting to see the guys walk in. She smiled at the elderly couple standing inside the store.

"Mrs. Taylor, it's nice to see you." Jillian hugged her neighbor. "Mr. Erickson." Only a nod for him. "I never thought you'd set foot in my store. What do you think of the place?"

She steeled herself for his cantankerous response. The old man did not disappoint.

"Big deal—it's a bookstore. There are books and places to sit to read the books." He scowled at the shelves teeming with the odious materials of which he complained. "At least there ain't no pesky brats in here runnin' around makin' all kinds of noise. I really don't like kids, you know."

Ethan had come in behind the couple, snorting at the old man's comment. He moved across the room to join Becca, who cast a warning look at her husband.

"Henry, be polite." Mrs. Taylor patted his arm. "Jillian worked hard to create this lovely space so children would have a comfortable, safe place to read." She gestured around the room. "I'm sure she doesn't allow them to run around, causing a ruckus in here. She was a teacher, you know. Teachers know how to make children follow rules."

"Don't worry, Mr. Erickson. The two rules in my bookstore are to use quiet voices and no rowdy behavior."

He opened his mouth, but Mrs. Taylor shook her head. "Henry, tell Jillian something nice about her store." She leaned in, lowering her voice. "We've talked about this. You need to work on being more positive."

"Um ... well, the place is ... uh ... colorful and ... uh ... organized." Mr. Erickson's face flushed as he stammered the coerced accolade.

"Why, Mr. Erickson. Thank you very much." Jillian winked at Mrs. Taylor, who flashed a demure smile.

"See? I can give a compliment," Mr. Erickson muttered under his breath.

Only when he's forced to.

"What brings you in today?" Jillian led them deeper into the store.

"My daughter and her family will be here Friday. I'd like to buy a few books for my granddaughter Molly to enjoy." Mrs. Taylor's eyes lit up.

"I hope I get to meet them." Jillian headed to the fiction chapter book section. "Molly is ten, isn't she?"

Ethan cleared his throat, drawing attention to himself. "I'm sorry to interrupt. Did either of you happen to see anyone messing with my police car earlier?"

Mrs. Taylor beamed at him. "Hello, Detective Harden. I don't think—"

"Yep. Sure did." Mr. Erickson sucked on the toothpick he'd jabbed in his mouth.

"Henry, throw that disgusting thing away." Mrs. Taylor censured his rude behavior.

Ethan ran his hands over his face. "So, sir. You saw someone by my car?"

"A woman. She came out of this here store—dropped her purse by the back tires, then bent down to get it." His face broke into a mischievous grin. "Don't ask me what she looked like. Never noticed her face. I was too busy staring at her legs." He let out a low whistle.

Mrs. Taylor frowned at her companion. "Oh, Henry."

At the man's silence, Jillian pounced at the opportunity to ask a question of her own.

"Did you notice her purse or shoes? You know ... since your attention was directed ... um ... downward."

"Shoes and purses. Is that all you women ever think about?" Mr. Erickson growled. "But yer in luck today, Book

Lady 'cuz I did notice. Her bag was red. She was wearin' them shoes with the tall, skinny heels. Same color as the purse."

Mr. Erickson rattled on about the woman's shapely 'gams', but Jillian had stopped listening. A tingle ran down her arms.

Sounded like their visitor from down south had vandalized Ethan's police car. If that was true, odds were she'd done the same to Amanda's. But why? And where had she stashed the flowers? She hadn't had them when she was in the store.

Jillian raised her eyebrows at Ethan.

C'mon, detective. You have to be thinking what I'm thinking.

Mr. Erickson's raspy voice snapped Jillian out of her musings. He continued to share information about their stylish visitor.

"—then she climbed into a sporty little green car. Raced off down the road. Turned south on Parker Avenue. Same direction they towed your cruiser." Mr. Erickson laughed. "She sure did a number on them tires, sonny."

"Did you actually *see* her slash my tires?"

"Well, no, but what else would she be doin' down there on the ground?" Mr. Erickson scowled at Ethan. "Sheesh, what kind of detective are ya?"

"As always, I appreciate your help, sir. If you think of anything else, let me know." Ethan grabbed Becca's hand, pulling her with him. "Could I trouble you for a ride to the station?"

Jillian scurried to choose a few books for Mrs. Taylor. "Molly will like these." She carried the books to the checkout desk. "Let's ring up your purchases, then you two can be on your way. Any big plans for the rest of the day?"

Before Mrs. Taylor could respond, Mr. Erickson chuckled. "I'm always tryin' to have big plans with this one." He crooked his thumb toward his companion. "She says we need to take things slow, get to know each other better. I told her the best way to get to know each other was to—"

"Henry! Do not say another word. We do not talk about private things in public." Mrs. Taylor's cheeks bloomed a rosy shade of pink.

Jillian bit back a grin, pretending to straighten a stack of bookmarks. She wrapped up the sale, dropping the books into a gold Whimsy & Wonder bag. Coming from behind the counter, she handed the purchases to Mrs. Taylor. "Let me know what Molly thinks of these books. If you have time, please bring her in."

"Thank you, dear. I will." Mrs. Taylor hugged Jillian. "My Molly will love this store. I only wish I were still a kid. I'd spend as much time here as possible."

"You're welcome to stop in anytime." Jillian handed her neighbor a flyer. "I recently opened two rooms full of books for adults—come check them out sometime soon."

"How wonderful," Mrs. Taylor said. "A great idea to bring more customers into your store."

"That's my plan." Jillian ushered her guests to the door. "You two have a great rest of the day."

She watched the couple hold hands, shuffling off the porch. Something Mr. Erickson said made Mrs. Taylor laugh. A breeze carried the sweet sound back to Jillian. A smile tugged at her lips. She was happy to see love knew no age limit.

Who would've guessed those two would become a couple?

Not me—but I hope they have many wonderful adventures together.

Jillian's thoughts of romance were disrupted by a woman who asked about books for a reluctant reader. More people entered the store, demanding Jillian's attention for the next two hours. She lost all track of time until Trixie waltzed through the door.

"You're early." She greeted her assistant with a smile.

"Hey there, boss. I've been up and at 'em since six." Trixie shoved her purse under the counter and rifled through the day's receipts. "Looks like you've had a busy day so far."

Would her friend and assistant ever stop calling her *boss*? The word grated on Jillian's nerves, but Trixie continued to use it to get her goat.

She refused to give Trixie the satisfaction today.

"Yes, business has been steady."

"Since I'm here ahead of my shift, is it okay if I sit at your desk to eat my lunch?" Trixie shook a greasy brown paper sack. "I ran a couple of errands, then stopped at that new place on Route 36, The Burger Barn. Today is their grand opening."

"Go ahead. I can handle it out here," Jillian said. "You should be warned. You'll have two furry friends begging you to share your fries. Don't give them any."

"No promises. They get me with those soulful eyes every time." Trixie shrugged. "Give me a holler if you get slammed and need help." She whistled a catchy tune on the way down the hallway.

Jillian studied her retreating form. Was there a little extra pep in her step today? Trixie's usual personality was positive and cheerful, but in the past few months, something had changed. She'd been moody, maybe even a little depressed, but she refused to talk about it. Whatever the reason, Jillian was glad to see a return of her friend's sunny disposition.

A steady stream of customers kept them hopping all afternoon. During the few breaks in the action, she filled Trixie in on the most recent events in Amanda's stalker case.

"Unbelievable," Trixie murmured. "I hope Ethan solves this case soon."

"Agreed." The Cheshire Cat clock on the wall meowed four times, drawing Jillian's gaze. "Are you kidding me—how did it get to be so late?"

"You should've been out of here hours ago," Trixie said. "Having the extra pair of hands was nice, though. Do you have plans for this evening? Maybe a hot date with your even hotter fireman?" Trixie leaned in, nudging Jillian with her shoulder.

"Trixie, you're too much," Jillian said. "Travis and I are going to Amanda's for a cookout. Cate, Wes, and the girls will be there too. Sam bought a Blackstone grill and can't wait to show off his new culinary skills. We're taking the dogs, so they can play with Poppy."

"Sorry, what? Who's Poppy?"

"Oh, that's right. You don't know." Jillian shared Poppy's story.

"Aw, she sounds sweet. I can't wait to meet her." Trixie loved dogs as much as Jillian did. "She'll be good company when Sam's out of town. Dogs can be a comfort when you're feeling stressed or anxious. Plus, they can provide protection for their humans. Until they find the nut job who's been harassing her, Amanda could use a guard dog."

"My thoughts exactly." Jillian appreciated how in sync her and Trixie's thoughts were most of the time. "However, this little girl isn't big enough to scare a flea. Maybe we could rent a dog—one that barks loudly.

Trixie laughed. "Having this puppy and training it will be good practice for when Amanda and Sam get married and have a few two-legged kids of their own." Her impish grin lit up her face.

"Do you think that will ever happen?" Jillian asked. "I mean, they've been together for close to three years. I don't know for sure how my sister feels, but Sam said he'd marry Amanda in a heartbeat if she'd just say yes. My mother would faint if Sam put a ring on Amanda's finger."

"Stranger things have happened." Trixie whistled a mysterious tune as she bent to unpack a shipment. "There are several couples who could get engaged in the near future."

"Do you know something I don't know?" Jillian arched a suspicious brow in her assistant's direction.

"Who, me?" Trixie giggled. "I don't know a thing." Her hands flew as the new books hit the shelf.

Jillian blinked, trying to decipher if Trixie's grin meant gossip or mischief. Was she referring to the proposal pool at McGuire's? Or something else.

Either way the truth wouldn't stay buried for long— Trixie was terrible at keeping secrets.

The door banged open. The bell tinkled. Mr. Erickson stood in the doorway holding his side, breathing hard.

"Mr. Erickson, what's wrong?" Jillian rushed forward, trying to help him to a chair. "Please sit down."

He batted her arm away. "I might be old, but I ain't helpless."

Jillian took a deep breath.

Lord, give me strength to deal with this man twice in one day.

"Is there something I can do for you?"

"I forgot to give you this." He shoved a folded, somewhat wrinkled piece of paper at her. "This was stuck in your screen door when Lizzy and I came earlier. I hurried over 'cuz she said you needed to see it."

Jillian stared at the familiar pink paper, knowing it would prove to be important. Disturbing, but important.

"Thank you, Mr. Erickson. I appreciate you hurrying to br—"

The door banged open again, sending the bell jingling like crazy.

That thing is getting a workout today.

Amanda burst into the store, red-faced and spitting nails.

"Hey, Amanda." Trixie greeted her. "I hear you have a new fur baby at your house. I can't wait to meet her."

Amanda had no time for niceties. "My stalker is messing with me again!"

CHAPTER SEVENTEEN

The store was free of customers for the moment, so Jillian could give this latest drama her undivided attention. After making sure Mr. Erickson was breathing normally again, she showed him out, then rushed to her sister's side, leading her to a stool behind the counter.

"Sit. I'll get you a glass of water."

"Can you put something stronger in it?" Amanda's top lip twitched in amusement.

She'd cracked a joke. Maybe it wasn't too serious.

Jillian set a glass in front of Amanda. "Okay, tell me what happened."

"My flower order should've been delivered by one o'clock. When it wasn't here by three-thirty, I called the supply place that's helping Rick's customers until his family gets their business sorted. Someone—my stalker, I'm sure—called and canceled my order, including the flowers for Cate's party."

Amanda downed the glass of water in one gulp. "The receptionist apologized—said they'd try to get my order delivered tomorrow, but some of my flowers had been released to other florists when my order was canceled."

"How in the world did someone know about your order?" Trixie asked.

"That's my fault." Amanda threw up her hands. "I've mentioned to several customers who were worried about their upcoming orders for weddings and parties that Wholesale Flowers was helping me out. They could've mentioned it to others. I have no way of knowing how many people heard about it."

"While canceling an order isn't a criminal offense, we should still tell Ethan." Jillian searched behind the counter for her phone. "With everything that's happened, this can't be a coincidence."

"I already called him. I'm not an idiot," Amanda snapped. "I can take care of myself, you know."

"No one ever said you couldn't." Amanda's tone stung. A change of approach was needed. "How can I help?" Jillian stood back, hoping her sister's response would be kinder this time.

Amanda stroked her right earlobe, a calming strategy she'd used since they were kids.

"Listening to me vent is a good start." She moved to the window and stood staring into the street. Jillian gave her some space. After a moment, Amanda continued.

"A supply company outside of Chicago could sell me the missing flowers—if I were willing to pay their ridiculous prices, which I'm not. So, I've swallowed my florist's pride and adjusted my plans for Cate's party. The arrangements will still be beautiful, just without breaking the bank. I'm not thrilled about it, but I'll make it work."

"Sounds like you have everything under control," Jillian said. "I never doubted you for a minute."

"I know a few missing flowers aren't a big deal—it's the whole situation that's frustrating. I don't understand what I've done to make this lunatic hate me."

"I wish I knew." Jillian joined her sister at the window. "I've been thinking about your vandalism and Rick's death—"

"You mean murder. He was murdered."

"Sorry, you're right. Good thing you remembered Rick was a leftie. That blew the suicide theory to bits."

"Yeah, I'm a real Sherlock Holmes." Amanda scrubbed her hands over her face. "Change of subject—my car is still at the body shop. I walked over here."

"Did you close the shop early?"

"No, I left Brianna in charge. All my arrangements are done. She can manage the shop until closing time."

"She was a good hire, wasn't she?"

"I'm lucky to have found someone like her with retail experience."

"Well, Jillian's taxi cab is at your service. Let me get my things together." By *things*, she meant the two wiggly bodies on leashes she retrieved from her office. They strained to get closer to Amanda, who always carried treats in her pocket.

She rubbed her furry nieces. "Sorry, pockets are empty. I'll owe you double biscuits next time."

Their bearded heads drooped in disappointment.

Amanda gave each dog a smooch on top of their head. "People think dogs don't understand what we say—they'd be wrong. You're both so smart, it's scary."

While Jillian hunted in her bag for her keys, Amanda invited Trixie to the cookout that evening at her house.

"Come over after you close. We'll save a plate for you."

"Sounds great, thanks." Trixie waved her goodbye as she hurried to assist a young mother before her three-year-old had a complete meltdown.

"Ah-ha. Here they are." Jillian held her keys aloft in triumph. "Let's go."

Following Jillian and the pups to the garage behind the store, Amanda sighed and shook her head. "Have I told you how jealous I am you get to park your car inside? Your car will never be vandalized—twice."

"Amanda, we *will* catch this crazy person. The important thing is they're targeting your property, not you."

"So far," Amanda muttered.

This is my cue. I need to tell her now.

Jillian took a deep breath. "Um ... before we go ... I need to ..."

"What are you stammering about? If you have something to tell me, do it." Amanda fisted her hands on her hips.

"I don't want to add to your worries, but I need to show you something. Now's as good a time as any."

Jillian pulled the folded piece of paper from her pocket carefully, making sure to only touch the corners.

"What do you have?" Amanda's voice quivered. "That pink paper looks familiar."

"I haven't read it yet." Her heart broke at the sorrow in her sister's eyes. "Mr. Erickson handed this to me as you stormed through the door."

"Read it." Amanda glared at the handwritten note.

Jillian unfolded the paper.

> *Roses are red, violets are blue.*
> *My patience is over—it's time that you knew.*
> *I wrecked your store and spray-painted your car.*
> *I made sure Tim didn't make it too far.*
>
> *I started the fire Rick put out so fast.*
> *I'll make certain your romance won't last.*
> *Your luck's been as ripe as a green four-leaf clover.*
> *That ends soon—your luck is over.*

"The note's longer this time. Looks like my poet has too much time on their hands." Amanda flopped into the front seat of Jillian's car.

"They sure had a lot more to say." Jillian pinned Amanda with her stare. "What fire? What are they talking about?"

"Nothing. A small trashcan in the backroom of the store." Amanda waved away Jillian's question. "Rick put it out—no big deal."

"No big deal?" Jillian's voice shook. "Your stalker came inside your store without you knowing it and started a fire. Seems like a pretty big deal to me. Why didn't you say anything about this?"

"I thought my glue gun fell into the garbage due to my carelessness. Now I know it had help." Amanda's shoulders slumped.

Jillian loaded her pups into the backseat. "We need to call Ethan and give him this note. We can fill the guys in on the latest at dinner if you still want us to come over."

Amanda catapulted forward in the seat and slammed her hands on the dashboard. "We, we, we. You sound like the three little pigs. If Ethan hears you talk like this, he won't be happy. You should know Sam invited Ethan and Becca to dinner tonight, so you better watch the 'we' talk."

Jillian stared at Amanda in disbelief. She'd never exploded like that before. Current events considered, Jillian was willing to give her a break.

"Great, saves me a trip. I can give Ethan the lunatic's new message when he comes to your house. Can we talk a little more about this note?"

"What else is there to discuss?" Amanda refused to look at Jillian. "The poet was clear. They didn't leave anything open to misinterpretation. Can we go?"

Jillian dropped the subject. Amanda needed time to process the threats within the note.

The drive to Amanda's fixer-upper was quiet. Jillian glanced sideways at her sister, noticing her eyes were closed. This was a clear sign she was mulling things over and didn't want to be disturbed.

Amanda found her voice as Jillian pulled into the driveway.

"I'm sorry I've been snippy with you several times today. I'm frustrated and angry, but I'm helpless to do anything about it." Tears pooled in her pale blue eyes. "This idiot is threatening my business and my relationship with Sam. I can't lose him." A single teardrop fell.

"I'm not going to say don't worry because you will—as would anyone in your shoes." Jillian took Amanda's hand and squeezed. "Ethan will figure this out. He will catch the jerk who's threatening you."

"And Sam."

"Yes, and Sam. This will be over soon, then your life can get back to normal."

"I'm glad you're all coming tonight." Amanda's words were calm, but her eyes, wide and haunted, reflected her fear. "I can use a relaxing evening surrounded by family and friends to distract me from all this chaos."

Jillian pulled up in front of Amanda's house. "We'll be here. Travis is picking up the sides you asked for from The Corner Deli. Abbey, Hayley, and Blaze are bringing Poppy a 'welcome to the family' present. We'll enjoy good food and even better friends. The night will end with one of Becca's new dessert creations. This evening will be great."

As long as your poet doesn't create another scene.

Amanda echoed Jillian's thought. "Good food and good friends—the perfect recipe for a fun evening. Unless my psycho stalker decides to make trouble."

"The police plan to cruise by your house every hour. Their presence should deter the lunatic from causing trouble."

Amanda let out a long sigh. "You're right. The cops will scare her off. My crazy poet can't continue to fly under the radar. She's going to slip, then we'll get her."

The use of the pronouns, *she* and *her,* didn't escape Jillian. "You definitely think a woman is threatening you?"

"Did I say she?" Amanda cocked her head. "I don't know. I guess—the poems, the slashed tires, the nasty word on my car—those all seem like things a female would do."

"Don't forget—Aunt Grace had that vision of an angry woman with blonde hair. We've met two strange ladies with—"

"Enough about the visions, Jilly." Amanda climbed from the car. "Aunt Grace's nutty premonitions can't be trusted. Do I need to remind you of her prediction about the man I'd marry? She saw a vision of me in a big, white dress walking down the aisle with Brayden Jackson." Amanda slammed the car door. "Brayden Jackson is gay. He came out in the twelfth grade."

"She doesn't claim to be accurate one hundred percent of the time," Jillian said. "I wish everyone wouldn't be so skeptical of Aunt Grace. Her intentions are always pure."

"We all love Aunt Grace, but you're a bleeding heart where she's concerned." Amanda reached in through the open window for her purse. "If you talk to Becca, tell her Sam's slapping the burgers on the grill at seven."

"I'll text her." She grabbed her phone. "I'm glad Ethan and Becca are coming. I'm eager to hear if he has any new leads. We can hope he's close to making arrests in these cases."

"Without your help—who would've thought?" Sarcasm dripped from Amanda's words like water from a leaky pipe.

"Very funny," Jillian said. "What can I say? I have a knack for uncovering clues and solving puzzles. Don't forget, I was an integral part of solving Maggie's murder last year."

"Yes, but your interference almost got you killed—more than once." Amanda's voice rose. "Steer clear of this. We're dealing with a couple of loose cannons here."

No, we're not.

Jillian kept the thought to herself, convinced this wasn't the work of two isolated lunatics. It felt controlled. Calculated. One person hiding in plain sight.

"I won't do anything to put myself in danger. I've learned my lesson." Jillian crossed her heart.

"Why don't I believe you?" Amanda mumbled under her breath.

A sudden flash of movement to the left sent Abbey and Hayley into a barking frenzy in the backseat. Jillian whirled around as Sam burst from the side yard, panic cloaking his face.

"Sam, what's wrong?" Amanda hurried to his side.

"I've looked everywhere—Poppy's gone."

CHAPTER EIGHTEEN

"Poppy, here Poppy." Jillian searched the neighborhood, her head on a swivel, watching for any signs of the furry pup.

She prayed the little dog would turn up safe. Sam and Amanda would be devastated if something happened to her.

Who am I kidding? I'll be upset too.

More shouts of Poppy's name rang out. Several of Amanda's neighbors joined the search. Jillian's heart raced, waiting to hear someone yell *I found her.*

They'd agreed to spend thirty minutes. If Poppy wasn't found by then, they'd regroup at Amanda's and plan their next step.

Jillian hated pulling back, but time was up. The others were likely already there.

She reached the driveway just as Amanda came sprinting from between the houses, clutching Poppy to her chest.

"I have her. Everything's fine." Amanda's voice cracked, contradicting this claim.

Poppy appeared unharmed, but Amanda still looked shaken. Something wasn't right.

"Where'd you find her?" Sam rushed in, scooping Poppy into his arms. He showered her with kisses.

"She was trapped inside Mr. Gillespie's tool shed yowling her head off." Amanda ruffled the dog's soft fur.

"Silly girl. How'd you get yourself stuck in a shed?" Sam flipped Poppy over to rub her belly. "Better yet—how'd she get out of the backyard? I'd tied her leash around the door handle. I was only inside for two minutes to grab a towel to wipe her muddy feet."

"Poppy didn't get stuck." Amanda swallowed hard. "Someone put her there."

Sam's head jerked. "Are you serious? Who would do that to an innocent puppy?"

Amanda held up a yellow carnation. "This was inside the shed with her."

Sam's friendly eyes hardened to orbs of steel. He put an arm around Amanda's waist, hugging her close. "I can't wait until Ethan nabs this psycho. I hope he lets me have a crack at this lunatic before tossing him in a cell and throwing away the key."

Him? Sam and Amanda differed in their opinion of the stalker's identity.

Jillian opened her mouth to point this out, then thought better of it. She watched her sister relax into Sam, putting her head on his shoulder.

This is not the time to debate the poet's gender.

Leaning on Sam comforted her. Amanda's heartbeat kept time with his, both racing in their shared anger over the crazed stalker's most recent offense.

"When is this insanity going to end?" Amanda took Poppy back from Sam as everyone headed for her house. "I want—no—I *need* this to stop before someone else is seriously injured—or worse. Not to mention, no one will enjoy Cate's party with this hanging over our heads." She settled Poppy on her new bed in the kitchen. The dog circled three times, snuggled in, and fell straight to sleep.

"Getting locked in a toolshed must have been exhausting." Amanda stroked the dog's head. "Poor, sweet girl."

Sam's angry voice jolted her from her musings.

"A party is the least of our worries, Amanda," Sam said. "Maybe we should postpone it."

"Not on your life, buddy." Amanda rounded on Sam. "I won't let this nonsense ruin Cate's special day."

"But, Amanda—" Sam's objection died on his lips.

"No. I'm not giving this person control over our lives. She's ruined property, injured poor Tim, tried to burn down the shop, and scared the pants off us by hiding Poppy." Amanda paced the distance from the fireplace to the dining room table.

"Burned down the shop? What's that about?"

Amanda gave a quick explanation of the trashcan fire on Monday.

"Seriously, Amanda. Why am I just hearing this now?" Sam's angry voice rattled the china in the buffet.

"Until very recently, I thought the fire was my fault—an accident with a glue gun."

"That's it." Sam slammed his fists on the table. "You're going to close the shop until this nut is found—and no party."

The temperature in the room dropped from the icy chill emanating from Amanda.

"I'm sorry, but it sounds like you're telling me what to do." She took a few steps closer, entering Sam's personal space. She poked a finger in his chest. "Listen, Sailor. This loony tune will not hold me, or any of us, hostage. My business will remain open. Cate's party will happen."

"This is a bad idea. You're not safe until Ethan makes an arrest." Sam straightened his shoulders. "He's had no luck so far tracking down leads."

"Well, maybe we should ask Jillian to put on her detective cap and get busy helping Ethan find the stalker." Amanda's sarcasm came out sharper than she intended, but her patience was wearing thin.

"Wait. Did I hear you correctly?" Jillian gaped at Amanda. "You *want* me to help Ethan?"

A sharp rap on the screen door announced Travis's arrival. He held two brown sacks in his arms. Cate and her family followed on his heels.

"Hey, look who's here." Jillian let them in. "Perfect timing, handsome." She took one of the bags from him, then greeted Cate, Wes, and her nieces.

"Yeah, I arrived just in time to catch the dumbest thing I've heard all day." Travis shot a stony glare in Amanda's direction. "I've obviously missed something that has upset Amanda, but there's no way I'll allow Jillian to put herself in danger—not even to solve your stalker case."

"You won't *allow?*" An angry scowl darkened Jillian's face.

"That's what I said." Travis crossed his arms over his chest.

"Uh-oh, Uncle Travis is mad. His face turned red, and what's wrong with his nose? The holes keeping moving in and out." Five-year-old Aubrey's eyes were wide.

"Hush, sweetie. This is grown-up business." Cate took her youngest by the arm. "And don't call Aunt Jilly's boyfriend *Uncle Travis.* He's not your uncle—yet."

Her final comment earned her a quick glance from Jillian.

"Travis," Sam said. "You don't have all the facts. There was another incident this afternoon."

"I don't need all the facts." Travis advanced on Sam. "The only one I heard was Amanda encouraging Jillian to become involved in solving this case. That's not going to happen."

"Now wait a minute, I can speak for—"

Sam cut Jillian off, unable to contain himself. "Who are you to come into our house making demands about what is and is not going to happen?" He stepped toe to toe with Travis.

"Guys, come on. Calm down." Wes attempted to defuse the tension. "Let's have a cold one and talk this over."

"Stay out of this," Travis muttered.

"Back off, Wes," Sam snapped.

"Both of you, knock it off." Amanda placed herself between the men. "First of all, it's *my* house. I shouldn't have said—"

"You've already said enough." Travis's voice increased in volume. "I can't believe you'd expect your sister to risk her life."

"Don't yell at her." Sam uttered a curse and jabbed a finger in Travis's chest. "Are you saying Jillian's life is more important than Amanda's?"

Laney squealed. "Ooh, Uncle Sam said a bad word, Mommy. He needs to sit in the time-out chair."

Again, Cate shushed her oldest daughter. "Laney, this isn't any of your business, and Sam's not your uncle until Aunt Amanda marries him. Honey, let's take the girls outside. They don't need to hear or see this."

Wes led his family away from the dispute, seeking refuge in the backyard where the girls could play with the dogs.

Having ignored everything around them, Sam and Travis's argument escalated. Their voices grew louder with each insult.

"No, I'm saying there's no way Jillian should become involved. I'll do whatever it takes to care for my woman and make sure she's safe." Travis knocked Sam's hand away.

"You do that. I'll take care of my woman too." Sam shoved Travis's shoulder.

"What is this *'my woman'* nonsense?" Amanda grabbed Sam's arm. "When did Jilly and I decide to date two cavemen?"

Ignoring the insult, Travis reached around her and returned Sam's shove with a hard push, sending him stumbling backward.

Amanda grabbed hold of Sam to keep him on his feet. She couldn't believe these two had let their disagreement become physical.

Jillian voiced her sister's thoughts. "Are you two kidding? You're going to come to blows over this?" She placed a firm hand on each of their arms. "Amanda doesn't need you Neanderthals pounding on each other. She needs our support, not your inflated male egos."

"You tell them, little sister." The two women high-fived.

"You," Jillian snapped at Sam. "Stop beating your chest like a primate trying to impress a female ape. If you want Amanda to know how much she means to you, propose already."

"Jilly, what are you doing?" Amanda's pulse quickened. Her question went unanswered. Or unheard.

"I'm not happy with you either, mister." Jillian rounded on Travis. "I take offense to being called 'your woman.' Until you put a ring on my finger, you don't have the right to call me that. Not to mention, I find the use of the term archaic and rude."

Sam hooted with laughter. "Are you gonna let *your woman* talk to you like that?"

"Sam!" Amanda shouted.

"What's wrong with you, bro?" Travis cuffed Sam on the side of the head.

The fight was on. Sam grabbed Travis by the shirt, getting in one good jab to the ribs. Travis used his extra five inches and thirty pounds to take Sam to the floor. There was a punch to a nose, another to an eye. A table fell over. A lamp was broken. The guys rolled around until—

"What are you two idiots doing?" Ethan barked. He and Becca had let themselves in when no one answered the door. "Get up right now, or I'll arrest you both for assault and battery."

The threat of sitting in a jail cell worked. Travis and Sam split apart like they'd been doused with a bucket of cold water. They stomped to separate corners where they sulked like disobedient children reprimanded by a parent.

"Thank you, Ethan. My living room, not to mention my nerves, couldn't take much more." Amanda hugged her savior.

"Would someone like to explain what happened here?" Ethan used both hands to point at Travis and Sam. "By someone, I don't mean either of you."

Amanda shared how they'd searched for and found Poppy trapped in the shed along with the yellow carnation. "When I made a stupid comment about Jillian helping you find the stalker, these two barbarians went nuts—trading insults and punches."

The blooming bruise on Sam's eye and the split in Travis's lip were evidence a few punches found their mark.

"You're all under a lot of stress." Ethan's cop voice brooked no interruptions. "Turning on each other isn't going to help. Amanda needs you to stick together, keep an eye out for anything suspicious, but, most important, keep her safe."

"I don't need—"

Ethan shook a finger at Amanda. "You no longer get to decide what you do or do not need. Until we've arrested your vandal, I'm calling the shots."

He spun on his heel and stared at Jillian. "I hope you listened to what I just said because it applies to you too. Your family might want you to help solve this case, but I don't. Stay out of my way."

Jillian brought her hands to her chest. "Me? What did I do?"

"It's not what you did—it's what you're thinking about doing." Ethan's attention turned back to the guys. "I was promised a juicy burger grilled to perfection. If you two could kiss and make up, maybe we could get this cookout started."

Ethan signaled Becca to follow him to the kitchen. She'd stood open-mouthed during her husband's tirade. Staring at his retreating back, she found her voice. "Is that man of mine sexy or what—especially when he goes all bad cop on someone."

She picked up the bag she'd set on the table. "I'm going outside with him. You might want to give us a minute unless you want to witness a ridiculous display of my affection for him."

"There are small children outside," Jillian called after them.

"On that note, can we trust you two to behave?" Amanda pinned Sam and Travis with a glare.

"I'm pretty sure we can manage it, don't you, Sam?" Travis reached out a hand.

"Yeah, we can handle it." Sam shook on it.

Despite the truce, neither man would look the other in the eye.

"Stop being such babies." Jillian stamped her foot. "You were both wrong. You acted like adolescents. Apologize already. Amanda and I are hungry too."

Both men raised their heads to make eye contact.

"Sorry, bro," Travis mumbled.

"Yeah, me too. Sorry," Sam said.

"I was wrong." They both blurted.

"You're finally correct about something." Jillian slipped an arm around Travis's waist. Placing her hand on his back, she pushed him out of the room. "Let's join the others in the backyard."

"Since you boys are done fighting, we should get out there too. We are the host—"

Sam pressed two fingers over Amanda's lips. "In a minute. I have something to ask you first." He reached into his pocket.

"Sam, what are you doing?"

"Amanda, you are the most—"

BOOM. CRACK. POP.

Loud explosions from the front yard drowned out whatever Sam had meant to say. One more earsplitting pop sent them racing to the door. A frantic Trixie wrenched it open, stumbling into the house.

She screamed. "Someone call 9-1-1."

CHAPTER NINETEEN

Flames shot into the air, turning the evening sky bright orange. Crimson leaves on a nearby maple caught fire, disintegrating into ashes sprinkling the ground. Gasoline and burning rubber assaulted their noses. Approaching sirens were barely audible above the popping and cracking of the heated metal frame of Sam's beloved 1965 Mustang.

Hearing the commotion, everyone in the backyard came running.

Jillian snuck a glance at Sam, who stood stoically—his expression blank.

Poor guy. He loves that car.

Her gaze was drawn to Amanda, whose head rested on Sam's shoulder, tears streaming down her face. Her previous anger toward him was now gone.

Three fire trucks screeched to a stop. Their air breaks hissed as the crews jumped from the rigs as if ejected from their seats. Masks were donned, hoses were pulled, and water flowed onto the fiery metal carcass.

"We should move inside," Travis said. Sam tried to object, but Travis stopped him. "Trust me—it's not safe to be so close once there's water on the flames. The steam can cause serious burns, not to mention the tires, shocks, and struts could explode becoming heat-seeking projectiles."

Deferring to Travis's expertise, everyone gathered in the living room. Since the conflagration in the driveway had interrupted their cookout, Cate, Trixie, and Becca offered to pull some food together in case anyone was hungry.

"If you don't mind us digging around in your fridge and pantry." Becca winked at Amanda.

"Dig away," she said. "My kitchen is your kitchen."

"We want to help. Can we help?" Laney and Aubrey bounced on their toes, begging to be of assistance. "Please."

"Of course you can." Becca took each girl by the hand. "You can be my sous chefs."

"Your what?" Their sweet voices chirped in unison.

"We'll explain once we're in the kitchen." Cate hustled her girls away from the grown-up talk in the living room.

"While they're cooking, I'll rustle up some drinks." Amanda wandered off in search of liquid refreshments.

"Preferably something strong," Sam muttered from his vantage point at the bay window.

Jillian stayed quiet in a chair in the corner of the room, hoping the other ladies would forgive her for not helping with dinner. She was more interested in the conversation than the cooking.

Ethan patted Sam's shoulder. "Sorry about your car. I know you and your dad put a lot of work into it."

Sam nodded, unable to find his voice.

"Good thing the fire department arrived so quickly—less chance of nearby houses, including Amanda's, catching on fire." Wes attempted to put a positive spin on this horrible situation.

"Any idea what might have happened—any mechanical trouble lately, making any weird noises?" Ethan's line of questioning caused goosebumps on Jillian's arms.

"No, nothing. She purred like a kitten." Sam shoved his hands deep into his pockets. "I don't understand. There's no reason why she should've caught fire."

Amanda returned with a pitcher of her famous raspberry sangria and a tray of chilled glasses. She'd overheard Sam's last comment. "I can think of one. My stalker's widening her circle. She's bored going after me, so she's targeting the people I love." She set the drinks on the coffee table. "I'm sorry, Sam. This is all my fault."

"Babe. Nothing about this is your fault." The despair in Sam's eyes had been replaced with tenderness as he gazed at Amanda.

"If the stalker set this fire—"

Ethan inserted himself into the conversation. "Let's not jump to conclusions."

"Would it help to have concrete evidence of the stalker's guilt?" Trixie had entered the room. She posed the question as she poured three glasses of sangria. "Don't judge—only one is for me. Becca, Cate, and I need this while we cook."

"Yes, we do." Becca took one of the glasses from Trixie. "We're reinventing those uncooked hamburgers by creating a make-your-own taco bar." She did her best salsa dance moves on her way back to the kitchen.

Ethan cleared his throat. "Trixie, you mentioned evidence."

"They're probably burned beyond recognition now, but before the explosion, I noticed yellow flowers scattered around Sam's car." Trixie faced Jillian. "Didn't you say Amanda's stalker uses yellow carnations as her calling card?"

"Yes, I did." Jillian's mouth formed a thin line.

"More flowers." Amanda latched onto this new piece of information. "There's proof my stalker did this."

A sharp knock at the door halted further speculation. Sam opened it to one of the firemen, dripping water from the tip of his helmet. "Wanted to let you know we've cleared the scene. Our fire investigations officer will take it from here. You all have a safe night." He pivoted and tromped down the porch steps.

"I'm going to join the fire investigator." Ethan shrugged into his jacket.

"I should be there too." Travis followed.

"I'm coming." Wes wouldn't be left out.

"Wait for me." Sam slammed the door behind him.

Becca rushed into the living room in time to watch the door close behind them. "What about dinner?"

Jillian stood in the doorway. Her mood lifted as Aubrey and Laney, followed by Becca and Trixie, marched into the dining room. Like a parade of culinary delights, the girls carried small plates of taco toppings and *botanas*—salsa, guacamole, and *queso*—while the grown-ups brought in larger platters of tortillas, taco shells, and meat.

"*Los tacos están listos.*" The younger sisters announced the food was ready.

"You spoke Spanish." Cate clapped her hands. "How did you learn that?"

"Trixie taught us." Aubrey grinned. "There's more. *Los hombres están locos.* That means men are crazy." This sent her into a fit of giggles.

"I know another one." Laney approached the table. "*Los hombres son un dolor de culo.* That means men are a pain in the—"

"Yes, I know what it means." Cate seated her girls in their chairs. "I think that's enough Spanish for one day. Thanks, Trixie."

"No problem." Trixie ignored the hint of irritation in Cate's voice.

Amanda pulled her nieces in close. "You did great, but let's not share your Spanish with the guys, okay? We don't want to hurt their feelings."

"Okay, we won't say a word, right, Aubrey?" Laney checked with her little sister.

"Sure, mum's the word." Aubrey zipped her lips.

Jillian chuckled.

We'll see how that works out. Discretion isn't part of their vocabulary.

Since the men were outside watching them tow away Sam's car, dinner would commence in shifts. The women and children ate first, enjoying the spur of the moment Mexican cuisine, sharing their impressions of these latest events.

"I couldn't believe how high the flames shot into the air," Jillian shuddered.

"The explosions were scary," Trixie said. "I could feel the heat at my back."

"I never realized a car could burn so fast." Amanda's brow broke out in worry lines. "Poor Sam. That Mustang meant everything to him."

When the men came in and sat down for dinner, the women pelted them with questions.

"Could you see the carnations?"

"Does the investigator know how the fire started?"

"Did he find any evidence pointing to the stalker?"

The answers came in quick succession—only burnt stems, not yet, and only burnt stems.

Amanda threw her arms in the air. "Great. She'll get away with torching Sam's car because there's no concrete evidence."

"You're frustrated. I get it. We're all frustrated," Ethan said. "I have officers knocking on doors, talking to your neighbors. Let's stay positive and hope one of them saw something."

Travis sipped the iced tea Jillian poured for him. "The fire investigator will examine the remnants—"

Sam sucked in his breath at the word *remnants.*

"Oh sorry, buddy." Travis squeezed Sam's shoulder. "The investigator's preliminary inspection of *the car* was cut short—too hot to search. They'll tow it to Shorty's where they can secure it inside for the evening to preserve evidence. He'll go back tomorrow when it's cooled off and give it a closer look."

When no tacos remained, Becca brought out her newest gastronomic creation—a lemon concoction with fresh raspberry sauce.

"This recipe is a cross between cheesecake and tiramisu with a lemony twist." She sliced large servings, plating them with generous drizzles of the sauce. "Let me know what you think."

Their answers came in the form of contented moans. Becca laughed.

"Thanks for your input. Cate, looks like we should add this dessert to the menu at the bakery."

The guys retired to the backyard with a couple of beers to watch the pups play. The women enjoyed a cup of coffee around the kitchen table. Their conversation circled back to Amanda's misfortunes and Rick's murder. With the information available thus far, they agreed the same person had to be responsible for all of the crimes.

"The question is *who* would hate both Amanda and Rick enough to do these heinous things?" Cate shook her head.

"I wish I knew." Amanda blew a curl from her face.

"They haven't been getting the carnations from you. I wonder where they've bought them?" Becca posed a great question.

"I've been wondering the same thing." Jillian nodded at Becca. "I thought of mentioning it earlier, but it slipped my mind."

"There are flower shops in Stonefield, Red Hill, and Livingston. She could've purchased carnations at any one of them," Amanda said. "Or all of them. I'm sure Ethan will check out that lead."

"We can ask him." Becca nodded.

"Sure, yeah," Amanda agreed. "All I know is—I won't be stocking those stupid yellow flowers in my shop ever again. They're banned from Blossoms & Blooms."

Amanda's attempt at a bit of levity barely registered with Jillian, lost deep in thought.

If the stalker is the same person who killed Rick, what's to stop them from going after Amanda?

This unpleasant seed sprouted in Jillian's mind, but now wasn't the right time to mention it to anyone.

"I'm sorry you're dealing with all this, Amanda." Becca's brown eyes shimmered with pity.

"Thanks," she said. "Having friends in my corner helps. I couldn't get through this without you guys." She cocked a thumb toward the backyard. "Those guys too."

"I wonder how Rick's widow is doing." Jillian snapped out of her mental musings. "From what Ethan said after his visit, she's struggling. No family here in town—hasn't lived here long enough to make friends either."

"We could all be her support system," Becca suggested.

"Sure," Cate agreed. "We could take turns stopping by—with food, things for the baby, self-care items for her. After I had each of the girls, I appreciated all the treats people dropped at the house, but the adult conversation is what saved me most days."

"I'll stop by and check on her," Amanda volunteered. "What a shame I'll be meeting Stacey under these circumstances. Rick talked about her, so it feels like I already know her a little."

"We could drop in on her tomorrow before our stores open." Jillian looked at Amanda, who nodded. "With a new baby, she'll be up early like us."

"Stop by the bakery on your way. I'll have breakfast ready to go." Becca rubbed her hands together. "I know just what to make."

Early the next morning, Amanda and Jillian strolled into Sugar & Spice. As promised, Becca had boxed their breakfast.

"I packed three slices of Denver omelet quiche, fresh fruit cups, and a variety of pastries from our customers' favorites menu." She patted the top of the blue carton. "I hope Rick's wife has an appetite. If she doesn't, I don't want to know." Becca sniffed at the thought of her food going uneaten.

Jillian hugged her bestie. "I'm sure she'll appreciate your efforts."

"Before you go, can you two take a look at Cate's birthday cake? I've done as much as I can until right before the party tomorrow." Becca bit at her bottom lip. "I want it to be perfect."

Amanda screwed up her mouth. "Becca, we're not aiming for perfection. We're aiming for fun."

"Then I need you to look at the cake to make sure it meets the *fun* standard." She pushed through the swinging doors leading into the kitchen. Having been given no choice, Jillian and Amanda followed.

Sitting on the stainless-steel island in the center of the room were four perfectly frosted tiers of the gorgeous cake Becca would assemble before tomorrow's party.

"Oh, Becca. This cake will be spectacular. You're hired to bake my cake if I ever get married." Jillian dipped a finger into the bowl of frosting. "Yum!"

The tiers of chocolatey goodness, not yet stacked, were covered with buttercream icing in a medium peach shade. Lying on bits of parchment paper, there were pink, darker orange, and white latticework and beading waiting to be applied to the sides of the cake once assembled.

Becca picked up a package of sparklers of the same three colors. "I'm using these instead of ordinary candles. Nice, right? I also ordered edible flowers for the top of the cake."

"Your masterpiece will look amazing—matches the decorations to a T." Amanda helped herself to a sample of frosting too.

"I'm glad you approve," Becca said.

"Speaking of the birthday girl, how are you baking and decorating this cake here?" Jillian cocked her head at her friend. "Where is your secret hiding place?"

"I'm not hiding it. Cate's seen me working on it." Becca shrugged as she put the frosting in the fridge.

"The cake, the party, *everything*, is supposed to be a surprise. We told you that, Becca." Jillian's voice contained a tone of censure. "Are you saying Cate knows?"

"Relax, the secret is safe." Becca chuckled. She worked on putting each tier into the cooler. "There was no way I could work on this cake without her walking in on me—it *is* her bakery's kitchen. I told her the cake is for a sorority sister's wedding this weekend."

"So you could work on the cake out in the open." Amanda gave Becca a thumbs-up. "Brilliant idea."

"I thought so." Becca beamed at the praise. "She even commented how much she liked the colors."

The three of them enjoyed a laugh at Cate's expense.

"Okay, here's your to-go box. I need to get some muffins in the oven. We're running low." Becca handed the hefty blue box tied with a satiny white ribbon to Amanda. "May this bring a bit of cheer to Rick's wife's day."

On their way out, they could hear Becca singing her personal theme song, *Girl on Fire*. Jillian shook her head.

Alicia Keys, she isn't.

Don't quit your day job, Becca.

Leaving the bakery, Jillian noticed the older gentleman she'd met, or almost run over, a few days before. He wore the same clothes and carried the same ratty knapsack. Head down, feet shuffling, he wandered from storefront to storefront, stopping to stare in each window. His hunched shoulders exuded an air of sadness. Her heart broke for him.

Was he homeless? Did he have family in the area?

Jillian knew it was none of her business, but she hated to think this man might need help but not know where to get it. A mental note was made to talk to Patty Martin, the mayor's liaison, about available social services.

She decided against mentioning her thoughts to Amanda. Listening to a lecture about minding your own business was not on her agenda for this morning.

They pulled into the gravel driveway of the ranch-style home Rick had shared with his wife. Flowering ivy obscured most of the brick façade. Grass clippings—a telltale sign someone had mowed—were scattered over the flagstone sidewalk leading to the front door.

"I hope she's not upset we didn't call first," Amanda said. "I didn't want to give her the chance to say no. I have this strange need to check on her."

Jillian stepped onto the small porch, preparing to knock, but stopped short.

"What's wrong?" Amanda bumped into Jillian.

Jillian's voice dropped to a whisper.

"Shh." She pointed at the door someone had left ajar. "Don't you think it's odd she left it open?"

"Not odd if she's home." Amanda knocked on the cheery yellow door.

Jillian stuck out an arm to block her. "Something doesn't feel right." She rubbed at the goose pimples on her arms.

"What do you want to do then—pull it shut and leave?" Amanda raised her palms to the sky and shrugged. "What if Stacey's inside and needs our help?"

Jillian silently cursed Amanda and her common sense.

"Fine. We'll go in."

Jillian put her hand on the knob and pushed the door open wide, stepping into a living room shrouded in darkness. No lights were on. The curtains were pulled shut.

"Hello? Anybody home?" Her voice echoed in the stillness.

She fumbled for a light switch. When her hand found it, track lighting above a fireplace flicked on, casting a pale glow across the room. Her eyes scanned the space around her. A huge flat screen TV dominated one wall while a dark brown leather sectional sprawled across the opposite side of the living room. A blue receiving blanket had been thrown over one arm while a book lay open on the seat. A half full glass of what appeared to be iced tea sat on an end table.

Jillian reached out and tapped the side of the glass. *Still cold.*

"Jilly, what are you doing? I feel awkward walking into someone's house uninvited, even with an unlocked, open door." Amanda hung back. "Do you think we should call Ethan?"

"No." Jillian twisted around, pinning Amanda in her sights. "If this turns out to be nothing, we'll look silly calling him. Stop worrying and get in here."

Amanda caught up with her in the kitchen. She wrinkled her nose. "What a mess. Stacey's not much of a housekeeper."

A plate with half a bagel topped with cream cheese sat abandoned on the table next to a cup of coffee. The sink overflowed with food-encrusted dishes. A garbage can stuffed to the gills smelled of food long past its prime.

Jillian touched the sides of the coffee mug. "This one's cold too."

Amanda tugged at Jillian's sleeve. "We should've never barged in. Let's go."

"Hello? Stacey?" Jillian ignored Amanda, continuing her search. "Are you here?"

Nothing. Only stale air and the faint buzz of silence pressing in from every corner.

The house wasn't large, so it didn't take long to check most of the rooms—guest bedroom, home office, laundry room, and nursery. From the back door, Amanda checked the yard. Jillian opened the inside garage door and called out. No answer.

"The main bedroom must be on the other side of the house. Stacey could be sleeping." Jillian led the way. "If she's not here, we'll go with Plan B. Pull the door shut and leave."

"Great—wish I'd thought of it." Sarcasm rolled off Amanda's tongue.

Tuning out her sister's snarky remark, Jillian's ears picked up soft, snuffling noises. Following the sound to a closed door at the end of the hall, she gently pushed it open.

No lamps brightened the room. The shades were drawn. Jillian stood in the hall, listening for the noise that had brought her to this spot.

There it was again.

Once her eyes adjusted to the darkness, she took a few steps inside.

"Amanda, you'd better come here. Quick."

CHAPTER TWENTY

Amanda rushed toward the sound of Jillian's voice. The urgency she'd heard caused a sick feeling in the pit of her stomach.

Please don't let Stacey be hurt. Or worse.

One step into the main bedroom, Amanda's fear was replaced by a new one. Jillian stood beside a white bassinet, snuggling an infant wrapped in a blanket matching the one on the sofa in the living room. She swayed, singing the Irish lullaby their Grandma McClaren used to sing to them.

Stacey was nowhere to be found.

Jillian patted the fussy baby's bottom. "This poor little one is here by himself." His cries grew louder, more insistent.

"That's Rick's son, Benjamin. He liked to show me pictures on his phone when he made my flower deliveries." Amanda smiled down at the infant's cherubic face. "He was so excited to be a dad, but now this baby will never know his father."

A wave of sorrow washed over her.

"He's a beautiful baby." Amanda stroked a finger on his soft cheek. "He looks like Rick."

"I can't believe a mother would leave her child alone." Jillian held the infant close as he began wailing.

"Why's he crying?" Amanda paced the floor. "What does he need?"

"Why do you assume I know?" Jillian sat in a rocking chair, rubbing the baby's back. "He could be hungry, wet, tired, sick—where's Cate or Mom when we need them?"

Amanda gazed at her little sister. "Seems to me you know what you're doing. You look like a natural at this baby thing."

Jillian huffed out a breath. "Must be all the babysitting I did in high school."

"We should call Ethan." Amanda patted her pockets in search of her phone.

"Why? He knows even less about babies than we do." Jillian stared at Amanda as if she'd lost her mind.

"To tell him Stacey is missing—that we found her baby here alone."

Jillian smacked her forehead with the heel of her hand. "Duh. I should've thought of that."

"You're too busy playing Mary Poppins." Amanda winced as the baby's sobs grew louder.

"Maybe he's hungry after his nap," Jillian said. "Maybe there's a bottle in the fridge I can warm up." She tried to hand the infant off, but Amanda refused to take him.

"Uh-uh, you know I don't feel comfortable holding babies. I'm always afraid I'll do something wrong and hurt them. Besides, they throw up and need their diapers changed." She crossed her pointer fingers to ward off the baby. "I don't do those either. Never could get the hang of it when Laney and Aubrey were babies. You take care of him. I'll make the call to Ethan."

"Fine. I'll change his diaper *and* feed him." Jillian headed toward the nursery in search of diapers. "Thanks for all your help."

Jillian heated a bottle she'd found in the fridge, then sat in the recliner feeding the baby. Ethan stuck his head in the open door.

"Hey, I raced here as fast as I—" His eyes fell on Jillian.

"Hello, Ethan." Jillian smiled at him, then the baby. He'd wrapped a pudgy hand around one of her fingers. "May I introduce you to Benjamin, Rick's son?"

Ethan approached the baby as someone might a stray dog—with a respectful amount of fear.

"Amanda says Stacey is MIA, so this baby's alone." Ethan edged closer. He peered into the little boy's face. "Why does he look so goofy?"

"He's milk drunk." Jillian laughed aloud at the confused expression on Ethan's face. "He has a full tummy and is happy about it."

She used a kitchen towel to wipe a dribble of milk from his chin. She propped him on her shoulder and patted his back. Within seconds, he let out a hearty burp.

Ethan's eyebrows shot toward his hairline. "Impressive for a little dude."

Amanda came in from the kitchen. "Hey, Ethan. I hope you didn't break the speed limit getting here so fast, but I'm happy to see you. What should we do now?"

"We? You're starting to sound like Jilly." Ethan snapped on a pair of gloves he had in his pocket. He wandered around the room, picking things up and setting them down. "*We* aren't doing anything. I'll do my job—you two will butt out."

"What about this little man?" Jillian cradled the now sleepy baby. "What's going to happen to him until his mother can be found?"

"I called Child Protective Services on my way over," Ethan said. "One of their caseworkers should be here soon to take him into their custody."

"Y'all will do no such thing."

Miss Southern Belle stood in the open door, hands on her hips, glaring at Jillian. She took three strides toward her.

"Give him to me." She held out her arms for the baby.

Jillian hugged Benjamin closer, turning a protective shoulder toward the woman. "Why should I?"

"Because he's my nephew." Her fiery eyes latched onto Jillian. "Where's my sister?"

Amanda watched as Ethan stepped into cop mode, taking charge of the situation.

Here we go. Miss Georgia Peach better watch out.

The new name popped into Amanda's head.

Hah, I like that even better then Miss Southern Belle.

"Ma'am. I need to ask some questions to verify your story."

"I have a few questions of my own." She straightened her shoulders, ready to square off with Ethan. "Why are you—all of you—in my sister's house? Where is she?" Her gaze landed on Amanda. "You're the woman who owns the flower shop. Isn't that right?"

Amanda opened her mouth, but Jillian jumped in. "We're not sure where Stacey is. We brought breakfast to your sister to, you know, see how she's doing."

"We've searched the house, but she isn't here. The baby was alone, so we called Eth—Detective Harden." Amanda took several steps closer to Jillian.

"No, I don't believe that." Miss Peach gave a haughty sniff. "My sister would never leave her baby. If she's not here, something's happened to her."

"That's what I'm trying to determine." Ethan stepped between the angry woman and Amanda. "Could I please get on with my questions?"

Their visitor sank onto the sofa never taking her eyes off Jillian—and the baby.

"I understand, Detective."

"What's your name?" He opened his notebook.

"Deirdre Callaway, but I go by Didi. Stacey is my baby sister and little Bennie"—she pointed to the baby in Jillian's arms—"is my nephew." Her face softened as she gazed at the infant, but her tone remained cold.

"Could I see some identification, Ms. Callaway?"

She removed a Gucci wallet from her matching purse, handing Ethan her driver's license.

"You're from Louisiana." He leaned against the fireplace. "Can you prove the woman who lives in this house is your sister?"

Didi marched to the mantel. Reaching around Ethan's shoulder, she grabbed a picture frame with a wedding photo of Rick and Stacey. Standing next to the bride, wearing a pink bridesmaid dress, was Didi.

Amanda peeked over Ethan's shoulder. There in the middle of the photo, beaming at Rick, was his gorgeous bride. Amanda sucked in a breath as she realized she *had* met Stacey—the day she gave her a bouquet of tulips.

The mousy woman with the unwashed hair and baggy clothes was the beautiful bride in the picture. The bedraggled young mother from the flower shop was Rick's wife, and that baby was his son.

"Isn't that a beautiful picture? Daddy sure wasn't happy his little girl was marrying a Yankee, or that she was knocked up—his words, not mine. Look how he's gazing at her. There's no doubt in my mind that Rick was head over heels for my sister."

"When was the last time you spoke with her?" Ethan asked.

"Last night around eight o'clock. I called to check on her." Didi removed a tissue from her purse and dabbed at her eyes. "She was already having a tough time dealing with a newborn—doctor said it was postpartum depression—and now Rick's suicide. She blames herself, saying she must've done a bad job making him happy."

"No, that's not true. He didn't—"

Ethan cut Jillian off. "How did she seem when you spoke to her?"

"Tired. She's always tired. That's normal, or so I'm told, when you have an infant." She cast a sweet smile toward her nephew. "She's a good mother. There's no way she'd go anywhere without him."

Didi approached Jillian. "May I please hold Benjamin?" Her words asked, but the steely look in her eyes said she wouldn't take no for an answer. Jillian handed the baby to his aunt, who cradled him close, cooing to him.

Amanda shook her head.

Huh, I never would've guessed this woman has a soft side.

"Ms. Callaway, I'd like you to walk through the house with me. You might be able to tell us if anything has been disturbed or is missing."

"For you, Detective Harden, I'd be happy to."

As soon as they were out of earshot, Amanda snatched the wedding photo, shoving it at Jillian.

"Look at this. Does the bride look familiar to you?"

Jillian held the frame, looking at the smiling faces in the picture. "She's stunning. They look so happy. Wait." She pointed to the bride. "This is Stacey? She's the woman with the baby I saw outside The Corner Deli."

"She's also the woman who came into my shop—the one I gave the tulips." Amanda paced in front of the fireplace, frowning. "She's Rick's wife? I don't understand. The woman we met was so plain, but in the photo ... she's beautiful."

"Of course, it's her wedding day." Jillian fiddled with the empty bottle in her hand.

"Now she looks—I don't know—haggard." Amanda pursed her lips. "What happened to her?"

"Gee, Amanda. Let me see." Every one of Jillian's words oozed exasperation. "She's the mother of a new baby. She's exhausted from lack of sleep due to caring for that sweet little boy. She's been diagnosed with postpartum depression. Oh, and she recently found out her husband is dead. Doing her hair and makeup might not be at the top of her to-do list."

Jillian's voice had increased in volume during her tirade. Amanda closed the space between them in two steps.

"Lower your voice. Miss Peach will hear you."

"Too late." Ethan stood in the doorway.

Didi stood behind him, her face contorted in grief. "Yes, my sister let herself go since Bennie was born. She pours all her time and energy into caring for him. She's too exhausted to worry about herself. With Rick gone, I don't know how she'll get through this."

With a hard edge to her drawl, she turned to address Amanda. "By the way, you might want to change Miss Peach to Miss Magnolia. I'm from Louisiana, not Georgia. But all us Southerners must sound alike to you Yanks."

Ouch, the softer side was gone.

To be fair, though, Amanda deserved that.

"I'm sorry for—"

"I apologize if—"

Amanda and Jillian spoke at the same time. Didi held up a hand to stop them.

"I don't need your apologies." She pointed a well-manicured finger at Ethan. "I need you to find my sister."

"The Willow Springs police department will make it their top priority," he assured Didi.

"I don't like asking, but I could use help taking care of my nephew. I arrived in town only a few days ago. I start work on Monday, I haven't unpacked, and my place is a mess. I don't have much experience with babies, and don't know anyone here except my sister." Didi's eyes brimmed with tears.

For the first time, she exposed a vulnerable side, but was it genuine or just an act?

"We'd be happy to help," Jillian volunteered. "Isn't that right, Amanda?"

Oh sure, throw me to the wolves.

"Of course." Amanda swallowed around the lump in her throat. "Rick was a good friend. I'd like to help any way I can."

This time, her smile reached her eyes as Didi thanked them. "I do appreciate it. Stacey told me what a friendly town this is. She loves living here ..."

Didi's voice trailed off as a faraway look invaded her eyes. Amanda had a hunch she knew why.

The poor thing probably wondered if her sister would still love living here without Rick. Or whether Stacey was alive at all.

"Unfortunately, Ms. Callaway, until we have officially confirmed your identity and your relationship to this infant through the appropriate legal channels, Child Protective Services will take him into custody." Ethan's face looked strained. "I've put out a Missing Person Alert for Stacey, so law enforcement officials will be on the lookout for her. I need to knock on doors, see if the neighbors saw or heard anything."

Didi exploded. "What do you mean I can't watch my own nephew? This is ridiculous. I *am* his aunt."

"When that proves true, the baby could be returned to your custody or that of another family member while we search for Stacey. Until then, I'm sorry. The law is clear about this. Here—in case you need to get a hold of me." He handed her his business card. "I'll be in touch as soon as I have news for you."

"Thank you, Detective. I'm grateful for your help." Didi managed a weak smile, backing down faster than anyone expected.

The disappearance of her sister had taken the wind out of her sails. Who could blame her?

I'd be devastated if Jilly or Cate went missing.

After settling Benjamin in his bassinet for a nap, Jillian poured three glasses of iced tea she found in the refrigerator, while Amanda unpacked the goodies they'd brought. Jillian glanced at her watch.

Ten o'clock. Looks like we'll have brunch instead of breakfast.

She sent a quick text to Trixie, letting her know she'd be later than expected.

Amanda and Jillian sat at the kitchen table, nibbling the treats they'd brought for Stacey. The rhythmic ticking of the wall clock filled the silence. Didi cleared her throat.

"This food is delicious. Did you say it came from your sister's bakery?"

"Yes," Jillian said. "Cate owns Sugar & Spice over on Maple Avenue."

"I do believe I've gone by her shop on my morning runs." Didi smiled. "The shop looks darling. I'll have to go in one of these times."

Jillian noticed Didi picked at her food, breaking everything into smaller pieces but never eating a bite.

No wonder she's so thin. Runs every day and eats like a bird.

Jillian could learn a thing or two from their visitor, but not today.

She took a big bite of Becca's famous cinnamon swirl muffin.

"Ethan wasn't nearly as angry with us as I thought he'd be for barging in and searching for Stacey." Amanda helped herself to a slice of quiche. "I mean, how could we have known this was a possible crime scene?"

"Yeah, normally he'd yell at us about tainting evidence," Jillian explained to Didi. "This time he just reminded us to go to the station for fingerprinting—you know—to eliminate us as suspects."

"I suppose he meant me too." Didi sighed. "I'll do that this afternoon, but I could use your help with something right now." She ducked her head, looking at them through lowered lashes.

Was she serious? Demure and shy wasn't going to work on them.

Out with it, Miss Magnolia.

Amanda saved Jillian from allowing the caustic remark rattling in her head to fly from her mouth.

"We'd be happy to help. Tell us what we can do."

"As I mentioned when Detective Harden was here, I took a job in Willow Springs to be closer to my sister, and I start on Monday." More food was moved around on her plate. "Most of my belongings are in boxes at my rental. I've been unpacking a little each day. I don't have room for Bennie and all his things if he comes to stay with me. I don't really know much about taking care of babies ..."

She broke down, sobbing. Tears streamed down her face, yet her meticulously applied mascara stayed put.

Must be waterproof.

Amanda handed her a box of tissues. "Why don't you stay here—once Ethan verifies your identity? Benjamin can stay in his own home with all his things which will make caring for him easier for you."

"Oh, my goodness. Why didn't I think of that?" She dabbed at her tears. "I'll need to grab a few things from my place."

Make-up bag. Stylish wardrobe. All the things a girl needs to care for a baby.

Jillian mentally shook her head to dislodge these negative thoughts.

Why was she being so judgmental? Expensive clothes and cosmetics do not make the person. Maybe Didi would prove to be nice once they knew her better.

Jillian's eyes narrowed.

There was something off about this woman, but she couldn't put her finger on it.

While she'd been ensconced in her mental monologue, Amanda had offered to call Didi as soon as they had word from Ethan.

"Aren't you the sweetest thing?" she gushed. "I'm going to start packing a bag. Detective Harden should have word on me soon."

She grabbed her Gucci bag and rushed out the door, not even sparing a backward glance at her nephew.

Yep, definitely something off about her.

The antique clock in the living room chimed, drawing Jillian's attention to the time.

"Um, Amanda. I need to get to work, yet no one from Child Protective Services has come for the baby. Are you going to be all right here with Benjamin?" Jillian raised an eyebrow. "I mean—you weren't ready, willing, and able to hold him earlier. What if he cries? Or needs to be fed again? Or poops?"

Amanda's head jerked up. "Poop?"

"Yeah, babies poop sometimes." Jillian chuckled at the horrified look on her sister's face. "You'll have to change the diaper."

"I can't—stay, I mean." Amanda's head shook so hard, Jillian swore she could hear the marbles rattle. "Brianna opened the store for me, but I do need to go in and fill orders. We need a new plan."

Jillian threw up her hands. "Do you have any suggestions? I can't stay. The construction crew I hired to build the outdoor reading area is coming at noon. We can't take Benjamin anywhere—we have no car seat."

Amanda was saved from answering when someone called through the screen door. "Hello. Anyone home?"

CHAPTER TWENTY-ONE

Jillian glanced up at the woman who poked her head inside the room, taking in the oversized, gray University of Illinois sweatshirt, blue athletic shorts, and electric orange running shoes. A damp braid fell across her perspiring cheek and over the front of her shirt. Jillian's brow furrowed.

Another skinny, blonde jogger.

Let's hope this one doesn't come with a side of southern attitude.

"Hello." Jillian headed to the door. "Can I help—"

"Jen?" Amanda peeked around Jillian's shoulder.

"Amanda." The woman laughed. "What are you doing here?"

"I could ask you the same thing." Amanda smiled. "Come on in. Have a seat."

Questions raced through Jillian's mind.

Who was this woman?

How did Amanda know her?

Should they be inviting someone into Stacey's house?

"I was headed home from a run—I live next door." Jen pointed east. "I saw an unfamiliar car in the driveway. When I noticed the door was open, I stopped to make sure Stacey was okay. Are you friends of hers?"

"No, I wouldn't say friends." Amanda pursed her lips. "I knew Rick. He and I went—"

Jillian cleared her throat, hoping Amanda would get the hint and introduce her to their guest.

"Oh, I'm being rude." Amanda shook her head. "Jen, this is my sister, Jillian. Jilly, this is Jen Green. She and her partner, Babbs, have opened Yips & Clips, the dog grooming business next to the flower shop."

Jen gave a gentle shake of her head. "Uh-uh. We're a canine daycare and spa, catering to your pets' wellness and beauty needs."

"Ooh, I've heard great things about your place." Jillian smiled at Jen. "I'd love to bring my girls in for a day of pampering."

"Anytime." Jen dug around in her pockets, digging out the business card she hunted for. "I keep these with me whenever I go for a run. I bump into potential clients who're out walking their dogs." She handed it to Jillian. "Give us a call to schedule an appointment. We'll do our best to make you and your furry friends happy."

Bennie let out a loud wail from his bassinet, letting them know he needed attention. Jillian stared at Amanda, making no move toward the distressed infant.

"I'd better go get the little guy." Amanda spoke through gritted teeth, then stalked from the room.

"Besides checking out an unfamiliar car, what brings you to Stacey's this morning?" Jillian raised an eyebrow. "Are you two friends?"

Jen wrinkled her nose, followed by a deep sigh. "I thought so. In the short time Babbs and I have lived here, we've spent a good amount of time with Stacey—coffee at the kitchen table, cocktails on our back deck, things like that. Since the baby was born, things changed. She's become withdrawn, shut down—standoffish, if I'm being honest. We can't figure out what went wrong."

Jillian's amateur detective radar buzzed. Those were the exact words that had come to mind when she'd seen Stacey in front of the deli.

Amanda stepped back in the room, holding Bennie close. Jillian smiled.

See, big sister, you can do this.

"We've been worried about Stacey. Babbs and I check on her every day, trying to cheer her up, but nothing we've done seems to help." Jen absent-mindedly twirled her braid.

"Whoa, if your sparkling personality can't pull someone out of a blue mood, I don't know who could," Amanda said.

"You're here watching Benjamin. She must consider you friends." Jen nodded at the infant in Amanda's arms.

"I wouldn't use the word friend." Jillian winced, shaking her head. "We came to make a condolence visit and bring her food, but she's not home."

"What'd you mean, *not home*?" Jen's eyes widened. "She left the baby alone?"

"We've checked the entire house. She's nowhere to be found." Amanda handed the baby to Jillian.

"This little one was sound asleep in his mama's bedroom. Good thing he's too young to know he's been abandoned." Jillian stared into his innocent face.

"You mean ... wait ... you think Stacey isn't coming back for him?" Jen's face crumpled. "Rick bragged about what a good mother she was. How could she do this?"

"You and Rick were friends?" Jillian's radar went from buzzing to vibrating. "He talked to you about Stacey? Did he share anything else—anything we could use to find her?"

Or solve his murder.

"We talked all the time." Jen tucked a stray curl behind her ear. "Anytime he and I were outside, we'd stand at the fence and chat. He was a friendly, upbeat guy." Her face fell. "Hard to believe he committed suicide."

Amanda and Jillian exchanged an uncomfortable glance. Amanda shook her head at Jillian.

"Rick's death behind the flower shop has been a shock to everyone who knew him." Jillian took a deep breath, plunging headfirst into detective mode. "I'm sure you've heard about Amanda's troubles too. Have you or Babbs noticed anything odd—you know—since your shop is close to Blossoms & Blooms?"

"You sound like the detective who interviewed us after Rick's body was found." Jen tapped her finger to her chin. "Harden, I think, was his name. He asked a ton of questions—had we seen anyone suspicious hanging around, had we heard any strange noises, had there been any trouble at our store?"

"What did you tell him?" Jillian rocked the baby as she bounced on her toes.

"I had nothing to tell." Jen frowned. "Our store is closed on Mondays since we're open both days of the weekend. When we are open, there's a whole lot of noise." She grinned, cocking her head. "German shepherds, goldendoodles, and Boston terriers are not a quiet clientele."

Disappointment washed over Jillian. She'd hoped Jen might offer a fresh clue to these vandalism issues at Amanda's. As a sigh escaped Jillian's lips, Jen went on.

"I might not have seen anything at the shop, but there've been a few weird things here at Rick and Stacey's house."

The hairs on Jillian's arms stood on end.

"Weird things?" Amanda's voice cracked.

"Not with Rick, but with Stacey." An anxious look spread across Jen's face. "I feel bad gossiping like this, but since Stacey's missing ..." Her voice trailed off.

Jillian jumped in to encourage. "Go ahead, Jen. You can't call it gossip if it's true. Something you know might help find her."

"W-e-l-l ..." Jen dragged the word out, then chose to share. "Babbs and I have a new puppy—a sweet malamute we named Zoe. We take turns letting her out at night. We've seen Stacey outside many times in her pajamas."

"What's she doing?" Jillian asked. "They don't have a dog, do they?"

"We certainly haven't found evidence of one," Amanda said.

"No, no dog." Jen tilted her head to the side. "Sometimes she walks around in circles in the yard talking to herself. Other times, she stands there staring into the sky, dead still and silent. Some nights, she does this for hours."

"Oh, the poor woman." Amanda let out a shuddering breath. "She must be overwhelmed without Rick. Maybe she goes outside to breathe, take a pause from her life."

Jen shook her head. "This started before Rick died. He even came out once, put his arms around her, and walked her back inside. I don't think he saw me standing on our back porch. I tried to stay in the shadows. I didn't want either of them to be embarrassed or to think I was snooping."

"Stacey's sister mentioned she had postpartum depression. That might explain the strange behavior." Jillian turned to Amanda. "You and he talked. Did Rick mention anything to you?"

"Of course not. Why would he?" Amanda scowled at Jillian. "We weren't close enough to talk about personal things like that. We talked about flowers and whether the Cardinals would make the postseason. He showed me pictures of the baby—said they call him Bennie Boo. That's as personal as we became."

"I hope I haven't spoken out of turn. I don't want to become known as the neighborhood snitch," Jen said. "There was something upsetting about Stacey's behavior those nights we saw her in the yard—like she was in a trance or having some type of breakdown. Babbs and I were concerned, but we didn't know what to do about it."

"We won't know anything until she comes home." Jillian gave a firm nod. "Speaking of returning, shouldn't Didi be back by now?"

"Who's Didi?" Jen asked.

"Stacey's sister. She moved here from Louisiana for her job and to be closer to her family," Jillian said. "You haven't seen her around?" She moved to the mantle, grabbing the wedding photo to show Jen.

"Not here at the house, but I've seen this woman around town—she's hard to miss—at the bank, The Corner Deli, Henderson's Hardware." Jen paused, her eyes narrowing. "Wait a minute. I saw her standing in front of the flower shop Monday morning staring into your store."

"Yeah, we did too," Amanda said. "Jillian had helped me pull my Halloween window together. We were admiring our work when Didi walked by and complimented the display. We didn't know who she was then."

"Again, shouldn't she be back?" Jillian glanced at the clock on the wall above the fireplace. "She left over an hour ago. How long does it take to 'grab a few things' as she put it?"

"You've seen the woman. She's always dressed to the nth degree." Amanda rolled her eyes. "I'm sure it takes time to pack all those Jimmy Choos and Manolo Blahniks."

Jen curled her hands, clawing at the air. "Meow, ladies. I'm curious to meet the mystery sister, but I have to go. I promised Babbs I'd come in early—so many baths on the books today. Jillian, it was nice to meet you. Amanda, see you around." Jen shut the door on her way out.

"She's nice," Jillian said. "I can't wait to meet Babbs. We should invite them to our next girl's night."

"They'd bring a lot of fun to the evening." Amanda grabbed her purse from the recliner where she'd dropped it hours before.

"Whoa, where do you think you're going?" Jillian asked.

"I'm going to work. The flowers won't arrange themselves." Amanda had her hand on the knob.

"Don't walk out that door." Jillian's harsh tone stopped Amanda mid-stride. "Trixie's expecting me at the bookstore. When I called, I said I'd be late, not absent completely." She looked at the sleeping baby in her arms. "What are we going to do about Bennie?"

Amanda's somber mood improved when she stepped into her flower shop. She inhaled the familiar scents of jasmine and gardenia. The smell of honeysuckle and roses tickled her nose. She'd entered her happy place where all the wrongs in the world became right.

Well, not all of them.

Her stalker was still at large, and Rick was still gone.

However, she wasn't responsible for an infant she had no clue how to take care of. Jillian called Cate when Didi didn't return. She arrived in less than ten minutes and took charge. Her mom-gene was in hyperdrive. She promised to stay until Didi or Ethan, whom they'd also called, arrived at the house. They hadn't heard back from him yet. When they'd said goodbye, Cate was ensconced in the recliner, cuddling the baby, singing another Irish lullaby.

What kind of a mother leaves her child alone?

Although she hadn't ruled it out, Amanda had never given becoming a mother a lot of serious thought. Even so, she was confident she'd never abandon a child as Stacey had done.

Or had she?

While waiting for Didi, she and Jillian had discussed the possible reasons Stacey left. Their list included the pressure of motherhood, the inability to face a future without Rick, even some kind of mental breakdown—all plausible explanations for a mother running off without her baby. They'd also thought of a more sinister excuse.

Stacey could have been forced to leave without her baby.

They agreed this wasn't outside the realm of possibility. Whoever murdered Rick might have gone after her too. The question was why. Why would someone kill a floral supplier, then kidnap his wife? What could Rick and Stacey have done to incur someone's wrath?

While on the subject, what had she done to invite this same anger from her stalker?

Amanda inhaled again, attempting to shake off the negative thoughts making themselves at home in her head. She had no answers to any of these puzzles. Dwelling on them gave her a headache. Flowers—they would ease her stress and take her mind off unpleasant matters.

After receiving the morning update from Brianna before she left for class, Amanda tied on her green floral apron. She asked Alexa to play her favorite 70s radio station. The strains of Billy Joel's *Piano Man* filled the shop. She gathered an armful of gerbera daisies as she sang along.

The door jingled as she set the flowers on her workroom table, putting an end to her solo.

A teenager on crutches hobbled into the store. He grinned, raising his hand in hello.

"Tim." Amanda rushed forward. "Oh my gosh, how are you? Do you need to sit down? What can I get for you?"

"I'm good, Miss Amanda. I'm upright on this bum leg, yet downright handsome." He ducked his head, blushing a light shade of pink. "I'm trying out that line for the ladies—you know—for when I go back to school, and they ask how I'm doing. What'd ya think?"

"Tim, you're a great guy. You don't need a cheesy line to get girls to like you. Be yourself. They'll flock to you like geese to Magnolia Pond."

"You think so?" Tim grinned, the dimple in his right cheek becoming more pronounced.

"Yes, I do." Amanda pulled a handful of hydrangeas from the cooler. "Come sit with me while I work. We can talk about what brought you here." She laid her second load of flowers on the table before grabbing a Coke from the fridge. She slid it in front of Tim, who'd perched carefully on a stool.

Tim cracked open the can. He took a long swig followed by a loud belch. "Oops, 'scuse me."

Amanda rolled her eyes in his direction. A sheepish smile crept across his face.

"Have some cookies. Leftovers from Cate's bakery."

Tim grabbed a handful. He popped the first two into his mouth whole, letting the crumbs fall where they may.

Amanda cringed.

Were all teenage boys this crude?

"What brings you here today, Tim? You're in no shape to work, so there must be something important on your mind." She snipped the ends off some purple irises.

"Doctor says I'm on crutches for the next six weeks which means no driving. My mom dropped me off this morning while she stopped in the bank." Tim finished his other two cookies before he continued. "I'm real sorry I won't be able to help you out for a while. I'm hoping ... I mean ... I'd like ... I was wondering ..."

"Tim, relax." Amanda placed the first flowers into the vase as she started the arrangement. "What do you need?"

"Well, you know I appreciate you giving me a part-time job that works around my school commitments."

"Sure. Go on."

"My injuries will keep me from working ... I'm real sorry about that" He was stalling for time or courage. "I hope it doesn't put you in a bind."

Amanda waved her shears in a circle, urging him to continue. She cut lengths from the stems of three pink tulips before adding them to the bouquet. "Keep going."

"I was hoping you'd keep my job open for me because I like working here and you're a great boss and I need this job because I'm saving to buy a car but I'll understand if you have to hire someone else." He ran out of breath.

Amanda raised an eyebrow. "How long did you rehearse your plea?"

"Was it obvious?"

His mortified look touched her heart.

"Maybe a little." She smiled at the young man's discomfort. "Don't worry. Your job is safe—it will still be here after you heal. I'll do my best to manage without you in the meantime, but it won't be easy."

Tim hobbled over on one crutch and hugged her. "Thanks, Miss Amanda. You're the best." He snatched two more cookies along with his remaining crutch. He headed from the room, then stopped, taking a few steps back.

"Did you forget something?" Amanda arranged the last of the tulips.

The teen stared at the floor, scuffing the toe of one sneaker. He wouldn't make eye contact.

"Tim."

"Please don't be mad at me, Miss Amanda." The boy raised his head. She saw tears pooling in his eyes.

"Why don't you tell me what has you upset? I promise I won't be angry."

He swiped at his eyes. "The day of my accident when the van ran me off the road ..."

"Yes." Amanda's heart skipped a beat.

"Well, the van came alongside me, speeding fast." He took a deep breath. "I thought it was a buddy of mine wanting to play chicken with me. Us kids do that sometimes down by Douglas Farm."

Amanda nodded, remembering the times she'd done the same thing in her dad's car.

Nice to know some stupid teenage traditions don't change.

"I sped up, so did the van. We went back and forth for about a mile. Then, she came at me hard, hit the delivery van a couple times. I lost control—headed straight toward the ditch. As I spun out, I was able to see the other van's license plate—first three letters were BLR."

"That's great, Tim." Amanda patted his shoulder. "Not the racing part but seeing the plate. Did you tell this to the police?"

He hung his head. "No, ma'am. I thought I'd be in big trouble for playing chicken in your delivery van. Maybe they'd blame me for the accident."

In a wave of maternal instinct, Amanda put her arms around the forlorn teen. "The van rammed into you, over and over. There's no doubt in anyone's mind that driver is at fault." His shoulders relaxed under her touch. "I have to call Detective Harden. You know that, right?"

"Yes, ma'am. I need to tell the whole story—get it off my chest." Tim released his breath in a whispered whoosh. "Do you think he'd come to the shop to talk? I'd like for you to be here too."

She grabbed the cell from her apron's pocket. "He'll be fine with that."

"I'll let my mom know I'm going to need some more time."

Amanda and Tim both startled at a loud thump on the alley door.

"What the heck—oops, sorry. Dad told me never to swear in front of ladies."

Amanda waved away his offense. "No worries. I slip sometimes too."

"I'll check out the noise." The teen struggled to open the heavy metal door while maneuvering his crutches.

"Why don't you let me take care of it?" Amanda pushed the door open. She stepped into the alley right on top of a scattering of yellow carnations.

CHAPTER TWENTY-TWO

Amanda worked on her third bouquet of the day as Ethan listened to Tim's unedited version of the accident. She prayed he wouldn't be too hard on the poor kid. He'd beaten himself up over this enough already.

Ethan surprised her when he gave a half smile and patted the boy's clenched hands. "Thanks for coming forward with this info, Tim. This clue might break the case wide open."

"Really?" The teenager straightened in his seat. "Do you mean I might have helped you find the stalker and vandal? That'd be awesome, wouldn't it, Miss Amanda?"

"I'd like nothing more." Amanda sighed. "Tim, could you give Detective Harden and me a minute?"

"You're going to show him the note, aren't you?" At her nod, Tim hopped off his stool, grabbing his crutches. "I'll go out front—answer the phone if it rings—if that's okay?"

"Perfect." Amanda watched him hobble away.

What a great kid.

With such a kind heart.

"Took guts for him to come forward." Ethan scratched his head. "Now, what's this about another note?"

"After someone banged on the door, I walked out and found it taped to the alley door along with those pesky flowers you already saw. I know I shouldn't have touched the note, but it had begun raining ..." Amanda waited for Ethan to pull on his gloves. "I don't have the courage Tim does—couldn't bring myself to read it."

Ethan held the note between two fingers, taking care as he opened it.

Flowers are lovely, but they'll die on the vine.
Don't think you can keep me from getting what's mine.

Amanda sucked in a loud breath. "She thinks I'm keeping something from her? I have no idea what it would be."

"We're not dealing with a stable person, Amanda." Ethan refolded the note, placing it in the plastic baggie Amanda grabbed from her supply closet. "She or he—I'm not convinced of gender yet—*believes* you have something. Doesn't mean it's true."

"This means she's not finished with me." Amanda added some leatherleaf fern to the vase full of flowers. "I'd hoped this would all be over before Cate's party tomorrow. I wouldn't put it past this nut job to try something there."

"I don't know about you, but this copycat poet is on my last nerve. We will catch them."

"What do you mean copycat?" Worry lines broke out on Amanda's forehead.

"You remember last year when Jillian's teacher friend was killed. They used this kind of rhyming note to threaten her." Ethan took his car keys from his pocket. "Feels like your wordsmith is copying someone else's playbook."

Amanda gaped at him. "I hadn't thought of that."

"At least we can be sure it's not the same person—everyone involved with that case is either dead or locked up in prison. I checked." Ethan zipped up his jacket. "You keep on with the prep work for the party. I'll work on putting this case to bed."

"Thanks, Ethan." Amanda hugged him. "Jilly and I have a lot to do before the party. I'll try not to worry and let you handle the detective work."

"Could you convince your sister to do that too?"

"No guarantees. Her Agatha Christie gene will activate the minute she hears about this note."

"Great, can't wait." Ethan pointed to the front room. "I told Tim's mom I'd give him a ride home. Call me if you need anything." He stopped at the door. "You might want to talk to Cate. She has some interesting news."

"Wait. How do you know Cate—?"

The screen door slammed shut. Ethan was gone.

Such an irritating man sometimes.

Jillian sat in the backroom of McGuire's, waiting for Amanda and Becca. They would have an early dinner while going over the checklist for Cate's surprise party. She wanted everything to be perfect for her sister's birthday, but a persistent fear tugged at the edges of her mind. Jillian's worries didn't lie with playlists and appetizers, but with the looming threat from Amanda's deranged stalker.

Becca arrived first, all smiles. "Hey, bestie. How's your day been?"

"Not as good as yours from the look on your face." Jillian wrinkled her nose. "What's going on with you?"

"I have some good—"

Her good whatever was interrupted when Amanda swooped in and plopped in a chair. "I just finished a call with Cate. You're not going to believe what she told me."

She took a huge drink from the Diet Coke sitting on the table, then pointed to the glass. "Thanks for this."

"Don't tell us one of the girls is sick, and Cate's not coming to her own party." Jillian steepled her hands in prayer.

"You mean Trivia Night." Becca's face lit up with a conspiratorial grin. "Isn't that the ruse to get her here?"

"Yes, yes, it is." Jillian faced Amanda. "What did Cate tell you?"

"Didi never came back for Benjamin." She paused as her words sunk in. "Can you believe it?"

Jillian sat open-mouthed while Becca filled the silence.

"Who does this? Two sisters abandon the same baby on the same day—unbelievable."

"Wait, how do you know—"

"I had lunch with Ethan. He told me about his morning." Becca signaled to the waitress, who rushed over. "I'd like a Sprite, and we'll share one of Max's fabulous appetizer platters. Thanks."

Jillian finally found her voice. "What's going to happen to Benjamin? I assume they'll place him in a foster home until all this madness can be sorted out."

"Already has been." Amanda's sly smile didn't go unnoticed.

"What's with that goofy face?" Jillian asked. "You know something else, don't you?"

"Yeah, Amanda. What's going on?" Becca tilted her head. "Ethan says it usually takes up to a week to find a placement."

"Not when a licensed foster parent was caring for the child when the caseworker arrived." Amanda clapped her hands.

"No way," Jillian squealed. "Cate and Wes are going to be Bennie's foster parents?"

Amanda nodded. "You should've heard her. She's so excited—rattled on about the things she needed to dig out of storage to throw together a nursery."

"Aw, Cate's such a great mom. She'll take such good care of—what's with the face, Jilly?" Becca frowned at her.

"Face? No face."

"Liar." Becca and Amanda echoed the same word.

"Out with it," Amanda demanded.

"I'm excited for her. We all know how much Cate loves kids, but this whole foster care thing worries me." Jillian toyed with the rim of her iced tea glass. "You know how attached Cate gets. She's planning his nursery, for heaven's sake. What happens when Stacey or Didi come home and take him back?"

Becca blew a raspberry. "They both *left* him. No judge in their right mind would give him back to either one of them."

"Not right away, but the courts want kids with their biological parents when at all possible." Jillian had dealt with custody cases as a teacher.

"Cate and Wes are aware foster placements are temporary." Amanda came to Cate's defense. "They've been through the training. She wants to help kids in need— even if it's for a short period."

Jillian chewed on her bottom lip. "Have you forgotten Christopher?"

The waitress returned with Becca's drink and their appetizer platter. The smell of melting cheese, spicy BBQ sauce, and roasted garlic tickled their noses. Amanda and Jillian reached for a small plate, but Becca's appetite for gossip was stronger than her hunger for food.

"He was the cute toddler with red hair and freckles, wasn't he?" She took a sip from her glass. "I don't think I ever heard the whole story about him."

"We didn't talk about it for the longest time." Amanda winced. "Didn't want to upset Cate."

"Christopher was a foster they had before the girls were born. You and I were away at college." Jillian dipped her mozzarella stick into the marinara sauce.

"Right, I remember. What happened to him?" Becca reached for a wing.

"After nine months with Cate and Wes, the judge gave him back to his parents. They moved out of state to be near family who could help raise him."

"That's great. The system worked." Becca shrugged.

"His leaving devastated Cate. She'd become too attached. Since they didn't think they could have kids of their own, she'd dared hope they could adopt Christopher." Jillian could still remember how long Cate took to recover.

"She didn't get out of bed for days, wouldn't go to work. Mom and Dad kept Sugar & Spice open. Wes tried everything—flowers, evenings with friends, even a trip to Mexico." Jillian reached for a couple of stuffed mushrooms. "She'd been back to the bakery two days when she found out she was pregnant with Laney."

"You're worried she'll get attached to Benjamin like she did Christopher." Becca nodded. "Makes sense."

"Time will tell," Amanda said. "Maybe they'll find Stacey or Didi before that happens."

The waitress came to take their meal orders. While they waited for their food, Jillian started their meeting.

"Travis and I stashed the decorations, balloons, helium tank, and party favors in Bryan's office." Jillian ticked the items off on her fingers. "The tribute video of Cate's life is saved on my laptop—I'll bring it to the party tomorrow."

"I'll finish the last of the floral arrangements in the morning, including Cate's corsage." Amanda rubbed her hands together. "The flowers are spectacular—if I do say so myself—despite having to change my designs at the last minute, thanks to the jerk who canceled my original order."

Jillian heard the resentment in Amanda's voice.

She's not ready to let that one go. Can't say as I blame her.

"Max let me put the cake tiers in the refrigerator here. He even cleared space for me to finish decorating it." Becca eyed the kitchen door. "I think this means he loves me."

"I can't believe he's letting you in his kitchen. He's getting soft, but don't tell him I said that." Amanda grinned.

"Back to the party, you two. Wes will bring Cate at seven fifteen since she—"

Amanda cut in. "Um, Cate told me she'll be bringing Benjamin to Trivia Night. She doesn't want to impose on the sitter. Three kids can be a handful."

"That's great. There'll be plenty of arms to hold him, so Cate can have fun," Jillian said.

"Sounds like we have everything under control." Becca popped a mushroom into her mouth.

"Sure does," Amanda said. "I'll even take a turn or two with the baby."

"You?" Jillian's eyes widened. "You never hold babies— makes you nervous, you've said."

Amanda shrugged one shoulder. "Who knows how long Benjamin will be with Cate and Wes, but at least for now, he's part of our family. I will be as good an auntie to him as I am to Laney and Aubrey."

"You're great with them." Jillian smiled. "They love spending time with you working on all those craft projects."

Becca cleared her throat. "I'll help with the little guy this evening too. I do need the practice."

"Do you mean—?"

"Are you—?"

"I am." Becca giggled, then clamped a hand over her mouth.

The shrieks erupting from the backroom could be heard out front.

Amanda's headlights cut a swath through the darkness as she made her way home. She'd been delighted when Sam dropped her car off at McGuire's tonight. The body shop had done a fantastic job getting rid of the graffiti.

Listening to her current favorite podcast, she gave herself permission to forget all the negativity. On her drive home, she'd focus on the positive.

Life was good. She was in love with Sam. Her home remodel was almost finished. Poppy had come into her life. Blossoms & Blooms was showing a tidy profit this quarter.

"I'm not the only one whose life is coming together." Amanda spoke aloud into the darkness. "Jilly's settled in at the bookstore and in love with a great guy. Cate has a little one to look after, and Becca is expecting."

Things would be even better when her stalker and Rick's killer were in jail.

One of the podcast hosts shared little-known facts about the Statue of Liberty. Her attention returned to the show as he cracked a joke. Amanda laughed out loud as she signaled her left turn onto Cambridge Road, the last leg of her drive home.

A pair of headlights shone through the rear window, casting blinding lights in her eyes. She raised her hand against the glare, then adjusted the rearview mirror. The car behind sped up until it was riding her bumper. Amanda's heart raced. She moved over as far as she could, hoping they'd pass. The car stayed on her tail. When the car stuck to her like glue no matter what she did, Amanda knew who was behind the wheel of that car.

She put her foot on the accelerator, going from fifty to sixty miles an hour. The other car did the same. She hated going this fast on a dark road, but she had no choice. Amanda sped up even more. The other car kept pace as her speedometer read sixty-five, then seventy. Her pulse pounded in her head. Her mouth went dry.

Her last lucid thought was to call Ethan for help.

She wouldn't get the chance. The car tapped her—not hard—twice. Amanda tightened her grip on the wheel as it sped up and pulled alongside her. The car swerved into her lane, slamming into her from behind.

Everything happened fast. Her car lurched to the right onto the gravel shoulder. The other car slowed, pulled in behind her, and struck again, harder this time. Amanda spun out toward the ditch. As her head whipped around, she glimpsed the other car—a white van. This was the last thing she saw before the outcropping of boulders came into view in front of her.

CHAPTER TWENTY-THREE

Uh-uh, it's not going to end like this. Not today.

Amanda tightened her grip on the steering wheel, giving it a sharp jerk to the left. The car fought the sudden change in direction but obeyed. The right side of the car fishtailed into the pile of rocks. The rear window exploded, pelting her with glass shards. She squeezed her eyes shut. The scraping of steel on rock assaulted her ears. The car shuddered to a stop. Amanda lifted a shaky foot from the brake and put the car in park.

She rested her head on the steering wheel without letting go of it. A strangled sob escaped her pinched lips. She slowed her breathing to quiet her racing heartbeat.

Calm down. Breathe. You're alive. No major injuries.

She talked herself through the worst of her nerves. After a few minutes, she was steady enough to step out of the car and take in the scene around her. The back of the car rested on top of a pile of smaller boulders, the rear right panel ripped clean off. The entire wheel well bent inward.

So much for the bodywork she'd just had done.

A trail of plastic and metal lay scattered across the skid marks in the gravel and grass. One thing was missing.

The other car? The van hadn't stuck around to see what happened.

A police car screeched to a stop on the shoulder. A young cop in a starched blue uniform stepped out making his way toward her.

"Hello, Officer."

"Ma'am." He tipped his hat. "I'm Officer Hendricks. An ambulance is on the way. Come sit in my car until it arrives."

"No, thank you." Amanda pointed to her car. "Rear end collision—airbags didn't even deploy. I'm fine."

"Still. You could have injuries we can't see." He motioned toward his squad car. "Let's move away from the wreck."

"How did you know I was here—that there'd been an accident?" She squinted her eyes at him, suspicions floating through her head. At this point, she didn't know who she could trust.

"On-Star detected the accident, then notified local authorities of your location. I was the closest unit. Would you please sit in my squad car until the ambulance arrives?" He headed for his car, glancing over his shoulder to make sure she followed.

"I don't need an ambulance." Sirens could be heard in the distance.

"Detective Harden told me you'd say that." Officer Hendricks opened the front passenger door. "He told me, and I quote, '*Don't take no for an answer or I'll have your badge.*'"

"He can't do that—take your badge—if I refuse the ambulance."

"I'd rather not find out, ma'am." The officer's face paled.

Detective Harden, you play dirty.

Amanda slipped into the passenger seat of the squad car. The warmth from the heater did nothing to chase away the chill in her bones.

Amanda sat on a hard bed in the emergency department, shivering in the hospital gown a gruff nurse had insisted she wear.

"Your clothes are covered with bits of glass, young lady," the nurse said. "I'll put them in a bag. You can have them laundered." She whisked away Amanda's things.

The privacy curtain was wrenched open. Ethan, Sam, and Jillian rushed to her bedside.

"Are you okay?" Jillian gave her a tentative hug.

"You scared us to death—glad to see you in one piece." Ethan patted her on the back. "When you're ready, I'll need to ask you some questions."

Sam said nothing. He hung back until the others had checked on Amanda. When she looked up, their eyes met. He moved to sit on the side of the bed, drawing her into his arms. Sam placed his forehead against hers. His tenderness was her unraveling. The tears she'd held at bay since her car crashed into the rocks fell unchecked, spotting the scratchy sheet drawn across her naked legs.

Everyone remained quiet as she sobbed. Amanda was aware all eyes were on her.

When her hot tears had run dry, she patted Sam's arm. He loosened his grip and sat back, wiping the last tear from her face, replacing it with a kiss.

"Love you," he said.

"Love you more." She squeezed his hand.

Jillian cleared her throat. "You never answered my question. Are you okay?"

"Yes, I'm fine. The doctor said just some bumps, bruises, and scratches—no serious injuries." Amanda scrunched her face. "The nurse tells me it won't be pleasant when they pick the glass out of my scalp, though."

Her visitors all sucked in their breath. They could imagine how awful the experience would be. Amanda laughed at their grimaces.

"Relax. Mom always says I'm the hardheaded one in the family. That should help, right?"

The same brusque nurse returned with a tray of ominous-looking tools. "This might take a while, so everyone out. I'll let you know when we're finished." She dismissed them without argument. "Doctor will release her when I'm done."

"Go. Get some coffee," Amanda said. "Just don't forget about me."

Jillian and Ethan stepped into the hallway.

Sam leaned in and whispered, "You, babe, are unforgettable." He kissed her so she felt it down to her toes. "See you soon."

Amanda was home, settled on her couch after being tortured by the ER nurse. She sipped the hot chocolate Jillian made and stroked Poppy's soft fur. Leaning into Sam, she let go of a tired sigh followed by a yawn.

"I know you're wiped out, but could I ask a few questions?" Ethan sat in a chair across from her. "Then, I'll leave you to get some rest."

"Ask away," Amanda said.

"Try to make it quick." Sam put his arm around her shoulders.

"No problem," Ethan said. "Can you describe the other car?"

"A white delivery van, no logo of any kind." She fiddled with the fringe on the afghan stretched across her lap. "I couldn't see the driver or the license plate. Everything happened too fast."

"Walk me through the accident from the beginning." Ethan prepared to take notes on his iPad. "I hate this thing, but the department says my notebook is an outdated way to take notes."

Amanda recounted each nerve-wracking moment to her stunned audience. When she finished, the silence was palpable.

"Oh my gosh, Amanda," Jillian burst out. "You're lucky to be sitting here. If not for your quick thinking and stellar driving abilities, you might be—"

"Don't say it," Sam growled. He stood to pace the length of the room. "She's here. With only minor injuries. Her car can be fixed. All good."

"I don't know if I'd say it's all good." Jillian took a drink of her hot cocoa. "There's still a crazy person out there who has it in for her."

"I'll find the driver, Amanda." Ethan reached over and squeezed her hand. "I promise this will be over soon."

"Until then, maybe we should take—"

"Stop!" Sam's bellow cut off Jillian. "We're aware of the situation, but do we have to keep harping on it? She will not be out of my sight from now until her stalker is behind bars. I'll make sure nothing more happens."

"Excuse me." Amanda straightened her shoulders. "I'm sitting right here. Do I have a say in any of this?"

"No." Sam's answer was clipped.

"Hmm. Well, I'm not sure I'm good with that." Amanda stood to face off with him while Ethan and Jillian looked on. "I'm a grown woman who can take care of herself. I proved that tonight. I appreciate your concern, babe, really, I do, but we all have lives to lead. You can't be stuck to me like glue for—who knows how long."

"I can and *will* be with you twenty-four-seven for as long as it takes Ethan to solve this case. I'm not budging on this, Amanda." Sam crossed his arms over his chest.

"Be reasonable." She shook her head. "You have work. I have work. There's Cate's party—"

"Forget the party," Sam shouted. "I'm not letting you go to a crowded bar where this wacko could try something."

"You're not *letting* me go." Her voice quivered, rising in volume. "You must have me mistaken for someone else. I don't need your permission to go. Nor do I intend to ask for it. I'll go where I want when I want. If you don't like it—too bad."

Jillian and Ethan's heads swung back and forth from Sam to Amanda like they watched a tennis match. Jillian's eyes were wide. Ethan's face said he'd rather be anywhere but here.

"Amanda, please." Sam put his hands on her upper arms. "You could have been killed tonight. You were lucky this time, but who's to say what will happen next time?"

"There will be a next time, Amanda," Ethan said. "Your stalker will try to finish the job they started."

"You don't think I know she'll come at me again?" Amanda shook her fists in the air. "I'm not an idiot."

"No one is saying you are, sweetie." Jillian's tone oozed with concern. "We—all of us—want to keep you safe. Tonight was too close for comfort. Please let us help you."

Amanda's first reaction was to explode, unleashing her anger and frustration on them, but she'd be directing her feelings at the wrong people. That wouldn't be fair. She sank back onto the couch.

Sam joined her there. Sensing her presence was needed, Poppy crawled onto their laps.

"I'm sorry." She pressed a hand to Sam's chest. "Really, really sorry. I shouldn't have lashed out at you—any of you."

"We love you, babe." Sam placed his hand over hers. "None of us want to imagine life without you."

"If I agree to be guarded, I do have a couple of conditions." She peered at the three of them.

"I'm going to need to hear your conditions before I'll agree to them." Sam raised an eyebrow.

"Me too," Jillian said.

"If you're sharing them with me, make sure they're legal." Ethan's humor lifted the mood.

"First, whoever is with me has to stay out of my way. I won't have my daily routine interrupted by a well-intentioned bodyguard." She ticked off these demands on her fingers.

"Number two, I will not change any of my plans—including Cate's party. This person won't bully me or have control of my life. Can you agree to these demands?"

"Demands? You make it sound like a hostage negotiation." Ethan again laughed at his joke.

"You're forcing me to be under protective custody, aren't you? Sounds like a hostage to me."

"Do you think we enjoy this?" Sam's cheeks were red. "When Ethan called to tell me you'd been in a car accident, I thought—" He choked on his words. His voice came out in a strangled whisper. "I thought I'd lost you."

"Oh, Sam." Amanda pulled him into her arms. "I'm sorry. I didn't think."

They stayed wrapped in each other's embrace. Quiet sobs broke the silence.

Jillian nudged Ethan. "We're going to leave. I'll call you later, Amanda." She pushed Ethan toward the door.

Amanda waved to them over Sam's shoulder, watching them make a hasty retreat.

They were alone, holding one another. When Sam broke contact and pulled back to look at her, his eyes were red-rimmed.

Her heart broke and soared at the same time. This wonderful man loved her—completely and unconditionally. She loved him back with her whole heart. This was the kind of love she never thought she needed but thanked God she'd found. She wanted it all—marriage, kids, the happy ending—and she wanted it with Sam. At that moment, Amanda prayed they'd be together always.

He drew her close again, kissing her until she couldn't think straight. She returned his kisses with every ounce of passion she possessed. Sam finally broke the kiss, creating enough space between them that he could place both hands on the sides of her face. His smile lit his soft blue eyes.

"I love you, Amanda. More than you know." Those words were music to her ears. "I can't imagine life without you. I want to be with you until I take my last breath."

Sam took a small box from his pocket.

Amanda's hands flew to her mouth, a tiny gasp escaping her lips.

"This isn't the way I'd planned, but I'm not waiting any longer." He dropped to one knee. "Amanda, will you—"

The door burst open. Aunt Grace rushed in. "I stopped to check on—oops, I've interrupted something important. Oh, my stars, are you proposing to Amanda?"

"Not now," Sam grumbled, getting to his feet.

"Do you know how to knock?" Amanda glared at her aunt.

"I would've, Pumpkin, but ... well ... I was flustered by a vision—of you—in danger. I rushed over to warn you." Grace twisted the gold bangles at her wrist. "When I turned onto your street, there it was."

"What?" Amanda and Sam asked.

"You should look for yourselves—in front of your house."

Sam put his hand on the small of Amanda's back, ushering her to the window. A warm tingle under his hand sent her heart racing.

Don't forget where we were, Sailor. Aunt Grace can't stay forever.

Her musings were cut short by Sam's curses.

CHAPTER TWENTY-FOUR

Amanda stared out the front window.

No. No way. This can't be real.

She blinked several times, hoping to erase the scene in front of her. Nope, still there.

Sam's arm snaked around her waist. They stood staring at the dented white van parked half in the street and half in the grass, a testament to the driver's haste to get away.

"I don't understand," she whispered. "Why bring the van to my house?"

"Must be part of her sick game." Sam tightened his grip. "I'm calling Ethan. If this van wasn't here when he and Jillian left, the stalker hasn't been gone long and could still be nearby."

Amanda stole a glance at her aunt. Grace's eyes were closed, her arms slack at her sides. A low moan issued from her lips. Without warning, her head jerked forward, then back. Her eyes flew open. Her blank gaze focused out the window.

"You won't find her today," Grace muttered. "She wanted you to see what she's capable of, how close she can get to you."

Amanda reached out to touch her aunt's arm, but Sam stopped her. He put his finger to his lips.

"Wait. Let's see what else she says," he whispered.

Another jerk of the head. Grace continued. "She's angry you have him. She won't stop until she gets him back. It will happen soon. There will be flowers." She fell silent. Her body went limp. Sam caught her before she hit the floor.

They helped Grace to the couch, putting a pillow under her head. Amanda fanned her face with a magazine while Sam went to the kitchen for a cool cloth. After he placed it on her forehead, it took only a few seconds for her eyes to flutter open. Her focus landed on Amanda.

"Pumpkin, I'm sorry." Grace grasped her niece's hand. "I hope I didn't frighten you."

"Not me," Amanda said. "You might have scared Sam, though." Her attempt to make her aunt smile failed.

"Don't tease. This woman is crazy, filled with rage." She tightened her hold. "She wants him back. She'll kill you to get him."

"You said she wants *him* back. Who is he?" Amanda studied her aunt's worried face.

"I'm not sure. The picture is fuzzy, but I see blue eyes." Aunt Grace's voice trembled. "I assume she means you." She pointed at Sam.

"I can't believe this is about me." Sam swallowed hard. "I don't know anyone from my past capable of something like this."

Ethan and Jillian had made it across town when Sam's call came through. Ethan made a U-turn on Sweetwater in front of Whimsy & Wonder and sped back to Amanda's. Jillian was glad to be wearing her seatbelt.

"Sam sounded freaked out, didn't he?" Jillian said. "Wish he'd stayed on the line to give us more information."

"He knew we hadn't gone far." He signaled the left turn onto Amanda's street. Halfway down the block, her house came into view. "We'll find out what's—"

The sight of the battered white van in the yard ended his sentence.

"I can see why Sam called us in a panic," Jillian said.

Ethan parked his cruiser in front of the house next door. He radioed dispatch for a tech team. "Tell them to bring a couple of portable floodlights."

"What are those for?" Jillian climbed from the squad car.

"How else will they find evidence in the dark?" He slammed his door. "Amanda's exterior lighting—while nice—won't help the techs much. I don't want them to miss something and have this fruitcake slip through our fingers."

Amanda, Sam, and Aunt Grace waited for them on the porch. Poppy's howls from inside the house expressed her displeasure at missing out on the action. A cluster of neighbors gathered across the street.

"Cop cars with flashing lights—an automatic crowd magnet. Going to need some of this to hold them at bay." Ethan reached into the back seat, grabbing a roll of yellow crime scene tape. He began wrapping it around the nearest tree.

"Go stand with Amanda on the porch. I need to do a quick search of the van."

Jillian ignored his instructions, choosing instead to stand off to the side, out of his line of sight. Ethan attached a body camera to his jacket. Then, he grabbed a pair of latex gloves from his tactical kit and pulled them on. Approaching the van, he switched on his camera and the

Maglite he carried. The bright shaft of light sliced through the dark, landing on the driver's seat.

"Keys are still in it." He jiggled the door handle which gave way in his hand. "The door's unlocked." He swept the beam around the cab. Jillian crept up behind Ethan to get a quick peek, despite his previous directions to stay back.

"Amanda's stalker is a slob." A jumble of fast-food wrappers, empty soda cans, and loose papers were scattered over the seats and floor. "Looks like she was living in her van."

Ethan's jaw tightened. He spoke in a guttural whisper. "I thought I told you to wait on the porch."

"Did you? I guess I didn't hear."

"Sure. That's one excuse."

A pair of headlights illuminated Amanda's yard.

"Good, the tech team is here. They'll have to sort through all this trash." Ethan shoved a roll of yellow crime tape into Jillian's hands. "Since you're set on helping, wait and give them this, will you? I'm going to check out the back." He shoved the roll into her hands. Without waiting for an answer, he stalked off.

Jillian wouldn't be pushed aside. She moved stealthily behind Ethan, the yellow tape trailing behind her. She motioned for Amanda, Sam, and Aunt Grace to join her. As they approached, a finger to her lips cautioned them not to alert Ethan.

He tested the back doors. Unlocked but dented, it took a few hard yanks to wrench them wide open.

A grisly sight awaited their peering eyes.

A woman's body lay face down in a pool of blood. Her hair fanned out like a halo around her head. Ethan checked for a pulse.

"Is she ... dead?" He spun around at Jillian's unexpected voice in his ear.

"I told you to stay back." He scowled at their little group. "All of you need to move out of the way."

"Is she dead?" Jillian persisted.

"Yes, she's gone." He snatched the roll of tape from her hand, tossing it to the nearest tech. "Hey, Esposito. This van might have been used in an attempted vehicular manslaughter case. I also have a DB in back. String this tape in a wide circle around this area to keep the gawkers away—including these four." He jerked his head toward Jillian and the others.

"Sure thing, Detective." Esposito and another man grabbed thin wooden stakes from their van and set to work.

Before her access was cut off, Jillian edged closer. "Are those yellow carnations scattered around her body?"

"There will be flowers," Amanda mumbled, moving in to get a look. "Like in Aunt Grace's last vision."

"Who is she?" Sam asked. "The dead woman—do we know her?"

Ethan put out an arm and pushed Jillian aside. "Maybe I could make an identification if *someone* would let me do my job."

"Relax, Detective." She made a show of taking several steps back. "I—we—need to know. Amanda and Sam deserve answers."

"If I were left alone, I might be able to get them some," he muttered.

Amanda yanked on Jillian's sleeve. "Let him work so he can find out who she is."

Struggling against her sister's grip, Jillian strained to see into the van. "You saw the blonde hair, didn't you? Is that—"

Ethan rolled the body over. The woman's face came into view.

Jillian gasped. "Stacey."

Amanda's voice came out in a strangled whisper. "We thought she abandoned her baby, but it's not true. Someone murdered her."

Aunt Grace inched beside her. "Are you sure she was murdered?"

Ethan pointed at the body. "She's bound and gagged with a bullet hole in her forehead."

"This cannot be happening." Amanda stumbled backward. "Rick *and* Stacey murdered within days of each other. Why? Their sweet baby boy will grow up without his parents." She wiped away a tear.

Aunt Grace placed the palm of her hand on the door of the van. Her breathing became shallow. "Her aura is deep red with splashes of black. She has no soul. She won't stop unless you—" she jerked a thumb at Jillian—"do something."

"Me?" Jillian's voice cracked. "Why me?"

"That's how it has to be." Aunt Grace closed her eyes.

"Let's go inside—give Ethan some space." Sam herded the women onto the porch. "When he's finished, I'll take everyone out for a late-night supper. Some of us haven't eaten yet."

"Amanda and I had an early dinner," Jillian said.

"Then, you can order dessert."

Manelli's Italian Ristorante stayed open until eleven and was Amanda's favorite place for a quiet, romantic dinner. The eight chairs around their table hinted that this evening would be anything but romantic.

Anthony Manelli, the restaurants' owner, had seated them by the front window. His wife, Isabelle, brought baskets of warm garlic knots. Sam placed an order of appetizers—toasted ravioli, mozzarella sticks, and antipasto skewers. Two lovely bottles of wine—a robust Merlot and a dry Pinot Noir—would pair nicely with their pasta dinner.

"You ladies who ate dinner early can snack on these." Sam passed the platter around the table. "Or wait for dessert."

"It's been hours—I can eat a little something." Jillian unrolled the napkin and placed it in her lap.

"Why'd you ask for such a big table for the five of us, Sam?" Ethan plucked a garlic knot from the basket and tore off a piece.

"Because Sam's a thoughtful man." Becca scooted into the seat next to Ethan. "He invited me to have dinner with our friends since you didn't think to call me."

A flush of scarlet tinged Ethan's face.

"He called me too." Travis planted a kiss on Jillian's cheek and pulled out a chair. "Thanks for the invite." He gave Sam a fist bump.

Becca pointed at the empty chair. "Who's the eighth seat for?"

Aunt Grace waved at a silver-haired gentleman who stood at the hostess counter scanning the room. "You didn't think I'd come without moral support, did you?"

Her fiancé, Dr. Robert Madison, rewarded Grace with his million-dollar smile. He joined the group with the ease of a man who was comfortable in any social situation, radiating confidence.

Amanda eyed his dark gray trousers, chambray shirt, and Ferragamo shoes. He looked like he'd stepped out of a Banana Republic ad.

Aunt Grace hit the lottery with this one.

Robert strolled to their table. "Hello, everyone. Thank you for including me tonight. I'm sorry to hear about your rough day, Amanda." He patted her on the back, then kissed Grace on the cheek.

"Not much of a romantic date with the six of us here." Becca returned the doctor's warm smile.

Robert put his arm around Grace's shoulders. "I'll take whatever time I can get with this lovely lady."

Amanda noticed how sweet they were together. She hoped their upcoming marriage would be a happy one— Grace had waited a long time for Mr. Right to come along.

Her musings were preempted by the waiter's arrival to take their orders. Promising dinner wouldn't take more than twenty minutes, he left to deliver their orders to the chef. Conversation then circled around to the victim, the crime scene, and Grace's premonitions.

"I'm surprised how fast you cleared the scene," Travis said to Ethan. "Not much evidence to deal with huh?"

"Oh, I wouldn't say that." Ethan popped another piece of garlic knot dripping with marinara sauce into his mouth.

"What would you say?" Becca bounced in her seat. "We're dying to hear—oh, sorry—dying isn't a good word to use in this situation."

"We know what you meant, Bec." Jillian squeezed her friend's hand. "However, we would like to hear what you know—if you feel you can tell us, Detective."

"Since it'll be all over town by tomorrow morning anyway, I don't see why I can't tell you guys tonight." Ethan picked a skewer from the appetizer platter the waiter had just deposited on the table.

"How about less eating, more talking?" Becca quirked an eyebrow in his direction.

"I'm hungry," he mumbled around his mouthful.

"Ethan." The frustration in her voice had him set the chunk of salami he'd held back onto his plate.

"Fine. I'll put my own needs on hold."

He brought Becca, Travis, and Robert up to speed on how the van used to run Amanda off the road had been found dumped just a few hours later in her front yard with a dead woman's body in the back.

"That's awful. For so many reasons," Robert said. "Since you're involved, Detective, I assume the poor woman didn't die of natural causes."

"There's nothing natural about a bullet to the brain," Sam grunted.

"No, there isn't." Robert grimaced. "I do hope death was quick. Bleeding out is a horrible way to die."

Amanda shuddered.

Always a doctor. Even at the dinner table.

"The poor young woman was a new mother." Grace took a handkerchief from her purse. "Her sweet baby is an orphan."

"There's no father to care for him?" he asked.

"He's dead too," Jillian said. "A murder staged to look like a suicide four days ago."

Robert's brow wrinkled. "Are you saying the woman in the back of the van was the wife of the man who was shot behind the flower shop?"

"Yes, we are. Such a sad situation—especially for that innocent little boy." Grace sniffled into her hankie.

"Oh, my goodness," Robert said. "My daughter will be devastated. I'll need to be the one to call and tell her."

"I'm sorry. Your daughter?" Jillian's eyes narrowed.

"Yes. Stacey and my youngest daughter, Hannah, were college roommates. They were also bridesmaids in each other's weddings. Stacey was the one who told my daughter St. Francis was looking for an oncologist to head the new cancer center. I stayed with Stacey and Rick for one night when I came to meet with the Board of Directors." He took a long sip of his wine. "This is terrible—so many lives affected."

Their orders arrived—plates filled with baked stuffed eggplant, braciole, spaghetti with meatballs, and the house specialty, Italian wedding risotto—a combination of garlicky meatballs and spinach risotto drizzled with olive oil and covered in parmesan cheese. The smell of tomatoes, garlic and onion wafted in the air. The conversation about dead bodies and orphaned babies was put on pause while people enjoyed their meals.

"While I'm sure the food's delicious, and the company is pleasant, I'd like to hear the rest of Ethan's story." Jillian's inquiring mind was impatient.

"Only if I can keep eating." He made quick work of the last two meatballs on his plate. "Evidence at the scene indicates the victim was restrained with duct tape around her arms, legs—even across her mouth. She'd been shot with a 9mm. The coroner places the time of death within five to six hours of her body being left in Amanda's front yard."

"You mean she could've been in the van, bound and gagged—maybe already dead—when it ran me off the road?" Amanda's mouth hung open.

"Could be. No way to know for sure." Ethan shrugged one shoulder. "We've towed the van back to the state crime lab. They'll go over it inch by inch for fingerprints, DNA, hairs, fibers—anything to help us track her killer."

"The same person who shot Rick killed her," Jillian said. "Had to be."

"We don't know that for sure. They weren't killed with the same weapon. The gun used to murder Rick was left at the scene, remember?" Ethan drained his beer, signaling for another. "There's no solid evidence to prove one person committed both crimes."

"Right. We have *two* gun-wielding psychos running loose in Willow Springs, and they just happened to kill a husband and wife," Jillian scoffed. "Next you'll tell me Amanda's stalker is in no way involved with these two murders."

"No, I won't." Ethan sprinkled more parmesan on his spaghetti. "I'm investigating all three cases, but it's too early to draw any conclusions. So, I would never say anything like that."

Amanda looked from one to the other. She should intervene or those two would be going at it all night.

"You will have the bullets analyzed?" Amanda swallowed hard.

"Not you too." Ethan ran his hands through his air. "I don't need two Edwards sisters interfering in my case."

"I wasn't interfering, merely asking. I don't intend to stick my nose where it doesn't belong." Amanda backpedaled.

"Mm-hmm. I don't suppose you two Nancy Drews could lay off the bullets for a minute. You might like to hear what I found in Stacey's hand."

CHAPTER TWENTY-FIVE

Jillian listened, pulse racing, as Ethan told them of the silver charm bracelet Stacey had clutched in her right fist.

"Do you think it belonged to her?" Jillian asked. "Or could she have snatched it off the attacker's wrist during a struggle?"

"Either is a possibility," Ethan said. "The clasp was broken, but until we find the killer, we won't know for sure. Hopefully the lab will be able to lift fingerprints from it or something else left in the van."

"Describe it again." Aunt Grace toyed with one of her own bracelets dripping with charms. "A woman chooses the objects she puts on her bracelet because they have special meaning. Maybe the charms on this one will tell us something about the killer—if it belongs to her and not Stacey."

"That's a great idea, Aunt Grace. Your detective skills could give Ethan a run for his money." Jillian cast a teasing glance at him.

"Most of them were silver like the bracelet." Ethan opened his iPad to check his notes. "There was a tiger, an anchor, a rose, a triangle, and a backward seven along with two colored gemstones—one pink, one blue."

Dr. Madison coughed, choking on a bite of food he'd taken. Becca used the heel of her hand and hit him on the back. "You okay there, Doc?"

He coughed again, then cleared his throat. "Yes, my dear. Thank you."

Grace hardly noticed her fiancé's distress, too focused on her musings about the charms. "Most of those are straightforward enough—except the backward seven." She nibbled on her bottom lip, a sure sign she was deep in thought. "If I could hold the bracelet, I might get a sense of its owner."

Jillian chuckled to herself. There was no way Ethan would let her touch a piece of evidence.

Sorry, Aunt Grace. Not happening.

"That won't be necessary." Robert's voice was strained, his usual smile gone. "My two daughters have bracelets like the one you described—from their sorority at LSU—and it's not a backward seven. It's the Greek letter Gamma—they were in Delta Gamma." He released a long sigh. "They never take theirs off."

"Would you know if Stacey had one?" Ethan said.

"Yes, she did. All the DG girls receive bracelets from their Big Sisters on Initiation Night. Those mementos are a big deal to them." Robert rubbed at the back of his neck. "Grace is right. The charms *do* have significance. The anchor is their sorority's symbol representing hope. Their house flower is a rose. The triangle is the Greek letter Delta, and LSU's mascot is a tiger. The gemstones represent the house colors."

"Do you know if Stacey wore hers all the time, like your daughters?" Jillian couldn't help herself.

Ethan took offense. "I'll ask the questions."

"What?" Jillian shrugged her shoulders. "We're just talking."

"I'm afraid I don't know if she did or not," Robert said. "I was only around her a few times. I'll admit, I wasn't paying attention to the jewelry she wore."

Grace snorted. "Hmph, typical. You men—"

Her words stopped in a strangled gasp. Her eyes rolled back in her head. Her body went rigid. A low moan escaped from her lips.

"She was betrayed by the one man she ever loved when he chose another. She will have her revenge for being wronged." Grace paused. Her hands twitched.

Robert scooted closer, placing an arm around her shoulder. "Grace. Can you hear me?" His face was ashen.

"She won't answer until her vision is complete." Jillian touched his hand to reassure him. "I know it's hard to watch, but she'll be fine once it's over."

Grace took a huge breath. "The time is near. Someone else will die among the flowers." Her eyes closed. She lowered her chin to her chest.

There was nothing but silence. Everyone held their breath, waiting for Grace to regain her composure. When she did, her eyes flew open, and she glared at Sam.

"You." She jabbed a finger in his direction. "You've brought this evil into my niece's life. Who is this woman? What did you do to make her hate Amanda so fiercely?"

Sam's mouth dropped open. He shook his head. "I don't know who this woman is, I swear." His gaze turned to Amanda. "There's been no one but you in my life for years."

"What about other women you dated? Maybe one of them feels jilted." Jillian jumped in. The loud sigh from Ethan had her pursing her lips to hold back another question.

"I've only had one other long-term relationship, the one I mentioned before, which ended amicably. We both realized we weren't right for each other." Sam's eyes never left Amanda, who remained quiet. "I never dated anyone who attended LSU, so if that bracelet belongs to the killer, she isn't someone I know."

"Good point," Ethan said. "We all need to remember this person isn't stable. She might not be someone you had a serious relationship with. You could have met briefly, even once, and she perceived it as more."

"How am I supposed to know who it is then?" Sam's face crumpled.

Amanda's gaze remained on the floor. Jillian wondered if her sister was beginning to doubt Sam.

"We also don't know for sure the killer is a woman—"

"Ahem," Grace cleared her throat to interrupt Ethan. "Are you saying my visions are wrong?"

"I'm saying they are not irrefutable evidence." Ethan turned to speak to Sam. "I'm going to need a list of the women you've dated," Ethan said. "I'll start ruling them out one by one."

"All of them?" Sam's eyes widened.

"Have there been that many?" Amanda snapped. "I can only imagine how long your list will be." She crossed her arms over her chest, turning her back on Sam. Not before Jillian saw the tears brimming in her eyes.

Sam stood and placed himself directly in front of Amanda, then he dropped to one knee, taking her hands in his. "Babe. I'm sorry someone from my past is coming after you. I'd give anything to make this go away, but you *have* to believe me. I have no idea who she is, or why she has these crazy feelings for me. I. Love. You. Always have, always will."

Amanda didn't know which ached worse—her heart or her head. She'd sought refuge alone in Manelli's restroom and had a good cry. Now her temples throbbed. Her eyes felt gritty, and her nose ran.

Not a good look, she was certain.

After the awkward moments between Sam and Amanda at the restaurant, the entire group spent the remainder of dinner discussing what happened to Stacey. They speculated about where her sister, Didi, might be. They agreed the same person who murdered Stacey had grabbed Didi, but they had no idea why. They supposed the poor woman was being held somewhere, bound and gagged, just like her sister. The burning question—was she alive or dead?

At the end of the evening, Sam drove Amanda to her house in uncomfortable silence. She allowed him to hold her hand, but only to avoid further pleadings to believe or forgive him.

He'd promised to send Ethan his list of former relationships—no matter how short-lived—as soon as he could sit in front of the computer. Ethan promised to begin paring down the list ASAP. He planned to search Rick and Stacey's house for her sorority bracelet. If hers was still in the house, the one clutched in her hand belonged to a sorority sister—and her killer.

Sam squeezed Amanda's hand. He'd pulled his rental car into the driveway, turning off the engine unnoticed by her. He sat without moving.

"I should go inside." Amanda reached for the door handle.

"Please. Don't." Sam's whispered voice filled the cavernous gap between them.

"Poppy will need to go out." She attempted to pull away from him, but his grip stayed firm.

"We need to talk about this."

"Sam ... I ... can't. Not now. Not here." With a strength she hadn't known she possessed, she wrenched her hand from his grasp and bolted from the car. He caught up to her on the front porch, wrapping his arms around her. He drew her close, pressing his cheek against hers.

"Babe. I know you're scared. I'm scared too, but not of this crazy woman." His shoulders shuddered. There was a catch in his voice. "I'm afraid of losing you."

Amanda's throat tightened, preventing speech.

"I know you're upset but promise me you don't doubt my love for you. That would kill me."

Amanda felt his warm tears on her face. They were her undoing. She grabbed Sam, holding him tight.

They stood like this under the dim glow of the porch light, their silhouettes visible to anyone who might be watching.

Jillian had driven to dinner with Ethan, her car still parked behind the bookstore, so Travis gave her a ride back to Whimsy & Wonder. She burrowed deep into the puffy sweater she'd worn to ward off the evening's chill. This would've been a great night to sit around a fire pit, relaxing and toasting marshmallows, but no one would relax until these gruesome murders were solved.

And the killer's behind bars.

Snuggled in Travis's truck listening to his favorite classic rock station and craving s'mores, her mind wandered to Ethan's current cases—Amanda's vandalism, Rick and Stacey's deaths, and Didi's disappearance. Jillian was certain there was only one person committing all these crimes.

Now there was the mystery of the charm bracelet.

Did it belong to Stacey or her killer?

Her phone pinged, showing an incoming text from Cate with a picture attached. She opened the text, and the cherubic face of Rick's son, Benjamin, filled the screen along with Cate's message—*Up for a late night feeding. Can you believe how cute he is?* followed by a smile emoji and a blue heart.

Uh-oh. Cate was falling hard for this little guy.

Jillian rubbed her temples, trying to ward off the headache building behind her eyes.

"What's wrong?" Travis said. "If you're tired, we can call it a night." He signaled the turn into the driveway of her store. "You can get your car and head home."

"No way." She touched a hand to his face. "I've been looking forward to ending this crazy night with some quiet time with you."

That wasn't going to happen anytime soon.

Someone shouted at them from across the street. Jillian squinted into the gathering darkness and cursed under her breath.

No. Not tonight.

Mr. Erickson headed their way, waving his arms like he was landing an airplane right there on Sweetwater Avenue. All he needed was a pair of those orange batons they use on the runway.

"Hey, Book Lady," he shouted. "I need to talk to you."

She rolled her eyes at Travis.

"I hope to make this quick, so you can stay in the truck if you want." Jillian unhooked her seatbelt to open the door.

"I might need to offer my protection." Travis turned off the radio, then the engine.

"You think I need protection from a ninety-plus-year-old man?"

"No. I might have to protect Mr. Erickson from you." He placed a kiss on her cheek before jumping out of the vehicle.

Jillian came around the rear of the truck. She took a deep breath. Wasn't there a saying about girding your loins for battle? Dealing with Mr. E. made her feel that way every time.

"Well, look who else is here—The Book Lady's Fire Man." The older gentleman put out a fist to bump.

Travis returned the gesture. "Hello, sir. How're you doing tonight?"

"I'd be a heck of a lot better if I didn't have to keep dealin' with more shenanigans outside that store of hers." He spat something Jillian could only assume was chewing tobacco out of the corner of his mouth. The spittle landed with a loud splat just inches from the toe of her new Skechers sneakers.

Could he be more disgusting?

He spat again, then scratched himself.

Yes, he could.

Jillian shook her head. "Mr. Erickson, I'm so sorry I haven't gotten back to you about the commotion the other night. Things have been a bit hectic. I checked the store's video—wait, what do you mean *more* shenanigans? Did those teenagers who partied on my porch the other night come back tonight?"

As promised, Jillian had checked the security camera after her elderly neighbor had complained about a disturbance earlier in the week. The video showed a group of kids using her front porch as a late-night party spot.

"Wasn't nobody botherin' me," he said. "That dark-haired cutie of an employee of yours is probably singing a different tune."

"Is Trixie all right?"

"Yes, yes. Calm down. Assistant Book Lady's fine." He scuffed the toe of his worn work boot in the dirt. "She got herself a little scared, though."

"Mr. Erickson, can you tell us what happened? Please don't leave anything out."

The older gentleman hitched up his suspenders, puffing out his chest before he began.

Always a production with this one.

"I was standin' on my porch, enjoying the evenin' air puffin' on my favorite *Cohiba*. Someone—a woman by the sound of her voice—was knockin' on the bookstore's door. I figured you was closed 'cuz it was after eight." Mr. Erickson took a dingy white cotton handkerchief from his back pocket and blew his nose.

Jillian wondered if he ever washed that filthy thing.

"Assistant Book Lady opened the door. Don't know what was said, but their voices got loud. The woman said something to your friend. Musta startled her 'cuz she took several steps back inside the store—away from the crazy lady who screamed, 'Do what I say. Give it to her.' Your assistant slammed the door in her face."

"Sounds like a tense exchange," Travis said. "Anything else?"

Mr. Erickson jerked his thumb at Travis. "Get a load of this one, will ya? Of course, there's more. Whatcha in such an all-fired hurry fer?"

Travis bit his lower lip. "Sorry, please go on."

"Well, since you said please." His grin showed teeth stained from years of tobacco use and coffee drinking. "When Assistant Book Lady turned her away, the other woman stomped off the porch. She spotted Yours Truly and pivoted in my direction. That's when I saw it in her hands."

CHAPTER TWENTY-SIX

"A gun?" The hair on the back of Jillian's neck stood at attention. "This woman threatened you with a gun?"

"Well, I wouldn't say threatened. She was in such a snit, she just waved it around—kind of crazy-like. I doubt she even knew how to fire it." Mr. Erickson snorted.

If her hunch was correct, and this woman was Rick and Stacey's killer, Jillian was confident she did know how to shoot a gun.

While she'd listened to the old man's tale, Jillian noticed Travis on his phone. Certain he'd texted Ethan, she invited Mr. Erickson inside.

He looked at his Timex with the worn leather band. "Book Lady, it's way past my bedtime. I s'pose I could be convinced to come in if you had some sweets from your sister's bakery."

Before she could confirm or deny the presence of pastries, Ethan's cruiser screeched to a halt in front of Mr. Erickson's house. He climbed out, slamming the door behind him. With his cop face firmly in place, he marched across the street.

"Looky here. It's The Cop. He's wantin' to talk to me, I'm bettin'." Mr. Erickson spat a large glob of tobacco onto the sidewalk.

Ick, right where someone could step in it.

Jillian made a mental note to hose off the walk before opening for business tomorrow.

Nodding at Jillian and Travis, Ethan addressed Mr. Erickson.

"This is becoming a habit, sir—you in the middle of my cases."

"You think I like bein' dragged into the nonsense that revolves around this one?" He cocked his head at Jillian. "I'd much rather be at home in my La-Z-Boy watchin' a ballgame."

Jillian unlocked the door and silenced the alarm before leading the group into the store. Flipping on lights, she led them to a room where the furniture was more size appropriate for adults. She chose the one right across from the kitchen, so she wouldn't miss a word. She excused herself to gather a snack for her nonagenarian guest.

Ethan's voice began the conversation. "Sir, start from the beginning."

Mr. Erickson grumbled. "I already told them. I'm not happy about repeating myself."

"Unfortunately, they aren't the police—so if you don't mind." Ethan tapped his finger on the iPad. "What time did you hear the commotion here at the bookstore?"

"Why're you usin' that new-fangled thing?" Mr. Erickson sneered at the device in Ethan's hand. "What happened? Did ya go and lose yer little notebook?"

"Standard police issue. This is what we're using now." Ethan spoke with steel in his voice. "Can we get on with this?"

The grouchy old man launched into his second telling of the mystery woman's story—from the moment he heard the two women shouting to when the crazy lady approached him with a gun.

"Could you describe the gun?" Ethan coaxed more information.

"Not really, hard to see it in the dark." Mr. Erickson shrugged. "I could identify it if I saw it clearly. I'm a veteran, you know—Marines, part of the ARFF boys—"

"Arf, like a dog?" Ethan narrowed his eyes at his witness.

"A-R-F-F—stands for Air Rescue and Fire Fighting. Mr. Erickson was one tough soldier." Travis came to Mr. E's defense. Firefighters had to stick together.

"That's right, but I also know my way around weapons." The elderly man nodded at Travis. "I couldn't see hers, though. She wore all black—pants, shirt, hooded jacket. Once she was done waving it around like a flag, she pulled her sleeves down, tucking the gun inside so only the very end stuck out."

Jillian returned with a tray of sweets, setting it on the table in front of Mr. Erickson. Without waiting to be invited, he helped himself to a lemon tart and a frosted sugar cookie, taking a huge bite from the latter.

Ethan opened his mouth to ask another question, but Mr. Erickson wasn't finished.

"Before you ask what she looked like, I can't tell you that either." Crumbs rained down on his dingy white T-shirt. "She had the strings on that darned hood pulled so tight, the only thing visible were her eyes and nose. Smart if you ask me. She knew no one would be able to identify her."

"Okay. Did she talk to you?" Ethan continued digging for clues.

"More like screeching—sounded like that annoying parrot they keep out at the Senior Center. I can't believe the whole neighborhood didn't hear her carryin' on."

Jillian was certain Ethan would question all the neighbors to find out.

"She never got within a few feet of me. Again smart—making sure I didn't get too close a look." Polishing off the cookie, he started in on the tart. "She kept yellin' over and over—'Give it to her, give it to her.'"

"Give what to who?" The question was out before Jillian could stop it.

Ethan pursed his lips. "Thank you, Jillian, for that astute question."

She'd poked the bear. "Sorry, won't happen again."

"If you two are done?" Mr. Erickson waited.

"Yes, go on." Ethan directed.

"I have no idea who or what Crazy Gun-Toting Woman was talking about. She rushed at me, pointing the gun again. I thought she was gonna shoot me." He took a bite of the tart. A large dollop of lemon curd dripped onto his shirt. "I went into fight mode. I survived a war. This lady wasn't gonna take down Henry Olaf Erickson. We struggled. I knocked the gun out of her hand with my brute strength, but I musta been a bit off balance—landed on my keester in the grass. She threw an envelope at me, grabbed the gun off the ground, then ran off into the darkness. Scared the girl off, I did. She left me lying there wondering how I was gonna get up."

"You could've been killed." Jillian sat down next to Mr. Erickson, putting her arm around his shoulders. "Are you hurt? We should get you to the hospital to check for injuries."

"Uh-uh, I ain't goin' to no hospital where they poke and prod you, run a bunch of unnecessary tests, then send me a ridiculous bill. I'm fine. Don't need no doctor."

"I could look you over. I am a paramedic," Travis offered. "Would that be okay?"

Mr. Erickson glared at Travis. "No needles. I don't do needles."

"Don't have any with me, sir. You're safe."

With a nod, the old grouch consented to a quick once-over. While Travis gently prodded Mr. Erickson's head, neck, and back, Ethan prepared to leave.

"I should get started questioning the neighbors—if they'll open the door this time of night." He shoved the iPad back in its case.

"You better get out there and find that lunatic before she really does use that gun on someone." Mr. Erickson glared at Ethan.

"Thank you for the suggestion." The tips of Ethan's ears had turned red—an indication he was losing patience with his witness. "I do need that envelope from you—now, please."

Mr. Erickson shook Travis's hand off his shoulder and stood. "Follow me. I left it safe and sound on my kitchen table."

The old man shuffled from the room with Ethan close behind.

"You will come back and tell us what the note says, right?" Jillian called out.

"You'd like that, wouldn't you?" Ethan cackled but didn't turn around.

"She won't stop until she finds out," Travis shouted, earning himself a harsh glare.

"All in good time, Jilly. All in good time. I'll enter it into evidence and have it tested for fingerprints first."

Ethan's laughter rang in her ears. The door banged shut as he left with Mr. Erickson.

Men.

Crisp air and a clear sky marked the start of Friday morning. Jillian flitted about the store, straightening shelves and adding new books while she chatted with Trixie, their conversation punctuated with pauses when customers strolled in.

Just the way I like it—busy.

"Detective Harden knocked on my door really late last night," Trixie said. "After I answered his questions, he told me a little about what happened to our elderly friend across the street."

"Ethan is less than thrilled to have Mr. Erickson involved in another one of his cases." Jillian opened another box of middle-grade chapter books.

"I can't believe that woman accosted poor Mr. Erickson. I hope he wasn't hurt." Trixie shook her head. "I had no idea she held a gun in her hand."

"In your defense, our porchlight is burned out." Jillian made a mental note to replace the bulb. "You might also have been distracted by her screaming and banging on the door after hours like a lunatic."

"True, she was out of her mind." Trixie ran a dustcloth over the tops of the bookcases. "Took me the longest time to figure out she wanted me to give something to someone, but she stomped off before I could find out *what* she needed me to give to *whom*."

"Mr. Erickson told us she left our porch and headed to her car. When she saw him, her plan changed. She made him the object of her obsession."

Trixie gasped. "Did she threaten him with the gun?"

"He said she waved it around a little, but he wasn't worried. Not sure a gun would faze him anyway."

Jillian fluffed the pillows in the pint-sized chairs in the cozy reading corner. "According to Mr. E., he and Crazy Gun-Toting Woman struggled. He knocked the weapon out of her hands but fell on his backside in the process.

Still screaming to give something to someone, she threw an envelope at him while he lay on the ground, then disappeared into the night. Ethan has it now."

"Just like that she left? What a weird night." Trixie's eyebrows rose to her hairline. "I can't believe Mr. Erickson gave the envelope to Ethan willingly, without so much as a grunt or grumble. Is our crabby neighbor going soft on us?"

"We're a long way from that happening," Jillian said. "Still, I do believe his relationship with Mrs. Taylor is having a positive influence on him."

Love conquers all—even those with a cranky disposition.

"What was in the envelope?" Trixie's dustcloth stopped in midair.

Jillian's eyes narrowed. "Another note, I assume, but I have no idea what new kind of crazy it contains. Ethan insisted on taking it to the station to test for fingerprints before we opened it to read what's inside."

"That's disappointing." Trixie's shoulders slumped.

"Aggravating is the word that comes to my mind."

"I'm aggravating, huh?" Ethan strolled into the Main Room through the back hallway. "That's like the pot calling the kettle black."

Jillian jumped at his voice. "Ethan, what're you doing, sneaking in the back door?" She put her hand over her racing heart.

"I didn't sneak. The door was wide open." He pointed a finger at her. "You of all people should know not to leave that door unlocked."

"I probably didn't get it closed all the way when I took out the trash a few minutes ago." A sheepish look graced Trixie's face. "I'll be more careful next time."

Ethan's mention of the unlocked back door flooded Jillian with memories of her fight with an armed attacker last year who'd snuck in through that same open door. She shuddered thinking of how close she'd come to being killed.

"Duly noted, Detective. We'll be more careful." Jillian shot a saccharine smile at him. "Now, to what do we owe the pleasure of your company?"

"You *did* sort of sneak up on us." Trixie couldn't let it go. "Were you hoping to overhear something salacious?" She wiggled her eyebrows at him, bursting into giggles when his face flushed.

"Relax. We weren't talking about anything lurid." Jillian shook her head at Trixie. "We were discussing last night's unusual events, which I assume brought you here today."

"I was across the street talking to Mr. E. since he couldn't finish the interview last night. Then, I decided to come check on Trixie to make sure she'd recovered from her run-in with—what did Erickson call her?"

"Crazy Gun-Toting Woman."

Jillian's answer sent Trixie into a fit of laughter.

"That old guy is funny—all his made-up names for people. I wonder what he calls me."

"Assistant Book Lady." Again, Jillian.

"Mm, I like it," Trixie said. "I could have that put on my nametag. Oh no, a T-shirt, even better."

Jillian marveled at how Trixie could turn almost anything—no matter how horrible or ridiculous—into something positive and fun. Then, she remembered something Ethan said.

"Why couldn't Mr. Erickson finish your interview last night? Too far past his bedtime?"

Ethan looked at the floor. "He was having ... intestinal issues."

Trixie snorted. "Another burrito past its rejection period?"

Ethan stared at her in disbelief. "How did you know he said that?"

"Are you kidding? That's what he always says when he becomes flatulent in a lady's presence." Trixie wrinkled her nose. "Which seems to be often."

"I'm not a lady," Ethan said. "Wonder why—"

Jillian cleared her throat. "This conversation has taken a disgusting turn. Let's focus on my original question. I'd still like to know why Ethan used the back door instead of the front."

"You had a store full of customers. People get nervous when they see the police—I didn't want to drive away business. I waited back here until your crowd cleared."

"That was very thoughtful of you." Trixie placed books on a nearby shelf. "We have been busy this morning."

"That explains one mystery, but you still never said— did Mr. Erickson have anything else to say?" Jillian asked.

"You'd love to know, wouldn't you?" Ethan arched an eyebrow, clearly enjoying himself. "Lucky for you, I'm in a good mood, so maybe I'll share."

"How gracious of you, Detective."

"C'mon, you two. Play nice." Trixie smiled at Ethan. "Can't you throw her a bone?"

He gave them a devilish grin. "I can tell you this. Mr. Erickson gave a good description of the vehicle Trixie's late-night visitor drove off in—right down to the purple and gold Tigers license plate holder."

"There's the LSU connection again." Jillian threw her hands in the air. "This has to prove Amanda's stalker and Rick and Stacey's killer are the same person. But why is she after Amanda and Sam when they have no connection to that university? This doesn't make any sense."

"As I've said before, criminals aren't stable people." Ethan scrubbed at his day-old beard. "I will concede you make a good point, Jilly. The whole LSU thing might prove to be a connection between the killer and Amanda's stalker."

"Might be? You can't still be thinking we have two different psychos at work here, are you?" Jillian's eyes widened.

"There's no rule about how many wackos can be running loose in the same town." Trixie shrugged. "I mean, spend an hour or so walking the aisles at Walmart, then we'll talk." Her deep blue eyes sparkled with amusement.

"Let's hope none of the Walmart shoppers are packing a 9mm and trying to make Amanda, Sam, or both, their next victim." Jillian looked to Ethan for reassurance.

"I'm working to make sure no one becomes the next victim," he said. "If I can track down the owner of the dark green sports car Mr. Erickson saw —"

"Dark green?" Jillian's heart skipped a beat. "The first time Amanda and I met Stacey's sister, she was driving a dark green Jag."

"You said she's missing," Trixie said. "She couldn't have been here last night."

"We assumed she was missing when she never came back for her nephew. Perhaps she *chose* not to return." Jillian rubbed at the back of her neck.

"None of this makes sense." Trixie shook her head. "If you're thinking Stacey's sister—what's her name?"

"Didi." Ethan and Jillian answered together.

"Right, Didi." Trixie tapped her finger to her lips. "She couldn't have been the woman I saw last night. I mean, why would she be stalking Amanda? Why would she abandon her nephew?"

Ethan huffed out his breath. "I don't have answers to your questions, Trixie, but I will. Soon. Thanks again for talking to me last night—sorry it was so late."

"No problem." Trixie gave him a thumbs-up. "I had a late-night date with a pint of Ben & Jerry's and the wonderful folks at Downton Abbey."

"Maybe whatever's in the envelope will yield the answers we're looking for." Jillian drew them back to the evidence.

"Hoping I'll let you take a look at it, right?" Ethan grinned at her.

"That would be nice."

"Patience, Jilly. Forensics still has it—pulling fingerprints," he said. "I'm as eager as you are to read what's inside that envelope. This case has dumped two dead bodies and a missing person in my lap. If the contents can help us catch this psycho before any more people die or disappear, I'll be thrilled."

Amanda stood on the top step of a ladder to secure her hand-painted '*Happy Birthday, Cate*' banner across the doorway to the backroom of McGuire's. She descended the rungs, then studied her handiwork with a critical eye.

The colors were bright. Lettering precise. Her artwork was whimsical and fun.

"The sign looks great." Jillian put an arm around Amanda's shoulder. "As always, you've outdone yourself."

"We've never tried to surprise Cate," Amanda said. "I want it to be perfect."

"Look around." Jillian motioned to the decorated room. "Everything *is* perfect."

Spectacular floral bouquets in shades of pink, orange, and cream dotted every flat surface in the room. Cream cloths, delicate china, and sparkling crystal goblets covered the tables. The chairs were swathed in the same cream fabric, tied back with pink bows. Balloon arrangements in the evening's colors filled in the negative spaces. Thanks to Sam's amazing photography skills, black and white photos of Cate through the years adorned the walls.

Amanda nodded. Everything was perfect. She prayed it would stay that way. Her mind buzzed with thoughts of the recent murders, Didi's disappearance, poor little Bennie, and her poetic stalker.

She wouldn't put it past this lunatic to try something tonight at the party.

The hair on her arms stood on end.

Everyone she cared about would be together in one place—perfect for some crazy stunt.

Amanda shook her head to dislodge this negativity.

No. Tonight has to be perfect. Cate deserves it.

If the person behind all the threats and chaos thought they could ruin this evening—they were wrong. Amanda would make sure everything went smoothly.

Her attention returned to the present when Jillian jabbed her in the ribs. "Hey, you. I need your focus here in this room, not wherever it was a minute ago."

"Yeah, sure." Amanda moved to straighten the pink runner on the nearest table. "When is Becca coming to work on the cake?

"Ask and ye shall receive." Becca sailed into the room from the kitchen, carrying an unwieldy box. "Point me to my table. I'll assemble my masterpiece."

Jillian grabbed a corner of the box, guiding it onto the table. Hands free now, Becca threw her coat and purse onto the floor. "Let's unbox this beauty."

The removal of the lid revealed a culinary confection smelling of chocolate, vanilla, and almonds. The buttercream icing had been coaxed into a flawlessly smooth surface ready to accept Becca's cake decorating genius.

"Hey, this tier has six sides." Jillian marveled at the confection. "You made a hexagonal cake. I can't believe I didn't notice this at the bakery—never seen anything like it."

Becca beamed. "I do like to be different."

"Why a hexagon?" Amanda asked. "Circles weren't good enough for you?"

"Not good enough for Cate." Becca winked. "Circles are boring and make it look too much like a wedding cake. I wanted it to be special. Once I work my decorating magic, it will be." She patted the bag over her shoulder. "All my necessary tools are right here."

"I assume there's more than one tier. Do you need help bringing them in?" Jillian moved toward the door.

"No need," Becca said. "My kitchen elves should be bringing them in."

As if on cue, Travis, Sam, and Bryan walked into the room. Each carried a different-size box.

"Where do you want these, boss?" Sam smiled at Becca, who pointed to the cake table.

"There's one more at the back door. I'll go grab it." Travis made a move toward the door.

"Stop right there, buddy." Becca waggled a finger in the air. "I can't believe you'd leave a box of my baking treasures lying there for someone to step on or walk off with."

Travis held up his hands in surrender. "Down, girl. The box was sitting there when we all arrived. I thought you put it there."

"Are you nuts? I'd never leave—" Becca wheeled around and counted the boxes on the table. "That can't be right."

She rubbed the back of her neck. "All my boxes are here." She pivoted back to Travis. "You're sure there's another one?"

Before he could answer, Trixie waltzed in carrying a blue Sugar & Spice box. "You're lucky I closed the bookstore and hurried over to help. Which one of you left part of the cake on the sidewalk?" She set it next to the others on the table and removed the top.

Becca tried to warn her. "Uh, that's not one of my—"

Trixie's scream rattled the picture frames on the wall. The cardboard lid slipped from her hands and landed with a dull thud. For a moment, no one moved. Bryan was the first to step forward and peer inside.

"Ugh, that's disgusting." Bryan wrinkled his nose.

Amanda leaned around him, then recoiled at the sight. *Lord, give me strength.*

Everyone around her look rattled, so Amanda reached for humor—partly to lift the mood, mostly to steady herself.

"Looks like my stalker is angry she wasn't invited to the party."

CHAPTER TWENTY-SEVEN

Ethan arrived within minutes of receiving their call. He found everyone huddled in the backroom. Despite the colorful party decorations, the mood was anything but festive. He snapped on a pair of latex gloves to remove the lid Bryan had put back on the box.

Peering over Ethan's shoulder, Jillian shuddered at the four dead rats laid out on a bed of yellow carnations.

"Those nasty critters creep me out every time I look at them."

Ethan let out a beleaguered sigh. "Let's keep this between us. We don't want to ruin Cate's party or cause panic among the guests." He raised his eyes to take in the assembled group. "No one else needs to know about this box and its contents. Or the message inside."

2 Down, 2 to Go
Enjoy tonight's party—while you can.

"A bit vague, don't you think?" Sam put a protective arm around Amanda's waist.

"Are you kidding?" Jillian scowled at him. "Seems pretty clear to me."

"Would you care to enlighten the rest of us?" Amanda stared at her sister.

"Don't you see? She's threatening to do something tonight." Jillian huffed out an impatient breath.

"How did she find out about the party?" Trixie said. "The only people who know about it are standing in this room."

"We've kept the secret from Cate," Amanda said. "All the invited guests are in on the surprise too. Any one of them could have mentioned it in the presence of my stalker."

"Good point," Trixie said.

"Let's say Jillian is correct. What's the whole 2 Down, 2 to Go business?" Becca asked.

Jillian had the answer. "2 Down—she's already killed Rick and Stacey. 2 to go means she has two more people in her sights."

"I'm one of them," Amanda muttered. "Who's the fourth?"

"Maybe me—who knows?" Sam's voice took on a harsh tone. "This woman is nuts. She could have anyone on her hit list."

Travis cleared his throat. "What about Stacey's sister? She's still missing. Maybe she's lying dead somewhere, and her body hasn't been discovered yet."

"No." Jillian's answer was adamant. "The message said 2 Down. If Didi were dead, it would've said three."

"Hang on. What if Didi isn't missing?" Bryan raised a hand to stop any objections. "Hear me out. Maybe Didi is our stalker/killer, and she's laying low until she makes her move at Cate's party."

"You could be on to something." Ethan clapped Bryan on the back.

"Oh, when Bryan says the same person could be the stalker and the killer, you agree with him." Jillian frowned at Ethan. "I've been saying the same thing for days."

When Ethan failed to respond to Jillian's comment, Bryan continued.

"What I don't get are those rats. Why kill them, put them in a box, and deliver them to my bar?" Bryan shoved his hands in his pockets.

"Jilly might be right about the message." Ethan narrowed his eyes at her. "Those rats are meant to represent four people she wants dead, and she's making sure we know her plan."

This somber thought silenced the room. The quiet was broken when the front door burst open, and a deep voice rang out. "The sign on the door says closed for a private party. I hope that means us."

Like the true gentleman he was, Jillian's dad held the door for her mom and Aunt Grace. Robert followed close behind. Their arms were loaded with gifts wrapped in paper as bright as the smiles on their faces. One look at the younger crowd stopped them in their tracks.

"Something's happened." Joy moved toward her daughters.

"What's wrong?" Jillian's dad shut the door. He addressed Ethan. "Are you here as a partygoer or a cop?"

A low moan escaped from Grace's lips. Her grip on the gifts she carried faltered, sending the boxes tumbling to the floor. She reached for the brass railing around the bar. Her words escaped in a choked whisper.

"Other women have what she can't. She'll take what she wants because she deserves it. She'll appreciate it more than they do."

Grace's eyes had been squeezed shut, but they flew open before her last pronouncement. "Someone sleeps. It's so dark. All ends tonight." She let go of her grasp on the bar and slumped to the floor. Bryan rushed to help his mom.

The party was in full swing. Cate had arrived right on time. To say she'd been surprised was an understatement. She'd screamed, cried a little, and hugged every single person more than once. The decorations, photographs, balloons, and flowers were a big hit. Music filled the bar.

As usual, Max had outdone himself on the food, making sure to include Cate's favorites—sausage stuffed mushrooms, coconut shrimp skewers, pulled pork sliders, and bacon-wrapped, cream-cheese-filled jalapenos. The birthday girl ate, danced, and laughed the night away, unaware the rest of her family were on pins and needles, keeping a watchful eye on Amanda.

After Aunt Grace's vision, they'd agreed the party should go on as planned, but Amanda would not be left alone. The message in the box plus Grace's premonition were enough to have them all exercising caution.

Jillian leaned against the wall in the back of the room, her eyes tracking Amanda's every movement.

No matter what—we'll keep her safe.

Wes joined her there, holding a sleeping Benjamin in his arms. Jillian brushed a finger over the infant's soft cheek. How did babies snooze through all that noise?

"This is fantastic, Jilly. You and Amanda did an amazing job pulling this party together." He kissed her cheek. "Thanks for making Cate's birthday so special. This is a night she's never going to forget."

Jillian hoped that would be because of the party and not some disaster.

"She looks like she's having a great time." Jillian glanced at Cate dancing with their dad.

Wes smiled at his wife. "She can't stop talking about the flowers, the food—everything. Oh, and the cake. Becca's creation is incredible."

"Don't tell her that. We won't be able to live with her." A slow song came on. Jillian watched Sam take Amanda by the hand, leading her onto the dance floor. "Let Becca or me know when you're ready to cut the cake."

"The waitstaff will bring out trays of champagne around nine-thirty. I've prepared a short speech for the toast, then I'll give Cate her present. We'll serve cake after she opens it. Do you have the ring or does Amanda?"

"Amanda. She locked it in her safe at the store after Travis picked it up on Wednesday. Give me this sweet boy. You go dance with the birthday girl. I'll check on her gift in a few minutes." Holding Benjamin in one arm, she gave Wes a gentle shove in Cate's direction.

Before leaving her post, Jillian let her eyes rove around the room, checking on Amanda's security detail. Bryan was positioned by the bar where he could monitor any uninvited guest who might try to get in the front. Travis sat at a table near the back door, nursing a beer and scanning the room. Trixie and Becca were perched on stools by the gift table, their eyes never leaving Amanda. Ethan prowled the perimeter of the room, checking the two exits each time he passed to be certain they stayed locked. He'd also positioned three officers outside.

When the music changed tempo, Sam and Amanda returned to their table.

"You two looked great out there—very cozy." Jillian shifted Bennie to her other arm. "I hate to interrupt your evening, but Wes would like to make a toast before he gives Cate her fabulous gift. Is it in your purse?"

Amanda's hands flew to her face. "Oh my gosh. I left it in the safe at the shop. I'll rush over and get it."

"You're not going anywhere." Sam motioned around the room. "In here, you're protected from the stalker. Your guard dogs will chew her up and spit her out if, by some miracle, she managed to get in. But out there, you're not safe."

"I'll go." Jillian handed the baby to Amanda, who despite her inexperience with infants, snuggled him close, rocking from side to side.

Hmm. Look at that. Amanda's natural instincts just kicked in.

"I have a key." Jillian grabbed her coat. "Just tell me the alarm code and combination to the safe. I can be back in less than fifteen minutes."

"You shouldn't go alone. Take someone with you," Sam urged.

"Fine, I'll go grab Becca. We'll be back before you'll have time to miss us."

"If you're not, we'll send in the cavalry." Sam didn't sound like he was kidding.

The evening had turned cool, making Jillian and Becca glad they'd worn coats. Standing in the light of Blossoms & Blooms' display window, Jillian fumbled for the key ring in her pocket, dropping it on the ground. As she bent to retrieve it, a movement to the left caught her eye. She squealed and jumped sideways.

A chubby squirrel darted between two parking meters, then streaked across the grass.

"Geez, Jilly. You scared the pants off me." Becca grabbed Jillian, pulling her close. "Why're you so skittish?"

Jillian shook her head. "I don't know—just a weird feeling in the pit of my stomach. Or maybe it's the fact there's a killer on the loose."

"Then, let's go inside, grab the ring, and get back to the party." Becca took the key from Jillian and unlocked the door.

The fragrant smells of the flowers tickled Jillian's nose as she hurried into Amanda's shop. Groping inside the door, she flipped on the lights, then keyed in the code to disarm the alarm. The coolers were full to overflowing with blossoms of every kind and color.

Amanda received a shipment today, but not from Rick. Bet that was hard.

Jillian turned to close the door. Standing in the shadows across the street was a hunched figure. Her heart skipped several beats as she flipped the lock. Not wanting to scare Becca, she said nothing.

"I need to use the restroom—be right back." Becca threw her jacket on the counter and ducked into the hallway.

Jillian let out a deep breath, trying to steady her nerves—then froze. The hunched figure stepped from the shadows into the glow of a streetlamp.

The old man with the veteran's hat.

He stood motionless for a beat, then hobbled across the street straight toward her.

Should I be frightened?

He was a stranger. In a week filled with threats, was he one more?

Keeping the door locked, she waited for him to reach the store. She intended to speak to him through the glass, but he had other ideas.

With gnarled, dirt-caked hands, he pressed a note onto the door.

Help me. I'm lost and hungry.

Jillian wrestled with indecision. Letting him in probably wasn't the wisest choice—not after the week they'd had.

What if he really needs help?

Something in his eyes—fear?—sorrow?—tugged at her. Both.

Then came the whisper in her mind. *Go ahead. Open the door. The killer's a woman, remember?*

Lord, please protect me if I'm wrong.

Jillian let the old man inside and relocked the door. She pulled a chair from behind the counter, coaxing him into the seat. He still didn't speak, but the gratitude in his tired eyes was unmistakable.

Her plan was simple. Grab Cate's gift, then take it and this poor soul back to McGuire's. Ethan could help sort things out from there.

Using a few hand signals, she asked him to wait. He nodded his understanding.

Amanda's safe was in the storage closet in the workroom, so Jillian made her way to the back of the shop. A flash of light flickered across the window by the door, startling her, but it was there and gone in the blink of an eye.

"Must've been a car's headlights in the alley," she muttered to the empty room. "Don't know why I'm so jittery. You'd think I was the one being stalked."

She crouched in front of the safe, spinning the dial to land on the correct numbers.

"Left to 26. Right past 26 to 35. Left to 14."

A soft click signaled success. She pushed down on the handle, and the safe's door swung open. A small box wrapped in Lake Jewelry's signature silver paper and gold bow greeted her. She popped the box into her purse, then locked the safe.

"Mission accomplished. Back to the party." She stood, smoothing out the soft fabric of her navy dress. "What in the world is taking Becca so long?"

Jillian reached to turn off the light—then a sharp pop cracked the air.

Everything went dark.

"What in the world?" She groped for something to hold. "Becca, if that's you, this isn't funny. Turn the light back on. I can't see anything."

No giggle. No admission of guilt.

No Becca.

Jillian stood still, letting her eyes adjust.

Why hadn't Amanda's backup generator kicked on? Was the power off all over the street?

"Becca, say something," Jillian called out. "Are you okay?"

Again, nothing.

Moving at the speed of a snail, Jillian edged forward in the direction of the door to the front.

Bam.

Her shins slammed into the sharp corner of a large storage cabinet. She sucked in her breath—a curse escaping on her exhale.

"Man, that hurts." She rubbed at the sore spot. There'd be bruises tomorrow. "I must've veered too far right."

Pivoting left, she walked zombie-style straight ahead until her hands met wood.

"Hello, Amanda."

The voice, nothing more than a whisper, stopped Jillian in her tracks.

She dropped her hands and turned—

"No. Eyes forward. I have a gun, and I *will* shoot you."

A soft click floated through the darkness.

Jillian's heart raced. Her pulse roared in her ears.

Stay calm.

"You're making a big mistake." Jillian fought to steady her breathing. "I'm not Amanda."

"Pity. I'd prefer it be her, but you'll do for now. I can get her later."

Jillian had to play along with this woman's paranoia—but she needed to know if Becca was okay. What about the old man in the front room? Had this psycho already done something to him? Or was he part of all this?

Keep her talking. Someone will come.

"Where's my friend—what did you do to her?"

The voice in the dark cackled. "She meant nothing to me. I made sure she won't get in my way."

Jillian's stomach clenched. A wave of nausea threatened to overwhelm her.

"You'll pay for your sister's sins." The voice, scratchy and harsh, taunted. "She already had Sam. Then, she went after Rick. I watched them together—laughing, flirting—it was disgusting."

"No. Amanda loves Sam, always has. She and Rick were childhood friends, more recently business associates. That's all."

"You're a liar," the woman snapped. "You'll say anything to save your whore of a sister. One man wasn't enough for her. She wanted mine."

Hers? Rick belonged to her?

"I ... I ... I don't understand," Jillian stammered. "Rick was married to Stacey."

The woman's primal scream pierced the flower-scented air. "He was mine! She stole him from me! She couldn't love Rick like I could—it's her fault he's dead. No one can have him now. She didn't deserve that baby, either. I'll be a better mother to him."

This woman was unhinged. Jillian had to keep her calm while she figured out where Becca was—and how to get them both out of there alive.

"I'm sure you'll be a great mom someday."

"No." The stalker adopted a casual tone like she just wanted to have a conversation. "The doctors said I'd never have a child of my own, but I *will* have Rick's son. Stacey thought she could keep him from me. She was wrong. You won't be able to stop me, either."

This last came out in a savage growl.

"Doctors can be wrong." Jillian stalled for time. She hoped talking about children would keep her captor calm. "My sister, Cate, was told she'd never get pregnant, but she has two beautiful girls."

There was a slight movement, then a whiff of foul breath. When the woman spoke, her voice was close, right at Jillian's ear.

"Don't talk to me about kids. The only one I want is Benjamin, or Bennie Boo, as they called him. Stupid name." Footsteps sounded on the brick floor. The woman paced.

"He's at that party, isn't he? The baby is there with your other sister." Her voice would get softer, then louder, softer, then louder. Still pacing.

I need to do something before she comes completely unraveled.

"I could take you to him," Jillian said. "I'll tell them not to hurt—"

The voice screamed in her ear. "You're not going anywhere. I'm going to take care of you here—then go to the party to get my baby. If anyone tries to stop me, I'll kill them. Just like I killed Rick and Stacey. Like I'm going to kill you."

What happened next was a blur—it happened so fast.

The back door to the alley slammed open. A rush of cool air swept the room.

Jillian heard a soft double click over her left shoulder.

Then—the lights blazed back on.

Travis burst in, Ethan on his heels.

"Jillian! Get down!" Travis shouted.

There was a loud pop.

Jillian crumpled to the floor.

CHAPTER TWENTY-EIGHT

Pain radiated through Jillian's knees as she hit the concrete. The jolt knocked the breath out of her in a loud *oof.*

Holy Mother of—mmm, that hurt.

Men's voices drifted from the opposite side of the room. She attempted to get to her feet but stopped.

The gun. The loud pop.

Had she been shot?

Jillian let her hands rove over her body, checking for a bullet wound. She breathed a sigh of relief when no blood came away on her hands.

She tried standing again, but a pair of strong arms scooped her up. They held her in a constricting hug. Her nose smashed against a soft cotton shirt smelling of peppermint and Island Breeze fabric softener.

Travis.

"I'm fine. I'm okay. What about Becca?" The folds of his shirt muffled her words. He held her to his body, his grip like a vise. She wriggled to release the tension in his arms, but to no avail. "Travis, you're holding too tight."

He loosened his grasp enough to lean back and look into her eyes.

"You're sure? I heard the gun go off. I thought—"

"Yeah, I did too." She caressed the worry lines on his face. "Becca?"

"She's fine. A little groggy, but she'll be okay. The paramedics have taken her to be checked out. Ethan went with her." Travis cocked his head at the woman screeching like a banshee. "That nutcase injected Becca with something that knocked her out, then stashed her in the bathroom."

At the mention of the shooter, Jillian and Travis looked at Officer O'Neil, who had the woman face-down on the floor. He'd handcuffed her and was mirandizing her as she screamed and cursed. "If you cannot afford an attorney, one will be provided for you. Do you understand the rights as they have been read to you?"

A mumbled response might have been *yes* or another curse, but it was hard to tell with her face to the floor and her crying so hard.

Grabbing hold of his suspect's cuffed wrists, O'Neil hauled the sobbing woman to her feet. With her head bowed, long blonde curls hung in her face. Her identity was still a mystery.

Jillian couldn't wait another second.

"Look at me." She snapped at the woman. "I want to see the face of the coward who tried to shoot me in the back."

The woman sucked in a deep breath and spat on the floor. She raised her head, giving Jillian a defiant stare. Her steely blue eyes radiated hate.

The previous evening's excitement at the flower shop had brought Cate's party to an early conclusion. Jillian regretted her sister hadn't been able to enjoy the full experience since many of the party guests had been tied up at the police station or the emergency room until the wee hours of the morning.

Her family would want to hear the details, so Jillian made a quick phone call to her sisters. They agreed to continue the celebration on Saturday—Cate's actual birthday—in Amanda's backyard for an afternoon cookout.

Cate's Surprise Party 2.0.

The unopened gifts waited on a small patio table. The charcoal grill had been fired up. Coolers full of ice and cold beverages stood at the ready. A long table covered with a checkered cloth groaned under the weight of food and what remained of Becca's beautiful cake.

Jillian was aware everything would take backstage to Ethan because he held the answers to all their questions.

"All right, Harden. Time's up." Sam pointed a pair of grill tongs at him. "Tell us what you know."

Ethan leaned back in his Adirondack chair, taking a slow sip of his drink.

C'mon detective, stop stalling.

"I'm afraid it's a long story," he teased. "You sure you don't want to eat first?"

"No." They all shouted.

Ethan chuckled. "Then, get comfortable. This will take a while."

Wrapped in warm blankets, everyone settled into the nearest chairs. Jillian and Becca huddled side by side, never breaking contact with one another.

By the glow of the fire pit, Ethan unraveled the story of Amanda's stalker and Rick and Stacey's killer.

"This may come as a shock to at least one of you." He leveled a quick glance at Amanda. "We arrested Brianna Jordan for murdering Rick and Stacey and stalking Amanda." His eyes roamed the faces of his audience.

"I can't believe it," Amanda said. "Brianna seemed so sweet. Why did she kill Rick and Stacey?"

"Better yet, why would she hold a grudge against you?" Jillian said. "You gave her a job when she moved to town."

"Wait, I'm missing something," Trixie chimed in. "Who is Brianna Jordan?"

"The woman I was dumb enough to hire to be my assistant when she arrived in Willow Springs a few months ago." Amanda spat out the words as if they left a bad taste in her mouth. "She took orders, ran errands, and made deliveries when Tim was unavailable. I was even teaching her to make simple floral bouquets. If it hadn't been for me giving Brianna a job, Rick and Stacey might still be alive."

Jillian could see the guilt in her sister's eyes, hear the regret in her voice. She hoped Amanda could move past this—eventually.

"C'mon, Ethan. Tell us why she terrorized Amanda." Cate held Benjamin in her arms, rocking him to sleep while four tired pups snoozed at her feet. Keeping watch over a baby was exhausting work. Abbey, Hayley, Blaze, and Poppy took their jobs seriously.

"We also want to know why she killed Rick and his wife."

"All in good time, Bryan." Ethan took another sip. "During a brief moment of clarity, Brianna couldn't confess and make a deal fast enough when her lawyer explained she was being charged with two counts of first-degree murder, one count of attempted murder, two counts of kidnapping, one count of stalking, not to mention multiple counts of vandalism."

Wes let out a long whistle. "I'm a lawyer, not a mathematician. How many years do all those charges add up to?"

"According to the district attorney, three hundred eighteen if not served consecutively." Ethan snapped out the number. "We dropped the vandalism charge in return for information about Didi."

"Please tell us she's okay." Aunt Grace twisted her bangles. "I could never get a sense of her in my visions."

"Didi's fine." Ethan popped a handful of peanuts into his mouth. "Brianna subdued her with a drug called Propofol, then stashed her in a seedy motel in Stonefield, even stole her car—sporty little green Jag several of you have seen around town. One of my officers spotted that vehicle in the parking lot of the motel. We found Didi early this morning, bound and gagged, but very much alive. Brianna owned up to using the same drug on Stacey and Becca."

Aunt Grace exhaled. A quiet *thank goodness* escaped her lips. She cast a sympathetic glance at Becca. "How're you doing, Cookie?"

"Doctor says I'm good—no long-term negative effects. I felt a sharp stab right here." Becca pointed to an angry, red spot on her neck. "My head went all fuzzy, my legs were shaky. Then ... lights out. The next thing I remember was Ethan calling my name and stroking my face." Becca's gaze searched for her husband. "I can't believe that wacko drugged me!"

"How in the world did Brianna get her hands on three doses of an anesthetic drug like Propofol?" Travis asked. "Those medications are kept under lock and key."

"A nurse in the ER accidentally left a cabinet unlocked when Brianna was there for a sprained ankle—she apparently fell at the flower shop?" Ethan raised his voice at the end, questioning the validity of the claim.

All Amanda could do was nod.

"When the nurse left the room for a moment, Brianna saw her chance. She grabbed the meds and syringes and shoved them in her purse." Ethan moved to Amanda's side, placing his hand on her shoulder. "The nurse has been relieved of her duties at St. Francis, and her nursing certification has been suspended."

"Any first responder knows how crazy the ER can get," Travis said. "This nurse made an honest mistake, but she's lost her job—probably her career."

Another life ruined thanks to Brianna.

The crackle of the fire, the whisper of a breeze through the trees, and a lone owl hooting from atop the neighbor's shed provided an ominous soundtrack to Ethan's tale. With Halloween just weeks away, the night reminded Jillian of childhood campfires and spooky ghost stories told in the dark.

Ethan cleared his throat, bringing her back to the present.

"Brianna attended LSU and was a sorority sister of Stacey's." Ethan started at the beginning. "Rick and Brianna went on a few dates before he hooked up with Stacey. Brianna admitted she was in love with Rick—thought they'd marry and have a family."

"Wait a sec. If Rick dated Brianna, even briefly, why didn't he recognize her when he delivered flowers to the shop?" Jillian asked. "Did he ever say anything to you, Amanda?"

"Rick never saw her. Thinking back, I've realized Brianna always made herself scarce when Rick came to the store—running errands, leaving for class—things like that." She looked at Ethan. "Was she even taking classes at the junior college or was that a lie too?"

He shook his head. "There was no record of her enrolled in any classes. I'd wager that was an excuse she could use to disappear for a while whenever she needed to."

"To slash my tires, destroy my display window, torch Sam's car—" Amanda stopped. "You get the idea."

"I have a question, Ethan." Sam stood at the grill, placing hamburger patties on the wire rack. "When Stacey married Rick—what?—this woman couldn't handle it and went nuts?"

"We had to transport Brianna to the hospital after her arrest because she was threatening to kill herself. The district attorney asked the staff psychiatrist to interview her. The preliminary tests indicated she suffers from bipolar disorder. More recently, she discovered she can't have children, which the doctor thinks caused a psychotic break.

"Brianna moved to Willow Springs to get her man back. She finagled her way into a job with Amanda, so she could keep an eye on Rick. Hiding in the bathroom, she overheard Rick and Amanda laughing and talking one day when he delivered flowers. In her twisted mind, she assumed the two of them were having an affair. She thought by killing both Amanda and Stacey, she could have Rick to herself."

Amanda choked on her soda, some of it dribbling down her chin. "Rick and me—together? That's ridiculous. We've been friends since kindergarten."

"She's not in her right mind, Pumpkin," Aunt Grace said. "People suffering from mental illness don't always see things as they really are."

"I get that, but now, two innocent people are dead. I feel responsible. If I hadn't given her a—"

"Amanda, stop. You aren't to blame." Ethan interrupted her. "Her mental issues started years ago. In a phone call to her parents, I learned Brianna was diagnosed with her bipolar disorder in high school, then schizophrenia during her sophomore year in college. Her mother said her illness is under control when she's medicated."

"I guess it's safe to assume she went off her meds." Jillian reached down, picked up Abbey and placed her in Amanda's lap.

Snuggling a pup might help soothe her nerves.

"Her poor parents," Joy sniffed. "I can't imagine how they must be feeling right now."

"Her parents?" Becca shrieked. "What about Rick and Stacey's parents—their whole family for that matter?"

While Jillian could sympathize with those who'd lost loved ones, she still needed answers. "So, in her twisted, *unmedicated* mind, Brianna thought if Stacey and Amanda were out of the way, she could have Rick. Then why kill him?"

"She ran into Rick at Manny's Pizza Sunday night as he was picking up dinner. She followed him to his truck and confronted him, professing her undying love. He blew her off—her words, not mine. He told her in no uncertain terms they would never be together. She decided right then to get rid of him. You know—the whole *if I can't have him, nobody will* train of thought. She slipped a note pretending to be from Amanda under Rick's front door, luring him to the alley behind the flower shop, so she could shoot him. Brianna wrote the suicide note.

"Then, she moved on to Stacey. Brianna blamed her for destroying any chance she might have had with Rick. She terrorized Stacey for weeks—hang-up calls, scary noises outside late at night, and notes threatening to take the baby."

"That poor woman," Jillian said. "We talked to her neighbor, who reported Stacey's odd behavior. We chalked it up to postpartum depression."

"I wonder if she told Rick about the threats," Amanda said. "I guess we'll never know with both of them gone."

An unplanned moment of silence ensued. Ethan respectfully waited before moving forward with the story.

He turned his attention to Amanda. "In Brianna's psychotic state, she thought you'd wronged her too. She admitted toying with you by writing the poems, leaving the yellow carnations and rats, vandalizing your property. She directed her anger at many of the people you cared about. She wanted you to suffer before she killed you."

"Brianna should've won an award for her acting. I never once suspected she was behind all this." Amanda shook her head. "This seems like the right time to ask about the flowers. She didn't get those yellow carnations from me—where'd she get them?"

"She ordered them from a wholesale supplier online." Ethan was ready with the answer. "Brianna thought that was safer than walking into a floral shop where someone could identify her. The forensic team found all the receipts in a desk in her apartment."

"I never want to see another yellow carnation ever again." Amanda shuddered. "You won't find them in my shop, and I hope no one asks for them."

Jillian doubted customers would, especially after word spread about how the stalker used them.

"What was the deal with the rats?" Bryan asked. "Did she run around town killing rats to use in her evil plan?"

"She referred to Rick as *a dirty rat* several times during my interrogation, so I assume that has some significance." Ethan took a sip of his iced tea. "No, she wasn't out there murdering rats. She claims Willow Springs has an overabundance of dead ones lying around if you know where to look."

"That's gross. Someone needs to speak to Mayor Sanford about our rat problem," Cate said.

"What about Didi?" Jillian said. "Why kidnap her?"

"Brianna wanted a piece of Rick she could hold onto forever. She wanted the baby." Ethan's gaze fell on the sleeping infant in Cate's arms. "Didi was collateral damage. Brianna figured with both parents dead, Didi would get custody of Benjamin. Her plan was to kill Didi so she could have the baby for herself, but we arrested her before she could finish the job."

"How did you know I was in trouble at the flower shop?" The question had burned in Jillian's brain.

"Didn't we tell you?" Travis asked. "Your new friend gave us a heads-up."

"My new friend?" Jillian scrunched her face.

"An old man, kind of grubby, ragged clothes and knapsack. Army veteran."

Understanding dawned midway through Ethan's description. Jillian's mouth dropped open.

"Oh, my gosh. With all the chaos, he completely slipped my mind. Is he all right?"

"He's fine," Travis said. "Tough old bird."

"You let the old guy into the store?" Ethan gave Jillian a harsh stare.

"Yes." Her answer was nothing more than a whisper.

Ethan nodded, then continued. "When the lights went off, he heard Brianna threaten you with a gun. He hightailed it to McGuire's to find me. The old duffer knew you were in trouble."

"How did he know you'd be there?" Cate asked.

"Apparently, it was all over town about your party." Ethan shrugged. "Everyone knew."

"Everyone but me." Cate laughed. "Again, thank you all for a lovely evening."

"I'm confused," Jillian said. "The man doesn't speak. How did he tell you I was in trouble?"

"Oh, he speaks—it was painful—but he can speak." Travis rose from his seat to get another soda.

"Your friend had a stroke a few months ago. His speech is returning slowly, but his message was loud and clear." Ethan leveled his gaze at Jillian. "That man saved your life."

"I'd love to thank him. Return the favor by helping him, if I can." Jillian sat on the edge of her seat. "What's his name? How can I find him?"

Travis and Ethan exchanged an odd look, which was not lost on her. She steeled herself for whatever came next.

"The man's name is Liam Oliver Erickson. He's staying with his brother."

Mouths dropped. The only sounds heard were the ones nature provided.

Jillian placed her head in her hands, letting out a soft groan upon hearing the identity of her savior. She sat without speaking, letting everyone process the information Ethan had shared, including this last piece of news. The same thought ran over and over in her head.

Please don't let this Mr. Erickson be as difficult as his brother.

Amanda was the first to speak, fulfilling her duty as hostess for the evening.

"Sam, how soon before the food is ready? I'm sure everybody is getting hungry."

The aroma of grilled beef and marinated chicken filled the air. Jillian's stomach growled in response to the delicious scents.

"The burgers are done." He slid the last two onto a platter. "Just a few more minutes for the chicken."

Despite her hunger pangs, Jillian couldn't even think about food yet. There were too many questions that still needed answers.

"I can't believe my hero is Mr. Erickson's brother." Jillian stroked Hayley's soft fur. Poppy stood at attention, waiting her turn. "Is Liam anything like his brother?"

"Hard to tell at this point." Travis raised his palms in the air. "Once his speech is improved, we'll see."

Jillian sighed. "We need to hope those two siblings are nothing alike."

This garnered a laugh from everyone.

"Okay, Detective Harden. Brianna confessed to everything. Didi's been found unharmed." Becca broke the silence. "I guess all your cases are closed, right?"

"Almost," Ethan said. "I have to be in the courtroom tomorrow morning when the State's Attorney presses charges against Brianna. She will enter a plea—more than likely not guilty by reason of insanity. She'll sit in jail until her trial or until the two sides come to an agreement. Either way, Brianna will be incarcerated for a long time."

"So, it's really over?" Amanda's voice was a whisper. "She can't hurt anyone else?" Her eyes searched Ethan's face.

He smiled back. "The nightmare is over. She's never coming back."

Amanda let out a shuddering breath, releasing the tears she'd held back all day.

Sam abandoned the grill without saying a word. He closed the distance between them, drawing Amanda into his arms.

"Babe, you're safe." His voice cracked with emotion. "I promise to spend the rest of my life making sure nothing bad ever happens to you again."

He released her, placing a few feet between them. In one smooth move, he pulled a small silver box from his pocket and dropped onto one knee.

A collective gasp rippled through the air. Amanda's hands flew to her face to wipe at tears. A smile bloomed.

Sam cleared his throat. "I've been trying to do this since I came home from Italy. Now might not be the best time, but I'm glad I can do this in front of your family and friends."

He removed a ring from the box and held it between trembling fingers.

"Amanda Siobhan Edwards. I love you more and more with each passing day. I want to wake up next to you every morning and fall asleep with you in my arms every night. Will you please say yes to becoming my wife?"

The lump of emotion in Amanda's throat had stolen her voice. All she could do was nod.

Sam slipped the ring onto her finger—a perfect fit.

The next morning, Jillian and Amanda met for breakfast at La Casita—again. Trixie had the morning shift at the bookstore. The flower shop was closed on Sundays. Despite the calendar showing October second, the weather had dawned sunny and warm—hopefully a final nod to summer before fall settled in.

They sat at a table on the colorful patio, drinking in the sunshine along with their *agua fresca*. The waitress brought them a platter of warm *agujeros de rosquillas*—those little balls of doughy goodness they loved. Some had been dipped in dark chocolate while others were dusted with cinnamon sugar.

Amanda reached for one. Her engagement ring caught the light and sent a shower of sparkles across the table.

"Be careful. You could blind someone with that thing," Jillian teased. "That ring is gorgeous. Sam did a great job picking it out."

Amanda held out her hand, turning it to admire the diamond from all angles. A soft sigh escaped her lips. "Yes, he did."

"Have you two discussed dates for the happy occasion?" Jillian popped a donut hole into her mouth, licking the sugar from her fingers.

"A little, but I'm torn between a destination wedding or a more traditional one. Sometimes, I think it would be easier to get married on a beach somewhere. You know, let the tropical scenery be the decorations."

"Whichever you decide, I hope you'll include the family." Jillian signaled for the waitress. "Mom would be crushed if she weren't there. For that matter, so would I."

"I would never get married without all of you," Amanda said. "I want Dad to walk me down the aisle. I'm just not sure whether that aisle will be in a church or through the sand."

They placed their orders—huevos rancheros for Amanda and a breakfast burrito for Jillian—and requested drink refills.

"Whatever Sam and I decide to do, it will be simple, romantic, and stress-free." She brushed the hair from her eyes. "Aunt Grace can have an extravagant wedding. I'll keep mine low-key."

"Amen to that," Jillian said.

The sisters sat enjoying their beverages and the beautiful weather while they waited for their food.

"We've been so focused on the recent craziness that we haven't really talked in ages." Amanda helped herself to another rosquilla. "What's been going on with you?"

"Work, work, and more work—at the store and on the upstairs renovations." Jillian took hold of Amanda's left hand, raising it so the engagement ring captured the sunlight. "There's nothing exciting in my life, not like you, anyway."

"We'll see a shiny bauble on your hand one of these days. Someone has to win the proposal pool eventually."

"Maybe." Jillian laughed. "Travis did mention he'd like to talk about marriage."

"We could have a double wedding on the beach in St. Thomas."

"No, no. You and Sam deserve your own day—one without stress or drama, one full of love, laughter, and happiness."

Jillian clinked her glass against Amanda's. "To love."

CHAPTER TWENTY-NINE

Three weeks later, on a cool, sunny afternoon, the family gathered at the First United Methodist Church. The altar was adorned with cream, bright purple, and orange flowers. Each pew sported matching satin bows. Candlelight flickered off the stained-glass windows.

The organist struck up "The Wedding March" as Aunt Grace began her walk down the aisle. A vision in cream silk, carrying a cascading bouquet of bright, eye-catching blooms designed by Amanda, her face glowed with happiness. Her eyes met her betrothed, who looked dashing in his dark gray suit and purple tie. He winked at his bride, causing a rosy flush across her cheeks.

The prayers were brief, the vows were heartfelt, gold rings sealed the deal. After a rather steamy kiss, the minister introduced them to their guests as husband and wife. The happy couple strolled back down the aisle, arm in arm, smiling at everyone.

The reception followed at the boat club's event center. Aunt Grace had planned each detail to ensure everything was perfect. She wanted her guests to enjoy the party. Champagne flowed, a delicious buffet was served, and an incredible confection sat on the cake table—thanks to Becca, of course.

Aunt Grace was a traditional bride. Following the cutting of the cake, she gathered the single ladies for the bouquet toss. Amanda and Jillian tried to hang back, but she called them out.

"I mean *all* the single ladies." She pointed the throwaway bouquet at them. "That means both my unmarried nieces. Get out here, please."

Dragging their feet, Jillian and Amanda took a position way in the back of the crowd of women.

"I'm not doing this at my wedding," Amanda muttered. "How ridiculous to think if you catch a bunch of flowers, you're the next to get married."

"You're engaged, so of course, you'll be next." Jillian shoved her hands down at her sides. "I'll stand here, but she can't make me raise my arms. Let one of these other women get it."

"C'mon you two. This is just a silly bit of fun." Trixie bounced up beside them, rubbing her hands together. "I'm going to give it my all to snag that bouquet."

Aunt Grace held the flowers over her head. She wiggled her hips and warmed up her arm, making quite a production of it. As the women in the front of the group jostled for the best position, Grace lowered the bouquet, handing it to a handsome, dark-eyed man sitting at a nearby table. She placed a kiss on his cheek and whispered in his ear.

"Thank you for letting me be a part of this."

He returned the kiss, placing a soft peck on her cheek. "You said this would happen. You saw it in your teacup."

"The leaves are never wrong." Grace winked and stepped aside.

The man walked through the crowd of ladies, stopping in front of the one he loved. He handed her the flowers.

"I believe these are for you."

As she took them from his grasp, their fingers touched, sending a tingle of familiar electricity down their arms.

He removed a small box from his jacket pocket and lowered himself to one knee.

The entire room inhaled as one. Not a sound was heard until ...

"Hot damn! I'm gonna win me that proposal money." Mr. Erickson's voice rang out loud and clear. "I knew my birthday would be a lucky day. That's why I picked it."

"Hush, Henry. You're interrupting a romantic moment," Mrs. Taylor chastised in a whisper that could still be heard throughout the silent room.

The man on his knee hung his head, but the movement of his shoulders gave away his laughter.

The woman placed her hand under his chin, lifting his head until their eyes met. "I wouldn't have it any other way." She winked at him. "I think it's safe to proceed."

Opening the box and offering it to her, he said the words every woman dreams of hearing someday.

"Jillian Saoirse Edwards." Travis paused to clear his throat. "From the moment we met, I knew you were special. Everything about you made my life better—your laugh, your smile, your love for family, and yes, even your inquisitive mind."

A ripple of laughter undulated throughout the reception.

"I want to hear that laugh and see your smile every day for the rest of my life. I want us to be a family, build a home—fill it with children and grandchildren. I want to grow old together sitting on a porch swing with our dogs.

"Tá grá agam duit means I love you in your family's beloved Irish. Please say you love me too, and you will become my wife."

"Is grá me tusa freisin—I love you too." Though Jillian's words came out in a tremulous whisper, the silent guests heard every word. The entire room burst into applause.

Travis stood and slid the ring onto Jillian's finger. His next words were only for her.

"Us. Forever."

ABOUT THE AUTHOR

Jodi Casstevens-Short is a born and raised Midwesterner, proud University of Illinois alum, and a third-generation educator. After thirty-five years as an elementary teacher, she now spends much of her time writing her Murdered in Willow Springs cozy mystery series. Her first novel, *Murdered by the Books*, received the International Impact Book Award for mystery and suspense for 2024. She's currently working on the third book in the series along with a humorous memoir of her teaching career and several children's books. She lives in Central Illinois with her firefighter husband and two sassy schnauzers, Riley and Finley. *Murdered by the Blooms* is the second novel in the series.

MURDERED IN WILLOW SPRINGS SERIES